For Mark Snell and Hope Smith,
who do not know each other, nor
have they ever met.

The Fame Game

By Ben Paul Dunn

Oh, the fame.

They asked, and I came. And now I regret.

My first time in a helicopter, hopefully the last. The pilot is diving down then screeching up because he is a sadistic bastard under the pay of the producers of this crap. The side doors open, wind blowing in, four people I have just met screaming or faking cool. And the cameras roll like it matters what a group of bellends in red jumpsuits say when strapped to chairs in a perfectly safe helicopter.

The woman opposite me may be well-known to the public, but to me she sounds like a mouthful of marbles and the kind of adult to refer to parents as mummy and daddy. You don't need the money, you are clearly rich and about to inherit an oil dynasty of some unethical scumbag who dresses nice and feels better about themselves because they donate a few quid to some half-decent charity. She mentioned her name, and I smiled and thought, nope, no idea who you are. But it will be the same for them. I have done as little as most to be selected here. I'm not even the has-been. I'm the never-really-was.

I am not a celebrity. I know that although these people seem to think otherwise. I wrote a book, it was made into a film, I appeared on TV five times and the last was six years ago. I am not famous, and let's face it, I am not successful. I made my money, the royalties roll in and I live within my means.

God, I feel sick. The woman screams, I hope she pukes, poshly, down her front and onto the others. They maybe don't deserve it, but I have, as is my want, taken an instant dislike to the privileged tossers. Who the bloody hell are you people? It might shut-up the comedian whose patter of endless banter is eye-rollingly shite. A vaudeville act who cannot turn off. You cheeky-effing-chappy of Mary Poppins banter. Keeping the spirits up by forcing me to concentrate on not killing you. Great move. But I will, if you do not stop with the endless one-liners, slice off your face.

What have I done?

They asked, I said, yes, why not? It'll be fun. Well it isn't. I don't see how shitting my pants on the BBC at 9 o'clock on a Saturday night is anything but bullshit humiliation for the entertainment of the idiotic sat on their couches feeling superior and hoping for a fall-out.

The young lad, I think, is from a pop-group. If he isn't, he should be, with his blonde curls and perfect teeth, and easy cool, that has just gone out of the window when he made a sound like Michael Jackson has

4

had someone cup his balls. Your teenage girl fans will be wild for that on social media. Oooo, look at non-descript, bland, passable singer being all brave in a perfectly safe helicopter with no chance of death. That I would now take, a crash into a ball of fire, my name forever connected to the deaths of people no one ever cared about. A soap, somewhere, will need a new storyline – or a storyline - and celebrate the demise of a barely able actor by ending the credits five seconds early with the name of whoever that aged woman is with the awful plastic surgery – you are not kidding anyone, love, you are seventy – with her date of birth and date of death and name. People will say, how sad, and most will try and think of cramming her death into a tasteless joke that hopefully involves tea-bagging they can tell down the pub and get a giggle from a pissed up mate.

I am not enjoying this.

I grin like a foreigner being polite.

I actually said yes to this shit.

We whoosh and they scream, and the comedian says something that must be a joke, as he laughs and gives a wink. I stare at him hoping that my telekinesis ability now works and I can, through thought alone, explode his big grinning face. I try, but his cockney gurning carries on unabated. Tonight, I decide I will shit in his pillow.

I've watched the show a little, I know the score, and we all know what will happen. It is a popularity contest and punishment. Are you a dislikeable annoyance? Then the public will make you lick the balls of a dead kangaroo, while a boa-constrictor slithers up your arse. The two cheeky presenters will make a joke they recycled from the 1950s, and Bob Monkhouse will regret being dead as his material is now comedic gold in their hands. A couple, who clearly hate each other. Man and wife who have been doing this for years and have grown jaded and tired with the constant grinning and endless banter. Oh, the banter. They absolutely love the banter, if not each other. A series now and again with one of them missing and replaced with someone with actual talent. A year they went into rehab, were under arrest for a suspected killing, or the year the man went mad and ran-off with a glamour model. All forgiven now of course because if it weren't they wouldn't be able to ride this cash-cow to its inevitable death that really should have happened before, but I am now resolving to force in the next three weeks.

We are coming in to land, in a field, in the middle of nowhere, with absolutely nothing to keep us safe other than a massive film-crew,

5

ten minor, but irritating celebrities, a contract guaranteeing our well-being, and the cheerful japes of the most irritating comedian in the world. He might as well say, cor blimey guvnor and vanish in a puff of utter farce while dressed as a chimney sweep.

The old woman says, "That was fun, wasn't it?" They all laugh in response, except me, who smiles and makes a promise to God that I will make sure this woman gets dysentery on live TV whilst swimming with sea serpents. Ten minutes I've been here, and I am already contemplating the effect on my career - or lack there of - if I become the first contestant to be filmed before, during and after a mad killing spree of celebrities people vaguely remember.

We were split into competing groups, which is easy to do as five of us are in red boiler suits and the other five in yellow. I look at my group and believe that were my life to depend on these people in any difficult situation I'd be dead, very quickly, quite possibly at my own hand. However, were we to be pitted against each other in a new angle of fighting to the death, that comedian is a deadman, and possibly the retired snooker player whose only claim to fame is that he blew all his money on coke and ex-wives. I've lived my life to the full he has often been heard lying.

We whoosh and turn and spin and do not vomit, not yet, that will surely come. We land and bend and crouch and walk away from the helicopter in a field, near a river in Australia, where, as it is commonly known, the devil keeps all of his pets. Their hamsters here will eat you, there are no zoos as the lions won't step foot in this insane land of killer animals.

We stand, each of us miraculously not covered in our own puke. I look to the comedian hoping for some signs of sickness, but all I see is a fifty-five year-old has-been with manscara. Yep, that knocks the years off and in no way makes you look a bellend, you bellend.

We are greeted by one of the two hosts, the husband, a burly Welsh man, once very attractive, now muscled and large and greying and eyes wrinkling from the sun a mild alcoholism and the inevitable effects of age. He has been famous since he was eleven on children's TV, he is now forty-five and losing his fight against growing old gracefully. He must be wearing a topper, the hair has been on that receding line for more than a dozen years. Still thick too, I wonder if it is real human hair bought from a street urchin in old London town.

The helicopter zooms off, gusting us and tipping us but thankfully no longer the obvious means of transport. It is time for cheeky Welsh man, who is too old for the patter to joke and smile and tease and refurbish old jokes for a new audience who weren't alive when they were originally spouted back in the sixties.

"Hello," he says, all smiles and Welsh, his teeth glistening white and large and false. Veneers they say, so porcelain teeth to hide his original teeth which were teeth that looked like teeth, not these that look like a massive white gumshield.

"Welcome," he goes on as if Australia is his country. "I think it is time to get started. You'll notice you five are those in red jump suits. Your companions in the yellow jumpsuits are in another part of the country, close by, and you will need to race them down the river to the camp. First ones to arrive get to stay, the second get to rough it for the night. Away you go," he says while waving us toward the river, which stinks and is the perfect place for man-eating alligators to lurk looking to eat humans. Luckily we are dressed like illuminous ice pops to give a clearer idea where we are.

The Welshman leaves, the camera crew do not. We all look at each other. It is a group interview situation and we are all trying to figure out who is the leader and boss. Some even look to me, the idiots.

Cockney comedian geezer claps, and we look his way, my eyes first then my head because they are rolling at the realisation he is taking charge and I will probably have to follow his orders. "We don't know each other, really," he says, then looks to me, "and some I don't even recognise." This raises a laugh from the other three minor celebrities, or failed sports stars, or that one person who I think is "famous" because they were on some young dating show in which they were massively disliked by the other contestants, the public and unfortunately themselves.

"I remember you," I say. "I used to watch you on TV, when I was a kid, thirty years ago. What have you been up to since?" I ask.

This is a new tactic that has dawned on me. I absolutely loathe this situation already. I'll be awful, rude and then get voted off and go home, cash in hand and no harm done.

He starts to say something about theatre, doing good deeds, travelling the world and some such lies. The fact is, he was unfunny and shit. I knew that when I was teenager, even my grandparents thought he was awful and they believed the royal variety performance to be hilarious.

"We can catch up at camp," I say. "What's the plan?"

7

We look at the river, there is a raft, some paddles, and life-jackets. It appears we have to paddle downstream, as a team, on a flimsy raft. It would be quicker to walk the river bank, but cockney geezer leads us to the water, instructing us to get on. We try, and fail, and the raft drifts off because it isn't tied to anything. We are all holding paddles.

"I have slept rough before," I say. "If park benches after Tennents Super can be considered rough sleeping. I'm OK with that."

The group stare at me, and I feel their combined hate. I feel better. I am not long for this show, nor this earth if their murderous eyes are anything to go by.

To clarify and seal my popularity, I add, "That was, of course, my way of saying, I'm not going after the raft."

Cockney wide-boy swears, which definitely won't be cut from the TV show, and wades into the river. By the way he squeals and tries to tiptoe his way forward, I'd hazard a guess it is a tad cold in there.

"Hurry up," I shout.

He turns to me, manscara slightly running, gives me a look a child throws before a fight and turns to be back on his way to the raft which is breaking all laws of physics and sitting still, in one place on the surface of the river. I look along the river bank and see the wooden stake and the attached rope that disappears into the water. It was tied to the bank after all. I walk over, not saying anything because my new best buddy is in the water with his scrotum now so small from the cold it is residing within him, and pick up the rope. I look out into the water and see cockney fun-boy is about to reach it. I pull on the rope just in time to see its length surface and be visible. I then pull it, just as the hilarious one reaches out to grab the raft. I try and time it right, and pull with force so the raft just moves out of his reach at the last second. I start reeling it in, slowly enough so that London geezer never gives up chasing.

He shouts something I can clearly hear but chose to ignore. The woman whose face is a testament to how bad plastic surgery used to be, walks over and says, "He said stop pulling so he can grab the raft and be dragged back in."

"Is that what he said?" I ask. "I don't think it was," I add, pulling on the rope.

I pull quickly and the raft beaches once again. The grinning cockney isn't grinning as he wades in the water towards us.

"Hurry up," I encourage.

He says something, under his breath.

"Do you need a hand?" I ask as he nears the edge. But he rather rudely refuses my offer and crawls on all fours onto dry land.

"Luckily it is hot," I say, "you'll dry out in no time," I add just as the sun disappears behind some very big clouds.

We step onto the raft, one by one, and I watch each with interest.

First up is the old woman who had spent a lifetime playing the same character in a soap set in a town that doesn't really exist, pouring fake pints, in a fake pub while actors came and went, mostly into obscurity, and she started to change her look by botox, exercise, shagging younger men, and paying big money to have the skin stretched across her face. She speaks as if she has suffered a stroke, but I think it is just botox facial paralysis, the fact her lips are inflated to four times their natural density, the fact she is older than most other women alive and finally that she is a bit thick. For whatever reason, I like her. She is clearly going to get an easy ride as there isn't a hope in hell she is medically fit to do any type of challenge without the clear and present danger of dying from any type of fright. I help her on by chivalrously holding her elbow and providing no actual support. She doesn't fall into the water, which is a shame as that would have been great TV. Her name is not Brenda, as it was in the show, but Georgia. Tall, bingo-winged, a neck like a turkey's ballsack, and a face as smooth and as swollen as a fighter after a heroic loss to a heavy handed champion.

Next is young pup, Anthony, who, he has told us in an unusual bout of words, likes to be known as Anthony, because, one assumes, he likes to make people very aware from the off that he is a total fucking wanker. He is a blonde beauty and effeminate charm and has no problem pulling the ladies – I reckon he doesn't even have to get drunk, become leery and try it on with all females in the hope of at least one of them giving in through sympathy like the rest of us normal folk. He is something of a sensation on the internet, probably not pornhub, but something gives me the idea he's a fan of the site and is particularly fond of the more dark areas. He smiles a lot, has said nothing, and appears to be thirteen. He isn't, as that wouldn't be allowed, but he still looks like he needs to finish puberty before he can go off and get a proper job. If we have to do a bit of celebrity boxing, I'm choosing him as my opponent as beating the living crap out of an ancient plastic woman would probably affect the sales of my next book, in a negative way, probably.

Third is a woman who has taken the same plastic surgery route as Georgia, only she is twenty four and in no need of looking younger, so has I think, asked the plastic surgeon to take her natural young and pretty

9

face and make it look utterly fucking ridiculous. Her lips have never been the lips of any human in history, they have however, in a previous life been two Cumberland sausages. Her nose has been sculptured away from its original shape into the long straight version I see, only it appears the artists design was made by a five-year-old from playdough. Luckily she is able to apply much makeup to hide the utter clusterfuck of her once normal face. Her skin is somehow glowing silver and her eyebrows appear to contain no hair despite taking up half her forehead. She looks like Metal Mickey half way to transitioning to a human. Her breasts are equally ludicrous, they do not move, bounce, wobble or sway. They sit there whatever she is doing like two solid lumps of silicon, which they are. Fortunately for every teenage boy watching, she has managed to set her jumpsuit up so the top is open and her cleavage is on show, and I, along with every other person, male and female, cannot help looking to see if I can see some nipple.

"Do you need any help," I ask her left tit, as I ease her onto the raft.

I think, briefly, that I see a nipple, but it is a mole, and in the wrong place. It would have been a third nipple, and I could have called her Scaramanga. I laugh to myself, and they all look at me as if I am a drunk tramp and need to be avoided. Her name is Chelsey, which isn't her real name, and she has clearly made it up on her own because it isn't even fucking spelt right.

There are open air, cold showers, Chelsey is going to be here till the end if she wears a white bikini and spends at least three hours in the water every day.

Last is the comedian, although now smiling less and very wet. He is called Robert, but insists on Bob. He has thirteen jokes and I've heard them all. He is also a self-proclaimed 'prankster' which roughly translated means he is the 'fun' one who everyone wants to fuck-off out of it and could easily be described in the simple terms: irritating prick. He'd swap your salt for sugar because he is that type of guy. He is average height, dyed black hair thinning on top, chubby with food and booze and at this minute absolutely livid. I offer my arm for him to step on to the fun raft with the cool kids but he slaps my arm away, and I want to do an exaggerated OOooooo, but think twice as that would make me him. I look suitably shocked and give the shrug of shrugs.

"Are you ok?" I ask.

For whatever reason, which he keeps to himself, he doesn't answer.

I am not Mr. Popular.

We are on the raft and all standing as the thing is barely breaking the surface and sitting down would mean getting wet on stagnant, green algae water. We paddle, and by that I mean we have each placed our paddles in the water and are moving them about like we know that is what to do but are doing it all wrong like a young teen trying to stick his erection into a belly button. We are all doing it wrong in different directions and we spin slowly, the natural flow of the river laughing at us as we make absolutely no headway. Bob starts singing some type of maritime song that he believes is humorous, and would, in my world, result in his being assaulted before the chorus. No one joins in, no one smiles, but he keeps on going like a drunk dad at Christmas oblivious to the angry embarrassment of the audience. At some point this guy is going to set light to his farts. I listen and it's a sea shanty, I think, of sorts, and one I shall always relate to the sensation of struggling not to cave the back of a man's head in with a solid wooden paddle.

"I think we are sleeping rough tonight," I say in an attempt to stop the man with the talent to get a minor role in the local village production of Oliver from singing any more.

"Why would you think that?" Bob asks, and I may be paranoid but I am sure I detect a little hostility.

"Because thus far we appear to be on a prolonged audition for being the first choice team to represent Britain in the special Olympics," I reply. "I'm not too sure of the physical prowess of the other team but I'm guessing they are able to at least drift downstream rather than paddle the wrong way, in circles, away from where we would be going if we actually just stood and did nothing."

"Go on then, big man," the comedian says, "you take the lead."

And despite myself and any self-respect I may have had, which was essentially none, I arrange my crew mates. Two either side, paddling forward and the old lady at the back who on close inspection appears to have a bit of muscle going on under her loose skin, to steer. We start moving in the right direction because that's what happens when you all do the same thing in unison.

"I don't actually think I want to sleep rough," I say. "The actual camp is rough, rougher than that and I imagine we'll be sleeping in a puddle with baby alligators. Or, even worse, have to sleep in tents with actual scout leaders. That would be rough, and dangerous, and possibly result in inappropriate touching."

"Do you like anything?" Anthony asks, and I'm shocked to hear his voice. It is actually pleasant, lovely tones. A voice for radio, and a face for modelling, and a body that would quite possibly prove to be too enticing for the most ardent woggle wearer.

"I like chocolate," I say. "And beer. Chocolate beer would be great, a gap in the market there. A business idea. I could drink that all day."

"I don't drink," Anthony blasphemes.

"Are you not eighteen yet?" I ask.

Georgia giggles, Anthony snarls.

"I'm twenty-five," he says.

"Do you have that illness from that film?" I ask.

"What?" Anthony asks.

"The film, you know, the curious incident of Benjamin's bottom."

"The curious life of Benjamin Bottom?" Chelsey says, happy to make me look like an idiot – as if I am not capable of doing this on my own.

I smile, and reply to both her breasts at the same time, "Maybe I watched the Porno version?"

Georgia laughs, and I am growing to like her even more. Anyone prepared to laugh at my jokes is fine by me.

"How we coming along there, Georgia?" I ask.

"I can hear the other team," she says. And just like that, from a river running into ours, or two rivers joining together, a raft appears, a very similar raft to our own, only with people dressed as yellow wankers instead of red, and at a cursory glance, a bonded team, working in unison, and singing along to the same bloody song Bob was blaring out tunelessly before. Bob smiles and looks at us all. Bob, it just means they are all fucknuts too, I don't say. They are quite a way ahead, and moving smoothly. A woman is at the back steering with her paddle, and her face, bless her, tells me she is ready to kill her crew. We are done for and sleeping rough in an inevitability.

"I think we need to paddle faster," I say. "But together, at the same time, in the same direction. Think of it as the anti-university boatrace, instead of Oxford versus Cambridge we have yellow retards versus the red morons in a test to prove how unathletic we are and just quite how stupid celebrities can be. My money is on three of us drowning."

"Why are you here?" Bob asks.

12

"To provide encouragement," I say. "Come on, guys," I add encouragingly.

And they do. We speed up, more or less at the same rate, and I notice the yellow team are struggling, caught in a little vortex, whirlpool, whatever the fuck it's called, circular movement of water. Their singing has stopped and they are looking shocked. We are moving up on them and they know it. As we pass them, and their stupid shocked faces, Bob, I just know, is going to start singing it, I just know. Wait for it, I think, two more seconds, and I'm only slightly off.

"Row, row, row your boat gently down the stream," he sings, vaguely in tune, and he laughs along with absolutely no one else. No one else would have thought of that, Bob, I successfully try not to say out loud. I bet in Venice, on a gondola with his mortified family, he belts out the cornetto song, the prick.

But we are winning, drifting ahead, the yellow team are eventually popped out of their circular stagnation and are a few metres behind us. And even I, the man who will not do it for the sole reason because you told me to, starts to paddle harder. The team, the yellow team, with their bullshit colour and their bullshit members who I don't know, but really dislike mainly because they are in a different colour and likely to steal my sleeping bag for the night, need to be defeated. I look at my team, and sigh in disappointment, but then realise, as pathetic as we are, the other team is the same. Their sports star played snooker, so he is only familiar with Coke and fags and booze. They have a young TV presenter who is trying to make amends for being arrested getting a blow job from a fan on the motorway while driving his Range Rover at 90 miles an hour four years ago. They never made it as a couple, surprisingly, what with her being someone he didn't give a shit about, and him being married. But now divorced. He appears to be vocal, which makes sense, as his chat show consisted of him talking about himself to his guests. It was cancelled, very much like him as a person.

I look ahead and there is a tape across the river. This must be our finishing point. We are ahead, we are paddling relatively efficiently for a group of people who have already reached our physical limits. The tape draws closer, I look behind and see the yellows, drawing level as if they are on a hovercraft and we have inadvertently already thrown an anchor overboard. We drift and they race, the tape coming closer and them getting alongside. We paddle faster, instinctively wanting to win and getting those others to sleep rough for the night. The tape arrives and we hit the finishing line in unison. I believe we won, but the jumping on the other raft indicates they are of a different opinion. They are hugging, we are stood swearing quietly under our breath. Anthony I can clearly hear say, Wanker, and I assume he is speaking about the other team in general and Bob more specifically. We drift, and are told by a booming Welsh voice from the river bank to make our way toward him. We all reluctantly put our paddles back in the water and start to paddle, moving quickly and swiftly in the opposite direction to where we need to go.

"A victory lap," I say. "Good thinking."

We arrive at the river bank, having spent longer than the race turning around and getting there. The big Welsh man booms a hearty hello, and his wife, Molly, dressed ever so fashionably in tight mini-skirt, tight top, and tight tights, saunters sexily about. She has made a career out of sauntering sexily, and only ever been in trouble when she was involved in the murder trial. It wasn't her fault her best friend killed two people and then sought an alibi from the sexy lady. Probably didn't help that she couldn't remember facts, and didn't want to incriminate a childhood friend in a knife crime. But still, friends are friends even if they have a tendency to slaughter people who have dissed them.

"We have the results. And, would you believe it?" he asks. "It was," and here he makes a dramatic pause, for way too long, I believe he is actually waiting for adverts to finish, "a draw, which means we have no team to go to sleep rough."

"That's a relief," I say, trying to hurry things on and avoid the quite clear and obvious negative that is rapidly coming.

"A relief to some," he says and laughs and Molly laughs along, which is her role mainly, which is daft as she is much funnier, smarter and better looking than her husband.

"But we can't let our special place be left empty, so each team needs to pick a member to spend the night sleeping rough. You have a few minutes to decide."

I turn to my team, ready to discuss intelligently and steer them to unanimously voting for Bob, but I am confronted by them saying, "Ben," "you," with a pointing finger at me. "Yep, Ben." And an "absolutely you," from Bob, the cheeky smiling cockney wide-boy.

There is no discussing that, which comes as a disappointment.

I turn to The Welshman, "I've volunteered to go for my team," I say.

"Very honourable of you, Ben. And why is that?"

"Because they want me to," I say.

14

"That's not volunteering though is it?"

I think for a second and say, "I don't understand your point."

My attention is drawn to the other team. They actually like each other and have found some type of chemistry. Except the woman with the scowl. A journalist, I believe, one that would generally be considered, opinionated. They are actually having a genuine discussion. In my head, I am too along the lines of why the hell am I here.

We are asked to stand in our two groups, either side of the hosts. The male host has a piece of paper. He appears to be reading off it.

"So the results are in," he says. "Ben, for the red team. If you'd like to step forward there, mate," he adds as if we have actually had a past. "How are you feeling about that?"

"Well," I say, dragging the word out so I can think of something pithy and intelligent to say, "I didn't want them to suffer unduly," I mumble like a berk.

"And the yellow team have chosen, Jenny. How do you feel about that, Jenny?"

"It'll be an adventure, I'm sure," she says while pulling a face that should be a smile but looks like she is holding together a bursting bladder.

"Ok," Welshman says, clearly having hoped for something slightly more interesting, "if everyone but you two get themselves together, and you'll head over to camp, while you two lovely people," he says, describing me and Jenny in a way that has never been used before, "follow the other path there to the alternative sleeping arrangements."

The eight celebrities drift off leaving me and Jenny alone, in a clearing in the middle of a forest in Australia with a film crew following and us with microphones strapped to our bodies.

"I'm Ben," I say.

"I know, you've done some interesting stuff," Jenny tells me.

"Really?" I ask.

"Yeah, a long time ago, but it was interesting at the time."

"You are very good at compliments," I say.

"You could try some."

She has a point so I have a go.

"That TV show, where you try and stick it to the politicians that are dumb enough to come on, what's that called?"

"In the Week," she tells me, but I knew already.

"Yeah, In the week, on TV at the weekend, that has some lovely intro music."

She smiles, she actually bloody smiles. And did I hear a stifled laugh?

"Oh, that is so kind of you to say," she says.

"Thanks, I'm presuming the outro music is the same, but I couldn't be sure as I never get that far."

She laughs now, a proper laugh.

"I was lying about your previous work," she says, smiling. "It was all actually shite."

I laugh this time.

"I knew you were lying," I say.

And we walk into our home for the night, and I really hope it is for just the night because it is, essentially, our bags, in a clearing, on the floor.

We stare at it as if we have missed something. Then stare some more becoming aware that we have missed something, the something we have missed is where the fuck we are actually supposed to sleep.

"Which bit would you like to take?" I ask.

She ponders for quite some time, "You know, I'm just not sure which part of the mud will be softest," she says.

"Probably the bit I cry on," I reply.

We have the facilities to cook, apparently. But it looks like wood and metal pans. But we have rice and that is it. We boil it up in our pans having set the fire with the matches provided. We are silent mostly, knowing what to do, and where to sit and how long to wait. We have beans too, but not the Heinz, actually beans that need boiling, that are white, or grey and look like fuel rather than food. It takes a long time to soften so we can suck it, chew quickly and swallow the stuff. It isn't bad because it isn't anything. No flavour, no substance, but our food. The night starts to set, and we have washed our metal bowl with handle. We have chatted and exchanged a few words about the place but not each other.

"I'm shattered," I say. "I'm going to try for sleep."

I have a sleeping bag and ample floor space. Jenny does too, but we end up less than a metre away from each other, near the fire, the weather still warm, the dark already in, noises of animals we do not know and the realisation we are being filmed by night vision.

"Had a good first day?" I ask.

She rolls onto her side to face me.

"It has been, quite frankly, awful. The people, they are like kids meeting up for the first time, all excited, all being so very friendly, and too

16

much. Mates for life they are thinking," she says. "They've watched this so many times before and know what they want."

"Yeah," I say. "My group were the same."

"They didn't seem to like you much," she says.

"I may have been slightly annoying. Possibly could have reeled that in a bit."

"And where would be the fun in that?" she asks. "My group were the same."

I give her the rundown on the four colleagues I paddled with and she knows them, or of them, and she smiles. And she tells me of hers.

The snooker player is called Gary, or Gaz, or if you really want him to be your friend, Gazza. He has a wig, no real teeth, and she assumes from the fags, booze and drugs, a heart that is operating on man-made chemicals. Lovely bloke, she says, if you like geezers with deep-rooted misogynist beliefs. They won't, I assume, become lovers.

Blow job on the motorway man is called Kieran. Tall, fit, good-looking and confident. The man, she says has never known disappointment, or rather, has never accepted anything he has done or said could be considered disappointing. He has made mistakes, he said, and is here to test himself to see if he is really back to his best. She won't, I assume, be grabbing his balls.

A curly haired, chatty, nervous Pop singer called Racheal was next. She had won a TV talent show, had a single hit, and then done the rounds on TV. This was her fourth reality TV show. She sings a lot, and speaks in tunes. Lovely lady, lovely figure, beautiful eyes. I assume they won't get frisky, although I hope in a way that the half-my-age, sexy lady is into older, grumpy men. She isn't, I know that, but I'm of an age where I dream and hope and embarrass myself.

The last is a TV presenter who has been on TV for thirty years. He did his children's TV, the adult morning shows and quizzes and talk-shows, and travel shows and cookery shows, and documentaries and pretty much anything and everything there is to do with TV. He has been on a sabbatical these last few years, with his highlighted hair from the early 90s. She knows him, she says, has worked with him, she adds. Absolutely fucking hates him, she spits, which comes as a relief because a man more in love with his own image I have never come across in my life. He is called Brian.

"I wonder what they are saying of us?" I ask.

"That we are definitely the first two to get voted out."

"After today, I bloody hope so. Why the hell I signed up for this, I don't know."

"The money they offered?" she points out accurately.

"Yeah, and the longer I stay the more I earn. I'm just thinking the initial sum is more than enough."

She laughs. "Me too," she says. "How much did they pay you?"

"Fifty thousand."

"Oh," she says.

I don't like that response.

"Oh, as in too much or Oh as in you got paid more?"

"Oh as in I got more."

"What? How much more?"

"Twice as much," she says and smiles.

"You are worth twice as much as me? Bullshit."

"It is the market rate."

I sit there pondering who is the cheapest here, and it doesn't take too much pondering, it is me, the has-been writer with a brief explosion of popularity to fade away into obscurity when I opened my gob once too often.

"Well, the only way I'm making more than you is if I make it to the end, and to do that I need to be the man here, and gain favour from the audience."

She looks at me and shakes her head, nicely, very pleasant about it all, but clearly not convinced. She smiles, not achieving 100% patronising but as near as damn it.

"That's you fucked then," she says.

"I've got a plan," I say.

"Nope," she replies.

"You don't even know what it is," I say.

"Yes, I do."

"So sex is off the cards then?" I ask.

"Yep."

"A hand-job?"

"Nope."

"A blowy?"

She sits up on her elbow. "You have just put hand job above a blowey. You clearly know nothing about sex so no chance I am sleeping with you. What a strange order."

I think, nod a bit, "Yeah, don't know what I was thinking there. I'll work on that."

"Alone and quietly if you can, I'm off to sleep."

She rolls over. I do too. The ground remains hard.

THE PRESENTERS: END OF DAY 01

"This is the last year," Molly says.

She knows she has said similar before, she knows he will try and convince her otherwise but she knows it is time.

He listens, sipping red wine from a clear plastic cup. He nods and smiles, the smile she loved years ago but has changed since they were young into something unnatural, something to turn on when required.

"You say this a lot," he says, and his Welsh accent is not as strong as in front of the camera.

"I don't want this anymore," she says, and she feels the tears coming. "Over here, two months of my life every year in a hotel in Australia, earning money I don't need, talking about celebrities I don't like, and reading jokes off the autocue I didn't write, and don't find funny."

"It is still at the top of the ratings," he says, and he is right, popularity counts, figures count, money counts.

"I don't want it. We are rich, stupid rich. But we do the same things, win the same awards, year after year by doing the same things."

"People love it, they love us," he says, reaching out to touch her knee.

She looks at the hotel room, the height of local luxury, the expense they don't have to pay, the view spectacular through the window that is the whole wall. The penthouse, a dream she had as a child. Fame and fortune and the ease of everything being done for you.

"I don't love it. It's the same thing again and again. A routine. This isn't real life."

He moves now, across to her and sits on the arm of the large soft chair in which she sits. He places his arm around her shoulders.

"We've done so much," he says. "We are as popular now as we have ever been. We have been through so much and managed to be us all the way. Why stop now?"

"Because I want real-life, I have had the fame, the popularity, the awards. I've done it. What I haven't done is life."

"This is life," he says. "Our life."

"I don't want it anymore," she says and stands and walks to the window.

19

He watches her back, as she stands and straightens her dress of creases.

"That Ben is a bellend, isn't he?" he asks.

She turns to him. "No, I think he is the only one there, except Jenny, who actually gets it. Gets the absurd fakeness of it all. Celebrities trying to be liked, or get a career back on track, or make money."

"They want the experience too," he says.

"Of chewing on a kangaroo's bollock?" she laughs. "No, they are all here for something else."

"Ben will be the first to go," he says.

"Probably," she agrees, "but that would just make it perfect. The man who thinks it is a load of nonsense – because it is – getting voted off first because no one wants to acknowledge that is what it actually is."

"He comes across as an idiot," he says.

"No, we all come across as idiots. He comes across as someone who won't play along. Someone who isn't in it for the game, but here to just take the piss."

"That is not what people want to see."

"It is what I want to see," she says.

He smiles, knows he is on a losing side tonight.

"The numbers and votes will be in soon enough. The team will be checking social media. We'll see how popular his routine is," he says.

"It isn't a routine, he is a grumpy man who thinks, like me, that all this is ridiculous."

"It has made us rich," he says, and she realises there is no arguing with that.

DAY 02: MORNING

I wake up when it is light, which is early as birds are singing, insects are rubbing legs together and grass rustles. I don't like the grass rustling as that could be anything deadly, they are all deadly here but I fancy my chances against a spider, snakes less so and rats are going to freeze me. I awake slowly, not exactly the hungover agony of waking up but not wanting to, but it is close. Instead of a mild paranoia about what I did and said the previous night, wanting to phone people to see if they are actually unoffended with me, I realise I'm here, in a jungle, on TV and it is hell. I look across and Jenny's sleeping bag is empty and I think maybe she made a run for it in the night, went mad, possibly stripped and covered herself in mud. That would definitely get her kicked off as well as a book

20

deal, permanent paparazzi following and an embarrassing reputation for every single member of her family.

You're related to Jenny, are you?

Okay, well I'll give you a wide berth as if you share genetics you are obviously mental too.

But I see her, drinking water from a tin cup, staring at me, not smiling.

"You snore," she says.

"I know."

"That's it. You know? No apology? All night you kept me up."

I go to speak. "Nope," she says, "I do not want a crap sexual joke."

I smile.

"Grumpy much?" I ask.

She rubs the back of her neck. "Why are we here?" she asks.

I have no answer, not today. It seems strange, an absurdity, not what you see on screen. There are people lurking, with cameras. We are not alone. The presenters are close by, waiting to tell us something, or speaking to the viewers at home, making jokes about one of us, or all of us. I wonder what they say about me. Then tell myself I don't care, even if I do.

And this is how the day goes, hour after hour of absolutely nothing but me and Jenny and the camp and no information. We talk, chat, then run out of things to say. Chat a little more when an idea pops up but mostly quiet, mostly thinking, and I prefer this, Jenny seems to think so too. We have nothing to read, nothing to write and nothing really to say. The highlight clip will be me and her silently lying against soft sleeping bags, propped up on trees not talking but being in each other's company like a first teenage date, only we don't have a cinema to do the talking for us, we have an assortment of noises from whatever is in the jungle and they all scare the shit out of me.

"You don't like the animals much, do you?" Jenny says.

"It is not so much the animals as the thought about how they can kill me in so many ways. There is a spider, I believe, that when it bites you, your body slowly stops working until the only thing left is your awareness of being helpless and your lungs no longer working. But I doubt I'd get that far as some other horrific beast would come and chew me to death, probably starting with my penis."

"We are celebrities, we are safe."

"You say that, but at some point, to boost flagging ratings, and we all know it isn't as popular as it once was, they are going to kill one of us

21

off. I'd volunteer to save everyone. With the exception of Bob. Bob can go first. Then me. I wouldn't sacrifice myself there, I'd think that maybe his jokes would also die with him."

"What don't you like about him?"

I think about this, as I have thought about it already a lot. "I don't not like him, I just can't stand the eternal fake jovial nonsense. It grates, like a brillo pad on my nipples."

"You've tried that?"

"Not yet, but I'd choose it over a night with Bob."

"He, and possibly others, don't like you either, you know?"

"I am aware of my ability to cause dislike in others."

"You go out of your way to be rude."

"It's not rude, it's honest. There is no malice. . ."

"No malice? You are kidding me. You are just rude and obnoxious."

"I prefer the term witty," I say, and before she can make other valid points about what an empty shell of a man I am, the two presenters shuffle through the undergrowth and appear, all smiles and funny walks. I think we are live.

"No swearing," loud cool Welshman says as he enters what is being called 'our camp' but what is, in effect a large, solid pile of Australian dirt.

He smiles and winks, but he is being serious so I stop myself from pointing at him and calling him a cunt, which is a very difficult thing to do when faced with such enthusiasm and fake hair.

"I'm sure you two would like to get back to the main camp, right?" The lady says.

Presumably she is contractually obliged to wear high-heels because they make no sense otherwise. I notice Jenny doesn't answer the question at all, which surprises me because if I were her, stuck with me, in silence, with rice and actual beans to eat, not only would I want back to camp, I'd want a psychotherapist.

"How are they doing back there?" I ask, as if they would tell me the truth.

Oh, you know, they are faking liking each other, being pretend friendly, not killed anyone yet but all thinking of murder.

We have all lived with people, all hated them at some point, all of us fallen out or been grumpy, but you aren't allowed to do that on TV if you are a celebrity. You can get caught doing it in the street, be taken to court and forgiven. But if you have been filmed doing it? Nah, goodbye career.

"They had a good night. Ate, chatted, bonded. That sort of thing."

I can picture the scene and prefer where I am, but I'm guessing it would be too easy and too boring to keep us here so I listen for what we have to achieve to get to a place I don't really want to go full of people I really don't want to see.

"To get back to camp," the very lovely lady says, "you need to pass a challenge. A jigsaw," she says while laughing.

She knows what is involved, and if she is sniggering at it then it is going to be bad.

"A jigsaw?" Jenny asks.

The Welshman smiles and speaks as it seems only he is allowed to converse with the females. His wife gives him the subtlest of looks. I don't think she trusts him. I wouldn't, he strikes me as a weird type of vampire, feasting on female sexual exploits to remain mentally young. From the outside he just appears to be Peter Pan in need of fanny.

"You won't be alone," the Welshman says.

"If you'd like to follow us," the wife says.

We are led to another clearing, there is a door into a small hill, manmade or not I do not care, what is inside is important. Jenny is quieter than before, and she had been almost silent then. She looks a little ashen, I notice a little trembling.

"Are you ok?" I ask.

She nods, her lips pressed tightly together in an unconvincing smile.

"So, you'll enter through this door," the Welshman tells us. "Inside are three rooms, in which there are hidden six jigsaw pieces. All you need to do is find the pieces and put them together in the central table. You have five minutes from when you enter. If you fail, you'll be back at your camp alone tonight. Success and you are back at main camp."

He isn't selling this to me, I don't want to go to main camp.

"Are you Okay, Jenny?" the wife asks.

Jenny nods and I think is on the verge of being sick.

I put my right hand on her back, for what reason I do not know. It seems to snap her out of her thoughts.

"We'll be ok," I say. "The really horrific stuff is later on in the episodes. They start off light. We'll be fine. Probably a bit of dark, an occasional non-poisonous snake, a lizard on tramazipan and a gay millipede. Easy."

The wife laughs. I don't like her as much as I did.

"At any time, you can play the celebrity card, shout joker and we'll get you out as soon as we can."

I feel confident stood at the door, Jenny at my side. But this is because we are not inside, inside I may actually pass out. We are dressed in cargo pants and red t-shirts with our name on the back, and all other information the viewers require to vote us out or leave abusive texts because everyone likes an abusive internet rant.

We enter, the door opens up into a dark room. No lights other than the rays coming from outside. The walls appear to be moving as does the floor. Insects, cockroaches and some other small things all able to crawl into my bottom and start a new community that eats my rectum. The Welshman will tell us what and how many. A gazillion ants and ten trillion worms, none of which can hurt you are in the room. Oooooo, how scary.

They interview you before the show, asking what you like, dislike and are afraid of. It was an intense set of questions designed to draw out your fears and worries and hates. They take all the information and make sure they are included in some way to the challenges you randomly face. It was an hour long interview and throughout every second I lied. I told them I was scared of things I do not mind. Pretty easy really. They could have asked people who know me well, who care about me, but actually want me to feel uncomfortable for the laughs. But no such people exist. They could have interviewed my ex, she'd have told them my fears, but then I can't imagine they are about to shove me in a room with her without escape so she can destroy my soul through words alone, the lovely, lovely lady that she is.

I feel Jenny's hand in mine, and I think it is me who reaches for her. I am not trying it on. I want to make sure she is OK, and it is about to get very dark, and I don't actually want to be alone. I've got lost in my own bedroom in the pitch black, I couldn't even find the wall, I had been drunk. I cried. It had been a bad moment in my life.

"Ready to do this?" Jenny asks.

I squeeze her hand.

"Nope," I say.

"Well, that's comforting."

The door shuts and light vanishes. The room is dark and we hear the Welshman. And I hate him, I genuinely hate him.

"The time will start when I say. There are three rooms, a door between each one. Find the two pieces in each room to move to the next. You may have realised you are not alone. The room you are in contains sixty thousand cockroaches, eighty thousand crickets, and over a hundred thousand earth worms. Anything to say?" he asks.

I'm guessing go fuck yourself isn't going to make me popular.

"No," I say.

"Jenny?" The Welshman asks.

"All good," she lies.

"Then away we go, your time starts now."

I put my hands out in front of me, releasing my hold on Jenny. This, I rapidly conclude is a mistake because when I instantly go to grab her hand again she has gone.

"Jenny?" I ask.

"Still here," she says.

"Where is here?"

"Just get looking."

I scramble around two arms outstretched like a blind Frankenstein wanting to touch something. Through my earpiece I hear the two presenters laughing. Wankers. They cut out and I know they will be back with lovely snippets of information. I step forward in to what I do not know, and I scream as someone adds at least a million extra cockroaches into the room by pouring them on my head. How utterly hilarious. I squeal like a little girl on opening a Barbie at Christmas, and my earpiece opens with laughter and, "are you Okay there, Ben?"

"Just great, love them cockroaches and the way they have no respect for personal space."

They are crawling all over my body as if I am actually naked. I feel them. But they are insects, as uncomfortable as they are, they don't bite, can't kill, and only look disgusting. I can't see them so that makes it better, I think.

"Have you found anything?" Jenny shouts from somewhere in the room.

"I haven't even touched a wall," I say.

And then I do, a writhing, insect covered slab of slime.

"Oh you filthy bastard," I say.

My earpiece kicks in.

25

"The walls have a special covering of goo," the Welshman giggles. "But if you feel about there are a few holes. Inside two are the jigsaw pieces. Thirty seconds gone.

I find a hole in the goo and the insects, who are almost certainly being annihilated in their billions by me, the goo, and the embarrassment of being on this show. I take a deep breath and thrust my hand into the space. I feel around in even more goo and find nothing other than a sticky substance that clings and drips in unison, which seems impossible until you have your arm up to your elbow engulfed in the shite.

"You found anything?" I ask Jenny.

"I think I have a piece," Jenny says, "And cockroaches taking up residence in my arse."

"Better place than living in the goo," I say.

I thrust my hand into the next hole which is conveniently right next to the first. I rummage around and find nothing.

"You might want to try in there again," the Welshman helpfully suggests as I pull my arm out of what I imagine it feels like for a vet to artificially inseminate a cow.

I slide my right hand into the cave again, up to my shoulder, swirling my arm about.

"I can't find anything at all," I shout.

"That's because there is nothing in there," The Welshman hilariously says.

You utter dick, I don't say.

"I've got the second piece," Jenny exclaims.

"Next door is opening," the wife says.

I hear the door open, but I don't see it as the next room is as dark as the one we are in.

"Where is it?" I ask.

"To your right," the wife says, so I shuffle right and shout loudly, a very rude swearword that will be beeped out of the broadcast. Jenny screams too because we have walked into each other. I reach forward and feel the edge of the door. I grab Jenny's left arm with my right hand and wish I hadn't because it is coated in three inches of gross, thick gunk. I walk through and Jenny comes from behind. We hear the door close. I hear the sounds in the room.

"Jenny?" I ask.

"Yes?"

"When you were interviewed for this show and you had to answer questions about what scares you most, what did you say?"

"Birds," she says. "I absolutely hate birds."

"Right, and you told them this, did you? The truth?"

She doesn't answer because she hears the cooing of pigeons, just like I do. The flapping of wings, their movement in an enclosed space.

"Oh shit," she says.

And very well she might because if I, like her, had been dumb enough to tell the truth I would have expressly said, I am terrified to my very soul of birds, and specifically pigeons.

"You are in a room with forty pigeons," the Welshman helpfully explains. "Two pieces are laying on their perches," he adds, almost wetting himself with the fun.

"Let's get this done quick," I say. "We don't want you too scared," I add, pretending I'm speaking to that utter fricking imbecile Jenny.

The pigeons fly around, and I crouch and I don't speak to Jenny because I no longer care about her and her fear of pigeons, that she admitted, and told the producers like an utter bellend.

The pigeons don't like us, the space they are trapped in, nor the dark, so they are flying around without direction, incoherent in their travels, back and forth, over me, into me, on me – they actually start landing on me. They are making noises that seem like cooing but sound like, in my head, kill the man. They are communicating, and betting, telling each other that they will give a prize to the first one who successfully shits in my mouth.

"Have you-" I start saying but finish "urglamafao."

"What?" Jenny screeches.

"Aburshimymo," I say badly, spitting.

The Welshman comes on the headphones. "You okay, Ben," he asks absolutely without any trace of sympathy.

"What's going on?" Jenny screams.

"A bird has just shit in my mouth," I helpfully explain, and she bloody laughs, as does the world at me eating bird poo.

"How's it taste?" Jenny asks.

"Well, considering it is actually a combination of wee and poo, it tastes like both of them, mixed together and dolloped onto my tongue, with a tangy aftertaste of diarrhoea," I explain, truthfully.

She laughs again.

"I've found a piece," she says. "That was easy."

"Where's the other piece?" I ask the Welshman. "Come on, I've actually swallowed some of it."

His voice comes through, laughing his booming laugh. "Reach your left hand out to the side and it is there," he says.

I follow his instructions, but not too carefully as I expect there is to my left a guillotine that will humorously slice my arm off just below the elbow. But no, he was telling the truth. A jigsaw piece. I put it in the special fanny bag I have been given so I don't drop it.

"Next room," I shout, and a door opens, I feel forward and there is the frame and I walk through alone as Jenny and her fear of birds can look after themselves.

"You have to wait for Jenny," the wife says.

Jenny can fuck off, I think.

"Come on, Jenny," I say. "This way."

She follows and we hear the door close behind us. The room is silent.

"A word of warning," the Welshman says. "Be quiet and move slowly. You are in a room that contains six small tanks. In each tank are several snakes of various description. Within two of those tanks are the two pieces of the jigsaw. Do you prefer pigeons or snakes?"

"Snakes actually, you welsh bastard," I want to say. But reply with, "Snakes are terrifying."

They aren't, but I don't want to put my hand in a tank of them. I'd like to shove your smiling botoxed forehead in them though, Welshman. Although if they bit you, they'd die what with all the paralysis poison you have injected into your facial muscles, you vain bastard.

I reach out with my left hand and lo and behold there is a tank. Right next to me, no searching needed.

"Have you found a tank yet?" I ask Jenny.

"No, nothing yet," she says, clearly making no effort to locate a writhing mass of non-poisonous snakes.

I put my hand in very slowly.

"Careful, Ben," the Welshman says, making me jump and not be careful.

"I was," I say, and not adding, "until you spoke, you Welsh prick."

I reach my hand in, pushing slowly to the bottom, and rather surprisingly actually find a jigsaw piece.

"That was easy," I say.

For the next two minutes Jenny doesn't find a single tank, and I suspect she isn't trying, while I find them all, put my hand in each of them, find absolutely nothing until the very last one, in the very last corner, having avoided being bitten until I grab the jigsaw, which a snake loves so much it draws blood from my hand as I remove the thing from its grasp.

"You absolute motherfucker," I tell the snake in English. "Got the piece," I tell the Welshman.

"Excellent," he says.

A door opens and it is light. I can see, briefly, before the light blinds me and I can't see anything but white for ten seconds. I finally see a table, and it is here we have to put the jigsaw together, which we do as it is six pieces that are a map, as drawn by a three-year-old.

"Stop the clock," the wife says. "You've done it. Out you come."

I look at Jenny, and she at me. Our eyes lock, we smile, we've done it. Earned food and a better bed, a hammock even. We embrace, we each raise a leg behind us, I whisper in her ear, "Fucking pigeons?"

"Shit eater," she replies.

I think I actually like her.

DAY 02 : EVENING
We walk into our base through a thicket of trees, on a well-worn thin path of dry mud. Each country in the world has a version of this, and they all come here and they all play the games and every country with TV has unlimited minor celebrities to humiliate by dunking us in fish guts, lamb offal and the liquid from popped whales eyes. I think I might hide out and wait for the Swedish edition as I am sure, based on my every childhood dream, that it would be constant nudity from lithe blondes who just want a bit of middle-aged Brit. On entering the clearing I see a group of people in the same suits with numbers on the back, and an overwhelming stink of sweat. I am definitely in the British edition of loud, obnoxious arrogant wankers. And I think I should fit in. I see the two hammocks left for us.

"Which one do you want?" I ask. "The shit one over there near the tree-line, or the shit one over here near the celebrities?"

Jenny looks at them both, shrugs and takes the one in the centre.

The celebrities are sat around a fire that isn't lit on long log benches, and they are silent. We appear, as do the cameras, and all of them stand, all of them form a group and they all hug, squeezing, kissing my cheeks, slapping my back and shaking my hand. It is as if we have been mates for life, bonded through war, given our lives for each other. A brotherhood of man united against the perils of the forest. It's like I'm Justin Bieber and I've been spotted by the most bizarre set of fans.

I think it'll take me twenty minutes to fuck this up.

Jenny is standing like a board, and they hug her more than me, which is nice. Chelsey has drifted away, which is bad, because being hugged by her may be the high point before I am voted out tomorrow, but also the start of a low point because any more of her cleavage on me and a semi might have broken out and my career, as low as it has fallen, would plummet to new depths only experienced by celebrities who have been caught on film masturbating over a web-cam. Not even this programme can bring those back.

I move to my hammock after the general buzz of new arrivals has waned and they are all sat again around the log fire.

Jenny comes across.

"Enjoy the reception?" she asks.

"I was mildly disappointed no one grabbed my junk. But there is always time. Pretty sure aging DJ felt my arse though."

"Enjoy the boobs being rubbed on you?"

I smile.

"I put that down to her being so stupid as she forgot how to shake hands. And my overpowering masculinity."

"Obviously. I'm surprised she doesn't collapse every now and again because she misremembers how to stand."

"She clearly can't work a zip."

"Saw you have a good look in there. See anything you liked?"

"Yes, a pair of massive tits."

"They aren't real."

"Neither is this jungle experience, but by day seven three will be crying because they miss their loved ones back home, like they've never been away for a whole week before. One will have had a mental collapse over not having had a ploughman's lunch in a week, one will be sent to hospital as a precautionary measure having developed a psychosis and two will have fallen in love and be having sex, discreetly, off camera behind the showers."

She stares at me, for a very long time as I grin away.

"The last two will be us," I tell her.

She smiles, and with her flat palm, she smacks me in the balls. Nothing hard, nor violent, a friendly smack, one between friends. But I still drop to the floor, on my knees holding my groin.

"I prefer it gentler," I say.

She smiles down at me.

"You can't help yourself, can you?"

I start to say something, but she shushes me.

"Just don't say anything. Nothing."

DAY 02 : STILL BLOODY EVENING.

God, this is painful. Everyone sat round, darkness setting in, we are all around the fire, the comedian lit it, telling everyone about his scouting days, and how he didn't think the skills he learned back then would be useful now.

He lit a match and held it near some dry wood. The dry wood set alight. Going camping in the middle of the Lake District and trying to avoid being inappropriately touched by a single, middle-aged man in shorts and a blue shirt, has paid off with the ability, beyond anyone else's, to strike a massive phosphorous stick against the box it came in, and set fire to a material humans have been using as fuel since we were all but orangutans. A few people clapped because he was able to use his free hand as a wind shield. I think about matching his amazing life skill demonstration by taking a massive dump in the cooking pot and showing them I am able to wipe my own arse with the toilet paper provided. I choose to nod my congratulations, praying the multi-talented man doesn't break into a song he ad-libs on the spot. Sadly, God is not listening. He sings a song he has just made up. And by sing, I mean he says words that would be a normal sentence like, I have set light to our fire and now we can cook. Words that don't readily fit together in a coherent rhyme, nor provide any great insight into the human condition. Club Tropicana it isn't. But because he is singing them, shitly, everyone giggles in delight. I put this down to everyone still trying to be nice. Give it a couple of days and his cake hole will be stuffed with an iguana at the merest hint of singing words he could easily just fucking say.

"Would you like a tea?" the seventy-year-old asks.

"Yes, please," I reply, thinking I have made a friend.

"Me too, but we haven't got any," she tells me.

She turns to her audience and they all laugh at the brilliance of the set up and pay off. Roaring.

I smile along too, but in my head I have smacked her unconscious with her flabby right arm.

I seek out Jenny with my eyes, and my heart rises with the sight of her rolling her own. I assume she does this to quieten her desire to tell them all to simply fuck off.

31

"What are we eating tonight?" snooker man asks.

"We won some food in a challenge today," Jenny says. "Dark room, underground. And a pigeon shat in Ben's mouth."

Oh, they liked that. They all laugh. Hahaha, some excretion landed in his mouth. Oh, how funny.

I not Oscar Wilde and not as witty and insightful as could be, but I've said a few zingers already and received nothing but vacant stares. I think I need to lower the bar and say anything dumb or insulting about me because then the whole place erupts. I should probably take this as a message or meaning in some way, but I choose to take it as an insult and the obvious conclusion that none of these people have a sense of humour. Especially the comedian. He isn't funny at all.

DAY 02 : THE EVENING IS DRAGGING OUT

The presenters appear and everyone turns on their charm, their smiles, their smarm, their best side all presented to the male Welsh man and his tight jumper and muscles. I look at Molly and she smiles, but it is the smile of a lady who has to stand and giggle as her husband gets drunk, talks mince and spouts mildly racist politics in a crowded bar. I feel her hate. I like her.

"Guys," he says, and they fawn, and giggle and cheer.

And he soaks it in like the messiah on a hill, totally missing the fact he is a knobhead in a clearing. His hair, however, is perfect and would have looked lovely on the head of the eastern European woman who sold it to feed her family.

Nineteen million people used to tune in for this. Most of the adult population. Year on year the numbers drop as they watch ever decreasing popular people turn up and act like cocks. I'm on it so I'm guessing they were unable to acquire the services of the semi-corpse of the actress who had a periodically reoccurring role in the 1960s soap, Z-cars. People will be tuning in, saying, oh, look, there is that guy that got a blowey in his car, stood next to that guy who I don't recognise. They'll google me and find my Wikipedia page that is full of lies and the assentation that I am in fact a prick. My ex changes the content regularly, but at least I am no longer supposed to have married my cousin called Colin. Let's face it, someone as non-descript and unknown as me would never have made the long-list back in the day, competing with girl bands, actors, and politicians and that porn star. We have all watched, all know what is coming, and all think we can make it. It is only twenty days. In a clearing. With food. It really can't be that hard. But it is, and Snooker man is cracking.

"Can we eat?" he asks. "When are we eating," he also asks. "What are we eating?" he further enquires. "Can we eat?" he asks, despite there being no food, no promise of food, no pots boiling or indeed anything to eat other than grass.

Thirty-six hours it has been away from the all-you-can-eat buffet they had at the hotel. Thirty-six hours and already his body is collapsing under the absence of incessant pizza slices, kebabs and because he is a proper Londoner, toad-in-the-hole. I bet he eats Jellied Eels with his hands. But I see a little sweat on his brow, recognise the moment, and know he is without doubt, craving alcohol. He smokes roll-up after roll-up, and he does this off screen, out of camp away from prying eyes because while it is Okay for him to swear, be sexist, rude and condescending and firing out jokes like he has memorized the routine of Bernard Manning in the late seventies, it would be criminal to see him inhale on a live show. He nips away, puffs and comes back. If it is a hunger suppressant, either he is not inhaling or he is one ravenous tool.

"We have a special treat for you all, but we have two people here who earned food. And they have a decision to make."

He looks around the group, each of them worried, the snooker player sobbing, I imagine in the memory of chewing through his twentieth chocolate bar instead of a spoon full of beans and the eight litres of saliva necessary to dissolve them into something that would constipate Japan.

"You two can eat, or you can take on the night trial, where all of you work to try and get enough food for the whole camp," he says.

I turn to Jenny.

"There is obviously a dynamic here. We are new to camp, we need to make friends, and we have to live together, grow, bond and work for each other in the pursuit of a common goal," I say.

She rolls her eyes at me.

"But, I think, it would only be fair if we ate it all, possibly right in front of their faces, and then when full, throw the rest of the untouched stuff away, but in such a method as to leave it inedible. What do you think?"

"I can see your point," she says, "and while it is an interesting one it would ultimately leave us as pariahs and I'd have to spend the time remaining here conversing only with you-"

"Win-win," I interrupt.

"-and then return to the real world having to explain why I behaved in such a horrific way toward my fellow man."

I rub my chin, ponder, nod as I pretend to mull over her wise words.

"So, possibly?"

"This conversation is being recorded, you do understand that, right?"

And I do, I understand my every utterance is recorded for posterity, and available on all streaming services for as long as people pay. I understand that I might come across as a bit of a dick at times, and maybe say the wrong thing. But, and this is possibly what Jenny doesn't quite understand, nor really appreciate, nor grasp, but I genuinely do not give a flying one. I'm here, I'm not recovered from my break-up, I'm stuck. I quite fancy Jenny – based on the fact she hasn't yet punched me in the face - and I want to go home, but I also actually want to stay as spouting bollocks to this random woman, who, if she has any type of brain will hate me, makes me feel happy. I was never good at emotions, being open, or rather bizarrely tennis. I believe these connected as I was Somerset's under Twelve squash champion and due for a long career by being quite sporty in a niche area, like a posh kid representing Great Britain at fencing. It is not an area where you face too much competition from the gifted ones at the local comprehensive.

"Oh, what sport does your son play?"

"He fences."

"Ooo, does he? From a-top a fucking pony?"

I stare at her, gurning, attempting to smile and achieving the look of a man trying not to reveal he has farted out solids.

"If you even try to keep this food for yourself, I will once again smack you in the balls," she says.

I pull the perplexed face which has served me well in life, especially when in in a workplace and being told to do something with simple instruction, not wanting to do what is being asked and just acted dumb. The only way I could increase this image of being a true intellectual moron would be to affect a mildly strong Bristolian accent. I have never met anyone from Bristol – and I have visited a couple of times just to boost my flagging belief in my IQ – who sounds smart. Could be a neurosurgeon, Astrophysicist but if you start spouting with those dulcet tones, I'm just hearing full on retard.

"I think it was less a slap and more a good old feel," I say, managing to complete the words and smile before she bollock punches me again.

But I am toughening up because this time I don't collapse, I bend forward and hold my groin.

"Have you made up your mind?" Welshman asks.

I nod.

"We would like to try and feed the rest of the group. To do otherwise would be selfish," I say.

"What made you come to that decision?" Welshman asks.

"She promised me a handjob," I say.

"This is going out live," he tells me.

"Well, you'd better cut away at about ten tonight," I say, straightening, and then bending back as she karate chops up and with great skill slices right between my balls.

"Motherfucker," I say on live TV, but it's Okay, it is after the watershed, and as we all know, no one under the age of eighteen has free access to the internet on their phone for the rest of the day. They can watch anything at any time and certainly do, but oh no, no nipples or swear words, or anything that would upset old people who died in the late nineteen eighties. Nope, that would send the press into collapse.

DAY 02 : STILL THE EVENING : STILL HAVEN'T EATEN

The game, the wonderful game.

Molly tells us in her tight skirt and tights and heels and a coat because it is blustery. It isn't done up as that would mean viewers complaining about not being able to see her cleavage. Mr. Norris from Southport has written in to say he will not be watching again until she gets her boobs right out. It is after 9 pm, I deserve, and in fact demand, wobbling top boob in my female presenters. Just have them in polo necks by the time Good Morning Britain is back on, yours sincerely, Colin.

We are in the dark, we walked to the nearby artificial lake that through the wonderful work of some student prop people, has fake weeds, reeds and smoke on the surface. I lagged behind, not in a sulk but because that is where Jenny was and everyone else was treating me as if I was the single thing that could end their career in seconds, the buzz of which was keeping me warm.

"Why are you here?" Jenny asks.

I open my mouth and she holds up a hand to stop me.

"No, seriously, why are you here?"

35

I take a deep breath.

"I was going through a rather dark time," I say.

"Were?"

"I was a lot worse in the summer. Cider does that to a man. A temporary high, leading to a prolonged low and a red bulbous nose."

"Woman?"

"Yeah, I hold my hands up, I maybe wasn't the best, in fact, arguably the worst. And we were coming to an end, I guess. Certainly a moment."

"So?"

"So, I got hurt. It is the way of things."

"You don't strike me as someone who gets hurt."

"Well, I don't intend to let it happen again."

"By being as repulsive as possible to all females?"

"And males?"

"What?"

"I'm non-discriminatory: I hate all genders and types with equal contempt."

"Maybe the only one you truly hate is yourself?"

"That is an easy thing to do."

"So you just try and make them all dislike you and your opinion is confirmed."

I want to say something, anything really. But I don't, she nailed it. This is who I am. And obvious with it too.

I now wish I had walked at the front.

Molly and The Welshman tell us what we need to do on the back of jokes they set up in the afternoon. They are looking for a running gag that sticks and will define the series. They won't be basing any on me as I will be one of the first to go, I have to be.

There are ten boxes, inside are ten exercise bikes, there is a long LED display along the top of them all. Each one is separated from the next with Perspex partitions, and we each sit in one. We have to pedal, and make the LED light get all the way to the end. If we hit the big number eight, we all eat because me and Jenny have a free pass.

Snooker Star Gaz is rallying the troops with encouraging team talk.

"Nobody fuck this up," he encourages. "Because if you do, I'll fucking die, and it will be your fault," he pep talks.

He has, I think, motivated me to a higher performance by at the very least zero point zero, zero, zero percent.

"Can I just say," I say not waiting for permission, "that I am, like all of you, inspired by those meaningful words, and thought provoking utterances but-"

"Shut the fuck up," Snooker boy tells me. "I'm hungry. I need to eat."

"But," I continue, "Snooker man-"

"Gaz," he shouts. "Gaz," he shouts again. "My name is Gaz."

I nod, pull an apologetic face, hold up my hands, and correct myself. "Snooker Gaz here," I say, and am unable to complete, as I am rugby tackled to the floor.

He is solid, yet soft, like a massive ball bearing covered in velvet cushions.

He is also a wheezing mass of rage. I think his lungs may be the size of tennis balls and the consistency of marmite. He squeezes me for at least three seconds, then rolls off, onto his back exhausted and done.

"I'm guessing you are, in the old bedroom department, a bit shit," I say, lying next to him in what some internet troll will meme into a post coital joke.

"I'm a fucking stallion," he tells me, not through a voicebox but by manipulating rasping exhales into vaguely familiar sounds.

"I'm less of a lover and more of a fighter," I tell him, lying on my back, throwing ridiculous punches up into the air.

He laughs at me. "More of a prick," he says.

"Yeah, quite a bit of that."

I stand up and offer him my hand. He takes it and stands.

"You realise that even if we do win, they are only going to make us skin, boil and then fry a hundred feet of Koala cock."

"I'm so hungry I don't think I'd even need the ketchup," he replies with utter seriousness and quite a fair amount of desperation.

We sit on our bikes, and Sexy Welshman is looking increasingly uneasy with the way the series is going.

Every year for the last decade it has been a massive love fest between the stars, a bonding programme where everyone is on their best behaviour, trying to show a public that everyone is fun and cool and calm at all times.

I've been here a day and I think Snooker Gaz genuinely would have harmed me if he wasn't more concerned with avoiding coronary failure or, indeed, causing commotion to postpone the delights of a meal cooked from parts of animals we didn't know were edible, or that those animals actually existed.

Tonight you have to figure out how to cook the Pituitary gland of the previously extinct giant sloth. Gordon Ramsey probably has a recipe somewhere in one of his three billion TV shows, that consists of the phrase, Fucking slice it, then stick it in the fucking pot and then fucking fuckety fuck fuck. I could do that for a living, stand and insult people from a position of false arrogance, shouting in their faces like a monumentally maladjusted child, in fact, I do that, just not frequently on film, and not paid to do it either. I should take this brief sojourn in the wilds of the Australian outback as an audition. In need of a seriously grumpy, massively untalented gobshite? I'm your man. I'll even go on kiddies TV and insult puppets, then I am your middle-aged man. Jackanory, oh, the things I could do with Jacka-fucking-nory.

I am sat on a bicycle, goggles on because obviously they are going to pour billions of animals that crawl and bite and slither and pinch and look to make home in arse orifices for the entertainment of all. Back in the day they had Superstars where actual sports people with talent took part in physical challenges to find out who was the best sportsperson of all. Nowadays you'd just get the best Judo practitioner in the universe to do as many sit ups in a minute as they possibly can while half-submerged in blended fish bollocks.

This is progress.

I look along the line of people, each one more blurred than the last as the Perspex, while transparent, is not perfectly so. Snooker Gaz is next to me, short of breath because he has, in the previous five minutes, moved. Then the rest of the fools who, like me, are in goggles, sat on a spinning bike. The half woman/half breast implant is laughing because she absolutely adores spinning, has a personal assistant who tells her she is fabulous at it and could have, in different circumstances been semi-pro. Are there actually professional spinners? Or do they fall into the all-encompassing professional group, who genuinely need a Union, the professional tits? I assume the different circumstances would be her being someone completely different and with a totally different upbringing. She pays him big money to enter her house, tell her to use her gym, and spout lies in the form of platitudes so she feels better about how she is keeping the annual cost of liposuction down through breaking a minor sweat while the silicone in her chest sloshes up and down to her gym instructor's delight. Semi-pro my arse. The rest are sat silently as Welshman talks us through it. Five minutes of peddling to charge the lights. The more lights, the more people get to eat something other than beans and rice.

"We are not playing for food, we are playing to find out how many of us can eat," I say to Snooker Gaz.

He looks forlorn, like a child actor who spent his twenties smoking crack and is now aware of just how stupid that was.

"I can't peddle for five minutes," he says, honestly and without much point.

"I'm surprised you can breathe for five minutes. But yeah, neither can most of us, and especially not when the creepy crawlies start raining down, along with the slime, and what other hilarity they deem fitting to slop on our heads."

"I'm really hungry, Ben," he says, and I am not sure if his desperation has hit such a low that he is now praying to me as some type of God, or if, as I suspect, he is in some type of hunger, alcohol deprived psychosis.

"How exactly did you prepare for coming on this show?" I ask, out of genuine curiosity. "As it appears, to me, that you have trained yourself up by drinking your local brewery dry and consuming the entire content of your fridge, freezer and pantry in a prolonged bout of binge eating. Then, basking in the afterglow of ten trillion calories trying to find a way through your large intestine, deliberately infected yourself with bacterial Tuberculosis and topped off the left-over healthy tissue by dousing them in diphtheria."

He looks at me, probably pondering how I can say so many words without collapsing in an oxygen deprived coma, with the glazed eyes of a man who just wants to eat.

"What is diphtheria?" he asks because that is clearly the important point.

I would like to tell him of the bacteria and its Latin name, the fact that vaccines have eradicated the horrific disease in the western world but that it is still prevalent in countries which have a much lower vaccination rate. But I can't be arsed.

"Lung knack," I say.

"Ooo, nasty," he replies in the same way he might dismiss a bad outbreak of acne.

"Are you ready?" Welshman asks in a shout of masculinity.

"Yes," half-woman/half-silicone says with the enthusiasm of a female who would be quite comfortable wearing a fluorescent pink

39

leotard and matching headband at a funeral for a close colleague in the industry.

The others, and me, grit teeth, clench cheeks and resign ourselves to the fact we are all going hungry. I won food, I want to tell them, with my own bravery and ingenuity. But I have given that up to form some solidarity with you utter wankpots. And yes, that does make me the biggest tit here, including those two rock solid mounds enthusiastic lady.

"As you may have guessed," Welshman says, sniggering like a school boy who has just heard a PE teacher say balls. "You will not be alone in there. Can you hazard a guess, Ben?" he adds with his booming deep laugh made up in equal parts of arrogance and conceit.

"Is it porn stars?" I ask.

He doesn't answer.

"Naked female porn stars pouring gallons of free booze?"

He stays silent.

"Naked female porn stars pouring gallons of free booze and smoking Crack cocaine?"

"No, Ben. None of those things."

"Well they are all on the list I gave of what scares me most. Ultimate nightmare, dark room, naked adult industry employees, female obviously, a fountain of Belgian lager and a smouldering pipe. That would be the end of me. You would never see me again. I'd stay there, quaking. The fear. Oooh, it-"

"Shut up," he tells me. "Anyone else, who doesn't want to be cut from the broadcast-"

"We are live," his wife tells him.

His smile instantly returns, his big numerous teeth all shining and gleaming and beyond white. Were you to go in to a paint shop and ask for that exact same colour, you'd be told it doesn't exist. It is made up. Fake.

"There will be insects, slime and fish guts and if you get far enough, rotting fruit and veg."

"Don't eat that," I tell snooker Gaz. "It'll give you the squits."

"I don't like fruit and veg," he tells me.

"Or water, I'd guess."

"No, can't stand water," he tells me, disowning the one thing only slightly less important than oxygen in keeping us alive. "Meat and if it isn't alcohol, I drink energy drinks," he adds, speaking like some health guru on hallucinogens.

"How are you not dead?" I ask. And I am serious. How is he not dead?

"Look after myself," he tells me, and I actually can't tell if he is making fun or is ignorant. I go with the later as this wouldn't break the pattern.

A buzzer sounds and we have to pedal.

We all start moving our legs as fast as we can like a group of non-athletes starting off a marathon by assuming we can sprint the whole way at full whack.

Ten seconds in and snooker Gaz announces, "fuck this," sweating like his forehead is Niagra falls. He tries to stay on his bike but through exhaustion he appears to have morphed into Stephen Hawking and he slides to the floor unable to activate any muscle in his body. Were this a water tank challenge he would now be quite content to drown.

I look along and everyone is flagging. What we need, as a group and inspiration is an event, an aligning of the stars, an epiphany. What we get are sixty thousand green ants – the biting kind – seventy thousand meal worms (what are they actually for?) and some insect that when crushed lets off a proper rotten stink. We all scream in unison, and someone, somewhere, and I believe it is comedy gold man, cockney geezer, manscara male, shouts, "come on guys, they can't kill us!"

They can if I ram them down your fucking throat I say in my head while smiling, and trying not to inhale while simultaneously attempting to blow several thousand biting ants from my face. I pedal like I have never pedalled, as when I did actually used to pedal, I was on a new-fangled BMX and just trying to impress girls with ever increasingly risky skids. I never pulled, but I did take the skin off both knees and cry. In front of people. Who mention it to this very day. Which isn't as bad as the kid who pissed himself on the school mini-bus because he was too shy to ask to stop so he could wee-wee. He left town at sixteen and is not even traceable on facebook. I got off lightly. My BMX took an absolute kicking though as it was clearly its fault.

I am pedalling and Welshman shouts, "Two!" which I take to mean we are a quarter of the way there. He skipped one so maybe he is just going with even numbers. Or maybe he was distracted by flirting with his wife in a manufactured love-in they have perfected over the years.

I look to my left and Snooker Gaz appears to be dead. A cigarette may revive him. I see his chest rise and fall, and his legs twitch so not deceased, just having a stroke or seizure. This will gain him popularity and public votes. I contemplate feigning a manic episode and running amock and killing the production team but assume this may not be the quickest

41

way to the nation's heart, unless of course I am able to do it with a cheeky grin, then I'll be on all the chat shows.

"Three lights," Molly says, giggling and she exchanges a pre-scripted joke with big sexy Welshman who has his instant off-the-cuff remark memorised and they rock back and laugh, all belly and spittle.

I hazard a guess that they were talking about adding extras to our cubicle of delight because upon the first guffaw a tsunami of slime cascades down from above. It is green, thick but still able to run freely under my clothes, into my ears and coat every single blade of hair on my head. It also covers the pedals and my feet fly off, and as I am not exactly sat, I fall an inch or two and clout my arse on the hard plastic seat. I scrape the slime from my goggles and peer over at Snooker Gaz who is lying face up as the last of the slime drips down onto his face where the rest of it landed a second before. He wipes some of it away so he can continue to inhale.

"Four lights," Welshman shouts while, I assume, flexing his biceps through a tight fitting black jumper.

I regain my footing and pedal more.

"I think Snooker Gaz is dead," I say.

"No, I'm fine," he gargles, raising a thumb.

"Five lights," the woman shouts, which is pointless as there is no way this test is genuine.

The pedals and lights are in no way connected. They are clicking on lights, giving us false hope, begging us to go faster, when the actual numerical climb is controlled by someone off screen, waiting for us to react. I pedal more.

I look across and see the woman of silicone with her arse in the air. I ponder, briefly, if she has had some work on that, in the sense of implants rather than an extension. It appears she is pedalling to the rhythm of a song in her head. A song with a beat every two seconds. Left pedal, hold pose, tense buttocks, face pout, right pedal, hold pose, tense buttocks, face pout, repeat. I think I see Jenny staring at her, green goo sliding down her face into her top. I see her mouth move, and hear her voice very clearly in my ear.

"Stop pedalling like a tit," she says.

God, I think she is fantastic.

"Six lights, but only two minutes left," Molly shouts as a god awful stench encases my nose.

I take a deep breath, at the wrong time, and a bit gets in my mouth.

"Fish guts!" Welshman says with glee.

And they are fish guts, rotten fish guts, really rotten, gone-off fish guts.

I look across to Snooker Gaz, only some of him is visible, mostly his stomach. He raises his thumb. All is good in the world.

I pedal more, increasingly sure there is absolutely no electronic attachment to this glammed up exercise bike.

"Seven lights," The woman shouts. "Seconds left," she adds.

Thank Christ I think. A few more seconds till the end and the outcome they have had planned all along.

"Time's up!" The Welshman shouts. "Let's get you cleaned up and out here," he adds, Welshly.

We are let out of our boxes, the doors opening outward and letting slop flow freely. We march, covered in insects drowned in goo and taunted by rotting flesh. We shake and scrape slime and dead animal's intestines from our clothes and skin. I hear a few retches, swear words and a belch. I look back and see Snooker Gaz isn't with us. I walk to his cubicle and see him on the floor.

"It is over, Gaz, " I say.

"Did we win the food?" he asks, thumb pointing up.

"No idea, mate," I tell him. "The results of our endeavours are about to be made public."

I reach down and grab his hand and pull him to his feet. What appears to be half the haul of a medium sized trawler falls from his body to the floor.

"I gave it my all," he says.

"Which is uncannily like absolutely nothing," I say.

He nods, blood and possibly a carp's anus dropping from his ear.

We are told our results. Seven lights, one short of the maximum.

"Ben and Jenny, you had already earned your meal ticket-"

"What?" I interrupt. "If you had actually said that before, I wouldn't have bothered. I'd have lay down with Gaz and wallowed in gunk."

"It was the best approach," Gaz assures me.

"Which means we have seven tickets to our evening's meal, away from camp. But there are eight of you. Normally we'd ask you to select who doesn't go."

Seven people say "Gaz," in unison. Gaz says, "Not Gaz," but the Welshman ignores us all.

"You all need to head back to camp, clean up, and get ready for the evening of dining ahead. Except you, Gaz. You need to get ready to eat beans. No ticket, no entrance," Welshman says.

I truly believe Gaz is going to cry.

We sit around, cleaned and smelling better. We have new clothes as the ones we had need to be burned. Gaz is sat alone, a few murmurs of him deserving no food. The hunger after two days killing them all.

Gaz smiles, sweating, beads forming on his forehead.

"You alright Gaz?" I ask as he appears to be even less popular than me right now, which is quite a weird sensation for me, and I would hope, for him.

"Yeah," he says about as convincingly as a teenage boy who has been dumped and just discovered his ex is now, twenty minutes later, in the early stages of a new relationship with his best mate.

Welshman and wife march into the clearing, and it is dark now, the fire going, a few studio lights shining so they don't need night goggles to see semi-celebrities. Seven people rush toward them like they are the tag-team messiahs and they are lepers asking for salvation. Jenny stands back and watches me and Gaz. She walks toward us.

"How you going Gaz?"

"Yeah, all good," he lies.

"I'd bring you back something but we aren't allowed."

"I'll manage on tobacco."

We turn our attention to the booming voice.

"Well done, Guys," he says like the local village want-to-be opera star. "Here are your invites, all nine of them."

The seven celebs, who are verging on hysteria having eaten only rice and beans for a whole forty-eight hours, snatch the big red card from the Welshman's hand.

They are jumping and giggling and excited. Some turn and look at Gaz, and they look solemn and sad, but then they turn away again and the jumps and the fun starts.

The Welshman walks over, chest puffed, arms out to his side as if his massive muscles stop him from moving normally. He is fooling no one.

"Here you go," he says, handing over the two A4 sized invites in red to the 'Jungle Party'. "Invites to the main event."

44

He looks at Jenny then me then Gaz. He taps the side of his nose with his left index finger. "Just between you and me. There will be a little booze."

I hear Gaz's lips smack and his heart break.

"These don't have our names on them," Jenny says.

"But they will get you in the same. You just need to have one to gain entrance. So don't lose it," he laughs, "or all that lovely food and drink will be lost to you forever. So say your goodbyes, and follow me."

He turns and walks off.

Jenny stares at me.

"You going to be alright, Gaz?" she asks.

He nods.

She walks off with the group, trailing behind.

"What do you think it'll be?" Gaz asks.

"They seem to be deluding themselves it'll be champagne and a three-course meal cooked up by Nigela Lawson," I say.

"She is fit," Gaz assures me.

"But I'm guessing it'll be slices of White Rhino buttock served on a platform of hedge, which I can't say I'm partial to. Yourself?"

"One of my favourites. Second only to a Sunday roast."

"Controversial," I explain.

I look at him, see him withering away in the pain of hunger.

"Fuck it, have my invite," I tell him.

"I can't accept that," he says, taking the invite from my hand and folding it into his pocket.

"You just have though," I inform him.

"You don't fancy the food?" he asks, standing and walking away.

"It's the company I can't stand," I softly tell the space where he used to be. "They are all boring."

I walk to my hammock, I get my rice and bean ration, I set up the water on the fire, that I needed no organised scouting experience to figure out, and wait. I lean back in my Hammock, alone and peaceful. Exactly how I like it. I try and think about where I am and what I am doing. I smile and laugh because I know the answers exactly. I like Jenny, weird how those sensations creep up on you. Gaz is Gaz, and there is no way to change that. The others are all annoying, but then so am I.

It's a shame I'm going to be kicked off in double quick time. I could do with the extra cash.

THE PRESENTERS : END OF DAY 02

They sit, The Welshman and Molly in their apartment room, sipping on wine, relaxing, taking a break in dressing gowns and slippers. They are new for this season and specially produced by the hotel for them, like a Spa retreat of serious exclusivity monogramming every toiletry to try and justify the exorbitant prices.

They are sat, thinking and waiting on the numbers from producers, numbers that dictate what will happen.

"What do you predict?" Molly asks, sipping on wine and smiling in the first glows of stress chemically beaten back by grape.

"Ben played the invite card well. That might have earned him some points. I didn't expect that. Selfless. Weird."

She laughs and he looks at her, a flash of anger. He doesn't like being mocked.

"He isn't fussed about hunger, not yet. It doesn't look like he is a food monster. He genuinely couldn't face sitting at a table with the others," she says. "He is weird."

"If you were watching, away from here, a neutral, what would you think?"

"I'd think I want to see more of him. He might wear thin, he really does only actually moan a lot, and be rude. But I'd like to see where he goes. I'd actually like to see him crack. Collapse. Isn't that bad?"

"Not for ratings. That would be amazing for ratings."

"They still dropping?"

"Not free fall, but bit-by-bit, slowly and surely, less and less."

"Because no one famous comes on anymore. And they are all pally and happy. We need more arseholes for views to increase," she says, and she knows she has had a glass too many. "We should call it a day, go out while it is still something rather than nothing. It has become boring."

"It isn't that unpopular," he says.

"But it is stale. We are stale. Same old, same old."

"See how you feel at the end. When it's done. When we get nominated for awards. When we get to kick back and the public tell us how great we are. We'll win awards."

"We always win awards. We do our silly routine, tell the jokes we planned to tell. The crew writing our material."

"I write the material," he says, slightly louder than he should.

She smiles, and sips her wine, happy that she has riled him.

"No, you don't. Most of what you suggest gets binned."

"I'm being creative, taking chances."

She laughs again.

"No you aren't, you are rehashing jokes from comedians past as if you are the new line in modern comedy."

"I pitch it to the audience."

"Which is slowly walking away."

He goes to speak, and defend and talk until she asks nothing more, but his phone beeps, a message pops up telling him the feedback and numbers are in. He tells his wife, she walks over and sits on the arm of the sofa he has been lounging on. He opens the email and reads.

"Viewing figures up. More on the second night than the first," he says, as proud as a pushy parent seeing their son win the primary school sprint.

"What are the numbers on the contestants?" she asks.

He scrolls through.

"Standard, no real move. All in the order they were. Gaz has dropped, but not by much." He pauses, staring at his screen. His wife notices and smiles.

"Ben on the up?"

"I'll quote you something. A general response, something said again and again. I'm not sure I like him, certainly wouldn't want to be stuck with him, but at least he is honest. I look forward to hearing more of what he has to say."

She laughs. "I think we have struck a winner here."

"He won't win."

"He won't win, a female always wins. But he'll be about until he cocks things up majorly. Which is going to be difficult as he has set the bar quite high. He has insulted everyone, clearly doesn't like being here, doesn't like us, thinks the whole premise is a joke-"

"But clearly has a thing for Jenny."

"Her ratings?"

"No change, lower half, but the comments are good. They want to see how she copes with Ben."

"I want to see how she copes with Ben," she says.

"I think we could manipulate this quite well."

"The surprise guests?"

"All ready. I don't think it works the way we thought it would, but it will work. Another day and we can drop them in."

"Is this really the way we want this to go?" she asks.

She tries at worried, and knows it is cruel, but she wants the whole thing to end.

"We have paid the money, they know what is coming. They are prepared."

"I don't like the direction," she says, but without venom. "But I think we might actually make this season have some actual interest beyond seeing celebrities try to swallow blended camel's vaginas. And then retching onto each other. It would be a good way to go out."

He turns to her, smiling. "We needed to switch things up. This could be our new direction."

She smiles too because she thinks this will be the end of the show forever.

"Yeah, maybe we should change things up a lot this year. Go in a different direction. See where that goes. Flagging ratings are flagging ratings after all."

He smiles, and nods.

"We are too popular to fail," he tells her.

DAY 03 : MORNING : VERY BORING

We are sat around doing nothing which is a particular speciality of mine. I have spent years of my life asleep, and then doing nothing of any interest until I can sleep again. But I usually did this alone, here I am surrounded by theatricals and people scared of silence, unable to hide away inside their heads. They need the acclaim, the noise, the attention. And they speak and ask and talk and chat and reminisce about other celebrities, better celebrities.

The man-child pop-star appears in shock, his face a picture of someone who can't unsee what has occurred before him. He looks like a boy who has just been flashed by his high-school geography teacher. Why is it always the geography teacher? I ponder this and break up the current conversation of what's your favourite fruit? And other such amazing insights. Comedic Cockney is all about the Melon he says. Someone has rather mischievously thrown in a raspberry and I believe Jenny, judging by the stares she is giving to the middle-distance wants to choke half of them to death with a passion fruit.

"Why is it always the geography teacher who is a perve?" I ask, breaking into the conversation I am actively being left out of, and having absolutely no sequiturs. They stop their fruit-based banter and stare at me. I look up.

"You know, the wrong-un at school, why was it always a geography teacher?"

"I didn't really go to school," Snooker Gaz tells us.

"You surprise me," I say.

"Me neither," Cockney wideboy, banter boss tells us all. "I grew up in the business."

"You'd have met some right wrong 'uns then," I say.

"It's a different world," he tells us all, standing, looking as though he is going to break into song and make this series the unnecessary alternative musical addition.

"I imagine it is. Bit weird though, right?"

"I don't know any different."

I think about that, how he was schooled in that environment, how he was constantly on a performance, how he was always trying to be noticed. I look at the rest of us and see we are all the same, publicity chasing, attention seeking, please-like-me-everyone people.

"So have you got any dirt on anyone?" I ask.

Tall good-looking but almost cancelled man starts to speak.

"Yeah, we all know yours," I say, holding up a hand.

"I wasn't going to say anything about my mistake," he says very very defensively.

Yes, we all read it and wallowed gleefully in your downfall. It is what we do, as a public. Ah, famous, talented, good-looking bloke on TV, turns out he is a bellend, and quite happy to use his fame to get sucked in his car on a motorway. Millions of people crying, What a wanker, with a fair few hundred thousand thinking, I wouldn't have got caught.

It is like the overweight sports writer castigating a professional footballer for being out of shape. I know you have to write something, but have a modicum of self-realisation.

"Was it worth it?" I ask.

He flusters and blabs and says nothing.

"It was a one-off error of judgement," he party-lines me.

"Oh come on, it was not. It was the first time you got caught. Obviously since then you've repented, done your time away from the camera, and obviously grown up."

"It was a mistake," he says.

"But which bit?" I ask, genuinely interested. "The cheating, the danger, the using someone, which bit? Because there are loads who would be like, fair play, what's the problem, two consenting adults – just."

49

"Have you never made a mistake?" he asks, and I think his eyes are welling up.

"Of course I have. Everyone has. The latest one would be agreeing to come on here. But I'm not important. No one really cares about me or what I say or what I do. I don't have paparazzi chasing me from my front door so a picture of me with a stain on my top makes the news. Oh, Ben the dickhead drops toothpaste on his shirt before going to the corner shop to buy booze at eleven a.m. on a Thursday morning. Literally – and I hate that word and its misuse – but literally, why would anyone care? Is it because they can feel better than me? They should because they already are."

"That's the same for me," he lies.

"No it isn't. I'm a knobhead, I've never pretended to be anything other than me. I annoy me, so I am aware of how much I annoy others. You and others like you portray yourselves as some type of goal for people. Look at me, be me, try and be me, buy my products and be more me. And then the big reveal, actually there is no superiority there, he is just a fickle, thick, pervy bastard, but just a good looking one with a nice line in patter. And the papers, always on the look out to knock the rich and famous down, jump on it."

"You got cancelled too," he says, still smiling, still trying for a positive.

"Yes, no one invited me onto shows or asked my opinion because they got bored of me saying what is in my head. I'm not stating I know everything, nor that I am the oracle of life and the epitome of all that should happen. I am very aware I am a gobshite who says the wrong thing. But that is the reason they asked me onto stuff in the first place, and ultimately the reason they stopped asking me. I gave opinions, my opinions, right or wrong, and they wanted me to say something that I didn't want to say. So I promised I would and then on live TV said what I actually think. Invites dried up. Oh well."

"I've done my time," he says, and I realise we are all being stared at and that popcorn, were it readily available would be crunching away in the mouths of eight people.

"You didn't commit a crime – well, you did, receiving fellatio at 80 mph on a motorway, while not directly addressed in the highway code, does indicate a lack of care for others and is, most importantly, 10 miles per hour over the speed limit."

"I was doing seventy, it was on cruise control."

"Oh, well, that's alright then," I say. "Our mistake, we take it back. It isn't about punishment, it is about rehabilitation. Essentially, are you still a dickhead, or have you just learned to mask the knobbish behaviour behind a well-crafted veneer of media savvy utterances and appearances?"

"I'm a better man for it," he says.

"For the blowjob? Being caught? Or for having thought and reassessed. Because if you think the only problem was being caught then no problem, but don't pretend otherwise. It is like that American evangelist, telling everyone to lead wholesome lives and family and honesty and respect is everything and then it turns out he is blowing millions given in charitable donations on hookers and coke. The guy actually went back on TV and cried and repented and blamed God for working in mysterious ways. He was forgiven. Can you believe it?"

"It was a simple mistake."

"Being caught always is."

Jenny appears in front of me.

"Are you always this grumpy in the mornings or do your breakfast chats involve less insults on a normal day?"

I look around the camp, the stares and smiles, them all thinking, well, he has blown that, he won't be on the show much longer. I think they are right. I have also covered most of them in spittle.

I take a deep breath, smile, realise most of that conversation would have been better left inside my own head or been better expressed through an inane grin and a series of ironic nods.

"Anyway, going back to the previous chat," I say, "were I to replace any part of me with a fruit, it would be my right knee which I'd swap for a pineapple."

I walk to the coffee pot and make sure I don't make eye contact with anyone.

The next couple of hours I am ignored by the rest of the celebrities. I like calling them that, makes me feel vaguely more important. Jenny looks across and I catch her glancing often. I smile as does she but we don't speak, and she doesn't come near me either. It's like I have been doused in minor celebrity repellent. Young pop-star boy-child-man looks sometimes too but I don't think it is at me, it appears he has forgotten to put on his rather strong glasses and can't focus on a thing, has been hit so hard on the head he is in a constant state of concussion or, as I suspect, upon signing a contract with Big Music Firm, he was, as a means of control, forced to undergo an anaesthetic free lobotomy.

If there is a quiz challenge I'm voting for him just for the giggles.

What is the capital of England?

England?

Ahhh, but I think I will be gone by then.

I lay in my hammock, the weather lovely, a warm sun but humid under the canopy of big green trees that probably only grow here. I've never seen them before, but they are tall and the branches spread out and birds sit in them and I watch them. I feel like I would at home on my sofa, pissing away the day, drinking coffee and procrastinating while thinking about stuff that I'll never get round to doing or achieving but loving the thoughts all the same. The only thing missing is rain tapping on a window and the low bass tones of some bloke telling me about a property up for auction and the potential yield and the travails of turning the lump of damaged bricks into a rental home for students. I could do that, I am sure but I lack the will, the desire, the money and the skills.

I am a single bloke, middle-aged, no mortgage, a fair whack of money, no ambition, no partner, no real happiness and a level of fake contentment that historically could only be found in the highest quality opium den.

I think about my rant this morning, the words flowing and washing over the good-looking bloke. I could have said anything to anyone, but I chose him. I am as absurd, more even. I smile at myself. I can't help it and I need to stop. I don't want them close, don't want them to see me as I am. I don't want anyone close. I think I'm scared people will see me as the pretty empty dull man I believe I am. And everyone here is the same, maybe everyone in the world. We all set up barriers to hide behind and shields to protect and deflect, it's just mine are better, and I enjoy them more.

My peace and doze is broken by the squeals of the silicone lady on seeing someone else she can speak to. The Welshman and his wife walk into the clearing and everyone is on their feet. I manage to lift my head and open an eye. They stand waiting for us all but I actually can't be arsed so I prop myself up on my elbow. I think we have been here three days so getting voted off is not yet on the cards. There are a few trials and a few set-ups to cause friction or make us all bond and be besties, and hopefully I won't be involved in any.

"It is time for the first trial," Molly announces as Welshman stands with his arms wide.

He shoots her a look, but the smile never goes.

"The public have chosen two of you, the two they would like to see the most. And we will tell you the names in double quick time."

She looks at her husband.

"We just have to run through a few jokes the production team wrote last night."

I smile, the Welshman has either been possessed by the peak Robert De Nero, or he has absolutely no idea what is going on.

"Well, I helped with their construction," he says.

"But did you really?" she replies and skips off to the middle of the camp.

"Last night's meal," she continues merrily, was a great success. Snooker Gaz ate a burger."

"I don't want to know what was in it," Gaz shouts.

She laughs and twirls and if it were not ten in the morning I'd swear she was tipsy.

"I don't think you chewed," she says. "And Ben, so courteous in giving up your ticket. Why was that?"

She asks this almost directly into my face as surreptitiously she has waddled sexily to all-but on my bed.

"I am made up of equal parts empathy and beauty," I make up. "And I saw the opportunity to be alone, and just had to take it."

She smiles and shakes her head like a primary school teacher outthinking a child.

"Ah, but our viewers have noticed a little bit of interest. They are convinced you have something for one of the other contestants."

Have they really, ooo, what could possibly have given them that idea?

"Is it because I keep looking down her top?" I ask.

"Wrong contestant," she tells me apparently using only teeth.

"Jenny? Would that be – and I'm only throwing this out there because it seems some of the viewing public might not have picked up on the subtlety – because I asked Jenny to have sex with me on live TV? I tell you, you can't put anything past these people."

She smiles again and I look at Welshman who is listening to something being shouted into his earpiece.

"Certainly was a clue," the wife says just too loudly and with way too much enthusiasm. "So as many are asking back home, is there something there?"

I would like to answer but Jenny appears and her face says, another mention of me and someone is losing an eye.

"Are we at school?" Jenny asks. "Have I somehow travelled back to the third year disco where your mates not so discreetly ask if you fancy someone?"

She is not happy and this, for whatever weird reason not even Freud could fathom, gives me a buzz. A tingling. I am obviously weird. But absolutely not a pervert.

"I have found over the years that due to my overwhelming air of Alpha male crossed with deep thinking wise man and all round hero figure, that woman-"

Jenny shuts me down.

"Is this why you live on your own in the middle of nowhere, without a partner and only a dog."

I feel just a little spray of spittle on my face.

"I thought it only fair to give other males who possess less dynamic magnetism a chance. It is tiring pleasing all women, all the time."

"You are a deluded individual."

"Who people think has a special attraction for you," the wife adds unhelpingly.

"That is not what was said," Jenny states despite having no access to any information beyond Comic genius' little asides and humble brags.

She turns to the wife.

"What has been said?"

"The early positives are that you guys are a point of interest."

The Welshman appears, pressing his right index finger into his ear listening to voices from production teams about what he needs to do and say.

"We don't usually reveal any outside secrets," Welshman says grabbing his wife's arm.

"No, but this year I thought it fun if we give a little lead on the opinion of people watching."

The Welshman stares at his wife, smiling but not happy.

"Do we need to do the joke about hungry snooker players?" she asks.

Welshman pushes his finger to his ear again.

"You two guys need to make your way along the path, you'll find a clearing and instructions," he says.

"However, be very very aware that everyone is rooting for you," the wife says and I am sure she has had some type of fit.

54

Everyone is staring at her now, the celebrities, me, Jenny, her husband, and every single crew member.

"Is this live?" I ask.

"We are always live," The Welshman says.

"Makes for great TV," the wife adds. "And you two guys are the most popular so far."

"Not THE most," Welshman adds. "But the ones with the most comments certainly. We, me and you, we are the most popular."

Of course you are, Mr. Popular of Popular street. The man just will not be second best, which is weird as he isn't even the funniest in his marriage.

"What type of comments?" Jenny asks.

"Have you guys planned this conversation because I am not following at all. Was there a morning drinking session I was not aware of?" I ask.

I look at all the other celebrities and as a collection of faces I'd say they resembled hate.

I don't want to be this popular, I would like to shout, I'm not used to it. I don't like it. I don't want to win, I don't want to steal your limelight. I want to annoy some of you, sure. Possibly become the least popular person ever to appear on reality TV. Maybe have a slang word for irritating named in my honour. But I do not want to be popular.

I look at all their desperate faces.

And I change my mind because that will be more annoying.

I slide out of my hammock and stand tall near Jenny, who looks like the person you really need to avoid later on a Saturday night when everyone has had a few.

"Jenny, I just think we have to accept the scientific fact that true, genuine personalities, full of warmth humour and love like ours – with sprinklings of insane intelligence, and charisma, and so much other stuff for which words are simply not enough but concepts of enlightenment come close – are always going to rapidly rise up and be the people all people want to be. We are, I believe I have rightly assumed, the modern role models for the great British public and obviously requiring a spin off show."

Jenny is staring at me, fists clenched.

"It would be like this," I say, indicating the clearing like a Shakespearian actor chewing scenery, "just much better and funny. It would involve multiple holidays abroad in which we chat and charm our

55

way through cultures, you in a bikini and me in budgie smugglers, educating as we go and making sure that we leave each place with-"

"Shut the fuck up," Jenny mentions, loudly, in my face, with staring eyes.

I think, realise she is not liking where I'm going with this TV pitch idea, and decide that I should take a step back and ease the situation.

"We could call it, Beniffer on tour," I tell her, ignoring my own sage advice.

"Seriously, shut up."

"Ben and Jen do the world?"

"No."

"Too arrogant?"

"Let's go," Jenny tells me.

And she tries to grab my arm but I move quickly and we hold hands. She tries to let go like she has accidently placed her hand on a turd, but I'm quick to it and grasp tight. She shakes her arm very violently for one so small but I don't let go. And it looks for all the world I am providing her with electric shocks through the form of physical repulsion. After a few seconds of her whirling arms, and tugging, I agree to release her because she is winding up to a sack slap and trying to melt my mind through evil thoughts.

"Too soon?" I ask.

"Why are you such a prick?" she asks.

"Well, so when I was five-"

"Just stop."

We enter a clearing having walked a mud path that loops out wide and then comes back. Another clearing with a line of high-school lockers, a massive wooden board covered in photos of our fellow celebrities, and a table with a large fake parchment. We haven't spoken, nor touched. I asked a couple of questions but was answered with withering looks of utter contempt, but I'm used to these and I think nothing of being disliked. I'll turn it around by doing exactly the same as before but just turned up to a higher level. I have always been surprised at how often this works. It's like they give up and I am able to break through the barrier of distaste into a free-zone where people just leave me to do and say as I want.

It is ace.

I have few friends.

"I'll read it," I say, snatching the parchment from the table.

I unroll the script and its dodgy colouring to make it look old like it has been dipped in coffee and burned at the edges to indicate age because the producer believes that all things eventually go brown and survive at least three house fires.

"Welcome to the first day challenge," I read loudly imaging myself with a laurel of olive leaves and wearing a sheet.

"You have been chosen because you are, without doubt or debate, the most intelligent and sexy of the cont-"

Jenny snatches the script away from me.

"Just pack it in!" she suggests with the air of a teacher who is no longer allowed to beat her students and the allure of the job has gone.

"You can't stand the comedian and yet here you are doing the same patter," she tells me rather accurately.

"That bad?" I ask.

"Yes," she nods.

"I'm sorry," I say and mean it. "I'm kind of a bit of a gobshite when I'm happy."

She looks at me.

"And also when I'm grumpy," I add, covering both my mood groups. "And, bizarrely enough, I like you."

I hold up my hands at her look of repulsion.

"Not in that way – at least I don't think in that way, is it that way?"

"Keep going," she tells me.

"I talk too much."

"You moan too much."

We read the instructions in silence, but one of the crew tell us we have to read it out loud so the viewers understand.

I unroll the parchment again.

We have to identify the other contestants by their baby photos, we have to attach events from their lives, only these events are hidden in the lockers where surprises exist.

"We have all day, so keep it slow. Otherwise we have to go back to camp."

"Hopefully we will be bringing back a treat," Jenny says.

From previous seasons I know that this treat will be a single custard cream each, or three twiglets or, as is most likely the case, absolutely nothing at all because we answer a random question wrong and the treat gets eaten in front of our faces by a massive bearded man who allegedly lives here but is in fact a jobbing extra they have brought in to look stern and say nothing as words mean extra money.

I am sure I remember him from a training film in the 1990s when he was fresh-faced and filled with hope. The intervening years have dulled his eyes so he cannot hide his self-disgust at trying to earn coin by being an actor and failing at the age of sixty.

Just that one big break that is all you need. A line we all feed ourselves.

I smile then realise I am dressed in a red boiler suit with my name and a phone number stencilled on my back about to be splatted by gunk while I try and flirt with a woman who thinks I am a dick.

I'll win her over, I imagine, even though I know I won't.

I've fallen for very few women over the years. Three as it happens. I don't know why, don't know the connection. I know they all ended badly and that maybe, after such an abysmal time – and let's face it, I don't linger on the happy moments, I dissect the disasters – I should give up the hunt. And I have tried, but always, always, the idiotic part of my mind says this one will be different. And they are, but ending the same, all twisted and nasty. The fair share of blame on me. I am, I know, an irritating fucknut with a selection problem. They are looking for someone like me, and I am looking for someone like them. But we should all be looking for someone different. But we chase the same and end the same and feel the same disgust. And for some reason, one that definitely demonstrates that some celestial being somewhere is a drunk, it gives me the biggest buzz. Congratulations biology and all the nonsense you give.

I look at her, see her smile, or at least see something fun, and tell myself, she is definitely not like the others. Beyond being female. I've had disastrous relationships but none of them have driven me to the other side. I'm not a lonely penguin. There are still some women who find me alluring. I hope. Probably. Please? I'm aging and hardly a model, or an intellect, or vaguely interesting after I've told my first five stories, but surely, I have qualities more alluring than my middle-aged competitors.

I look at Jenny, and she is looking at me. She looks tired which we all do, only some have snuck in makeup and are hiding the lines and the pale skin under very expensive products. Someone has a lip gloss that contains snake venom, which makes your lips swell due to the poisonous nature of snakes. This, I find, is quite frankly bizarre. I have no doubt there are men spreading this on their penis in the hope a bit of swelling occurs without the gangrenous effects of being bitten on the cock by a python.

A box opens on a handmade wooden wall. The first picture appears and while I'd like to take an hour or two to decide who it is, the choice is very limited. We are not in camp with Adolf Hitler, but the black and white photo tells us the picture is old. The white frilly clothes, looking like the doilies my gran insisted on knitting, are reminiscent of a child born before the advent of electricity, world peace and any idea of fashion.

"Georgia," we say in unison.

"Not that we are being ageist," I explain to the ones of people who would be interested in watching me, "but no one born after 1962 was ever made to wear that."

"Agreed," Jenny says.

"It doesn't look like her," I add.

Jenny looks at me, raises an eyebrow.

"Because," I add for clarification, "she has had more work done than the roof of the Sistine chapel, and probably spent many a Saturday night with a face like a plasterer's radio."

"Innocence is fleeting," Jenny says.

The next box opens, we have guessed correctly. A photo pops out and Jenny laughs.

"Jesus Christ," she says. "That's even worse."

We are looking at a picture of a four-year-old boy in the tightest of blue hotpants, with a matching blue top, which in itself isn't too bad, but the unfortunate little boy has made the error of choosing accessories of a plastic cowboy hat, a holster and gun, open red sandals and white socks and the expression of a very very constipated goat.

Jenny laughs, and I smile along.

"Who the hell is that? And who the hell would let their child dress like that AND take a photo?"

She laughs more, and turns to me and my grinning face. I think there are tears in her eyes. Hopefully she has squeezed out some pee.

"That would be me," I inform her, "and the answer to the second part is my parents."

She doesn't speak to me for a few minutes, but not from embarrassment, but because she is laughing too hard and pointing at me whenever she can lift her hands from her knees.

"Wait til we see yours," I say. "But more importantly, how the hell did they get that? There is one copy, I have it. It is in a safe place. No one knows but my- Shit."

59

"Ex?"

"Yeah."

"Oooooo," she says. "Do you think they have anything else on you?"

I nod, slowly and in a certain level of unease. If they have spoken to her, I am in the deepest of deep. They wouldn't have done that. No, that would be nasty. Really unpleasant. They would do that, they really would. Public scrutiny of me, on the word of her. Oh, I really don't want to be here.

"Still dress as a cowboy?" Jenny asks.

"Hotpants just don't suit me anymore," I tell her as my stomach shatters into pieces at the panic ripping through my body.

The next photo pops up and it is a young baby, sex difficult to tell as they are draped in a yellow towelling ensemble of obnoxious design that is not defined by any generational fashion as it is yet to become a thing. Possibly made by a grandmother who has decided they can create clothes through the fact they are retired, old and immune to criticism because they have accumulated more money then the rest of the family combined and the relatives are waiting for the moment of inheritance.

Oooo, that's a lovely, and unique, design, Vera, thanks, we'll try that later when we get home, just before we throw it in the bin next to the home sweet home disaster you crocheted last year as our main Christmas present, when what we really needed was you to finance our redecorating.

No, no, put it on them now or you are out of the will.

I look at the background and see some bland furniture, beige stuff and wooden cabinet with carvings. It isn't pine.

"Judging by the furniture and colour selection, we are looking at new. And bland, and unimaginative. In twenty years, people will be, ooo, that bathroom, in brown and grey tiles. How common, how out of date. We'll rip that out and get some lime green in there. Very new, got to be a youngster."

"How are we classifying youngster?" Jenny asks.

I think, and want to say, younger than me, but on reflection that eliminates no one but the two old bastards, leaving anyone but me.

"Twenties or younger."

"Chelsey."

"What?"

"It is Chelsey."

"How do you know that?"

"They look the same."

60

"What? How? Chelsey doesn't look like she did three years ago let alone when she was three. Her face has been altered."

"It's Chelsey."

"Yeah, you can say that, but why? She is what? Twenty Four and has already had fifty percent of the facial procedures that the thirty-year-old Michael Jackson had undergone."

"Michael didn't have his boobs done."

"He wasn't interested in boobs. He probably had his chest implanted with young boys' balls."

She stares at me as if I am liquid evil poured into a boiler suit.

"They'll cut that bit out," I say hopefully. He has a lot of fans, I don't want them slapping me about with their gloved hand and fingers covered in plasters.

I look to the crew and they are all smiling and shaking their heads.

I stare at them and tell them to go fuck themselves, then realise I am, in effect, staring at the British public through a TV camera and expressing my thoughts.

Ten quid says I am the first out.

"It is Chelsey, you can tell by the shape of her face."

"The shape of her face? That kid is what, two? It is a round face, with chubby cheeks and a ridiculous lemon towelling cap. The shape of her face?? Are you mad? Her cheeks are prominent because some bloke who studied medicine sold his soul and now shoves shit under skin so things look bigger. Ooo, are you a medic? Yes, a plastic surgeon. Oo, so not a medic at all, just a human mechanic. You are just guessing."

"You can see clearly it is her. The shape of the eyes-"

"It is a baby, her eyes are chubby and half closed. That baby, looks nothing like Chelsey. Chelsey looks nothing like Chelsey. At school reunions people will be whispering, who is that? And people will be like, no idea. In fact, when they look at her name badge, they will be like, Chelsey, who is that? And why can't you fucking spell?"

"It is Chelsey."

Jenny turns to me and speaks to the camera.

"We have decided it is Chelsey."

"No, we haven't," I say as the door on the wall opens in recognition of Jenny randomly guessing the answer.

She looks at me, doesn't say a word, although I just know she wants to say "I told you so."

"Lucky guess," I say.

She shakes her head.

61

"I got the last one before you."

"Because it was you," she tells me.

"Still counts. One-one."

"It is not a competition between us," she tells me, not realising that she is wrong.

"It is now," I tell her. "Lucky guess."

The next box opens and a photo of a boy who would not look out of place in a Dickens novel, all rags and black on his face, pops up.

"Bob," she shouts confidently and in my face.

"What? You can't just shout out the answers before me."

"That's what we have to do. And it is a competition, so that is exactly what I'm saying."

"I say it is Bob too," I state confidently trying to bluff my way to a draw.

"Congratulations on copying me to the correct response."

"That's a draw."

"I called it first. I won."

"Those are not the rules."

"There are no rules. I shouted the correct answer first. I win." She turns to the camera. "It is Bob," she says.

"Dressed like a tit," I add for no reason other than needing to throw my annoyance at someone I dislike.

The next box opens and Jenny shows me two fingers, points at me and shows one. I genuinely love that she is rubbing this in. Does this make me a masochist? Does it mean she actually likes me? Am I being friend-zoned? Please, please don't say I am being placed in the zone where only friends reside and there is no escape into the hallowed, naked, sexy uplands of relationships that are actually meaningful.

The next photo appears.

"Anthony," we say in unison as a picture that is clearly Anthony pops up. Possibly, in the photo he is three, maybe four, but as he has yet to genuinely pass through puberty he looks like a smaller version – only slightly smaller version – of the silent, inconceivably popular child in the camp.

"He hasn't changed much, has he?"

"Remarkably similar," Jenny agrees.

"And he is considered attractive?" I ask, hoping she will say no, but you are, and then grab me, wherever she wants quite frankly, and lead me away to a caravan somewhere and molest me sensitively.

"Yeah, something about him," she says in, what I assume is a way to piss me off.

"How?"

"Just got that certain something?"

"Bum fluff?"

She shakes her head.

"The body of an eleven year old?"

She smiles.

"The intellect of a shoe?"

She laughs, but at me, not my words.

"It's OK," she patronises, "you have your traits too."

"Go on," I encourage.

"You are," and she pauses and thinks, and then thinks a lot more. She opens her mouth, closes it, and thinks even more.

"Shall we get onto the next one," she asks, grinning away like the hilarious human she thinks herself to be.

"Masculine," I help.

"Hmmmm," she says non-committally, like an arse.

"Are you?"

"Some would say that, yes."

"They'd be wrong though, wouldn't they?"

The next picture pops out.

"Gaz," we say together. He appears to have had the face of a craggy smoker, cocaine addict, alcoholic, heart-attack-waiting-to-happen since the age of five.

The kid is also in a snooker hall, so it wasn't difficult.

The next we shout, "Kieran," as whoever volunteered the photo likes him. He looks cool, is barely younger than ten and just achingly good looking. I would bet money this kid captained every team, was the dream of every girl and the teachers he had forgave his every indiscretion, the absolute wanker.

"Racheal," we say, as a picture of Racheal pops up. She looks happy, in a princess dress, holding a baby, suspiciously perfect like it was a publicity shot.

"Brian," I shout before the last photo comes out. It is Brian, it has to be. It isn't.

"Me," Jenny shouts, and a girl in a pink bikini appears on a photo, in the summer on an English beach surrounded by English people not really knowing what to do on sand, in heat with a deckchair.

"Cute," I say. "Brian," I then shout, again.

"I'll let you have that," Jenny informs me. "Makes it three-two, to me. Loser."

"Nice bikini."

"Says the gay cowboy."

THE PRESENTERS : DAY 03 : NOT HAPPY

The Welshman moves, foot to foot, agitated but wanting to remain cool. He likes being cool, always needs to be cool. Molly smiles at him and knows. She knows everything about him, everything he shows in movements and words. She has seen them all and read the signs and made a dictionary in her head of all the meanings his sentences and expressions define.

She smiles to herself because outright mocking will result in a verbal lash and now is not the time. Live TV would be the time. But it would need more than here, his defences are stronger in public.

"What were you doing?" he asks.

The crew have vanished, they are on their own and the question finally comes.

"Mixing it up, changing the routine. It was fun. I bet the ratings are up."

"We have our routine, we do what we do. We have set it up. It works."

"It just feels like a different year," she says.

She wants this to be true. The staleness of the last few years, the jokes by numbers, the same sentences by the same people only less famous.

"We don't need anything new," he tells her.

"I need something new," she says. "I'm bored. We are boring. We are middle-aged and not moved on."

"The Rolling Stones kept going," The Welshman says as if the fact a group of men pretended to be sixteen well into their seventies is the put down to destroy all arguments.

"And became sad old men chasing young women and never growing up. They lived as teenagers their whole lives. They are not my role models on life. I'd hate to be them. Are you planning on being this way all the way through till you retire?"

He doesn't answer because Peter Pan is strong in him. He tells himself that he lives in the moment, but he refuses to see himself dragging the moment out like someone not ready to hit the working world and extending out education until they can't be reasonably seen as a student any more.

"We have more to give," he says.

"We are just squeezing the last part out of a seriously dry formula. No one has come along to replace us because they are all about the reality TV. Our competition comes from lumps of surgically altered plastic, or men on steroids – more than you – who can barely read off the autocue. We have no competition, but we aren't what people want. I'm not what I want."

He looks at her as if she has spoken to him in ancient Greek.

"Don't destroy this because you are having a crisis," he says, because he is a man and thus anything mildly contradictory a woman might say just has to be a crisis.

"A crisis? That's what you think? Oh, she is moaning because she is having some unexplained crisis. I bet you don't like the tone either."

"I don't as it happens."

Molly shakes her head.

"How many times have you told a man, you don't like his tone? Don't even pretend to think about it, the answer is never. You don't like what they are saying, but it is only women – specifically me, whose 'tone' you can't stand. Which makes you a misogynist."

"A what?"

"Look it up, or get a runner to come back with the answer you want."

"What is going on?"

"You haven't listened. I'm not playing anymore. I'm not doing this the same way, the same gurning, the same lines only slightly different."

He stands thinking his size means more than the empty words he can conjure.

"We've got two people," he says," – weird people – doing something different on the show. Let them be the difference and we can be what we always are, the rock, the humour, the-"

"- deluded individuals we have always been."

"We can get through this," he says. "We are the best at what we do."

She shakes her head.

"I'm going for a walk."

"Do you want me to come?" he asks.

"No, I really don't."

DAY 03 : AFTERNOON : DRAGGING THIS OUT SO WE DON'T HAVE TO GO BACK

We have the photos of the other contestants. Ten including us.

"Who do you think they'll bring in as the surprise celebs?" I ask as I sit down aiming for a breather against a tree.

"Have to be someone at least a little famous. We aren't exactly setting the world on fire with fame are we?" Jenny tells me, with a lot more thought than I thought she'd offer.

"Could be a royal," I say, stretching my feet out.

"They are not that desperate for popularity."

"A disgraced politician trying to show how reformed they are?"

"Nah, career suicide," she says coming and sitting next to me. "Coming on here means your career is dead, you are looking for a way back into daytime TV and a regular pay check or your life has fallen to shite and you are unable to make any rational logical decision and accept an offer to come and show your every failing on live TV because you think you have recovered when you haven't."

"That would be me," I say. I turn to her, excited, lifting my index finger as if I am making a meaningful point. "Or, you are so utterly arrogant, and have always been told how wonderful you are, that you assume coming on is a guaranteed win and an easy path to British cult celebrity status."

We sit and think and acknowledge where we are and why. We lean against the base of a tree, probably in an ants nest, almost certainly within fifty feet of an animal that looks all cute and fluffy but would, given the chance, try to impregnate me.

"I think it'll be a boxer," I say after way too much considered thought. "A retired boxer with anger issues."

Jenny smiles. Shakes her head but keeps looking forward.

"Nah, a former children's TV star turned dark and gothic with tattoos on their face and a series of nude photo shoots in her recent past."

I nod my appreciation of her input.

"A former politician," I say, "who has been paid by the Russian government to influence the powers that be and is now trying to manipulate thoughts through afternoon chats and fish slurry challenges on the sixth most popular show on mainstream TV."

She shakes her head. A weak effort. She is disappointed with the idea and I am now too.

"One of the Prime Ministers many ex girlfriends?" she says, very surely.

I like the idea and look at her.

"That would be ace. Spill the beans. Tell us all."

She smiles and impersonates a vacuous squeaky voice.

"Oh, but I can't, as I signed a non-disclosure order and received ten trillion pounds to keep my mouth shut and accept his denials. Although I am allowed to infer how bad he is in bed."

"That's it," I say. "That has got to be it."

She looks at me too, her imagination going.

"Or," Jenny says, on a roll now, "some massive right-wing imbecile who has made it on their own because their family of billionaires gave them a multi-million pound trust fund at eighteen, but they have absolutely made their career on their own."

I laugh. I've met some of them.

"The afternoon debates would be better," I say. "Instead of would you rather have an egg as a chin or a fish as a tongue, we could talk about why are your views so repulsive you spoilt little, isolated twerp?"

"Footballer's wife."

"Pretending she is in some way an integral part of why her husband is a filthy rich sportsman and how she was attracted to him, not because of his endless revenue, but because he is such a down-to-earth guy. And a great father."

"She will have a podcast on fashion and gossip."

"And Chelsea tractor, no real friends, and a misplaced self-regard."

We see the crew waving and indicating the lockers. A flashing light is on and may have been going for some time.

"What do you think that's about?" I ask knowing the answer.

"I think they are getting bored with our deep and meaningful debate and want us to stick our hands in disgusting stuff, watch us retch, and then try and win a single crumb of jammy dodger for everyone at camp."

I stand and offer her my hand. She takes it and I pull her to her feet.

"Nice grip," I say, smiling.

"Don't bloody ruin it."

"The moment?"

"The what?"

"The moment. We just had a moment."

"You are a desperate, desperate man."

"I felt it. I think the viewers would have felt it. You clearly-"

She is staring at me now. A fist clenched, low down. I step back.

"I thought it was a lovely, friendly chat. Shall we crack on with the hilarity?"

And what could be funnier than this?

I have to reach into lockers through a hole, just big enough to get my arm through, and rummage around for a piece of parchment which has a quote. Each quote is something one of the contestants has said in their life and we have to match them up. One of us has to stand under a shower head while the other places the quote next to a picture. If they are wrong, a tsunami of illuminous green gunk containing ingredients banned in most of Europe for causing skin to permanently change colour flushes down on your head. This is going to be a long day.

I go first.

I slip my hand through one of the thirty holes – only ten contain parchment – and rummage around until I grab something, and despite my best efforts, I can't let go.

The electrical current is powerful enough to give me a painful shock, like licking a fence in a field with cows only to realise it is connected to a battery and now your face. The current forces all my muscles to contract, and so I squeeze the metal even harder. I try, with all the effort I have, not to shit my pants.

I say something which in my head is, "I say, I think you may have set the current at a level just a bit too high and I am, albeit without any medical knowledge, on the edge of having a fucking coronary." It comes out, however, as "Umghrhggy, fuck." Which means I can't speak but can swear when on the edge of death.

The electrical current ceases and I pull my hand out as quickly as possible, in fact quicker than I would have imagined possible, possibly troubling Einstein's idea that nothing travels faster than light.

"I think you might want to turn that down," I say. "A bit of a kick to it."

"What was it?" Jenny asks.

"A rough guess of five hundred thousand volts, give or take a volt or two."

"Any parchment in there?"

"You are very welcome to double check."

She indicates I need to hurry up by spinning her index fingers around each other.

I stick my hand into the next hole, slower than is actually necessary, using the back of my hand to check for metal. I feel something, smooth and solid. And that thing feels me, decides it doesn't like me touching it – presumably because I contain more charge than a lightning bolt – and uses what feels like a pair of massive blunt pliers to grab my middle finger, not in a pinch and release but in a grab and squeeze until it breaks. I pull my hand back, but the hole is too small for whatever creature from the Jurassic era is on the other side, and it smashes against the wall with such force that the only logical action to take would be to release its hold and fuck off. However, whatever is currently gnawing through my knuckles doesn't understand logic and holds on even tighter like it is on the waltzers and some man with three teeth is shouting the tighter you hold the faster we go. I smash the bastard thing repeatedly against the inside of the locker and it will not let go. I look around, seeing little as my eyes are filled with tears of pain, except a man in a crocodile Dundee hat loping toward me with a claw hammer.

"Fuck off!" I shout. And the animal appears to understand English and lets me go.

I pull out my hand and my finger is oozing blood and is half way to being the same size as a small pony's hind leg.

Hat man looks at my finger.

"Strange that," he says. "They don't usually let go. You'll be grand," he adds patting me on the back.

"Are you a doctor?" I ask, knowing that if the answer is yes I am not visiting any hospital in the entire country.

"No. I'm an actor," he tells me.

"An actor? You aren't even an expert with animals?"

"I was born and grew up here," he says suggesting with his incredulous face that geography is the only qualification you need to treat wild animal attacks.

"That's your expertise. You were born and grew up here? I was born and grew up in Cornwall. I don't know how to make scones, nor welcome holiday makers. What the actual fuck?"

"Go easy mate. They aren't poisonous."

"What aren't?"

"The giant crab that just bit you. They are pretty docile usually. Never bitten anyone before."

69

"Well they have now," I say, showing him my middle finger in a way I hope he understands.

"Looks like a red cucumber that," he tells me, as if red cucumbers are an actual thing.

"Your turn," I say as I turn to Jenny. "I'm under the shower."

She walks across chooses a hole, puts her hand in and pulls out parchment. Of course she does. Of course she finds parchment. Had I put my hand in there I'd have found an escaped alligator that only feasts on Brits.

"What's it say?" I ask, as I move under the shower head.

"I will become the country's best prime minister. Aged twelve."

"Aged twelve? What type of imbecile has the ambition to be the PM at age twelve?"

"Your guess is as good as mine."

"Has to be an absolute tool. PM? At twelve?" I think, pondering who of the people here would be such a pompous prat, and I can exclude myself. "The presenter. Brian," I say.

Nothing happens. No slime appears and I smile and relax. I nod and feel good. Nailed it.

There is a slight hissing sound, and I can't quite place where it is coming from. I look up and within a second I am crumpled on the floor as several metric tons of goo splash down not in a shower way but a structural collapse of the biggest dam in Europe way. The single positive aspect is the producers have seen fit to remove the monumental chunks of aged concrete. Regardless, I am crushed.

I stand, gingerly, holding the floor and looking for my breath and hoping that my lungs still function. I would guess my internal organs are no longer where they should be, some of them, particularly the spleen may now reside in my Y-fronts.

"Not the presenter then," I say. "Have you got an idea?" I ask.

"I'm fairly sure," Jenny assures me, "that the person who said this was, in fact, me."

I stare at her even though I can't really see as my eyeballs are on fire like a happy chappy has sandpapered napalm into the iris. But I stare all the same as blinking, against all evolutionary nature and their sole function, seems to impersonate the sensation of a having my cornea lacerated by mini Stanley knives.

"Just come to you has it?" I ask. "That you might have said that. Forgot did you?"

"Sorry," she doesn't say. However, I take her nonchalant shrug as some type of erotic move meaning I need some immediate and deep therapy and that Jenny is very much into me. It is essentially what inexperienced teenage boys do: inflict pain and humiliation on those they like. Could have done without the bruised liver and internal bleeding though. But hey ho, young love and everything.

"Do you want to pick or stay under the shower?" Jenny asks.

I rise from my crouch and step forward in a way a newly born horse might find uncoordinated and embarrassing.

"I'll find some parchment," I lie to myself.

I step up to the next hole and thinking that speed is best I slip my hand into the box in the belief that I have hit my pain threshold and above this nothing else will matter nor cause any more agony as there can be no more torture. I'm at zero Kelvin on the pain scale, there can be no more. I am pained out. Fingernails being removed with pliers would be a soothing tonic right now. Electrodes on my nipples would be a break from the agony.

I place my hand in and other than a pleasant spray of moisture over my bare skin I feel nothing. I am imaging this is the cold spittle of a very angry Komodo Dragon waiting to strike upon me accidentally trying to open a small sack in which parchment lies but is in fact his sagging scrotum. But I'll take the risk. Apparently their poison kills you slowly until you can breathe no more. Right now I'd take that over being here.

"Nothing," I say. "Nothing at all."

"Go to the next one," Jenny tells me.

I pull my arm out and stare at it. It is my arm, I can see that. Clearly my arm attached to my shoulder and fingers moving when I request. However, it is now bright blue.

"What the hell?" I ask my arm as if it can reply and explain its new colour as a fancy dress mistake for a night out.

I rub my arm with my normal hand.

Nothing happens, it isn't even damp. I lick my fingers and rub, but the blue remains.

I turn to Jenny.

"It is permanent dye, isn't it?"

She smiles and nods, not quite as erotically as I had hoped, but why would she be turned on by a man who has an arm that resembles a blue whale's cock? I absolutely hate this place.

"Next one," she tells me.

"I have a plan," I say. "I'll find them all, lose a finger or two, get bitten by a rabid prairie dog, have small insects have sex with my skin and contract ebola – all in the interests of entertaining the middle classes at home in their Ikea houses – then we can place them and do the shower thing. I'll even stand under the shower as why not take fifteen years off my life expectancy and trigger early onset dementia through repeated concussions? It is all for fun, isn't it?"

"Are you ok?" Jenny asks me.

I stare at her, vision returning, my eyes cooling, my arm, I would say, is flashing like a police light and I am about as threatening as a drooling Labrador.

I set myself to the task. Eight to find. I give myself five minutes to do it. As much as I want to spend time with Jenny, away from camp, and not in earshot of comedian London man, I also want to have at least a small area of me that isn't covered in bruises, is my natural skin colour and that hasn't been licked by a poisonous beast. I wonder how they take me to the emergency room?

The first I'm bitten by ants, like rummaging round in a bag full of nettles. My blue arm all bumpy like I have a hundred mini blisters. I swear and curse and ants die. Ratings probably soar. The second contains stupefied snakes, which I don't mind and none of them bite. A parchment is found and I drop it on the floor, moving to the next. A sensation box of warm, sticky blended animal. There is no one to tell me what it is so I'm guessing it is mince from a butcher made up to look like shredded human bowels. Parchment is found, writing illegible. I'm on a roll. The next I am shocked again by electricity which I am sure is too high to be safe. I shudder and shut down but feel relatively little. I'm working on adrenaline and my body is accustomed. My mind not so much as I fade out of consciousness briefly. I look like I'm thinking, which I am of sorts, I'm thinking of slipping into a nice cosy coma. But I'm back in seconds, alert and on task. Obsessed somewhat with getting the parchment. The next few are animals, all small, all slimy, all disgusting like rifling through a moving block of that hair you find when unblocking a bath in a student accommodation after six years of hippy use. Lovely. Parchment is flying out. The last couple I am stung, and my arm loses feeling, all the way up to the shoulder. I have read about heart attacks and this is the wrong arm, and no tingling, but no sensation at all. I clench my fist and while I know I'm doing it, I can't feel the touch.

"What the fuck was that?" I think I ask, but I might just have said something only a Glaswegian drunk at the end of an all-dayer in Spoons could understand. The world is becoming a dreamland.

And that is them all.

"Right, you sort these phrases out and I'll take the shower," I barely illiterate to Jenny.

"You ok?" she asks, which I find insulting as I am, other than the dye, the pain, the numbness, the concussion, the smell, the incoherent thoughts and the vague hallucinations, doing pretty damn well, thank you very much.

"Yep," I lie and walk under the gunge tank.

She picks up parchment from where I have thrown them. She unrolls the first one, reads it, and I can't quite make it out as I am trying, ever so subtly, to stop myself from being violently ill. I am shaking and the numbness is creeping up from my shoulder to the right side of my face.

"Gaz," I shout, because I am aware I need to say a name. He could possibly have said the quote I have not heard, even said them all. Who knows? They are all probably made up by the production team or the contestants. It is just a random guess, no one can ever really know, it's like heads or tails for punishment. Brilliant concept I think as a tonne of liquid green shite deluges onto my head like a fifty weight of jelly. I collapse, think about staying put, think better, stand and shout "Racheal." Nothing happens, my luck is in. I smile. "Racheal," I say smiling, "good old Rae-" I don't finish.

They must have been recharging the gunk tank. Green gunge falls as if shot from a cannon and only seemingly able to hit me on the cranium. I smile but don't fall. Just stand, rocking from side to side.

Jenny is in front of me.

"Are you ok?" she rather annoyingly asks again.

"When are you going to understand that I am perfectly OK," I think I say, but judging by the expression on Jenny's face I may well have become confused and said, "I would like to jizz on your tits."

Her face is not a happy one.

I try to rectify my possible mistake with further deep thoughts on relationships, and I manage to make a noise, possibly a word, but I don't finish what would have gone on to be a world-wide phenomenon and base for a new religion as I collapse to the floor unconscious. My last thought as I drift from the world, hitting the floor hard is, please don't piss yourself. And then I am gone into a deep sleep brought on by a combination of many things, but the most important being that this year they have chosen to kill a celebrity.

DAY 04 : ABSOLUTELY NO IDEA WHAT TIME OR INDEED WHO I AM

I wake and I'm warm and I feel as if the plot line to Dallas all those years ago when an entire season of twenty-two hour-long episodes was wiped away because it had all been a dream actually could be a real occurrence. I'm wrapped up warm, feel nothing but bliss and the horrendous nightmare of a celebrity torture show was just a very vivid cheese-induced psychosis. I'm hoping Jenny was a real thing though. And while this makes no sense in any logical way, I'm still dozing and drifting so the real world physical laws are yet to kick in.

"Are you awake," a soft sultry voice asks me.

I smile, I think it is Jenny, or a hot nurse in a fifties uniform that are still available on specialist websites, although exclusively made in rubber. Why is that? Is it not too sweaty? I open my eyes and feel the warm touch on my shoulder, a comfort and a connection.

I look up and it is a nurse, dressed in green baggy uniform, hiding all the curves of the body. I smile our eyes locked. It is a nurse. A male nurse. A male nurse with a beard.

"I'm good," I say truthfully. I feel great, the intravenous drip I see stuck in my inner elbow is clearly pumping my body with some really good shit.

"What happened?" I ask

I have a vague recollection of being in significant pain, hallucinating a bit and being blue. I look at my arm. I am indeed blue.

"Am I ok?"

"You will be," sultry voiced heterosexual nurse tells me. "But I am going to recommend you stay with us for a day of observation, just to be sure."

"No more show?" I ask.

"In my opinion, no, which is a shame. I have family in the UK, and they are intrigued as to your injuries. I can't say I know a thing about who you are and what you do. Famous is stretching it apparently. But they are all in on you and a woman. They say they haven't enjoyed the programme as much in years. But I've been instructed not to tell you anything. Which I can't as I don't watch the show. But you were becoming very popular."

74

I feel a warm glow, a bond with this lovely man. He is telling me everything I would like to know. I don't think he is flirting.

DAY 04 : PRESENTERS : HAVING A TIFF

"You did what?" Molly asks.

They are standing in a clearing in the forest. She has checked her microphone is off and he has removed all equipment from his body. She had made him walk with her.

He holds up his hands like some chancer in the pub who thinks they are so cool and can't possibly fight. Her face is red, her fists are clenched and she is pushing up close to his face. If she were taller she would crave chest to chest.

"You nearly killed him. You. Understand. That? Someone nearly died."

"He didn't though, did he?"

"Well as long as your attempted manslaughter didn't pay off, it means it doesn't count."

He smiles and stands back. "I didn't try and kill him. Just made it more painful than it normally would be."

"You asked the tech guys and the animal guys and the insect guys to make it a little more juicey. You nearly killed him."

"The ratings are through the roof," he tells her. "They repeated the show an hour later, we are talking nearly midnight, and the same number of people watched it. Do you understand that?"

"I understand that millions of people tuned in to see our show accidentally nearly kill off a gobshite. That isn't popularity that is macabre elderly hoping to watch real pain."

"It worked though, didn't it? We got them all tuning in."

"And then eliminating the only interesting person in this place – and yes, I include you in that – forever."

"We are looking into that."

"Looking into what? Resurrecting the dead? He is not fit for the show."

"We can bring him back, have him rest, not involved in activities, and see where he goes."

"He collapsed on live TV. We called an ambulance. Our medic guy thought he was dead."

"He isn't a real medic though is he?"

"No, he isn't, which means we would be absolutely taken apart if he is even remotely permanently damaged. Do you realise what you have done?"

"We need him back. The next part is kind of based on his reaction."

"We destroy him physically and now we take him down mentally? This isn't a programme called medieval prisoner show. We don't tend to genuinely torture people to the point of collapse. We just humiliate them and then send them on their way to do daytime talk shows for a month. Occasionally someone wholly undeserving gets a TV show out of it despite them being talentless wankers. We, however, do not try and kill contestants."

He pulls his phone from his pocket. He presses something and looks into the screen and it lights up.

"Look," he says. "Look at those figures. Look how many are watching. This is our new start, our new direction. This is what we can do. A revamp. A new philosophy. We can and are making this show different. Evolving."

"Evolving into torture porn is not a direction it's a crime. I'm not having any part of it, and that bloke needs to stay in hospital."

He smiles and looks to the ground.

"What?" she says. "What the hell have you done?"

He holds up his hands, palms out in anticipation of her answer.

"He might be on his way back."

"Here? To us? After we just forced him into a deathbed. Is he mental? Are you mental?"

"It is what he wants?"

"Is this a done deal?"

"It is what it is," he says.

She turns, but doesn't walk away. She pauses, thinking, trying to come to some decision, something, some control, some sign, something that means something to someone. She turns back.

"This weekend's papers are going to be full of us," she says.

He looks confused but happy, newspapers with his name. The fame, the front pages, the excitement of knowing you are being spoken of throughout the land.

"I'm moving into a separate room in that bloody expensive hotel. And the press are going to know. And if they don't figure it out quick enough, I'm leaking the information."

"It'll make us more popular," he says. "Boost ratings. I'm cool with that."

She stares at him, this guy who evolved into this. She thinks and she isn't sure, not really, not one hundred percent, whether he has evolved at all. Maybe it is her. Maybe it always was. She walks away.

"Come on," he shouts, and he thinks he'll win her back.

DAY 05 : MID MORNING : ON THE COMEBACK TRAIL

"They talked me into it," I say.

"How?" Jenny asks, staring at me as if she could spot an illness through how I frown.

I walked into the camp and a few said hello, Comedic Bob sang a song about a returning man that may be in a musical somewhere, if a local village gives the director's role to an imbecile with no talent. But I'm guessing he is making it up as the words sound like sentences. But he can hold a tune, for a really long time, in a single note until all air is expelled from his lungs and any hope of him dying fades.

I walk over to Jenny and she tells me she thought I was dead. I smile and tell her I am resurrected.

"How?" she asks again.

I try to think of an answer that is plausible and thus untrue.

"I felt that I should come back and earn my money," I lie blatantly.

"Bollocks. They offered you more money, didn't they?"

"No, I wanted to return and they, the production company and their lawyers, who are worried I will file some type of suit, agreed and due to my overwhelming empathy, they dried their eyes and patted me on the back and said that it would only be fair if they made me richer, in comparison to how much you are being paid. So, as it happens I am no longer the worst paid non-celebrity here."

"How much are you getting?" Bob asks, not in song, but in a faux friendly, come on mate way.

"Can't tell you that. The lawyers made me sign a non-disclosure order barring me from revealing the cash, or making any type of medical claim, and I think, the small print means the Production company and by extension Rupert Murdoch own my very soul."

Jenny stares at me shaking her head and Bob is trying to think of a rhythm he could mould into a demand for information.

"I think I got a good price as my soul – as they will find out soon enough – is worth about fifty old pence."

"Jenny told us you were out of it," Snooker Gaz says.

The group are gathered around me and I feel vaguely important, all of them listening in to what I say, which means I am interesting or they are so bored of sitting in a clearing having to converse with each other that their brains have searched out any stimulation that isn't words that try their very best to be non-controversial.

"What's it like out there?" Rachel asks.

"Very, very similar to how it was when we came in to the point I'd say it is exactly the same."

"Any news on how the show is going down?" Presenter man with late-eighties highlights in his suspiciously thick hair asks.

"It is being shown in the UK. We are not in the UK. No one in this country is watching and let's face it, we are arguably the least celebrity group of the increasingly crap level of celebrities to appear."

"Well, I don't think that is the case," Comedy Gold Bob says, ignorant of the fact the younger generation of internet and streaming have absolutely no idea who he is, unless they like variety performances in small venues in London, in which case they will be aware of his myriad of talents.

"It is," I correct him, "I am not recognised in my local hospital let alone one in a different continent half-way around the world. They were more interested in the camera crew."

"You were filmed in hospital?"

"Not by this lot, by the British press. Paparazzi snapping away, writing articles. They probably thought I was a member of the royal family as I was blabbering incoherently."

"No news on who is popular this year or anything?" half-woman-half-silicone asks me.

"I didn't really get to chat to anyone, other than a lovely nurse, but I did overhear some people talking about spinning and how after watching something they would absolutely smash it. But that could be anything."

She seems pleased and bounces off in her boiler suit all ready to be enthusiastic and bubbly to whomever can't get away.

They are all still hovering like being close will give them a sense of the outside world they haven't seen in just over ninety-six hours. I've stayed in my house moping for longer. I managed. And this clearing is a damn sight cleaner and tidier than my front room was at the time.

I lie down in my hammock.

"The doctor said I should rest," I tell them, pulling a cap over my eyes, "And due to the pain of almost dying to feed you, I have a medical exemption from all activities until I give the green light, which I will, just before I leave here."

They start to walk away and then it dawns on me. "What did we win in the challenge?" I ask the backs of those walking away.

"A chocolate finger," pre-pubescent popstar squeaks me.

"A chocolate finger? One each? Is that it? I nearly lost a lung, kidney and two thirds of my brain so you could all have a single, solitary chocolate bloody finger?"

"It was the best one I have ever had," popstar says in a voice that hasn't broken.

I sit up and before I can speak, Jenny pushes my shoulder and forces me to sit back down.

"Shush," she patronises me. "Poor little Ben needs a sleepy sleep. Can't get all stressed. You might die."

"True," I say, happy that she cares.

"Because if you don't shut up with your moaning, I'm going to suffocate you."

"A chocolate finger?"

"Yeah, they were stale too."

"I hope they gave you all the shits," I shout because through injury I have some leeway with group insults for the time being. I plan to milk every moment of it.

DAY 05 : THE PRESENTERS : STILL HAVING A TIFF

She paces up and down the set, a platform over a safe spot where green doesn't grow as it is in perpetual shade and cables for electricity and optics run riot in coils. The edge is barricaded with scaffold bars hidden under hessian cloth and wrapped in plastic vines. She has walked this many times before, and she knows hosts from ten different countries come here and do the same. A new chamber to humiliate guests here and there, and each country having their favourites. The Brits loving snakes, rats and eating vile concoctions. The Italians loving the psychological breakdown of faded stars, and the Germans wanting to see whose opinion infuriates who. She has never watched the Scandanavian show but her husband says it is bordering on soft-porn. It does here too when they can entice a model who was once well known through adverts or a quiz show to come along and try to revive past glories by showering in white bikinis and lathering firm tanned, albeit middle-aged bodies. A simple trick and the means by how they made their fortune. It's all good, all fair. You can only resort to what you know.

79

He is late arriving.

She sees him on the other side of the rope bridge, grinning and smiling and flirting with staffers. It doesn't matter if they are male or female, he flirts away not wanting their body but needing their attention and gaze. He elicits that through giving them a hint of something he won't give to the men but without doubt would give to the ladies.

She thinks about the opportunities he has, and they are limitless. Were he single, with no me, she thinks, then every day would be the chance for some woman new. She has never checked, never searched a phone, or had him followed. They are together almost always, work and home, holiday and rest. Together, always together, no escape from the partnership that the public love and want to claim as their own. They made us is what they think, and to a degree they are right. They made us this because we give them what they ask, and we change little beyond taking feedback from random interviews and social media opinion on what is the prevailing positive trend of the moment. We are us but moulded to them. At some point, a soon point, we will break and search for who we are again.

She thinks she will struggle, but she is sure he will make no attempt to revive the person he had been. He can't separate the TV showman from the fragile kid he has always been. A Stockholm syndrome, but not to a captor, but an audience.

He sees her and waves like they have only recently parted. And they have, but the words she left him with are hidden away and not shown in his face.

He walks across the bridge and it sways, and he is timing it perfectly. He walks and the countdown begins. The man behind the camera counting back from ten, at five his voice is silent and he knocks off the remaining numbers with his fingers. On zero he points at her and a red light blinks on top of the camera, and her husband, all regal smile, tight black jumper and thick hair walks into shot and starts his spiel.

"Good evening," he starts in a voice she is finding increasingly whinny and a trigger to her right fist smashing his face. "We have seen the greatest recovery in the show's history."

He pauses and looks right into the camera.

"Just how did Ben do that?" he asks.

"By contractual obligation, extra cash and the wonderful effects of opioids?" she responds.

He guffaws like they have rehearsed this opening for hours.

"He just wants and needs to get back for Jenny, is what the word is," he corrects as he winks at the audience. "Middle-aged love."

She looks at him, smiles and shakes her head just so slightly that someone somewhere will notice and set social media alight with conspiracy theories about its meaning, which would be weird because the conspiracy theories in this context would actually be true.

Many years ago, a tabloid plastered a photo of him dishevelled but rugged and looking sexy of a morning walking out of a hotel, ever so close to an equally dishevelled and good-looking woman. Crisis headlines, cheater, marriage over splashed everywhere and people worried that the grand old British institution that was them was crashing down due to such obvious infidelity. However, much to everyone's disappointment, it was a cropped picture, the cropping having taken Molly out of it as she was pointing at the imbecile with the lens who was sat in a car a hundred metres away on a Sunday morning looking for a photo he could sell to a trash mag for a few quid.

They had a story, they had a picture, cut her out of it and it would get the story. No others appeared.

To go on holiday anywhere other than a remote, expensive and secluded walled resort, they had to broker an agreement with the paparazzi to do a day, or a few minutes a day, of natural, but oh-so-unnatural photo shoots. Walk on the beach in bikini? Ok. Candle lit dinner? Ok. The fake poses passed off as real. Which is essentially what they are and do.

"Do you think he can take any more punishment?" he asks her, apparently rhetorically because he leaves no pause. "I don't think so. Especially not after our new guests arrive. Here is a snap shot." He points to his left and they cut to a pre-recorded mystery guest segment, where their identity will be hinted at with word games and long-shots so the social media world can cause a frenzy and people can make loads of shit up about how a friend of a brother's mate, who is having an affair with the wife of a production member's cat, has seen a famous actor in the vicinity of the set, and while he can't say precisely who, as this would get said person in trouble, their surname rhymes with PiDaprio. And other such nonsense.

They once had a very famous person on the show who, we can only assume, had thought they were going on something entirely different, like an all-inclusive holiday at a sex island. This fact has been milked for a decade. No one famous is coming on.

"You are going ahead with this," she asks, knowing the answer and wanting the outcome herself.

"We are going ahead," he tells her, his smile not breaking,

DAY 06 : MORNING : GENUINELY BORED

We sit around, well, I do. My medical exemption is a dream come true. A get out of pretty much anything card I can play at any time. I lay in my hammock and pass the time staring and thinking. My moment gone. I'm fading, I know that. But I made more money, had a brief flirt with actual real fame, and now it is time to kick back and watch them all perform and prance and play. I think I have a few days in me, a couple of votes before I go.

The morning is cool. A tea or a coffee we earned made on a fire and sipped and swallowed despite being bitter. There is no milk, and I wouldn't drink it if it appeared mysteriously in a metal camping jug. I'd use it to top up my tea, comment on the strange taste and texture, and then have hilarious Welshman bursting through the bush to guffaw at me half-swallowing, half-chewing what turned out to be half-a-cup of monkey spunk, or koala cum, or giraffe's jizz. I try to think of more but can't, think about asking the camp for more animal-seaman combinations, think better of it and slip back to watching the tree canopy. It's like camping, I imagine. Even if I know what camping is like. It's like this, nothing to do, outside, grumpy bored people everywhere, and I have to shit in a bucket.

We run out of things to say quite quickly, except Comedy gold Bob, he never runs out of words, or banter, or song, or unfortunately breath. We then wait until two people are selected for the afternoon activity, the one, I remind people regularly, in which I nearly died so they could all eat a chocolate finger. I think they like the story, I do go into detail.

Then we wait debating what the treat could be. We sit around and discuss. I don't join, I stay in my hammock, but I try to be as helpful as I can by shouting suggestions to the backs of the others as they huddle together ignoring me.

"It'll be fig rolls, or a thin slice of processed cheese in a plastic film. Only you aren't allowed to eat it unless you squish it into a ball," I suggest, and maybe my voice doesn't carry as no one replies.

The moment arrives and blonde highlight, traces of a mullet, former TV star, currently washed-up has-been TV presenter, Brian and Racheal are selected to go off. And we watch them, and we cheer and say good luck. And then they are off, and we all go back to doing nothing, moving little, and saying sod all.

Former famous man Brian is sooo excited. I know this, as we all know this because he keeps bloody saying it. "I'm sooooo excited. Are you excited? I'm excited. It's exciting isn't it?" he says, asks, shouts, whispers, murmours and repeats.

They walk off. I think he tries to hold Racheal's hand and she shrugs him off like she has been touched by an old pervert, which is exactly what has happened there.

"What do you think will happen?" Snooker Gaz wheezes.

I look into the distance and give this more thought than I naturally would, considering options based on my own experience and hopes and the accumulated knowledge of life. I turn to Gaz, I have the answer.

"I think he drowns in a stagnant pool of horse piss," I say.

I am assured of everyone's agreeance by the prolonged and deep silence.

"And wins us something that isn't made up of a tasteless chewy lentil that requires me to find other people's saliva to fully turn into a swallowble paste," I add as it has become awkward now.

"I hope it is a drink," Gaz says. "A gin maybe. Win a bottle of gin."

He wipes his forehead and licks his lips because he thinks this is an actual possibility.

"It will probably be a cream cracker that you have to eat with some type of exotic jam made from a fruit that only Tucans can eat," I say, and clearly I'm losing my touch as no one even nods.

We sit around some more. I have a doze and am woken by Jenny.

"What do you want?" I ask, genuinely incredulously. "I was having the best dream."

"We've divvied up the jobs on camp. Me and you got the short straw," she tells me.

"Medically exempt," I tell her, needlessly adding, "from the injuries I sustained while-"

"Oh, shut the fuck up," she tells me, attempting for anger but hitting rather sexy. "We have divvied up the jobs and you and I are on toilet duty."

I know what this means and it is the job the least popular moron is forced to have.

"Keeping the paper supply topped up, making sure, it is there?" I ask.

She shakes her head.

"We are to empty the Dunny."

I lean back in my hammock. This is bullshit.

"I understand why they chose you," I say. "But why me? I nearly died-"

She punches me in my upper left arm. It hurts more than I think it should. She carries some power.

"That is getting old really quickly."

I shrug, look away and up like an arrogant posh Londoner.

"Still mileage in it," I say.

We wait, sitting around, doing little. Someone starts a quiz, but it fades away as we all have knowledge just not on each other's subjects. I know nothing of journalism, Jenny knows little about writing and Bob knows the absolute square root of eff all about comedy.

We wait for the telephone to ring and a question to be asked.

We wait for what seems like twelve rotations of the sun, but is probably around twenty-five minutes. Time has taken on its own journey, and right now it has stumbled over rocks and knocked itself unconscious on a tree root because time has not moved forward. We are trapped in stasis with nothing to say or do. This programme is a test of patience, and despite my best efforts I can't seem to sleep twenty-four hours a day.

The phone rings and we are all awake and alive to the possibility of having a treat. I now understand how my dog feels when I am standing vaguely close to the drawer with his special biscuits inside. I am alert and absolutely sure I'm going to get something nice to chew on that isn't a bowl of crunchy tasteless pellets of man-made chicken flavouring. I'd eat a dog treat right now. Drag out the flavour sensation for minutes as I suck out the beef dripping and all the other bits that are in there because they are not fit for human consumption.

I once saw a man eat a full can of cat food at a party. I knew him. He thought it funny because we all laughed but we were just freaked out. We would have laughed the same had he tried to chew glass and thought him no less weird.

Gaz sprints for all of two metres, realises he can't, stops and walks toward the ringing. He picks up the phone designed in the fifties but built recently in cheap plastic. It is red because it is important. He listens.

He then asks, "What?" then, "I don't understand." Next he waits and says. "That isn't even a word." "Speak properly," he tells the phone.

Jenny takes it from his hand and listens.

"Got it," she says.

84

She places her hand over the mouthpiece.

"Ok," she says very loudly like a headmistress trying to bring a sports hall under control.

"Is it thirty-four percent of men, or fifty-four percent of men who would like to shave their bum-crack?" she asks.

"What?" Gaz asks. "That isn't what he said. No man is going to want to shave his bum-crack."

"Despite myself and our history, I am going to have to agree with Gaz. The answer is as close to zero as it could possibly be. No man is going to want to shave his crack."

I look around and motorway man is looking sheepish.

"Are you a shaver?" I ask.

He shakes his head in a way that screams, yes, I do and I like it.

We all roll our eyes and look away. We will discuss this later. But at the very least he trims his ball fluff.

Half-silicone pipes up.

"Hair is so unnatural," she tells us based on her PhD in Biology I assume.

"What?" I ask.

"Hair," she goes on with her revolutionary theory, "it is disgusting and unnatural. I shave it off. Don't like it. Don't need it," she assures us.

I step forward as the illogic of the statement is destroying my very soul.

"Are you actually saying that having absolutely no body hair is so much better than thousands of years of evolving our body hair for its intended use? Like eyebrows and hair for warmth?"

"Yes," she tells me, with such conviction I have to stop and think if it is me who is going mad.

"But jamming plastic under your chest to create unnaturally large and bizarrely shaped boobs is natural? And that expanding your lips into a permanent expression of whistling is normal and no wrinkles are all perfectly ok. But no to body hair as that is weird?"

She looks at me as if I have just spoken to her in tongues and let a snake bite my face.

"Obviously," she says. "You have to fight aging."

"But not stupidity it would seem," I say, out loud and to my surprise.

I shake my head and I see Jenny laughing and I think, God I like her. I turn as staring at Jenny might put her off.

Back in the day, men padded their calves for sex appeal and they used mice fur as fake eyebrows. How we could laugh at how stupid humans had been, despite me being near a man wearing mascara, a woman who was fifty percent altered and every single woman on TV having undergone some type of lift. There are Hollywood male actors in their fifties, and some over sixty without a single forehead crease. We got them beat. Silly people with their big calves and fake eyebrows.

"Bob?" I ask. "What are your views?"

"Definitely not," he says.

Mascara is fine though, I think.

"Thirty-four," I say.

Everyone nods.

"Thirty-four," Jenny says into the old handset.

She places the phone back on its hook.

"Well?" Gaz asks.

"We have to wait till they get back."

So we do, on edge, on logs around a fire.

We hear them coming through the bush and nearing camp. We all know if they have won they will pretend they haven't as the extra disappointment will turn into extra cheer and they will have just that little bit more of ego boosting adulation. The pricks.

They walk down looking sad and disappointed. Of course they do. Although Racheal appears closer to barely suppressed rage.

"What number did you say?" former TV great asks.

"Thirty-four," Gaz shouts. "There wasn't an option for zero."

"Well, that's a shame. Because-"

He pauses for dramatic effect, and the most obvious of pay-offs.

"-because it was right."

They dance and jump and pat his back and they dance and jump more, congratulating past-his-best TV man. I look for Racheal and she is standing holding a wooden bowl with a lid. She doesn't seem happy, she doesn't seem happy at all. In fact, I'd go as far to say that she has rarely been this unhappy and that were she not on live TV that bowl would be repeatedly smashed into once-a-long-time-ago-I-was-cool celebrity old man.

"What did we win?" I ask, slowly turning to the mini-party of excitement and joy.

"Oh," old TV man says. "We won something awesome for you all."

I look to Racheal and she is slowly, but very clearly shaking her head side-to-side with the face of someone who is now ready to kill.

She steps forward with the grace of a ballerina, moving her right arm sweepingly forward and to the side. The beginnings of a courtesy. She lifts the lid on the bowl.

We all stare at its contents, the party losing its energy like we have all hit the point of too much beer.

"What was the other choice?" Jenny asks.

TV man bounces around not realising he has lost the audience, the group, any friends he thought he might have, and soon the breath within his lungs.

He smiles, serenely, misjudging us all with a level of incompetence only the monumentally arrogant possess.

"Strawberries," he says.

"With cream," Racheal adds, almost in tears.

I look into the bowl, hoping, beyond all hope that this is a cruel joke. I look at TV man from the eighties. He is smiling like the Dalai Lama.

"Some twiglets?" I say. "Two actual grown-ups chose a bowl of twiglets over some strawberries?"

"Oh, we thought someone might be allergic," highlight-hair TV throwback tells us. "And there was only one each. So, you know," he adds unhelpfully.

I wait and think, just like all the other people wait and think. I spend my time staring at the bowl, starting to hate dry bar snacks. I believe I want to punch the bowl in the knackers.

"Yes," I finally say. "And now, instead we all have a handful of burnt hedge twigs that taste of gone off marmite. Lovely. What the hell were you thinking? You chose the joke option."

"Strawberries," everyone says at least five times, and principally to their tastebuds.

"Cream," Gaz adds, saliva dribbling from every pore.

"Yes," Racheal says. "Was my choice but I was overruled by him."

She points and we all, for the briefest of moments have a collective thought about burning someone at the stake.

"I think it was the wise choice," soon-to-be-beaten-to-a-pulp TV man says.

"No," Jenny says, bubbling under. "I think I can safely say I would rather have eaten the off-cuts from Gaz's arse crack than these."

She takes a twiglet and throws it at TV man. He catches it like some human-cat combo ninja.

"I love them," TV man tells me, popping one into his obnoxious mouth and chomping down with his bleached teeth. His fake hair with out-of-fashion highlights doesn't move at all.

I am now no longer the most hated human in camp. I feel a little loss. I also feel like I need and deserve strawberries.

"It was a tricky challenge," the most hated man ever says. "I had to overcome some serious stuff. Fish guts, gunge, an animal that bites." He turns to me. "I didn't have to go to hospital though," he ends rather diggingly.

"You will if you don't shut your wrinkled pickled face," I say silently in my head while trying to maintain a grin that doesn't resemble a death stare. I look around the camp and I don't know why I bother to conceal. Everyone is frothing at the mouth and clenching fists. Tonight, around the camp fire may become a little frosty, or a live effigy may burn while we hum the theme to his Saturday morning children's show that ended three decades ago.

THE PRESENTERS : DAY 06 : ABOUT TO HAVE A PROPER BARNEY

"Are you genuinely sleeping in another room?" he asks.

"I would be sleeping in a different continent – my own – if I wasn't contractually obliged to stay. I don't fancy paying a six-figure fine so I can leave this dump forever," Molly tells him.

They are outside the hotel, there are people milling, the temperature is close to the point that kills old people, the sky is blue, all of it, no clouds and there are, in the distance, certainly paparazzi. But she doesn't care, the word is out, papers have run with the story of their falling out. Her agent has been contacted for extra information. He has been told and he will drip whatever he needs to keep the story going.

"Money is always important," he says, grinning in the knowledge a photo could be taken at any time and fierce-face when speaking down to your wife is never a good look.

"We have plenty, in fact I should say, I have plenty. I just don't fancy walking away, being seen as difficult and then never having an offer again."

"So career is important," he says.

"Yes, a career I want, when I want and how I want. Not this utterly stupid, and seemingly endless load of repetitive claptrap."

She is not smiling, she knows what it looks like. A couple having a fall-out. She is in a different room, the word is out, the fractures highlighted and the articles written. They don't know what they are saying, and the press don't know the circumstances, but that is how it always is. They will make assumptions on their words, decide who is right and who is wrong and who is the victim. They will assume and guess and nothing will be positive. She knows this, she knows the way it leads.

She has chosen her clothes to be bland and black, a neutrality in aggression. Tight but not revealing, a mourning suit, possibly for the relationship that is ending.

The Welshman doesn't believe it can end. If they break it is his career that suffers, their double act, their award winning double act, gone and forgotten, he would be alone, no straight man to keep him propped up. Those bands that break with each member believing they will make it as a solo artist but vanishing into insignificance. He doesn't want that and he is sure she doesn't either. There is something else going on. Maybe she needs a break, maybe a couple less projects. But the public love them, mostly. The things they have been forgiven for, the really bad choices they made that haven't always been reported. The information is there just not in the public domain. A little bit of compromise and an exclusive here and there to make the bad press disappear. Luck plays a part, popularity even more.

"What are you trying to achieve here?" he asks, smiling away like they are reminiscing about a beautiful day at the beach.

"I'm trying to make you understand I am done."

"But you love all this," he says, indicating the air in front of him as if it is magical.

"I loved. I'm grateful it happened, happy with the memories, but I'm just repeating the same thing. It is like holidaying at the same spot year-after-year. It is comfortable and the weather is nice. But there is no challenge, nothing. It is boring. I want out. This is the last year and I'm going through the motions to get to the end."

"And us?"

"If you keep on banging on about a future doing this, projects we can do when home to be on prime time and soak up all the adulation and awards, then we are done too."

"It is what we always wanted."

"When we were half our age. Things move on, we grow up. Life changes."

"We don't have the commitments of others, our life is different. We are the ones people aspire to be."

She laughs. "No they do not. People don't want to be us. They would take the money, the lack of work. But they don't want to be us.

We are people they laugh at and then move on. They probably realise we are pathetic. Doing all this for no reason other than to be famous and rich."

"We are famous and rich."

"And we always will be. We are known, we have money. So maybe we should just go and enjoy it instead of filming for ten months of the year on increasingly pathetic shows and then spend two months sleeping so we can get back to it."

"I like this life."

"I don't!" she says, throwing up her hands.

There is a flash and she smiles and she knows the photo will be in the papers tomorrow.

He knows too.

"We didn't need to do this here," he says.

"Everything we do is in the public eye, why not argue and break-up in front of them too. When was the last time we had any privacy?"

"It is one of the negatives of fame," he says.

"I don't want that any more. I'm not too sure I can say it again. I do not want it."

He stares at her and she at him, nothing to say, and another flash happens.

The Welshman swears.

"The ratings are good," he says.

She snorts and shakes her head.

"Not for us they aren't."

"Ben is still popular. Everyone is holding out for the love story to break out into physical contact."

"When are you dropping the new people in?" she asks.

"Soon, and hopefully Ben and Jenny have something going by then."

"That would definitely set ratings soaring," she says.

He smiles and nods like she is back in the game.

"Then you destroy it."

"Pure gold on TV," he says.

She nods and walks away, she has set up her trap, she has distanced herself and he doesn't know. She will claim this conversation was about the ethics of who the new contestants are, she has photos and articles to back up her lies. He is taking a big risk, and it should end the show. But knowing him, it'll work out wonderfully and the whole thing will become even bigger than before. But she has her out, the photos to a conversation that could be about anything.

"You still have to work on our script," he says.

She stops and turns.

"I think we should ad-lib, it makes for better TV."

DAY 06 : LATE AFTERNOON : BORED

They walk in but not together, not really. One of those moments when the pretence is not as good as the real thing. There is something off, a separation, a distance between them that is further than it has ever been. The lack of looking, the facial expression that doesn't quite fit. The Welshman is grinning like he has just been the recipient of a wedgie and he does not want to show the pain. Molly walks and doesn't look at him, not once. She looks ahead, calm and relaxed, smiling but with something close to real.

They seem to have had a fight and she came out on top, but then she would as she is smarter.

They are here to tell us who will have the pleasure of tonight's challenge, the idea to win food for people we don't like.

Aged TV star has played a blinder. His twiglet bullshit has set him up as the hate figure, a crown I reluctantly have to hand over, one he will wear with more aplomb. He must have thought, must have planned. The hatred we feel toward him can only be magnified a hundred fold by those who watch. He played the cretin card for a popularity boosts and played it as well as anyone could. I'd congratulate and pat his back, but I won't as I can't stand the irritating game player. The result of this vote is clear cut. Mr. Twiglet is going to be getting the popular vote to see him suffer. He knows it, he is smiling away sat on the log with his crocodile Dundee hat, rubbing his hands, waiting for the confirmation on his tactical move to be centre of attention. The man just does not care if it is positive or negative, he just needs to be under the spotlight. The only way he could be moved is if someone starts to be sick with fear, literally vomit through terror, or piss their pants. If someone wants to try that card then they will be the only choice for any scary stuff. The public are nasty bastards at times.

We are sat around and I have joined. The amount of time I have spent lounging around in my hammock may have started the early stages of bed sores.

We are all sat round and most are fake giggling, saying they hope they are not chosen when they really want the challenge. It will tell them they are popular, that the public actually know who they are. I'm immune.

"So," Molly starts, breaking with tradition and speaking despite not holding the small pieces of card that indicate you are the one with the information and script. "The public have voted. And here are the results. Ben, it would have been you, but it cannot be. But rest assured, you are still the overwhelming favourite to be placed into positions of pain and difficulty, through what some viewers call arrogant blather."

I turn to the nearest camera and place my right hand over where my heart should be. "Thank you," I mouth.

"Jenny," Molly says. "It isn't you."

Jenny, bless her cotton socks whispers, "Thank fuck," and she means it.

"Bob," she says, and Bob is alert, desperately wanting the confirmation of his importance. "It isn't you."

He smiles and wipes his forehead in an exaggerated way that would be overacting even in a pantomime. He is clearly gutted.

And on they go, wasting our time, until they say to Mr. Twiglet, "It could be you."

He smiles the knowing smile, his plan coming together like he is lead in the A-Team. He pulls on a fake cigar, and despite it not existing, I still want to ram it down his throat.

They go through the rigmarole of saying it could also be massive fake boob woman and she is soo excited, but tries for fear. She thinks she is popular but what she doesn't realise is that her votes are from pervy males who want to see if her boiler suit will, under some weird circumstance become transparent, along with all her other clothes. Or they will all snag on trees and bushes and be ripped from her body like she is an extra in a Benny Hill sketch from the seventies. If that were to happen, she'd cover her face and not her body in some faux embarrassment.

Molly drags the final decision out for what seems like the time it would take for me to train in martial arts, obtain my black belt and then use my new found skills to break Mr. Twiglet's legs. She doesn't half love the dramatic pause.

"It is," she says, waiting to tell us exactly what we all know with the exception of cleavage lady, "You Brian."

He nods knowingly and stands. I think each and every one of us, under our breath calls him by his new nickname, the C word.

I'm guessing we are all hoping that the trial will be one that has the possibility of going wrong and would result in total hair loss along with a permanent inability to speak. I'd join in with group prayer for that.

"We do need a volunteer to go with him, that person will not be involved in the activities in any physical way, under no stress, no pressure and certainly free from bugs and gunge. Someone to essentially help Brian avoid certain situations through answering questions and providing encouragement."

We are all silent as while it appears we could cause a little bit of bother for him, it would, in return, mean we spend time in his presence, possibly alone, and that, quite frankly is about as appealing as a pint of Gaz's belly-button sweat.

"Oh, come on, guys. Where is your spirit of adventure? I didn't think I was in a group of boring cowards."

I have to admit, he is good at being annoying. The words are nothing, pretty daft if I'm honest, nothing in them at all. But the way he says them, the arrogance, the superiority, the patronising tone of a man who is impervious to hate. It can't be me, he thinks. It has to be them. I don't want to do it, I can't. I really can't. I just want the quiet life.

"I can do this on my own," he patronises further, "I'll bring back the bacon for you all. With my great-"

I stand, and make him stop by putting my palm up and arm out. This wouldn't normally shut his arrogance up but I'm close enough for my sweaty palm to slap his face, and his fringe bounces up, revealing a significantly larger amount of forehead than anticipated. He steps back.

"Are you saying that the pain and humiliation this man – I forget his name, and his career – would be highly correlated to my own ability to answer stuff?" I ask, knowing I've bit and I will feel pathetic about it all later.

"That is exactly what we are saying," Molly says and turns to Welshman and they smile like they have trapped me, which they have. They played to my weaknesses and I hooked myself. Bastards. But I'm not changing, not going back.

"In which case, I am in, and then some," I turn to Mr. Twiglet. "Hospital here we come. Well, you, I'll just wave the ambulance off."

"Hahahahaha," he says in a way that the arrogant kid at school used to do with knowledge of no comeback as he would grass you up if you slapped him. "I have trained for this. I have been on an SAS course, eaten nothing but grubs. Eaten eyeballs. I am ready for this. I can take anything."

Rolling eyes is childish and a really base reaction that I have always thought to be even lower than sarcasm in the come-back stakes, but at certain times, there are certain people who deserve not your witty words or cutting lines, but just the total contempt of my eyes moving up and disappearing into my skull. The step down is blowing a raspberry, but I'm saving that for a special occasion, like his funeral, which I will inevitably crash with a steel drum band and carnival float.

I am an absolute fan of this challenge. I have never seen it before, never heard the name, "Spit of Shame," but I bloody love it. A lot. I think I need to stop bouncing like a six-year-old waiting on the main present at his birthday.

I am obviously there as a side-kick and confidant and safety valve to any pain. I love this power, and I start to see the early cracks in Brian's character.

"This looks difficult," he understates with a whimper, a smile sitting falsely on his lips like the phrase "I love you," said by a drunk at One a.m. to the barmaid. I see him swallow saliva.

A hot tub of dirty water and animals with a spit over the top, a spit to which he will be attached, and spun around, through the stagnant water until I am able to answer a question.

"I am not good at questions," I tell him like a shy girl depicted by Walt Disney.

But he has thought things through. Tried all his lawyer think.

"Think about the food," he pleads, smiling, assuming this will make me like him.

"I don't understand," I lie.

"If we fail this we don't bring any food back. Think of the camp, think of your stomach," he weasels on, and then places his hand on my left shoulder as if we are some type of brotherhood.

This is a fair point and one that I should take into consideration, and I do, briefly. But the problem is, I can see him, and hear him, and pick up on the patronising, arrogant vibes that flood from his body. This may be an effort to somehow negate the ones flying from my body, although little chance of that happening.

"I'm finding it difficult," I say in the worst set up for a pay-off this year but he eats it and nods, "to think of anything beyond you drowning," I finish, honestly.

"Why?"

I think he is being genuine, I'm sure he is, so a genuine answer is deserved.

"There are a multitude of reasons, a long list as it happens. Maybe I see too much of me in you, maybe I'm scared that in seven hundred years when I'm approaching your own age, I too might be a deluded, arrogant irritant with hair highlights. But I would have to say the main one is that when I was a kid, I watched your Saturday morning TV show and took an irrational dislike to you, and now, after all these years, I realise It wasn't irrational at all, it was justified and that I can now, though my own ineptitude, provide payback."

His hand is still on my shoulder.

"I could get hurt," he says, eyes welling.

"No, you'll feel nothing," I reassure him, "There is no pain in drowning. Most peaceful way to go they say. Although who answers that questionnaire is a mystery to me."

"Is this because of the food I chose?"

"I think your choice of salty savoury snacks over actual fruit and cream did contribute to my deep-rooted dislike, yes. As does your hair. And you. The words you use. The hair. What is it with the hair? I hate your hair. It insults me. It's a semi-mullet. But those snacks."

"We'll have to interrupt your team talk," Molly says, and we turn, having been lost in the deep, meaningful chat, we completely forgot we are not alone in a jungle but surrounded by quite a number of people in really ropey camouflage.

"Team talk?" Welshman asks.

I nod, "Just putting some tactics in and a few words of encouragement."

"We heard all of what you said," Molly informs me. "You are on mic."

I don't know why but I do keep forgetting this. Every utterance - and even I know seventy three percent of what I say is bollocks - is caught and broadcast. I'm not going to watch it all back. I'm not going to watch any. I'm probably going to find some way to never remember or speak of this moment in my life ever again, in the same way the designer of the Titanic never spoke of it again. But I haven't hit an iceberg, I've hit peak annoyance, that stage the old get to where they just say exactly what's in their heads and we all think it is because they have gone a bit doolally when in fact they have reached the point of not caring.

"What did you think of my play?"

"It was a load of insulting wank."

95

"Thanks, grandad. Maybe I'll do better when I move up to the big school."

This all passes through my mind and I'm stood looking into the distance like a student coming up on mushrooms on a Thai beach in a bid to discover their inner soul while financing their stay through a ten thousand pound present from their banker parents. I finally come back to the here and now.

"Does his hair annoy you too?" I ask, reaching up to touch it.

He slaps my hand away with such force that I yelp as his chop hits my wrist. It stings like a git.

"That's another question I'm not answering," I tell him.

"Think of the food," he pleads while being led away and strapped to the spit, smiling false courage all the way.

I wave at him with my good arm.

"Are you ready, Ben?" Molly asks in a shouty voice that startles me. I shudder.

"Absolutely," I tell her with a shiver.

"Are you ready, Brian?" The Welshman bellows.

Mr Savoury snack nods, but he looks at me through his diving goggles that are pulled tight against his face. Any gap and stinking piss water is going to splash through and cover his eyes with conjunctivitis, and at his age, despite the alleged SAS training – I imagine only done in secret – that might just be too much for his immune system.

I smile back, hoping it provides no comfort at all, and is, as I hope, as false as I feel and that through seeing my teeth through stretched lips he can truly take on board just how bad I intend to be at this.

"Here we go," Welshman shouts and Brian starts to turn, his hands tied behind his back.

The water has floats, with rope hooks. Apparently, and I could be wrong as I wasn't paying much attention to the instructions as I have little desire to be helpful, he has to bite the rope, hold onto it and I reach across and pull it from his mouth, read the word, and a question is asked on that subject. I will, invariably try to answer wrong as this adds disgusting stuff to the water. I didn't hear the word Crocodile, but you never know, they do love surprises on this show.

Brian starts to spin and he takes a massive gulp of air, which seems pointless as he is going to have to open his mouth at some point.

He goes in, vanishes for a few seconds and then reappears with a rope in his mouth. I lean across from the side of the pool, reaching but not far enough unfortunately, so Brian keeps spinning and is dunked under the water again. But on the plus side he won't have to try and bite any more rope as he already has one.

Around he goes, under the water, rope in mouth and I think there must be a leak in his facemask as his eyes are wide and staring, like he is trying not to blink. He pops up on the other side, the rope still in his mouth. I reach out and grab the blue float. His mouth is free and he takes the opportunity to engage in some banter. His sentence, which starts with a humorous bonding insult is cut short as he is submerged once again.

"What does the word say?" Welshman asks.

"It says, oo, I'm not sure. Hang on."

Brian pops up out of the water, no rope this time, just a mouthful of rancid liquid.

"What does this say, Brian?" I ask pointing at the white letters.

"It says Geography, you Wan-" he doesn't finish as he goes under the water, and I worry that he may not have taken a breath.

"Geography," I say.

"Ok," Molly tells me. "Geography. Are you any good at geography?"

I shake my head. Brian pops up again.

"Are you good at geography?" I ask him, wishing to know if he can help with this gap in my studies.

"Answer the question, you C-," he says, and I'm left trying to finish the sentence for him in my head.

"What is the capital of France?" Welshman asks.

"Is this like the, What's the Capital of Australia? Question. Everyone says, Sydney, but it isn't. It is like a weird place that no one knows as it has never featured in Neighbours or Home and Away."

Brian has gone round a couple of times. He has a rope in his mouth, which is just silly.

"No point having that, Brian. I haven't answered the geography one yet," I tell him, slowly.

He says something, but it is all mumbles and incomprehension like a pissed posh bloke trying to speak but the marbles too large to form vowels.

"Paris?" I say.

"Yes, next float," Molly says.

I reach across and grab the float.

"It says Entertainment," Brian chokes just before he is submerged again.

"I know some stuff."

"What are the British Academy of Film and Television Arts awards better known as?" Molly asks.

"Like the Oscars but for Brits, and TV," The Welshman tells me, presumably as some type of clue.

"So not like the Oscars much at all really then," I say, watching Brian go round and round, spitting out water every time I see his face. He isn't smiling. He is staring straight at me, his eyes never leaving mine until he goes under. He is a trooper, totally in the zone. It brings a tear to my eye.

"The fucking BAFTAs," Brian yells as he comes up out of the water.

I am about to ask him for clarification but he is under again so I wait.

"What?" I ask as he reappears.

"BAFTAs," he says.

"BAFTAs," I tell the couple who hate each other.

"Correct," Welshman says.

Brian comes out of the water but he isn't biting a rope.

"Come on, Brian," I encourage. "Don't give up. Think of-"

He tells me to be quiet, although he peppers the sentence rather unnecessarily in my opinion, with at least six swear words. He doesn't drop the C bomb so all is good.

He appears again, rope in mouth. I pull it before he has stopped biting and I may have dislodged an incisor. He screams in pain, which interferes with his breathing and he definitely doesn't inhale before going under again.

"It says Sport!" I say. "Not my speciality."

"What is the biggest horse race of the year? " Molly asks.

"I don't know anything about horses," I lie.

"Everyone has a flutter," Welshman says.

"Red Rum," Molly hints.

"That's Murder backwards," I tell them as I discovered that when I was in my forties and feel the need to tell everyone as I assume no one else figured it out either.

"Everyone knows that," Molly condescends.

"Grand National!" Brian splutters as he briefly passes through air.

"What he said."

"Correct! Next!" Molly shouts and I think she is loving this even more than me, and significantly more than Brian, who looks like he has fallen off the inflatable banana in Crete and been dragged around every single Greek Island at high speed before anyone realised he was being pulled by the chord attached to his ankle.

I feel a slight pang of guilt, just slight, remember not eating strawberries and think I'll carry on with the nonsense for a bit. We have, after all, through answering the easiest questions possible to ask, won a few meals already.

I try to imagine what animal, or more importantly, what part of the animal will be winched down from the sky, wrapped in paper and ready for us to figure out how to cook. It'll be fried, it is always fried. Stick it all in a pan, chopped up and fry it. We know this but we'll debate the point anyway. We could boil it but who wants boiled badger balls on a bed of damp lettuce? Not me. Fry them, it is the only way to fully appreciate the flavours. There really is only one way to fully extract the best of flavours from a badger's ball sack.

"He has a rope," Welshman tells me, and I look, and Brian stares back.

"I might have zoned out briefly for a moment there," I tell Brian, but he goes under water so I don't see the need to say sorry.

He has another, and the SAS training is paying dividends here. What a man he is. Or thinks he is. I lean across and grab the float.

"History," I shout and despite myself I'm getting excited, like the team building exercises where they take you to a go-Kart track and even though you are an adult and have no intention of becoming competitive, after ten minutes your sole aim in life is to beat the time set down by Barry from Accounts, the big Autistic bald bastard that he is, going fast and having an affinity with motor sports and spreadsheets, and no ability whatsoever to be comfortable in social situations.

"What is the name of the current ruling monarch?" Molly asks me.

"Queen Elizabeth," Brian shouts behind me.

"Am I actually needed here?" I ask, put out that my role has been relegated to passing on info.

"The second," I add smugly.

Brian is looking increasingly dishevelled. I am inflating my chest as if I believe I am now second favourite for this year's title of mastermind. The next question, judging by their difficulty so far, is going to be along the lines of, How do you spell your name?

"Three more minutes," Welshman says.

"Three?"

Brian pops up and I tell him in no uncertain terms to get a move on, the lazy git. I suggest he tries to find the one labelled literature next as that would be my speciality as I'm assuming there won't be a category title, procrastination. I'd never lose at that. I'd be the Muhammed Ali of procrastination, the GOAT. Undefeated and revered in every circle of people who like to waste their time doing nothing, which is, weirdly enough, not as many as you'd think.

I grab a float from Brian, and encourage him to try and bite two on the next roll round. He nods his approval, or maybe gags on water. But either way, he isn't good enough to do it.

"Quotes," I shout.

"Who said," Welshman asks, looking at the card in front of him, "and this is a difficult one, who said, 'I think therefore I am.'"

"Rene Descartes," I say, making absolutely no attempt at a French accent. Des Carts. I'm not saying Pizza with an Italian accent so foreign names are getting the same. Just as I do not visit Firenze but Florence.

I turn quickly and I am annoyed with myself. I am actively participating, doing my best to go at speed and be involved. I may, when watching this back, or being forced to by some half-wit on morning TV, be physically ill.

I grab the float that Brian has snagged.

"Literature," I shout as triumphantly as possible.

"How many novels did Charles Dickens write?" The Welshman asks.

"What!? What happened to the easy questions? How many novels?"

"How many completed works did Charles Dickens write?"

"I have so far been asked questions about as easy as if you asked a child to be simple-"

"Just guess!" Brian shout-gargles.

I turn and because he has opened his gob so far, a float drops out and starts to sink.

"Concentrate, you stupid tit," I mention in passing.

"Do you pass?" The Welshman smugs.

"No, the answer is fifteen," I tell him with levels of arrogance that just cannot compete with his teeth and hair. "I just think it unfair you asked a difficult question when all the others were so easy."

I turn and grab the next float and judging by the colour of Brian's face, the smell and the floating debris, Brian has been violently sick.

"Don't fall apart now," I sympathise. "Stick with me."

His eyes roll into the back of his head and judging by the pallor of his skin he appears to have died three days ago and been left to rot and bloat at the bottom of a cold lake.

He comes around again and he has no float in his mouth and quite frankly I think that is unacceptable.

The rotation stops, a few people rush to the pool and untie Brian, who helpfully doesn't move or react, and I believe he may even be asleep. They pull him to the ground and just as some massive bearded bloke with a beer belly is about to give him a kiss of life, he miraculously wakes up. He opens his mouth, I assume to thank me, but is unable to say a word, at least not until he vomits three litres of stagnant pool water down his shirt.

He looks around and finds me. He stares intently into my face.

"I am going to kill you," I presume he jokes with his face turning red.

DAY 07 : THE NIGHT : FOOD TIME

We wait for the food to arrive.

There is a lot more silence this evening, much directed at me as they have somehow, and rightly, deduced from Brian's description of the days challenge that I am implicit in attempted manslaughter.

They checked him over, he was sick a few times, his hair dried out and returned to how it had been before, perfect in its position if still looking somehow synthetic.

"He did that?" was a question asked a lot of his exaggerated descriptions. And I nodded as it was a fair assessment.

"Got you loads of food though," I explain as if meat will somehow balance out me being a total arsehole.

I'm left alone as the fire burns in anticipation of the huge frying pans being filled with delights only the truly indigenous could fathom.

Jenny comes and sits next to me on a log made for three but generally occupied by one, me.

"Did he really nearly drown?" she asks.

I nod and smile and reminisce about the waterlogged face of little oxygen and the emergency panic that unfolded after he was removed from the spit.

"Might be a little exaggerated," I lie.

"Shame. I cannot stand that guy," she smiles. "I wouldn't want to kill him, there are others for that list, but a good humbling would have helped him out many a year ago."

"If by humbled you mean drowned, he was almost humbled to death. Quite amusing seeing as he survived, but I don't remember the challenges coming this close to killing people before unless they cut those bits out."

She nods and looks at me.

"Yeah, it does seem more dangerous this year."

We can't chat more as the screams from our team indicate food is being dropped from above. Tradition has it that we call it down by doing something like a bird call and moving our fingers. I have, out of respect for myself and the innate desire not to look like a primary school tool, refused to do this at any point. And it doesn't matter how much Comedy Bob stares at me in disgust, I am not joining in. Jenny doesn't either and I'm sure we'll get punished with smaller portions, which is mostly a blessing. Snooker Gaz will scoff anything. I however have a boundary on what I'll put in my mouth. Penis being a no-no even if it is cooked and once belonging to a Bull.

The food is lowered and they call and whistle and do some weird thing with their fingers. A basket with a package inside wrapped in vine and cooking paper.

They open it up, and much to my surprise, if not many others, tonight's delicacy is not flying squirrel's snatch, but the tail of an alligator. Yum, yum, nobody thinks as we stare at an actual alligator tail still covered in green skin. It is revolting in a way that only those faced with the prospect of actually eating the shittest part of a reptile can truly understand.

Bob thinks it'll be great. I am not convinced. But I sit there, silently as I am tired and jaded, and Jenny sits next to me. We stay in silence watching an actual dinosaur fry. The others chat but my energy is gone.

It is finally fried after hours of prep and discussion, with a few vegetables that I will not be asking the local Tescos to stock thrown in to add colour and hopefully taste. Our cans are filled, our forks prepared and I chew. A lot. In silence as people stare at each other asking the silent question, What the actual Fuck?

Turns out the tail of an alligator is all gristle, bone, and the hardest meat known to man. It would have been easier to pulp up sand.

Jenny sits next to me grinding her teeth away.

"Shame he didn't drown" she asks.

I smile and nod, knowing that when I'm down I will be revisiting this memory.

"I cannot stand that man. I have worked with him, known many others who have worked with him and the general consensus is that he is an arrogant, woman-hating, tit."

"He hates me too."

She laughs.

"You aren't very popular here, you know?"

"I know. And I don't really want to be. You however, I'd be gutted if you hated me."

"Why?"

"I don't know. Maybe I rate you, think you are someone who is a lot closer to genuine than the rest. You don't seem to be playing the game. And if you are, wow, you are good. Got me fooled."

"I'm not playing. Regretting agreeing to come, without a doubt. Although meeting you has been fun. Weirdly. I don't know why. You are an irritating dick."

"Thank you."

"Pleasure."

We don't speak much more. I'm tired. I fall asleep somewhere along the line.

I go to sleep sicker than when I woke up.

THE PRESENTERS : DAY 08 : BLATHERING AGAIN

"We are bigger than we have ever been," The Welshman says, showing her his phone, flicking through page after page of newspaper headlines and graphs.

He has sat and read through it all, taken in every line on every chart and smiled all the way through. They were the number one show. The most watched, the most talked about. The number one trending topic on all social media.

"We are being investigated," she says without reading. She had seen them already. She always read the morning news and she always knew the ratings. "We have nearly killed two contestants, we are headlines on scandal sheets because of our break-up. They want to know if it is staged to increase ratings."

"It doesn't matter, if it is staged or not. It is working. We are being spoken about as much as them. People are tuning in to see if they

103

can decode our body language. Everyone wants to know if it is our break-up that is causing harm to the celebs."

"Brian is hated. Universally. I'd imagine each of his five ex-wives have tried to kill him. People would cheer his drowning. But you think us, what is happening with us, is a game? A ratings tactic?"

He drops his smile like he has practiced and done a million times in his life. She watches and rolls her eyes. She knows the routine.

"No, what we have is special," he says. "Admittedly we are going through a bad spot, as we have before and where we are and what we do right now is interfering with us spending time to work stuff out. But when this is all over and we have a break, we will get back on track. You know that."

She doesn't answer, she has spoken to her agent and she knows the articles are divided. Some for him and his dedication to entertaining the masses is a factor in the love the public have. She is a trouble maker, an uppity woman wanting everything and then a little more. She should know her place and role and be grateful for all that she has, as it is almost all off the back of catching him. Other papers, with less misogynistic journalists have taken a more female based approach and actually highlighted he is an untrustworthy cheating bastard with a track record of being a selfish, egotistical cretin. But the weight of opinion swings with every hour and there is no predicted outcome. It could go either way. The man who works for their good, or the woman who suffers in silence. People are reading and making decisions and formulating opinion based on gossip paragraphs written by people who have never exchanged a word with either of them. The media in overload, the golden couple, the people's couple, fragmenting and breaking up. They have all invested in their marriage, travelled with them every step because they have been on Television nearly every week of their married lives. They all know, they think, they have all become part of the relationship they see, the fake one of easy one-liners and written banter. And now that relationship, their relationship, is not what they want and sides need to be taken, careers are on the line.

She has spoken to her agent, tactics discussed, but even her agent questioned whether they were playing a popularity break-up with the reunion near the end of the show to boost ratings to levels only a royal wedding in the eighties would have met.

She had told her that she wanted out, that she needed an exit that left her with some chance of coming back as a single presenter, as a woman with strong morals and a desire to be independent. The agent is not her friend, she knows that, although she has information about all her life and thoughts. The friendship is a financial one. Were she to become economically unviable, someone whose ten percent was not enough to keep a bond, then she would be dropped. She knows this, knows that almost everyone she has in her professional life is there because of the popularity and economic means she possesses. They will fight for her as long as she wins and remains someone who can provide them with the money they crave. No one is doing her a favour through a feeling of friendship.

She looks at this grinning imbecile she married back when the journey looked an adventure. She knows he is plotting in the same way she is. But she knows he is wallowing in the belief that her success is only off the back of his. He is the major player in a relationship of comfort because she as an individual entity is so much less than the couple. But he, with his mature charm, his fake teeth, hair and personality will make it alone through the power of being an attractive man who can read jokes off a large bit of card.

Inside information is required and she has sent through more than she ever has. She made the decision, she is out, and this is the last. The popularity is astonishing. Two near deaths, a romance between two middle-aged, not-very-famous people in a jungle, with one of them being just about the most obnoxious gobshite that has appeared on the history of the show.

The public, it appears, love to watch people unravelling but need to offset their contempt with a redemption story of anyone, the underdog making it great.

"Are we ready to introduce them?" she asks.

She knows the answer, there can be no slow-down, no foot off the pedal. They have a limited time and they have to now throw everything at it. They are the most watched, most talked about show on TV. The last big thing on traditional channels. The streaming services can't compete with this level of intensity. The destruction of real famous people.

Everything they are doing, everything that shouldn't work, that should shut them down, should result in people switching off just isn't doing it. The evil Midas touch of turning pain and stupidity into viewing gold.

"We have to. People are tuning in to watch them. And us. Mostly us. We need to keep up our show too."

105

"It isn't a show," she says but knows he isn't listening. He is in total control he thinks. He has the final say on what happens between them. He is a fool. "We'll drop them in, and see if the chaos continues. Have you seen the ratings?"

"It is nasty."

"Nasty seems to be the new popular."

He is laughing, actually chuckling away at the evil he is promoting in the name of making him the face of Television to the current generation. She smiles inside. The gamble instead of letting it play out. Trust just isn't something worth its investment.

DAY : 08 : SLIGHTLY LESS BORED

And then the day came.

I woke up and said Hello to Jenny. I then said, "Why are you in my hammock?"

"Oh, shit," she replied, not in an attempt at sexy, more like waking up with a hangover, a vague recall of the previous night's piss-up and the realisation that you have spent the night in some random's bed and now need to get out quickly.

"This is not a good look," she adds correctly. "We fell asleep while talking?"

"It happens in a lot of my conversations," I add.

"Bollocks."

"Did we have sex?" I ask, a touch hopingly.

She punches me and stands up. The camp, each and everyone of them is staring at us and smiling.

Jenny points at them in one long motion.

"You can all fuck off," she mentions as she walks over to her own bunk. The first ever walk of shame on a reality TV show. I'm glowing with pride. I think I should walk around the embers of the fire high-fiving anyone who wishes to acclaim my manliness and talk about boxing and plumbing to drag out my moment of macho.

We all shower, me with my chest puffed out like a boss. We eat breakfast and have our coffee and Jenny doesn't speak.

People drift off, cleaning tins, tidying up, and doing the chores they have been assigned.

"Let's go, Stud," Jenny says in a futile attempt to degrade me through exaggeration.

It won't work. And the smile I have is not leaving anytime soon. She fell asleep with me. That is comfort and peace. That is a sign.

106

We are walking down to the Dunny, the toilet, the shed with a plank and a hole and a large bin below. The bin is full of celebrity shit watered down with celebrity wee. I'm sure this would make a profit on some dodgy fan site, like those people who buy used shoes on ebay not because they like the worn design but they get off on the smell of someone else's foot having been sweating in there. But I keep this thought to myself despite believing Jenny is able to read my mind.

"You are thinking something weird," she tells me, but doesn't go into detail, which is great, as I don't want her to have any.

"That is a general constant," I say with more truth than I am used to.

I look around, the path down to the shithouse is a long and windy one that takes you from the view of camp and luckily out of earshot. Changing from a western diet of processed crap to a jungle diet of inedible and half-cooked meat has had a severe effect on the production and spread of the squits. I had a particular problem with the after effects of the rice and beans. The alligator has, I think, remained sat in my stomach as I don't believe my ancestors evolved the requisite enzymes, acid or indeed desire, to break down the meat of apex predators. I come from a long tradition of take-away eaters. Chinese or Thai, it doesn't matter. We can deal with all of them without problem. The chewy fat of a camel spleen is however a completely different proposition.

But it is eerily quiet as we walk toward our camp job. We open a wooden door, drag out an almost overflowing plastic bin that sloshes as we urge. I have gloves, which stay clean for only a second. It takes two of us to lift and drag the thing and I think of all the worst jobs I had as a kid. The kitchens full of angry people shouting and sweating. The head chef having a cigarette in the corner as flour flies from a machine he has deliberately set off without a lid to hide his habit. The pot washer that I was, with half eaten food and sauces and bread and meat that all ran into one big ball of sloppy pulp. I'd rather eat that and date the insane lady who loved chopping veg into the smallest slices. She was destined to kill. I fear looking up her name. I fear her. But I'd take all that right now over trying to move a bin of human waste with a woman I really like while trying not to be sick.

"It is very quiet," I say.

Jenny nods.

"Always is down here."

"No, It is really quiet," I say.

107

We are being filmed, just not by people. There are cameras attached to trees, some seemingly new and recently placed. They have a red LED on top showing they are filming. There are microphones attached to us and to tress. We can't move without being seen nor speak without being heard. But almost always there is a couple with cameras and a long stick with a microphone. Not now though. It is too quiet.

"Are you always paranoid?" Jenny asks.

I look around, feel something that isn't right. I stop. The bin can move itself. My gloves can be burned. And I really need a new job. I turn to her. We are on the lane, bushes and trees all around. A breeze making leaves rustle and blow.

I think and it dawns on me.

"Shit," I say, smiling. "They have left us alone to see what happens. See if we get physical. Jesus, that's it. We sleep together-"

"Accident," Jenny interrupts.

"-and they leave us, no other people to see, and they expect your feelings to crystallise into a physical approach, a step toward the-"

I am smiling but not for long. Her face is aghast, absolute shock. Not quite disgust, just the face of someone who has been told after taking a sip of their pint that their hilarious mate with the massive shlong has, while you nipped to the toilet, dipped their cock in your lager.

I didn't think I had misread the room that much. I start to think as quickly as I can, which is not that fast at all when it comes down to pressure situations. I just need to start, with a word, any word and then let my literary talents take over, ad-lib my way through a monologue on how I was joking – but make sure I actually wasn't and that there is still the possibility. I think and choose. My first word is "A," which is a dodgy choice. But it matters little as upon my first sound, Jenny screams and my world goes blank as a hood is wrapped over my head and I see nothing but black as the bottom is pulled tight around my neck.

Fight or flight is a part of our genetics. However, just as my ancestors prefer kebab over hunting and killing their own deer, they also seem to have taken a conscious decision to move away from fighting or running and firmly attached themselves to the possum approach and freeze like a big coward.

I grab at the hood, but a little too hard and pinch my own face. It hurts. I grab the underside of the hood and pull, which somehow makes it contract tighter and I choke under my own strength. I can think of nothing else to do so I stand rigid as my arms are pulled behind my back and tied.

It is part of the show, I understand this. A little later than maybe I should, but I realise all the same.

"You Ok Jenny?" I ask.

She may have replied, but I can't hear anything as someone smacks my head, a lot harder than they are contractually obliged to do.

Someone kicks the backs of my knees and I bend forward, falling but the same person pulls my arms toward them and I am dragged along, my heels scraping into the earth.

"Is this going to take long?" I ask, pretending to be so chill I can reverse global warming.

For my troubles, I am kicked in the upper thigh and it stings like a mother but then goes completely dead, which, in many ways, is a blessing.

THE PRESENTERS : DAY 08 : GLOATING

"There they go," The Welshman says, more joyously than his wife thinks appropriate for a staged kidnapping. "Our two star-crossed lovers are being dragged away to face an even bigger challenge. Fear itself."

What a bellend, she thinks. And she would be right. But she keeps her face neutral, short of loving for the cameras that are rolling. They are live and this, she thinks, is a big mistake for any show that wants a future. She doesn't want the future but she doesn't want the blame. The pay-off would be just as good without the macabre set-up. He has bought in conflict, and manipulated battles to bring in ratings. The aftermath will be a public period of reflection and the realisation that what is happening is cruel, that the nudge-nudge, wink-wink old-school humour of previous years was what made the show and the new, edgier stuff is fun in the short term. No one wants to see people tortured for long and no one famous is coming here again.

"It is something that might freak some viewers out. It has certainly shocked me," she says to the camera. "This has been organised by others. I hope they are aware they aren't actually being kidnapped," she adds. "That it is just one of your 'jokes'."

She doesn't turn her head, she stares straight ahead, trying for solemn and hoping she is close enough and not showing any of her internal smirk.

"We were all there in the meeting," he says with a giggle that fools no one.

"This was not discussed," she says. "The next part, if I am in on the actual plan, is the step I think might be the cruellest. I'm not sure we

109

should be doing this. But it is a democracy, and my vote was counted against by others."

She knows what she is doing. She voted against, knowing hers would be the only negative. He runs the company, has a say in who is hired, who is sacked and who gets recognition and money. Everyone, without fail, backed his decision. In previous years she could have talked, taken the rough edges off. People could express their worries and she could modify his thinking through manipulation. But she wasn't trying now. She spoke, but in a way she knew would rile him into going that step further, that one move more just so he could say he stuck it to her.

He is such a tool, she thinks and has to stop her grin before it fully forms.

The production team had been there, had heard her voice, had come to her and spoken of their fears. She had promised, like she always had, that she would speak to him, that when he would describe what needs to happen before filming the extremes would be removed, logic and empathy would prevail. She had listened just like she always had but this time she didn't present like a union representative. She spoke, bashing his ego and his intelligence in ways he wouldn't realise but she knew would flame his desire to prove he was right.

And now they are here with a production team wide-eyed and scared, her telling the live audience she was not supporting the day's actions and him smiling away like he knows best and that every creative choice is without doubt the most genius, audience-increasing brilliance of all time. She thinks it would be like deciding to go all creative and make an episode of Coronation Street be performed through the medium of mime.

"Let's get back to them," he smarms to the largest number of viewers they have had in five years. "I'm excited to see what happens," he adds and no one behind the camera cheers.

DAY 08 : STILL MORNING : GETTING KIDNAPPED

They drag me for a bit, and by bit I mean at least ten minutes. I'm pretty sure the camp isn't that large so I guess I've just been going round in circles, arguably carving a ditch deep enough to plant potatoes. It certainly seems that every two minutes the same large rock hits my knees, and I make the same scream. They don't speak so I have no idea if they are local or British. They are obviously part of the production company as I think had some mad far-right terrorists wanting to make a statement about unregulated immigration, they could have chosen someone more important than me and a show that is actually watched in Australia. I hear a few noises, birds, a click, a clump of something heavy hitting the ground hard like an oversized elephant just took a dump off a cliff. I am lifted further and thrown with not inconsiderable power, and my stomach slips up into my throat as I fly for a little too long and the floor has become further away. I hit the ground, my hands are free and I sit there for a long time waiting to be cuffed around the head.

"Ben," I hear.

"Yes," I respond like I've just been called in a doctor's waiting room.

"You can take your hood off."

It is Jenny, and I'm relieved at that.

"Am I going to see something I don't want? Are there big hairy men, naked, oiled and looking for love?"

"Just take your hood off," she insists.

Reluctantly I start to oblige, although my wrists are very sore and my fingers feel and work like a set of boiled parsnips.

"For Christ sake," Jenny tells me and pushes my hands away.

She fumbles around and slowly pulls the cover off my head. I see we have been placed inside a small entrance to a cave. The opening above is a rectangle of blue light from the sky. I turn and behind me is an entrance to an even darker recess of the underworld.

I prefer the blue sky and look up. A big hairy faced man with a cowboy hat appears and he is flipping the door. He closes one side as I smile inanely at him. He closes the other side too with a comforting thump. The room we are in becomes pitch black.

"It was arguably lighter with my hood on," I say.

"I thought you were exempt from challenges," Jenny tells me.

"I think they want to kill me."

"Oh, we don't want that," an irritating voice tells me through a speaker hidden somewhere in this man-made underground space. "We have a surprise for you."

The voice, while disguised with an attempt at a speech impediment, is about as convincing as French when spoken by Clousaeu.

"If it isn't cash and a first class ticket back to my house, I'm not going to be happy," I say.

The male voice laughs, and I detect the edges of insanity, that slight unhinging like the man in the pub who has learned to control his shaky mental health issues when sober, but is now on his fifth pint of strong European lager and the eyes are starting to slip into pure insanity

111

and his sentences are starting to contain worrying references to things that have not been said nor ever happened.

"You may have noticed a cave entrance behind you when there was light," he lisps fakely.

"Was the kidnapping actually necessary?" Jenny asks rather pointedly. "You could have just asked us and we would probably have come along anyway. And I can tell it is your Welsh voice, you are hardly going to get a job on Spitting image."

"That is a reference the kids won't pick up," I say.

She hits me, which is impressive as I can't see my own hand, yet she can clip my ear with great precision and force.

"Ow," I say.

"You may have seen you are in a cave," the Welshman continues gradually losing the will to talk like a prick – at least with the voice of an actor who thinks impersonating a disability gives a character depth. He'll start playing the cello next to show he has an emotional side even though he doesn't and it is a cheap gimmick to portray more than the two dimensional character he has become, or indeed may have always been.

"You need to pass through the cave into an open area where the next stage of your escape will become apparent."

"What was the point of the kidnapping?" Jenny asks again.

"Creative choice," the Welshman's wife says in her normal voice but with the undertones of boredom.

"Off you go," The Welshman stammers and lisps again adding further stupidity to his accent.

"Can you see?" I ask Jenny.

"I'm getting there."

"I'll follow you then."

"Yes, because you can't see and not because you are scared and think the lead person will get the horrible stuff first."

"This may have passed through my mind, yes," I say having been caught out by Jenny the mind-reading freak. "However, you were the fool who admitted they hated pigeons and birds in general so I am guessing the next room contains a flock of geese."

"Skein," she says, and it is a word, I believe, she has either made up or mispronounced because she is shitting her pants.

"What?"

"A skein of geese, not a flock."

112

I pause, thinking, rubbing my right thumb and index finger against my chin, which is redundant as no one can see me other than the viewers who will be watching this in night vision green.

"We are in a dark cave," I tell her, "having been kidnapped by a group of hairy men, led by a man with a faked accent and pretending his tongue doesn't work properly, and you choose this moment to be pedantic?"

"It is important to be correct."

"After you," I insist, pushing her slightly and I may have, possibly, placed my palms upon her arse.

"Touch me again and I will snap your wrists."

"Carpus," I correct her. "It's import-"

"Fuck off."

And she horse kicks me in the shoulder.

We crawl on all fours along the dusty floor and into the darker part of the room. The doorway is low so standing and walking is right out. Nothing happens, nothing at all. No gunk, no bugs, no pain nor humiliation, just two middle-aged nobodies crawling through tunnels in total darkness for minutes. I'm preparing for an electric cattle prod to be forced against my armpits, but nothing happens other than a crawl in the dark.

"This is boring," I say.

"I'll take boring over needing to shower for ninety minutes to remove the worst effects of being dunked in fish shit."

"Yeah, but this feels like a massive build up to hell."

The lights come on and I am blinded, in a different way from being blind in the dark, this is a painful blinded, a scratch my own eyes out blinded.

Jenny swears and I do too, only she is more creative than me and I'm impressed with her ability to put seemingly random words together to insult even the most Welsh of things.

We are in a room, made to look like a cave, and in front of us is a pond. The edge of the pond has large swimming masks and no snorkels. Each mask has our name on it.

"Swimming?" I ask. "Really?"

"You need to place your goggles on, make them nice and tight. You will need to swim for twenty metres."

"Under water? Piss off," I correct. I can swim but leisurely and always in breast stroke.

"Every two metres there is a surface point where you can collect oxygen," the stupid, idiotic voice blathers on.

"In a bag? Or do you mean breathe?"

"He means breathe," Molly says.

"I mean collect oxygen," the Welshman says in what is edging toward, as all faked accents do, a vaguely racist version of Indian.

"You can pack in the façade now," Jenny says. "We know we haven't been kidnapped. We know we have to do a task and win a treat for camp in the shape of a quarter of a mildly stale baby bell."

"Hahahahahaha," the Welsh/Indian voice actually says, like a supervillain in any 60s spy film. "You are wrong."

"It'll be more twiglets," I say.

"Hahahahaha," he bellows again like Brian Blessed's deeper voiced dad. "No, we have a surprise for you at the end of this challenge."

"You have a surprise," Molly corrects. "I'm nothing to do with this."

"Hahahahahahaha," he cackles, this time in an attempt to audition for the fake monster in Scooby Doo. "Let's get wet," he adds, and every school boy in the country is trying not to giggle and thus give their thoughts away to their parents who are sat watching with them.

"The water is well lit, you will be able to see, which is both a help and a hindrance as it will not be just you two down there," Molly says.

"A seal, twenty seven penguins and eight killer whales?" I ask, not as jokingly as I would have been.

He laughs again and the routine has not just worn thin, it has worn away to reveal a ball of irritation.

"There are baby alligators, dozens of eels, plenty of fish, and water snakes," he explains, his accent now not readily attached to any place that has ever existed. It may be old English but it could equally be a long lost dialect of Cumbrian tribe. Whatever it is, he sounds a dick.

We snap on the goggles, oblivious to the fact we can just ask to stop. But there are two of us and neither wants to be the one to walk away, which is ridiculous as we both want to walk away. I'll analyse this later, probably in an ambulance or more likely coffin.

"I'm taking my boots off," I say as I sit down cross-legged. Jenny does the same. We are fully clothed otherwise, like two kids who are doing their gold-badge lifesavers exam and we are required to wear clothes and save people in a swimming pool. Most choose pyjamas, we have chosen heavy cotton cargo pants and t-shirts. This may prove to be a mistake.

We stand and walk to the water's edge. I dip a toe in and regret the decision. I have swum in the English Channel and come out with my lips blue and my skin so tight plastic surgeons would gasp at the stretch. This water however, appears to be breaking the laws of physical state, as it is easily at a temperature of minus ten but still happily sloshing around in its liquid state. It probably isn't water at all but liquid nitrogen poured in to send us into a state that Walt Disney is rumoured to be. We could wake up and be shivering but in season four thousand and ten of this god awful programme.

"Ready?" Jenny asks.

I shake my head. I look into the water and it is clear enough to see steps leading down like a Jacuzzi but scarier, so like a Jacuzzi with people in it that I don't know and that are talking to each other. I would never get in that Jacuzzi. I don't want to get into this one.

I hold Jenny's hand and we step down, and I am dreading that moment when the surface of the water hits the level of my bollocks. I'm right to dread it. I inhale sharply. Jenny looks at me, I smile and she nods. She knows my pain.

We are up to our chins in water, I release her hand and I dip below the surface, and then, very quickly, some might say immediately, I surface again.

"Cold," I say. "And you can see the creatures."

Jenny dips down, and in an attempt to break my speed record is quickly above the surface again.

"Many creatures," she says. "Are we on a time limit?"

"No," I say. "We can stay down here for as long as we want."

My mask is steamed up, and I can't see any more. I take it off, spit in it because I saw someone do this in a film, and then put it back on. It doesn't really work as it is still quite steamy but also covered in spit.

"Dip it in the water," Jenny tells me.

I do as instructed and the condensation goes, although quite a lot of the spit dribbles into the corner.

I go under again and push out into the water.

It is well lit, and there are creatures everywhere but they seem more scared of me than I am of them. They move away like the big dog has just entered the prison yard. They will smell my fear soon enough, just hopefully not in the scent of my piss from me urinating in terror. They all swim off except the baby alligators who appear to be absolutely off their tits on mushrooms. They are the remedial alligators I presume as they are pressing their noses up against the glass of the tank in an

115

apparent animal attempt at licking windows. They lounge about at the point where I need to go for my next breath of air about two metres away. A break in the surface.

I nearly choke when I see the massive killer whale at the other end of the tank, floating under the surface, bubbles popping from its mouth, I almost turn and swim back before I realise it is in fact a human in wetsuit with an air-tank, sat watching, waiting for me to show distress so they can come and save me. This I find reassuring, until I think about it more deeply and realise he is there as there is a significant risk of drowning. The water snakes less so. They don't seem to like the alligators enough to stay close so they are now swimming around, quickly and some in my direction. I do breast stroke under water and within three awkward pulls I am below two baby alligators and the room of air above. I push up and my head breaks the surface. I am face to face with a child alligator that breaks the general rule that all babies are cute. It is a monster with many, many small pointed teeth. Jenny pops up seconds later and the alligators start to shake about.

"Deep breath and lets go," I say, worrying that one of the two might snap my face off.

Jenny pushes one of the snappy jawed fuckers away and I stare at her.

"Alligators, no problem, a punch on their snout. Pigeons however."

"Let's go," she says, dropping under the water.

I don't follow but then one of the baby dinosaurs winks and while I am no expert on animal kingdom body language, I assume it isn't flirting and is making a subtle sign for me to get right out of its face.

We swim, slowly, but it is three strokes to the next air hole. There are plenty of eels, I think. Snakes have bigger heads. They are going to be harmless I lie to myself. They are almost certainly electric, or biters, or stingers or something. Probably all carrying concealed weapons to stab me for entering their street or something similar. I break the surface and gulp in air even though I am not short of breath. I'm no fitness freak but holding my breath for ten seconds is not a bind. I do it often when trying not to shout obscenities at people who have annoyed me. Mostly in Supermarkets, and mostly the elderly, and always near the milk.

The eels special skill is swimming around and touching me and slithering across my arms and bare flesh like massive coils of snot pulled from toddler's noses. I think I'd prefer to be eaten.

"These things are disgusting," Jenny informs me.

"I know, I am here also," I inform her in return. "Worse than the alligators on tramadol?"

"Let's go," and under we go again.

The killer whale man points us to his right, a bend in the tunnel. I swim round as elegantly as a sack of potatoes drifting in the current, and see steps up and out of the water. I speed up, pushing my hands quicker and kicking my legs faster and somehow managing to go slower. Jenny glides past while I seem to be moving all my limbs in different directions and effectively staying stationary. I feel a push, and the whale man has shoved me forward. I drift to the steps and climb out.

I walk into a large lit cave. Manmade, the walls are clearly fibreglass and the vegetation plastic.

Jenny watches me crawl out of the water.

"This is all very dodgy," she says. "What are we supposed to be doing? We aren't collecting anything, the rules are not anywhere to be seen. What is it that this is about?"

"Punishment," I tell her because I have been thinking about this while trying not to drown. "It is punishment. Someone, somewhere has decided to torture me – and you – for the amusement of the masses. I am totally done. I am about to quit."

I wait to hear some voice, the Welshman or the wife, or the stupid character he is playing. But there is nothing. A silence broken by our own deep breaths. I look around and there is nothing to show us what is next.

PRESENTERS : DAY 08 : REALISING IT IS RUBBISH

"This isn't working," Molly says smiling.

She wants it to fail, knows that it really should. And he is throwing a hissy fit of silent grumps because his big plan is clearly a load of nonsense. Oh, poor boy, she thinks, what a shame. Your big idea falling to pieces. And it is. The kidnap was a badly thought out plan. They didn't believe it, no one was fooled, and his stupid bloody, inconsistent accent made him look an utter tool. She smiles at the memory and how that clip will be played over and over to humiliate him on any show. He'll be interviewed on a satellite channel's morning program, watched by ten thousand right-wingers from the Home Counties, who are waiting for the news report as read by one of Mussolini's distant cousins. He sounded

Indian come the end and there is nothing quite as bad as being called a racist.

At least he didn't black face, which even he wouldn't be stupidly arrogant enough to do. Although he did once dress up as a Nazi in a fancy dress party, which he somehow managed to wiggle out of. He claimed ignorance, and she was never sure if he meant he was totally ignorant, he didn't know what a swastika was or that he was simply unaware of modern history between 1930 and 1945. She imagined it was a strong combination of all of the above. She had once worn a vegan shirt and been the recipient of death threats from men who told her eating meat was healthy. As was wife beating apparently, and sending obnoxious messages on social media. Her husband had impersonated a high-ranking official in the holocaust and been given a minor reprimand, boys will be boys, while she had recommended eating vegetables and been threatened with death. But this is rapidly falling apart and he has the face on like a five-year-old child who has been told off by the class teacher. It is amusing to watch a grown man be a child. She hopes the silent treatment will continue for weeks, if not years. Arguably forever.

"There appears to be absolutely no point to what they are being asked to do," she says.

He turns away, his arms crossed across his chest. Suck it up, big boy, she thinks, a big cheese-filled grin across her face.

"We need to cut to the chase, possibly? Hit the pay off as this is just getting them to do stuff just to do stuff. There is no suspense, just torture."

She can't help herself, she is having the time of her life. She giggles.

He spins around, eyes wide with anger. She has seen this before. He'll start ranting silly stuff that makes no logical sense, like when he is drunk and claims he will achieve anything he puts his mind to, like winning the lottery, despite being rich.

"What was your idea?" he spits. "Your idea was to do nothing. Your idea was to just watch this show fade into cancellation."

"Everything has its life. We are very much heading into retirement. The show is done."

"No, it isn't. We need a change of direction. We have been the most popular presenters – as judged by the public no less – for thirteen straight years! Thirteen. We are untouchable. We do not do failure."

A lot of Welsh spittle sprays her face, which is, she thinks, preferable right now to getting litres of the stuff through kissing. She can't remember the last time they kissed properly. She tries to remember, pulls a disgusted face, then sacks that off to concentrate on the present.

"It is your creative decision. We have had a fake kidnapping – for no reason, a danger-free underwater swim. No actual challenge and yet here we are, waiting on you to pull the trigger on what you think is the biggie. I don't get it."

"Everyone here backed me yesterday," he shouts, pointing at the crew who all look to floor or into cameras.

"They didn't back you, they just didn't oppose, which is a totally different thing. Was, is and will be a bad idea. It makes no sense," she tells him with as much honesty as she can muster. Her enthusiasm has long since left the continent and she is wondering if it will soon be followed by her pride.

He tries to say something, but nothing comes. His lips are clamped together and he is vibrating his head side to side like it is a bomb on the verge of explosion. He does this for an uncomfortably long time as they all watch waiting for something, anything, maybe not a stroke though as there is a segment to film quite soon, and his voice is required, his normal voice, not that of a white man getting all method and pretending to be ethnic.

He uncrosses his arms.

"Fuck off," he says and walks away.

She turns to the crew.

"Get them to the last part as quickly as possible," she says. "We need to get this done."

She nods to a camera man and he nods back. There is nothing showy, it is almost hidden. He is telling her he has it all on film, and she needs it. She needs evidence for her way out. It might not be enough, he has Tefloned his way out of a lot of trouble in his time. Avoided anything that may stick, things other celebrities could never survive. Things she shouldn't have put up with. But she had sold her soul too. She knew this. Whatever the reason he is loved, it'll need some serious weight to shift opinion. And after all, she is the woman, the wife, the person who should be dutiful and grateful. She will be, she thinks, if she can get out of this unscathed.

119

DAY 08 : AFTERNOON : THE NONSENSE CONTINUES

A voice comes through the air.

"You have made it to your place of punishment," the voice says, trying for a deep voiced Brian Blessed but ending up nearer Tiny Tim but Welsh.

The inconsistency could, I believe, be the effects of the rather late onset of his balls dropping. Or he is just very bad at accents. Maybe both. Maybe I no longer care.

"Look, mate," I say, in that way British people do when addressing someone they think is a nob. "I'm done."

"No, no, no," the Welshman says, his accent gone and panic ringing through. "No quitting now."

"Well, actually, he can quit when he wants," Jenny tells him. "It is written into the contract."

"Yes, but there is the biggest of surprises for you just around the corner."

"Ohh," I say like I am the campest Drag Queen in Sheffield. "Is it wrestling with a hungry Lion with a roll of Clingfilm to protect me? Or do I have to whip naked down a slide that has been made entirely out of old, used razor blades? Or do I have to eat the testicles of a boar while they are still attached to its living body? This is all a nonsense. I have absolutely no idea why I am here, what you people are doing, or why any of this, particularly today, is entertaining on any level."

I lie back, exhausted, in the dirt they must have shovelled in when constructing the place. It smells of bleach.

I look up and Jenny is smiling down at me, no sarcasm, no contempt, just a smile.

She reaches down and offers her hand. I take it and she pulls me up. We are face to face. We look at each other and I have this aching desire to kiss her, not like a slobbery French kiss at the school disco when you are twelve kiss, but a peck, on the lips, nice and slow, what I imagine would be loving and full of care but that she would almost certainly take as an attempt at a physical assault and reply by destroying me both mentally and physically with words I have never heard combined in such ways and short sharp jabs she has learned from growing up with rugby playing siblings.

I chicken out and revert to type.

"Nice grip," I attempt at a joke.

"You just don't have the confidence, do you?" she tells me smiling.

"You scare me."

"Good."

She squeezes my hand like two old friends who think this may be the last time they meet. If she pats me on the back I am in friend-zone hell with no way to return except through bribery.

"You can't leave," The Welshman pleads. "Not for a while anyway. Jenny has to finish her little challenge-"

"We don't know what it is!" she shouts, but still hasn't turned away from me so I get the warm breath and spittle into my eyes. She mouths sorry and I accept her apology as she is still holding my hand and I am not too sure she doesn't know some weird Vulcan death grip. I plan to stay on her good side.

"All will be revealed," he lies as he makes stuff up on the spot. "You, Ben, can sit and watch and maybe, just maybe change your mind upon seeing the prize."

"Yes, maybe, I could. But if the prize is not my fist repeatedly smashing into your face to the sound of Flash Gordon by Queen, then I am afraid I am not joining in."

"Jenny," he says, ignoring me and my empty threats. "You need to walk to the water's edge and your instructions will be given to you."

She walks over, having let go of my hand. Not in a long lingering look, with hand still out like we are participating in a re-enactment of scenes in Dirty Dancing, but a drop, huff, inhale and stomp across to the water.

She stands there and nothing happens. Several seconds pass until the surface is broken by the wetsuit man. He removes the oxygen tube from his mouth and saliva drips down and he takes off his goggles revealing a creased, wrinkly from water face with a massive red mark circling his eyes. I've never seen his face before but if he spends his time looking like this when out and about round the pubs, he is a man who would spend the evening receiving slaps. He has a proper strop on.

"You need to go over to the secret door," he says, pointing at the wall where there is vegetation and no clear escape. "It is hidden behind the plastic vegetation," he adds with the voice of a man who has spent the last week attending three funerals a day. Go through and you'll find out what you need to do."

Jenny stares at him. I stare at him. He shrugs.

"There was another contrived challenge to do, with absolutely no logical reason to find the door," he informs us. "But we are skipping that part, unlike the first bit, which is a shame, as the first bit should have been avoided too."

He holds up his left hand. "One of the snakes bit me," he says.

"Looks painful," Jenny informs him with her non-existent medical knowledge.

"It was initially, but now it is numb, as is the entire arm."

"Hospital?"

He nods and falls back into the water.

Jenny looks in, squinting in the hope this will give her the ability to see well through water like an arrow fish or X-man.

"He is swimming," she says.

"He's probably seeking revenge on the anaconda."

"He's gone."

"Forever?" I ask.

She smiles, and I am sure, in that not-sure-at-all-but-I-am way of a teenage boy too scared to actually ask because he doesn't think he could carry the rejection, that she likes me. She turns to the fibreglass wall and walks over.

I lie back, star fish on the floor, the starting position to make a snow angel but I have zero intention of moving. I am out. I should never have been in. It has been fun, and while I don't think I have made too many lifelong friends, and will be forever known when they all meet up during festivities to talk about how they survived the jungle like it is comparable to having been one of the lucky ones in the Second World War, I will be referred to as That Dick. This warms me more than it should. Being disliked by people I dislike has a lovely glow to it. It makes me proud.

I smile at all the things I have done, like slopping liquid faeces over my hand, nearly dying in hospital and showing more composure than I realised I had when keeping words and thoughts in when I'd really like them out. I smile. I think I have cracked it. I am betting Jenny will see me on the outside, which is about five-hundred metres in any direction really.

I'll have that leaver's interview with the presenters and they'll show me clips of my escapades and ask questions about whether I meant any of what I said. I'd like to do that. The first one out, and I get to stick around, do interviews and appear in those magazines that appear in dentist's waiting rooms. I'll be associated with teeth being drilled for years to come.

I've left my mark, I think.

"You are going to have to help me," Jenny says with all the enthusiasm of a high school history teacher three terms from retirement and phoning it in about the Tudor period.

We don't care, Sir.

And neither do I. Turn to page eight.

I sit up slowly and look at what she is doing. The wall has opened into a trap door, there is a winch of sorts, like pedals on a bike but for hands. She is winding slowly, but nothing is moving. I smile and see the problem. I walk over, grab the stick next to her and pull it forward. The winch starts to move as she pushes.

"A brake?" she asks.

"Safety, I'd guess."

I look down the shaft that has been revealed. There is a type of coffin attached to ropes and as she winds, the rope shortens and the coffin rises.

"Any ideas what's inside?" I ask.

"Food," she says. "Lots of good food. And by good I mean take-away food, burgers."

"A Chinese?"

"Fries."

"A curry."

"Coke."

"Gherkins?"

"Always gherkins. Why remove gherkins?"

"Food? Really?"

"What else can it be? The whole day has been pointless so far. Might as well reward us with something Bob doesn't have to cook, and Gaz doesn't have to figure out how to eat, and Chelsey doesn't try and guess at calories."

"It'll be too many."

"And she'll eat it all except the last mouthful and offer it to Gaz who will gobble it up and everyone is happy."

I inhale, deeply.

"You know," I say, wishing I had a pipe and a mantelpiece to lean against as a log fire roared away behind a protective metal cage. "I think our work is done here. We need let them go, let them find their own way in this wicked little jungle. Our job is done. We can do no more. Let our babies fly solo, while we go home and try and forget their names or even having met them, like parents pretending to have dementia."

The coffin is in fact a box, about six feet long and two feet across. It looks solid and there is a latch. Jenny winds the last of the rope in and the box hangs there, occupying almost all the space of the shaft from which it has been raised. I place the brake on.

"If it is worse than a barbeque burger made by a bloke named Dave who is wearing an apron and a chef's hat, and cooking off a stove that has been left outside all winter, I'm not eating it."

"That's a low bar," she tells me, bending forward and grabbing the latch. She flips it loose and places her fingers under the hinged lid.

"I like a low bar, gives me hope. Aim for the stars they used to say, and you might just hit the moon. Mrs. Maloney year five, Treeside Park Infants School. Stuck with me that, as has compulsory bobbing up and down freezing your undropped balls off in an unheated outdoor swimming pool, the sadistic Witch. She-"

I am stopped in my nostalgic reminiscing of old times in pre-health and safety schools where teachers were allowed to hurt you for doing such outrageous things as saying willy, not being totally still when they ask you, and being unable to write the letter e in joined up pen. Good times. Kids today are soft.

I am stopped mainly because of the most wonderful combination of swear words, objects, and their combination in ways that are so creative as to be the very first time they have been used together in actual language. She is the poet laureate of put-downs. I particularly like the way she insults the box in such a way as to destroy its masculinity in a short sentence that combines the C-word with a rarely used culinary implement. I want to applaud but I can't as I, more urgently, need to hold Jenny back from stomping whatever is inside.

I grab her from behind and by the shoulders and she is angry strong. She twists and turns but I manage to stop her. A man rather cheerfully sits up from the box. I recognise him immediately and his smarm hits me like a teenager's Lynx Africa on Boxing Day. I dislike him also, and everything he stands for, but I would stop short of taking Jenny's approach to a slimy tit-turd and not attempt to physically assault him upon our first meeting. I'd wait till the third, and possibly do it in a back alley and with no witnesses rather than on prime time TV and on film for ever. I'd probably use a mace.

I pull her back.

"Nobody likes a politician," I say. "No need to beat them up though. It isn't their fault. It's a genetic problem, exacerbated by their upbringing. They can't help being dislikeable, blathering tools."

124

She stops pulling and trying to reach for his throat. She relaxes and turns to me.

"Ben," she says, and I'm hoping she isn't about to add 'I love you,' as it is too early and it would make it awkward. How do you respond to that when you, in fact don't, but are just quite keen and would fancy figuring out your feelings though the medium of sweaty sex. 'That's nice," is not an answer that is going to cut it.

"Ben," she repeats clearly seeing that I have drifted off into the beautiful countryside of my imagination, "this is Jonathon Harvinger."

"I know, I have watched political shows during the last twenty years. Not for long, I grant you, and even less when he is smarming shite on a panel debate. But I know who he is. I read newspapers. Although never his column."

"Jonathon Harvinger, my very soon to be ex-husband."

I turn to her. Mouth agape.

"You aren't breaking up over me, are you?"

Which sounded a lot funnier in my head, which is the reason I giggle it out.

She is staring at me, no humour, but significantly less aggression than she showed Jon boy the go-to political insight man.

"I'm joking," I say.

I turn to Jon-boy.

"She barely touched me," I tell him. "When we slept together. She barely glanced my balls. Could have been by accident."

"Shut up." Jenny tells me.

And Jonny Harvinger smiles away, hair impeccable for a fifty-five year old man, white, slicked back and thick. The face of a man who has had to show no emotion in public for forty years. And the body of a man who has enough time to swim, probably in his own pool, in his monumental basement, next to his sauna. He looks like Roger Moore, but with Richard Gere's hair. He is one of those people you either hate or think is not too irritating. Nothing in between, and absolutely a total void of people on the liking side.

"How long?"

"Eighteen years and two children."

I would like to say something, anything. But eighteen years. With this guy?

"I hope he is less irritating in private. People have set fire to bus stops because his face is on them."

I look at him, and he says nothing, just smiles with white teeth, no gaps, all straight, mostly original. He is superior, in his mind, and many others. That public school level of knowing they are and always will be that class above. A confidence in what they say even if it is vacuous gob-spittle of the highest order in the queen's English and words which while obviously English in origin have been so sparsely used in the every day vernacular of the average person as to be as conspicuous in phrase as a man wearing an inflatable sumo suit to church.

Why use them?

Oh, but they are in the dictionary.

So is crapulous, cockalorum, and twattle, but if I used them I would also be a bellend, or as I am sure they say in Eton, a snollygoster.

I bet you say legal tender, don't you?

"There is another trapdoor," the Welshman says, as a Welshman and not as an Australian trying to pretend to be Scottish.

I think, trying to pick out a person who they could bring in who was a) going to annoy me to the point of violence and b) vaguely famous and c) someone who knows me. I can think of no one. I hang out with no one, have never been in a relationship with anyone more famous than me, and I am unknown throughout the land, and those that do know me are generally of the, oh, yeah, him, variety. There is no one. The only person who is remotely known to the public and would be able to stand me for more than five minutes is myself. And I find that very difficult at times. And also, I am already here.

It is going to be food. I open a part of the wall next to the hand pedal thing. There is a shaft, a rope and at the bottom a wooden box. The set-up is exactly the same. I release the brake and start winding.

Jonny-boy and Jenny stand in silence. Jenny seething and wanting to take a part of Jonathon's soul and Jonathon waiting for the right moment to spout rubbish, pretend to know stuff and say sentences that mean nothing, although they sound like they should.

I wind slowly and realise I have been coaxed in to participating again. I sigh but wind on like the sad pathetic man I am. Over and over and the box comes up, closer and closer, the cave I am in silent as Jenny and Jonny wait in that uncomfortable quiet like they are stood waiting to find out how the judge believes their finances should be split. I should really make this quick but I do not have the enthusiasm.

The box gets close, I put on the brake and lean down and undo the latch, and put my fingers under the lid. I really don't want to open it, I really don't. It is like walking into an abandoned warehouse on a dare

126

when drunk as a teenager. I don't believe in ghosts, and didn't back then, but I was still terrified of seeing one.

I open the box, look in, swear loudly but not with the creativity of Jenny, a simple, blunt insult to mothers, even though it isn't my mother.

"You aren't even remotely famous," I say when I have calmed down. "There are people who were eliminated in the first round of quiz shows on channel five who have more fame and who are more well-known than you. What the actual?" I finish, slamming the box shut, hoping to have caused physical harm, and maybe permanently sealed it.

I take a step back, think of what to say, no words come, I step forward, push the brake to release it, nothing happens, so I spin the pedal wheel winch thing and much to my own surprise, the box drops like a broken elevator in a horror film.

I smile at the sounds of a muffled scream.

"Ben!" the Welshman shouts through the microphones.

I turn, and Jenny is staring wide-eyed.

I turn back to the brake and pull the lever. There is a thud, followed by another quieter thud, and a barely heard whimper.

I smile.

"I wasn't going to let her get to the bottom," I lie bare-facedly.

I start to wind the mechanism that is not as safe as they would let us believe. The box rises slowly and I hear a few swear words emanating forth. I try not to show the huge smile I have growing inside.

The box reaches the top and I put on the brake. I lean forward slowly and I hear the very familiar insults a lot clearer now. It takes me back to times I don't want to go back to, ridiculous times when it all seems so important, and yet, on reflection was a silly game. Take the high ground, I tell myself.

I open the box, she sits up, I reach in and offer my hand. She takes it, a face I have seen scowl so many times. She stands, smiles, the beautiful shit-eater grin of contempt, which is her go-to expression when I am in her presence. She is stood in the box, she leans across, right up to my left ear, and, some would say, justifiably drops the C-bomb on me. So, being the mature grown-up I am supposed to be, I reach to the brake and release it.

She drops, falling into the box, screaming like she's been instructed by Wes Craven on the set of his new, but predictably familiar, horror film. The louder you scream the faster you go, I don't say, as she tries to hold onto thin air. I hope this is on the highlight show.

"Ben!" Jenny shouts reaching across and grabbing the brake.

127

The box shudders, the woman inside it bounces up, and, to me at least, satisfactorily slaps back down against the wood.

"Are you insane?" Jenny asks me, and I assume it is rhetorical. Jenny starts to wind the mechanism and the box moves upwards to us.

I look down the shaft and no one is dead.

"She'll be fine," I reassure.

"You could have killed her," Jenny explains, winding away looking like she is trying to break a world record.

A little bit of guilt is flowing in, I admit that, just a little. But not enough to show any type of contrition. No, that would take something magical, something quite absurdly impossible as to be the cause of my own downfall, not in general, just here with this person.

"But I didn't?" I want to say but end up asking.

"Jesus Christ. Why? Who is she?"

The box is at the top and the woman, that woman, steps out. She looks unsteady, a little wobbly on her petite little feet, and ashen faced, although she is pretty white skinned most of the time. A rarity in modern times, being a female that hates a tan, the sun, and less weirdly, me.

"I used to live with Ben," she says, and I can just feel her desire to spit and have a shower.

"But not anymore?" Jenny asks redundantly.

"Look, to stop the whole story being told, in detail and with my own sexual performance being brought into the world of live TV, I can surmise that we came to an agreement," I say very quickly and without inhaling, "In that we agreed, without many exceptions, or any at all really, that I am, when awake, or talking, so talking in my sleep is included, an insufferable prick."

Jenny stares at me. I look to the woman I lived with for three years, the woman eight years my junior, long blonde hair, pencil figure, unconventionally attractive, if not quite the beauty I had believed. Strange how falling out with people changes their physical presence in your own mind. I had thought her stunning once, not now though. Five feet eight, and a face with features that are attractive, blue eyes, blonde, full lips, but somehow they don't quite fit together. Maybe a few millimetres out, a nose just too big, a chin maybe not quite big enough, or vice versa. She would be a shoe-in for a Carnival queen in a small town, when in competition with only those in her immediate year group. Boys in the years above, boys with cars, would want her. I wanted her, and bizarrely she had wanted me. For a time. Then whatever had been happening reversed itself into animosity. And here she is. Bollocks.

"At least I am no longer the most unknown of all people here," I say. "Jenny, this is Kathryn, with a K."

"And what is it that you do?" Jenny asks rather pertinently.

"Oh," I answer for her, "she strips men of their dignity, masculinity and happiness. It's like a special power, but one that works slowly, over time. She is in the X-men comics. They call her the soul-crusher. She defeated Superman by luring him into a-"

"Superman and the X-men are in different comic universes," the oily ex-politician states loudly, his chest pumped up.

I turn to him, smiling.

"Thanks for that," I tell him. "But what you fail to understand is this."

I raise the middle fingers on both hands, and wave them around in circles, and why not? It was a classic when I was at school in the nineties and just like the lyrical genius of Jimi Hendrix and his guitar, it is timeless.

"To be fair," Jenny says, completely ignoring the warnings and speaking directly to Kathrine. "I have spent time with Ben here, and I am not saying you have no positive qualities, but I can through experience state quite honestly that I imagine living with you is one long fest of angry ranting."

"Exactly," Kathrine says, with her fucking irritating voice, a voice that I had once found fun and charming and cute. But now I have come to my senses I hear it as it truly is, an irritating whine of blather, much like mine but with less interesting insights into the essence of being, and the philosophy of modern man.

They've done me over. This show has done me over. I've been done. I repeat these phrases in my head, throwing in the occasional, you are a dick and spiced with, you absolute loser. I don't think I can be me in her presence. They've done me. God, I hate TV. And I hate all those that tune in to see people mentally tortured.

I know why she is here. She wants the fame, any shot at being known, with the added spice she will have the chance to bring her convincing arguments about my unsuitability as a partner, man and functioning human being in the modern world. I am doomed. But like the inability I used to have in leaving a party just in case something happened, and staying until it had long since passed boring, and I was scrambling around and even accepting shots of Malibu, I cannot leave. She'll destroy me in word and I won't be around to defend myself. Christ. You bastards.

129

I resolved the party problem by never attending another and sticking to the life rule of never drinking alcohol that has been made to taste like a combination of watered down shampoo and bleach. But I am here now and I now can't leave.

THE PRESENTERS : DAY 08 : BEING ARROGANT

Molly stands and knows the grin means he thinks he has won. The crew are on a break and she wishes she were with them. Many years ago she would sit with cameramen and staff and they would talk and actually speak to her as if she was almost one of them. Not anymore, and she knew she had a part to play in that. She had backed off, become less accessible, paranoia mainly, the belief that everyone was looking for an angle, a story or promotion.

She was always friendly, always kind, but the time she gave had dwindled to nothing. She ate alone and went to her caravan on most breaks. She was not rude, didn't believe herself superior – not like her husband – but she preferred the peace.

But there he was, grinning away with the confidence of someone who had bet significant cash on the horses because he received a tip from a dodgy source and went for it all the same. Only the dodgy source was himself, the information the lies he told in his head, and the outcome a piece of luck that he would call the inevitable conclusion.

"We are going mental on social media," he tells her, showing his phone, the screen only slightly smaller than a laptop, and the image more brilliant than TV screens that have yet to be invented. He doesn't pay anything for the thing, the freebies given are absurd, the advertising insane. Every day they are begged by companies to hold their product, wear their clothes, say something positive about their brand, and he does, and he is the best dressed, the most technologically up-to-date and yet he has not paid for a thing.

She has heard from her team too. Her agent telling her the news, the ideas, who is winning.

The show is on a high, everyone talking about who is who, what is happening. The new contestants. The politician is a coup. A man everyone knows and most hate. Hate is a popular feeling for any show to broadcast. Tune in, swear at them, watch them squirm, see how they really are through our craftily edited sequences. A fallacy of presentation unless the celeb is a genuine fool and then there is nothing to do but watch them destroy themselves.

The word is that they are riding a wave that cannot last. The celebs are making the show popular. Ben and Jenny the main characters in a non-descript cast of the usual semi-famous.

"It worked, see?" he says. "Never a doubt. Never a doubt in my mind."

"It can't last."

"It doesn't need to last beyond another ten days," he shouts and she expects him to spin and jump and yelp with glee. He shows restraint, but only just.

"We are on a delicate one," she tells him. "There is a lot of talk about the sadism, the 'oh-my-god, they can't do that,' is fine up-to a point."

"I was right," he says. "I was right and you, all of you, were wrong. This is what people want, the hardship, the pain, the challenge. We've seen them all wallow in slime, eat a rotting intestine or camel's foot. That is old hat. What the people want is personal challenge. And that is what we have given them. Simple but genius."

She watches him and he just doesn't see the end. They can't go anywhere else. There is nothing more to do on the climb through pain. They would need to end in maiming, a scar and then possibly loss of limbs to ratchet the conflict further.

He has set the show on its last run. The kickback when people have thought, considered and decided will be one of disgust. All those who watched the black and white minstrel show who later denied. The reverse of the World Cup final where millions claimed to have been in Wembley to watch, despite there only being thousands. Here everyone will deny they viewed and voted and laughed and encouraged the pain. But that hasn't come yet, but it will. Right now the voices of concern are from the usual softies that oppose all things that are not peace and love.

"Not everyone is backing this," she says. "There are many voices calling for this to end right now."

"Looney left. Those hippies and crusties all pretending to be right-on and morally correct while they drive around in converted buses and don't wash."

"Newspapers. Journalists."

"The weak ones, the ones that sell about four copies to liberals who just can't stand the modern world. That's who. Our viewing figures are better than at any point in history. Twenty million. Twenty million. That is half the adult population. Half. The FA cup doesn't get that. The bloody queen's speech on Christmas day doesn't get that."

She sees saliva at the corners of his mouth and she wonders if he hasn't at some point in the last week been bitten by a spider whose venom causes psychosis, and hopefully, with a collateral side-effect of immediate sexual impotency.

"We are creating history here," he continues on with his bizarre insight into how special moments are created. "We, or actually on this occasion, me, have combined celebrities in such a way as to be must-see viewing. Everyone is talking about us."

He doesn't understand it is a one-off, a single shot of mayhem. There is no series in this, no future where dumb people come here to be broken into small psychological pieces. This is car-crash viewing. But he thinks he has created the modern day Generation Game that will run and run until he is the elderly man the public love despite being a wig-wearing, joke-repeating, catchphrase blabbing, presenter who has done the same shtick for forty years. She knows she would be an old granny by then and no longer a screen presence because she would be evidently older then forty-five, have wrinkles, or a face so pumped and stretched as to appear like an inflated peach sitting atop of a neck made up entirely of wrinkly scrotal sacks. A turkey neck? Nah, this one could hold elephant's balls.

She smiles and lets him run. She thought the kidnap and reveal of exes would be the step over the edge, but he is hovering still. The papers back home speaking of politics on the front page, but each carrying a paragraph about how the celebrity world will never be the same.

She has made her bet. She believes this is the last throw of fame, the big bang of a blow out that leads to notoriety and then obscurity. The TV presenter caught on camera being vile, racist or sexist. The real them revealed when they thought the public couldn't see, and some make it back through a public relation campaign of cost and effort, and others never can come back because they will never be allowed.

She is sure this is the way it goes. She is involved but not attached. The leaks and her words showing her distance, her opposition. This is her way, her freedom. Maybe she will never be touched by fame again, maybe she'll end up flogging over-priced tat on a shopping channel for a basic salary in return for her pride. But she has more than she needs and knows it. But he can't live without the adulation, the fame, the recognition, the belief that he is number one. He'll crash and burn thinking there is always a way back.

She needs distance, needs to silently oppose and watch. He can't make it back from this, this is on him and the world is tired, looking to move on from the old school, and she knows that is who they are, to stand aside and let others in.

DAY 08 : EARLY EVENING : ENDURING TOTAL NONSENSE

Of course they like her. And him, with his media savvy, trained personality. Answering questions but never saying a damn thing. She gets by on a smile, a flirt and a laugh. Everyone loves a pretty lady who can giggle at even the most base attempts at humour.

Oh, did you make a pun? Brilliant.

Oh, a double entendre?

Oh, you cheeky thing.

Giggle, giggle.

She touches too. Upper arms, a little glance, a small squeeze, or simply resting her palm for that moment too long. In a pub, when men are half-cut, she could have drinks bought and be chased by anyone. It's a skill, as good as his, and they all fall for it. I would make fun of them, and call them fools, but I fell for it too, in a big way. And she is doing the chat, the twirls and the giggles and there is something inside me, something I do not want to call by name, but I recognise all the same as the jealousy it is. I absolutely cannot stand that woman but at the same time, for whatever reason, possibly because she has woven a trail of emotional thread through my mind, I think I want the adulation to myself.

I can, at times, not just make others sick with my presence, but myself too, which is annoying as wherever I hide, I find myself quite easily – unless, of course I hide under three bottles of wine, a couple of pints and a kebab sloshed in special sauce. Luckily I am in a booze-free jungle so there is little chance of getting drunk, insulting everyone, berating myself like a loon, and then waking up naked on a beach in a country I certainly didn't start the day in. Oh, how we pine for our youth spent pissed.

We are sitting around and we have new arrivals, and we needed them. We had discovered everything about each other, down to the point of absurdity. When someone asks, what is your favourite letter? And people consider and give an actual answer, you know you have reached a comparable point to a primary school teacher phoning it in without imagination at the end of term.

Let's all play sleeping lions for the next three weeks while my hangover and despair run riot.

I briefly thought of asking deep philosophical questions around the camp fire along the lines of What would you do if your left knee was an octopus, your middle name was Charlotte and you could only talk in tongues? I kept it to myself for fear of them all answering seriously. Oh, I'd definitely have plastic surgery the woman who is almost all plastic surgery would say. Without any concept of irony.

So we all have new information to elicit, new people to discover, new faces to associate with and fake friendships to form in the sake of a theoretical harmony. They all know him, you would have to have been in another country these last twenty years, or in the UK but exclusively watching quiz shows, soaps and programmes showing you how you too could buy, renovate and sell on houses for massive profits if only you had the desire, guts and drive of those who have taken the plunge, as well as their fortunes to invest or the backing of rich parents in the first place.

"How did you start out on this business of yours?"

"A combination of factors. I saw an opportunity, researched, found a gap, and then my family gave me five hundred thousand quid."

I could eventually become a successful property magnet given the finances to fail repeatedly until I learned how to do it, which, in my case would be to employ someone who knows how to do it, and sit back and watch, thus reducing my profits a little, but also the hours and stress almost to nothing.

"So, who are you exactly?" the lady with inflated lips, silicon monstrosities, and a liking for illuminous lycra asks them both.

They have actually answered this question, but in paragraphs that have gone off at tangents, covered a few other areas but ultimately contained all the information required to piece together who they are.

"This guy is the go-to political expert on TV," Bob says, pointing his thumb at Jonny-boy, man of the people, man of the masses, man who genuinely thinks you are all thick.

Jonny-boy smiles and nods, he has reached that point in life where he no longer needs to explain his brilliance as others are willing to step in and explain for him. The next phase in his evolution will see him curing diseases by selecting one of his numerous knowing looks from the vast collection of facial expressions he has collected over the years and folded up neatly in his mental filing cabinet labelled Smug.

"Oh," she says, in a way that seems to me to indicate she is unaware of the general concept, meaning, and application of the word, idea, and the actual significance of political.

She looks perplexed and I believe I need to help.

"When the government do something bad, they ask him to come onto the BBC and comment," I explain. "He says something unoriginal and an opinion widely published in the daily papers that morning, and everyone, despite already having read the opinion, had the opinion, spoken the same opinion out loud, and heard the opinion in their work place congratulate him on his insight, originality and his inside knowledge."

Jonny boy answers without words, like the Marcel Marceau of facial mime, he tells a joke, with a put down, through the artful manipulation of his eyes, lips and nose. Oh, how Bob laughs, in such a way as to make me think Bob may very well spend the evening coming up with new material based on silence, which, I hope we all pretend is magnificent and he spends the rest of the time in my presence gurning like he has the dual affliction of intestinal cramp and heartburn.

"It's like having an ex-prime minister with us," Anthony says, while rocketing up the rankings of today's biggest idiot, and firmly in the running for the title of stupid of the week.

"Yes," I say, "in the same sense that having Bob here is like being in the presence of Robin Williams."

"Thanks,"

"Sarcasm, Bob. Come on, keep up, comedy one-oh-one."

He tries for the facial mime but a few of us, with my own definite exception, are worried he is having a fit.

"Or, in another comparison," I say, looking at Chelsey, "that you are Helen Mirren crossed with a large dose of Marilyn Monroe. It isn't true. We are here because we are bog standard celebs. And yes, before you all raise the obvious point that I am the least famous of you all, I know this, you are not in the presence of the modern day Dickens – who is unreadable by the way. He, you might remember, is not in actual real politics anymore, as in an elected member of parliament, because he lost his seat. It is like me being sacked as the manager of my company because the staff don't want me and then being held up and paraded around as an expert advisor on how to manage."

He goes for the facial expression put down, but the response is muted, and if you remove Bob from the equation almost non-existent. I may have made a breakthrough.

"And what is it that you do?" Georgia, who has to stay away from temperatures above forty degrees to avoid the danger of melting asks.

"Me?" Kathrine giggles, and shrugs and plays innocent like she is the virginal lead in a stage production of the Wizard of OZ, despite her being filth. "I'm not a celebrity at all. In fact," she adds, crowding in, like a conspirator about to reveal the whereabouts of the Nazi's secret V2 rocket base, "I am here for the money, and the production teams desire to throw a spanner into the life of Ben."

Honesty is an approach that really shouldn't work here with these habitual bullshitters, but she has received some solid advice because they eat it up. They smile, and not even patronisingly. It is like they have associated her admitting to non-fame with the idea that she is not only somehow a newly born kitten but also the runt of the litter, the one they all need to help, feed and care for because she just won't be able to make it on her own. Ooooo, we'll look after you, we'll help you. Poor you, not being famous. Look at your big round blue eyes and the innocence they hold. It is a cruel world here in celebrity land, especially for naive young things like you. They crowd around her and throw arms around her shoulders as if saying I am not famous is the equivalent of admitting to having a terminal illness. God, she fucking annoys me.

"A spanner for Ben?" Gaz asks, and I feel he may have missed sections of the conversation by suffering from alcohol withdrawal hallucinations. He probably thinks we are currently trapped in an episode of Emmerdale Farm.

"Keep up," I say, wanting to answer all questions that relate to me and her. I find it best to speak first and let people form opinions off my own facts rather than other people's 'facts', some of which I wouldn't class as truth but more as utter bollocks, but some, more grown up and mature people could possibly refer to as uncomfortable words that reflect reality. The wankers.

"We used to date," I say, waving my arms around in that vague, non-committal expression of you know, fill in the gaps, positively, nothing to see here, no lingering emotional scar. I wish I were better at it, like an Italian, but I'm not and no one buys it.

"We lived together for three years," she says, quietly, nicely, and with compassion. But I know it is fake, and I will reveal this later.

"Advanced dating," I explain, "which, I can assure you is similar to basic dating but with all the life, enjoyment and self-regard sucked out by a big evil demon, who I believe many people around the world refer to as Satan."

"You pulled that?" Gaz asks, clearly not quite out of his head as I thought.

It was a common refrain. Apparently out of my league, as if dating is a sport, and I had somehow gone on a long cup run as a non-league team and was currently involved in my one-off, momentary minutes of fame against one of the teams from the lower divisions who nobody actually knows. Like Scunthorpe taking on Middlesborough in a dream third-round match-up in the much maligned knock-out cup in which the big boys let their under fifteens play because they are better than anyone else. We were not a dream team.

"Yes, I did, Gaz. I have my certain charms."

Katherine guffaws, she actually fucking guffaws as if I have said a funny thing in a Maths lesson with the head teacher, and despite it not being a particularly amusing comment, the situation causes an exponential growth of comedic response. Others, loving the vibe, laugh too despite them knowing shit.

I swear under my breath.

"What was that?" Jonny boy, million dollar man ears, political tool asks.

I look up, surprised anyone has heard. I see his teeth and stubbled chin.

"I said you are a wanker." I tell him.

He breaks from his mime and speaks.

"You are a deeply troubled man," he tells me as if he is a Psychoanalyst with a deep understanding of my character, and he isn't, to be fair, too far off the mark.

"Evening," a big, booming voice from the Valleys yells out as he marches in a way that indicates he would rather be skipping in celebration. His chest, despite it seeming impossible to achieve, is even more puffed up than previously. He is proper chuffed with himself. Molly walks beside him, seemingly like a chastised pet, her head down and not looking for eye contact, as if she has had a real dressing down from the head hamster. I exclude cats from that as they aren't pets, they are shitbags.

I get the shakes, not through fear, at least not classical fear, not fear of these people, but because I think it will endanger the very fabric of the space-time continuum with this many tits grouped together in such a small space. If they come closer, I fear a spontaneously formed black hole will erupt and suck in all egos, over-inflated self-regard, and cosmetic procedures from around the world. And hopefully all historical record of the TV show friends.

My heart sinks. I don't think I am up for another challenge.

"We have both good news," he bellows. "And bad news, also." He pauses to inhale the fresh air that seems to be giving him hallucinations and the idea we like and respect him. "The good news is that tonight, for one night only, is party time. We have a famous DJ."

He pauses here wanting the question to be asked.

"It isn't one of the old-school, is it?" I ask innocently. "Because they might take away from the vibe, what with them all being convicted paedos. And while I do not resemble a small boy, they are so old as to see young flesh as anyone younger than forty."

The Welshman stares at me, his moment, he thinks, stolen by my unfounded accusations against any man on popular radio from 1963 through 1999.

"It is a famous modern DJ," he spells out very slowly for a man so excited. "A personal friend, as it happens."

"Let's not go too far, eh?" Molly corrects. "You know him, in the You alright, mate? Sense of friends. He knows who you are."

Welshman stares at her, perplexed, and confused at how these facts don't make them best buddies, the absolute definition of BFF, unless of course the DJ loses fame, fades into obscurity and is of no importance anymore. In that instance he will be deleted from his contact list, or blocked, and any connection denied with all the expertise of a politician on TV swearing they have absolutely no idea why the population is baying for his resignation, or preferably death at the hand of a pack of foxes.

"The bad news," Molly says, stepping forward, "is that two of you will be leaving this evening."

She turns to some bushes a few metres from where she stands and points at them.

"You the viewer get to decide," she lies to the shrubbery.

I stare where she is pointing and can see the glimmer of light of a very well hidden camera.

"Phone or text," she says. "There are ten minutes remaining. All calls are subject to charge, and all texts cost one pound."

I think of the absolute fortune this ploy must make them. The millions of tools who think their vote actually counts and that the elimination is not based on who the production team want out because of ratings. I turn to debate this fact with my special friends, but they are all huddled and panicky as if hiding the numbers printed on their back will somehow remove them from the viewer's minds.

And it hits me. I could be out. Jenny could be out. Then I think. But that makes no sense, they have brought in our exes, have pressured us to be front and centre in a show they had us hired to be cannon fodder. Two people brought in to cause discomfort. I think the others

138

realise this too. They are looking in turn at me and Jenny, and Katherine and Johnny Boy, like a dog watching doubles at Wimbledon on a big screen TV.

Millions of votes a week from old men, old ladies, the middle-aged, the young, the stupid, the less intelligent than that. Phone apps used, plastered with advertising: drink beer, bet money, wear a sports brand, eat at a fast-food place that cares for your health because they sell fruit bags alongside the mounds of shite. Advertise surreptitiously, get a celeb to sip on a fizzy drink while they give an interview. Put a massive brand name behind their head while they get interviewed after a match. Link the fame to the brand and we'll buy it up because it might make us more like them, or make them more like us. Oh, how stupid we are.

"Two of us go, eh?" I say to the group who are ignoring me. "It'll be OK. We'll all meet up after the show has ended and be bestest friends forever. I feel we have bonded. A group hug?" I ask at the end, outstretching my arms into the air inviting them all into my warm bosom. But no one comes, no one accepts my heartfelt offer of communal love. In fact, Bob, red of face and shaking slightly at the prospect of being eliminated first and thus confirmed as the biggest failure of a group of monumental failures, says, "Fuck off."

But I forgive him the indiscretion as the whole set up must be his absolute worst nightmare, or maybe second to being forced into a double-act with another person who actually has talent.

I think they are plotting, or discussing a riot if it is not me who is ejected so I amble over to my hammock. Jenny spots me and comes over too. We sit, gingerly as I have still yet to master the physics of a suspended canvas sheet, and am as wary as when being introduced to an Alsatian by an owner whose eyes look mad and has just said, "Oh, he just barks, he doesn't bite," after it has backed me into a corner in the carpark at the local co-op and I'm too scared to ask, "Well, if that is true, why is your arm wrapped in a bandage?"

We sit, watching the group all discussing who it could be, and usually more who it should be and then looking in my direction with unadulterated fury. I wave, and this makes them turn away.

"Are you worried?" Jenny asks.

I laugh.

"I'm not sure how or why this has happened," I tell her. "But we have through accident, and absolutely not by design, become the focal point of this series. I think the exes drop in was to have us scream and collapse and leave and have some real old fashioned love fallout. But somehow it has morphed into this. I don't think they will let us go quite yet. They have some serious tension to crank up."

She nods and smiles. "It is like you are saying the whole thing is rigged," she says while laughing.

"I would never have thought it before coming on. Oh, no. Absolutely not. I think the millions of votes cast are totally genuine. Not binned and the creative decisions taken by the owners of this show. Oh, no. absolutely not. It is, without doubt the viewer who is doing this."

I hold an imaginary can of lager up to the shrubbery.

"Drink this lager," I say in my best voice over. "It will make you both sexy AND funny, not like other lagers that will make you retarded and ill. Buy my beer. More expensive but better."

"Looking for a specific contract or endorsement deal?" Jenny asks.

"Any really. Although I think my skills lie in the area of shampoo. Middle-aged man head soap, for all you wobbly out-of-shape men who have thinning hair but can't accept you are not attractive to the young girl in the office. Use this three times a week and just feel the realisation slowly seep in that you are past it and need to stop letching over women half your age. Grow a pony tail and buy a motorbike and become that cliché. Available at all discount supermarkets, in the middle aisle next to the industrial band saw and opposite the cheese."

She laughs, and while I know some of it is at what I am saying, the majority is at me, and how pathetically grumpy I am. But it is cool. We are sat on my hammock, talking absolute mince and smiling. It doesn't really get better around here, certainly not at night, when cooking nor during the day interacting with others.

"Do you want to go?" she asks.

"I think I'm like you. I think I was ready to go. Really ready. But then Katherine drops in and despite myself - and highlighting my abject lack of self-worth, I simply can't now. I know I should, know that being here with her is not what I want to do with my time. But I can't. It isn't winning-"

"It is winning," she corrects immediately and accurately.

"-yes, it is winning or rather beating her, but," and I can think of nothing. "Yeah, I just can't let her win."

"Sad, isn't it. But I know what you mean. Him of all people, coming here and being media savvy, smooth and slimy and charming, and intelligent."

"He really is irritating."

"Try living with him for half your life."

140

"Can he cook?"

"No."

"Good in bed?"

"No comment," she replies smiling, which means yes, and I hate the guy even more. I hate it when women talk about past sexual experiences in a positive light. Just lie and say you needed to take a combination of paracetamol, Tesco's own Ibuprofen and a litre of Polish Vodka to get in the mood. I don't want you to set me a high bar, I want you to lie and massage my frail libido.

"I'll give it a miss."

She is smiling at me, reading my mind, knowing exactly what she set off with her comments, knowing that this is to her hard-core flirting. Anyway, this is what I tell myself because if she isn't, I'm doomed.

"What is the deal with you two?" I ask, attempting a throw-away casual but managing to smack right into nosey, I'm desperate to find out. She knows this.

"Met up, had fun. Thought we were mature adults when we were newly graduated fuck-nuts. That sort of thing. You think, been together a few years, burgeoning careers, fair bit of cash, hit all those life markers and what's next? Kids. One of each and away you go. And then you realise that just because you had a bit of fun and can chat-"

"-despite the sex being awful," I add, looking for a nod.

"-despite life being out there, that maybe you are just doing it because there is nothing else to do and it is scary."

"He ended up being pretty famous," I say.

"He is smart. But don't believe for one second he has any true beliefs. He'll articulate a whole load of stuff. But he doesn't believe in much enough to defend it till he dies. He has stayed in the spotlight because he is engaging on most topics. But he'll back what is going to get him more time. He lost his seat remember?"

"I remember him falling over on that dance programme."

"I wouldn't disbelieve the idea that he did that to elicit sympathy."

"He got a lot of laughs. What isn't to like about a politician faceplanting a stage."

"And he talked his way into the nation's sympathies."

"He was up against an ex-footballer with dubious history in female relations."

"He would have analysed the contestants and calculated his move. He made us rich."

"Still love him?"

She inhales, pulls a pained face of squinting and teeth clenching, turns and looks at me.

"I'm not sure I even like him."

We sit there pondering on that depth of sentiment – me now feeling confident I have a chance - watching the huddle of nearly-quite-famous slowly break apart and take their seats around the fire. Jonny Boy is chatting and earning friends, while Katherine smiles like a weakling despite being able to eviscerate every single one of them, like Richard Dahmer but with tits.

"What about Katherine? What is the deal there?"

"We built something on rocky foundations."

She is looking at me, eyes wide, waiting for my confession, my therapist giving me space to explore my thoughts and speak out loud so the conversations in my head are given a real voice and flaws are more easily found.

"She was, at that time in my life, a lonely time for me, and my money, the one woman who could and would actually let me touch her boobs without the exchange of cash."

"You just can't do it, can you?"

"What? I haven't finished. I actually paid her."

She stares at me, contempt sinking into her frown.

"I did, in pieces of my own soul. She is essentially a prostitute who accepts not American express but the payment of another's self-respect and happiness."

She is staring at me now and there is no humour.

"Look," I say, "I've been in many relationships and the one thing they all have in common is that they ended. The other thing is that they all had me in them, being me, and as we can all agree, that is not a bonus of any kind. So, things happened, choices were made. Choices about sleeping arrangements, as in she wanted to sleep with someone else and so did and I just wanted to sleep. She didn't tell me this, although it was not exactly a brilliantly kept secret. I, as some males do, the ones who don't get angry and smash like the Hulk, became a self-pitying mess, blaming myself for it all."

"Do you still?"

"Yes. Look, I can also hear what I say, as well as how people react. I know when someone says, it isn't you, it is me, what they actually mean is, it IS you and you really need to just accept you are better off growing old as a single, pathetic man with a tendency to moan. A lot. About anything in an attempt to smokescreen your own deep-rooted inadequacies."

"You really don't like yourself very much do you?"

"Why would I? Do you?" and I instantly regret the question.

What if she says no, even if as a joke? How do I know she is joking? Would I just be fooling myself into believing it was a joke when it was in fact her real opinion? What if she says she does like me but that is actually a joke and some way to lure me into a trap in which I am humiliated and my soul crushed before these minor celebrities? What if she says yes, but just out of sympathy? How would she say yes if it were sympathy and not real? How can I interpret anything at all? But most fundamentally, why the fuck has my thought process in these situations not evolved even a single fucking day since I was fifteen and asking out a girl so clearly out of my depth as to be deliberately self-harming my ego? She had looked at me in maths and I interpreted this as she clearly fancying me. The absurdity in this was apparent from the off-set. The teacher looked at me a lot more, and he wasn't interested in me, because if he was an adult male interested in me, he would obviously be teaching geography, as that is where all the wrong 'uns go.

"What do you do?"

"I teach."

"What subject?"

"Geography at an all-boys school in the countryside."

"Oh, so you are a nonce."

"Come on," Jenny says, and grabs my arm, but gently, and ushers me toward the group from my sat position.

My face must be asking a question. We stop.

"You really are not very good at any of this, are you? How did you pull anyone?"

"Alcohol," I say. "Gave me all the confidence I needed."

"Gave?"

"I just don't need that level of confidence anymore."

She stares at me.

"And there is only so many times you should wake up on a kitchen floor, fully clothed with bottles of wine rolling about like you got drunk on a pirate ship."

"Bad?"

"I – man how do you get people to open up? – I just didn't have the resilience. A long line of crap with a full-stop on the end in the shape of Katherine, bless her cotton socks. As she told me, I should actually be thanking her."

"Have you?"

"Not in person, and not with thoughts and words that many would class as thanks, or coherent really. Some might even confuse it with insults but I know the truth. It is self-flagellation as punishment for perceived slights-"

"Perceived?"

"Ok, genuine slights. I've insulted a fair few people. Jeez, I'll be walking down the street and suddenly I'll have a choke of panic over something I might have done and said when I was twelve at highschool and bitterly regret even if no one remembers. Weird, isn't it?"

She looks at me, that sadness people get when I reveal some of my inner being by mistake.

"It is weird. You are weird. What you say is mostly weird - occasionally funny, mostly bitter – but in general I think most would agree you are weird."

I wait a second taking in the information, wondering if there are song lyrics that would describe this situation – if there are they should be sung by Elvis - or maybe it should just be represented by an instrumental, probably a solo piano played by an old, sad man whose fingers don't work as well as they once did and so can only play long, slow, reverberating notes. I feel, and I don't know why, a little choked up.

"You Ok?" Jenny asks.

I smile, no I am not, haven't been since a teen, I think.

"Yeah, really good thanks," I lie, smile, and nod.

I am, after all, just still a bloke.

We stand not moving, and I am staring ahead as I know she is looking at me, at my face, searching for a crack in the façade, a small glimmer into my very soul and where she thinks answers lie. The silence is absurd. I turn to her.

"Only occasionally funny?" I ask.

Her sad serious face breaks into a smile and she shakes her head in that way adults do when they thought you were mature but now realise their faith in you being grown-up was misplaced.

"Everything I said and that's what you pick out?"

"Often is the word you were looking for."

"Rarely."

I agree and smile, slipping back into my comfort zone.

144

We sit around the fire, which is lit. A semi-circle with the Welshman at the focal point two metres in front of us, like the smallest of theatres ready to hear the boisterous ramblings of a man convinced of his own genius. He again, is wearing clothes he has never worn before. Every day a new get up similar to those he has had before, the free-rolling skeff.

"Tonight," he says like he is the compere for the opening night of the royal variety performance in 1963, "We have the very first elimination. It could be any of you," he adds pointing forward and moving around the semi-circle like a slow motion disco dancer.

"Except it can't," Molly adds, once again reeling in the bullshit of her husband's words when exuberance takes over. "It cannot be Jonathon nor Katherine as they have just arrived. But the public have voted, just not for elimination. They have voted for two people to be immune from this being their last day."

"Now you may be thinking How do we eliminate?" The Welshman says. "And I will explain. The process is simple. Each of you will be given a piece of paper and a pencil. Each of you will be able to write one name from the group. We will collect the results."

I look around at the group, who are all worried, scared even about the eviction. I can see they are all worried, all not wanting to be the first out. Someone should speak, say how it is no shame to be the first to leave, even if it is. I choose this person to be me.

"How do you spell your last name, Bob?"

He looks up from the ground where he is taking time over doing up his laces.

"Prick," he mouths.

"Here we go," Welshman booms. "Each of you have a piece of paper. Each of you has a pencil. You need to write the name of that person on your paper. Then we will read them. Count them and then tell you the result," he says, I am hoping for the benefit of small primary aged children at home.

The process is quick.

Everyone has written the name they want to go. They all fold their piece of paper and hand them over to Welshman who places them in a jar as he walks around the group.

"Right," he says upon collecting them all. "We will keep count."

He pulls the pieces of paper out, one-by-one, saying the name as he goes. Hand in the jar. Unroll the paper. Read the name.

"Ben," he says, followed rapidly by,

"Ben."

"Ben."

"Ben."

He looks at me after this one. I shrug.

"Ben."

"Ben."

"Ben."

"Ben."

"Ben."

There is one left. He looks at me.

"Presumably this is the one you wrote," he laughs.

He unrolls the paper.

"Ben," he says.

"You voted for yourself?"

"Let's face it," I explain, "there is only one person who deserves to be booted out immediately. And while I will miss aspects of this show like the mind-numbing boredom of the day, having to remember to switch off my mic when having a dump, and eating meats from animals that are illegal to own. I have, justifiably come to the end, and I must say goodbye to you all, but I know, after spending so much time together that in the future when we cross paths at awards ceremonies, in the posh supermarket near the headquarters for the BBC, or on celebrity coach trip, or possibly later on when our careers have hit even lower levels of insignificance, on a new series of 'celebrities go for a shit', we will look back on our time together and simply ignore each other's existence. I shall leave my things here as a memento for you all, one that festers and smells and may, in the coming weeks start to become a sentient being as the katrillions of bacteria combine into a new species of-"

"I must stop you there, Ben." Molly says.

"But I'm on a roll, and I have a couple of questions for Jenny," I say.

I turn to her, mock outrage not concealed by my smile.

"You voted for me?" I ask, in a pathetic attempt at the raging Jack Nicholson in any film he has ever been in.

"You voted for you," she points out with insane accuracy.

"Yeah," I agree. "But I don't like me. I thought you did."

She smiles and stands hearing all the joke in my voice.

"I do. But I genuinely believe for everyone's sanity, and your own, that you leave."

There is no arguing with that.

146

"So, which way is out?" I ask with a level of relief I was not sure possible. It is like a high, the exam results not turning out to be abject failure but not bad at all.

It doesn't last long.

"Unfortunately for you, Ben," The Welshman interjects with a hint of phlegm in the vowels. "The viewers have spoken and the free pass is yours. And also Jenny's. Neither of you can be evicted today."

And as if we are the choral section in a modern Opera written by someone from the street, who is in fact grammar school educated and friends with the Posh, a unified and passionate, "What the fuck?" is said by all. Bob, obviously, misses his cue, but makes up for it by stepping forward and going solo with a free-style profanity. He appears to think this decision is "bullshit," and adds that, "the viewers, if it was indeed the viewers who actually voted to keep this dick on the show, are genuinely retarded."

I place my right hand on his shoulder.

"Bob," I say, like a father to a son on his wedding day.

But that is as far as I get with life lessons as he pushes me in the chest and I step back.

"You have ruined this experience for me," he says. "Absolutely ruined. I came on here wanting to have fun and all I have got is the idiotic, childish nonsense that comes out of your mouth. You are without doubt the most irritating, annoying, destructive man I have ever met in my entire life."

His fists are clenched at his sides, I think he is bouncing up and down slightly.

They all stare, silent, a hush like when the geeky kid who everyone bullies at school breaks and starts to shout and you realise that their angry voice is a squeaky whine of long words that only tits use.

It starts to dawn on him that he has broken character, revealed the anger that is normal in everyone. Anger being a quite acceptable emotion as long as it doesn't involve causing actual bodily harm. However, for a celeb this is an absolute disaster.

We stare as Bob calms and starts to look around realising he has blown it. He has broken the fifth or sixth wall of entertainment and actually vocalised his hate. He isn't, after all, the perpetual cockney chancer of quips and giggles. He actually has another side to him.

He starts to breathe.

"I'm guessing this wouldn't be an appropriate time to pitch you my new idea for the pilot to a sitcom?" I ask. "It is like the old Crosby

Hope road movies. Me being the funny one, who gets all the ladies through the laughs and you being the character no one remembers or cares about."

Bob steps forward, and I tense ready for the punch I realise I am trying to elicit.

His red face is right into mine.

"I. Fucking. Hate. You," he says.

And I realise that this is all I want. I also don't need to realise that this is how it has always been.

Me and Jenny are given a new piece of paper and a new pencil, which is just wasteful as we still have our first pencils. The production costs are just not cared about.

"It is up to you two to decide who goes," The Welshman says.

"Bob might be in the reckoning," Molly adds.

"Absolutely not," I say. "Bob is absolutely staying. No way am I getting rid of Bob."

"That surprises me," Molly says, and it might be the most genuine thing she has said in a week.

"I don't know why. I won't vote Bob out until he has come up to me and apologised," I say, and manage to get the last letters out before laughing.

Bob swears at me again, inviting me to perform a sex act on myself, which, biologically speaking is impossible, so who is the fool now, Bob? Get back to school with your misunderstanding of human orifices.

"Well, Brian is going," I whisper to Jenny.

"Why?"

"Because it will annoy him the most."

"That is your reason. Vote them off because it will cause them the most anguish?"

I think about this, trying to see a flaw or problem she might be trying to highlight without specifying it as if I am insightful enough to read her subtle suggestions. I think, I genuinely do, see no reason at all and say, "Yep."

"Oh, Jesus. You just can't help yourself."

"He is definitely on the list."

"The other?"

"Who do you think?"

"Georgia"

"What!?! She is actually nice. In comparison."

"What about the pop star?"

"Georgia. She wants to leave."

"How do you know this?"

"I know."

"Is this that Jedi shit women do? That, I know despite never having spoken about it, had a conversation or word at all in relation to it, but you just know."

"Yes. But it is not Jedi, it is being able to read people and understand emotions and subtleties of expression."

"It is black magic, and I suspect you are a witch. You are sure about this?"

She nods. And the world still holds so many mysteries for me.

The others are sat around the fire, mostly with their hands clenched.

I walk in, and for the first time I see they are actually waiting to hear what I say. I feel a buzz, that love of attention. It is weird. I never seek this out but I love it all the same.

I smile and start to speak as they hang on my every word. If this is what a public speaker or politician is all about, I want more.

So I go for it, standing in front of the group whose attention I have.

"After a brief discussion," I say. "We came up with a list. Two names. But before we say those two people who will be the first to leave, I would like to say a few words. These are two lovely names of people who have been here for as long as me. Who have spent their days here as we all have. Two people who many will remember, vaguely, into the very near future. Two people who once they have left will no longer be here. Unlike those of us who won't leave as we will still be here, in this place, doing things. Two people who will leave making the group ten instead of twelve. Two people who will be able to eat proper food tonight and sleep properly without fear of Bob "sleepwalking" and "sleep dangling" his schlong into our faces for the bantz-"

"That never happened," Bob says truthfully, but the information is out there now so people can decide on the verity after deep and disgusting discussion.

"Be quiet now, Bob. This isn't about you," I tell him.

"Two people who are humans, who have been here as humans, and will leave here in much the same way as humans. Two people who I

149

didn't know before coming here because I didn't want to and now as they leave I realise that when you spend time with others, here, in the jungle, you grow to understand the human condition through eating the sexual organs of Wildebeast, and I think it is these challenges that I would say I would still prefer to do rather than stay in contact with anyone here. But I shouldn't just keep on talking about two people, I must, and really should get to the moment you have all been waiting for, the moment of truth, the discovery of who the Two will be, the Two people who will leave tonight, right now in fact, without pause, walking away across the rope bridge into the arms of other people seeking fame and a moment on TV. Poppers and bangers exploding like you have completed a meaningful challenge like a marathon or saving homeless children from a fire. The two people who will be showered by the fake platitudes of the ones who remain and pats on the back and promises and the exchange of false phone numbers where we have deliberately swapped two numbers around, the last two usually, so that when you message or call, we don't receive the message and can, justifiably when called out on this blame you for writing it down wrong. We can then give you another number, also made up, with a couple of numbers swapped, and so we go on. This is the love that we have formed by being here together for a week and not really speaking to each other because people are watching and we need to pretend. Although we now know the real Bob, Violent Bob, angry Bob, violent angry Bob, who hides his pathological evil behind jokes stolen from George Formby. It is Okay, we still Love you, Violent Bob. But without much further ado, I segue into the important part, the part about how we as a group are without doubt the best group that has ever existed in this place – and I don't just mean the British version, I think I can say, without having watched a single second of any of the shows ever from around the world that we are the best. No question. I'd guess that the worst of the lot are the Italians. I bet they are awful based on my experiences of a weekend break in Tuscany in the late 1990s. And while now our group is reduced by two, from the magical twelve like the last supper, although actually I should count Jesus so that would be thirteen, but it is close enough, to the less magical ten, like Leeds United in a game after a player has been sent off, possibly the goalkeeper and they have to put the striker between the posts. God I might have to stop, I'm welling up."

I look up and I feel I have their attention now, my words of wisdom cutting through and sending their thoughts into overdrive to the point where they appear to no longer be listening and instead are hoping I either shut up or die, or shut up because I die.

"The two names we have decided should leave sadly, and it was a difficult choice, make no mistake. We debated this for many, many seconds, to the point where we could no longer say the names properly. So here we are."

I lift the paper up and stare at it.

"Would you like to hear our reasoning?"

No one answers they just stare at me, thinking, I assume, of ripping my face off from the inside.

"The first to go this year, this momentous year of record viewers and unbelievable drama, is – do I get a drumroll?"

The answer to that, it immediately seems, is a big fat Fuck off. I do my own drum roll by vibrating my tongue, although even I admit I sound like a drill.

"The first to go is Brian," I say.

He stands as tall as he can be and takes the decision with grace. It is almost as if he expected it, and in fact he says, "I expected that," thus confirming I am incredibly insightful.

Nobody moves or says a word, they are all still staring at me. I look blankly in response. "What?" I mouth.

Jenny snatches the paper from me, which is pointless as she knows the other name as she suggested it. Why does she need a memory jog? She looks at the paper and sees the name she suggested and I agreed to and that is written below Brian's.

"You already know the name," I say.

She looks at me as if I am the thick one. She looks at the paper again, that has the name she knows written on it.

"The second name is Georgia," and Jenny smiles sadly.

I look at Georgia and she nods, mouths "thank you" to Jenny and stands. She is immediately hugged by everyone around her. I wonder how it feels to be liked.

Brian sees his opportunity.

He has taken his microphone off and thrown it down. He comes up to me, he whispers, "you are never going to get anywhere in this world, I am going to make sure of that."

As threats go that is up there with, if you don't stop I am going to walk away and never come back, after your insults were directly intended for the recipient to go away and never acknowledge your presence ever again. I am banned from his section of the industry, an industry that runs afternoon shows on channels with fewer viewers than the ones that sell fake jewellery twenty-four hours a day.

"So I won't be able to be on old quiz show reruns, or participate in creepy anniversaries of ancient kids TV shows. Shame, I thought that would be my best market. I'll hold off on getting highlights to my fake hair then."

"I am going to destroy you," he says while smiling and appearing to be in pleasant conversation.

"My mic is still on," I say, and the dawning of the obvious hits him.

I feel he wants to punch me. But he takes his clenched fists and walks away as I wonder why I dislike him so.

THE PRESENTERS : DAY 08 : FINALLY KICKING PEOPLE OUT

Molly is sat at her fake jungle desk with its fake plastic vines and the camera is rolling. The Welshman is sat with his big white grin, like a student found a mistake on each tooth and decided to erase it all with Tipex.

"Here they come," he says, standing and throwing his arms out like he is about to hug a greeting to a son who has lived in faraway lands for the last three years.

Georgia comes first, limping a little and wincing as she walks.

She looks in trouble, Molly thinks. Hurt but not wanting to show it. She looks a little thinner than when she went in, but this is not healthy. Georgia smiles and sits down. Brian is a few steps behind and he has his big TV happy-face on. They shake hands and hug. The Welshman stands and they shake hands briefly. He sits down at the table and they all take a breath and sip on alcohol as if this is a moment to celebrate.

Georgia doesn't drink.

"Is there water?" she asks. "Fizzy?"

Brian takes her glass of alcohol and knocks that one back too, smacking his lips in pleasure.

"A few days in there – with Ben – and my god, it would turn any man to drink," he says, expecting a laugh for repeating a cliché. No one does so he laughs himself.

"Good stuff that," he says, showing his ignorance. "Champagne?"

Molly nods but she knows like the crew that it is fake Australian sparkling made up to look like a French classic. They never invite anyone on here who knows good wine from bad, or anyone who could actually recognise anything beyond the difference between red and white according to colour.

She smiles at the Welshman. He had his own vineyard because he was interested in wine briefly, about ten years ago. It was all the rage with celebrities so he dabbled. He was offered a glass of red on live TV, asked to taste and review. He did the whole swirl, sniff, slurp routine some fraud had taught him on a course that cost a thousand pounds and was simply pointless after an hour as everyone was drunk.

She smiles as she remembers his face, all scrunched up and disgusted. "Awful," he said. "Cheap nasty wine."

He spat it out. On live TV. Oh, it was a glorious moment.

It was his. He sold the vineyard at a loss six months later.

He has been speaking of Gin recently because a Hollywood star has a brand he sold for millions. She is pretty sure his level is bargain booze like a beer brewed in Birmingham and simply called Strong Beer and sold only in cans that are red and have the word Beer stamped on them in white comic sans. That would be his tipple.

She realises she has missed her cue.

"What do you think?" The Welshman asks her.

Georgia really does look ill, tired ill, tired and stressed ill.

"About what?" she asks, snapping out of her go to memory of Welshman's humiliation.

"About our time in there? It was very different to how I imagined. A lot tougher," Georgia says.

"Come on, you did nothing," Brian tells her.

Molly sees Georgia is struggling for breath.

"Are you OK?" she asks and Georgia nods, unconvincing, fooling no one.

"We can come back to her," Brian says. "I thought the experience, while short, and obviously that way because of Ben, and not because I am unpopular, a rather pathetic revenge on the part of the man, who is quite the simpleton-"

He realises no one is watching and he has missed the noise.

Georgia has rocked back on her stool, eyes rolling up into her skull, passed out, unconscious and toppled back onto the floor. The thud is sickening, but better than a crack. Her head whiplashed into wooden planks that make up the stage on which they are sat. There is a pause of confusion, an inability to understand what they see, and then, as Brian blethers on about how it wasn't him as a person or personality that caused his early exit, just the mean-spirited soul of an absolute nobody.

"Just shut up," Molly shouts, spittle flying, as she leaps from her chair and crouches down to hold Georgia's head.

153

"Shit," The Welshman says, and she isn't sure if it is because of the collapse or that he now has no script to work from. She looks at him, a glance and sees his red-faced panic setting in. People rush over, a medic from somewhere, an actual real medic, someone qualified in helping people, not some charlatan who pretends they know deadly animals.

Molly is moved away, the cradle she has formed with her hands to cushion Georgia's head is replaced with a medical support, all blue and seemingly firm.

She remains crouched as an oxygen mask is placed on Georgia's face, as space is requested, as oxygen is pumped, as people wait, staring and holding their breath. Her eyes white because the pupil is looking inside her brain. Her chest moves, her eyes roll back, and she coughs and inhales, rasping a little. They keep the mask and she sucks in huge lungfuls of a gas mixture that seems to be the elixir of life. She sits up, all on her own, smiling through the transparent plastic covering her mouth and nose. She raises a hand and gives a thumbs up.

"Thank the Lord for that," The Welshman says. "If she had died, that would have put a proper dampener on this year's show."

Molly spins on him, "You what?" she spits. "Put a dampener on the show? She nearly died. Are you an idiot? You, and by association me, nearly killed a former nations' sweetheart. How are you able to be such a monumental bellend?"

The Welshman smiles inanely, like the words have acted like an ice-pick in an early nineteenth century lobotomy on his frontal lobe.

"It might be good for ratings?" he asks, hopefully rhetorically.

"The death through asphyxiation of a woman who came on here to revive her career and possibly get a couple of runs at a pantomime in Blackpool? Are you without a soul?"

He shrugs in that way men do that means, yeah, I see what you are saying, understand a woman might actually have feelings about this, but I don't, what with being an arrogant male, and as such, I will shrug to show you I dismiss your warblings as inconsequential. I won't say this however, for fear of verbal destruction at your hands.

"A fucking shrug?" Molly asks.

"Excuse me," a voice, quiet and wavering says from behind the camera.

They both look up annoyed that someone dare interfere with a domestic.

"What?" they bark, faces mimicking the aggressive snarl of a pair of Dobermans.

"We are still going out live," the meek voice says as the owner zooms in on the lovely presenting couple.

The Welshman smiles, revealing his teeth, or the covers he has glued to them. He stares at the camera for three seconds, moving his smile back and forth by millimetres. She knows this is the slow moving of cogs in his brain. Live TV, the country watching, or at least those with nothing better to do than watch this abomination labelled entertainment.

His face hardens, he has a plan.

He points off camera, to his right, directly at Brian. The camera scans across and zooms in on the smiling, slightly tipsy face of the old has-been.

"He caused this," The Welshman says as Brian's face falls into dismay. "It is his fault." And the Welshman stands, and pretends to be part of the medical entourage that has just arrived to take Georgia away.

The nation fades slowly to a break in the broadcast watching Brian's gurning smile as his complete career dissolves into a toxic brew of ridicule and contempt. He smiles as his popularity drowns in the bile of the British public. He doesn't salute.

DAY 09 : MORNING : THERE IS MORE TO THIS

We heard the commotion, we heard the ambulance, and we heard the chatter and panic. We do not know the Who and the Why, but we all hope, as a silent collective, without prejudice that it is Brian in the hospital having his tongue removed and not the ever lovely, old and thus easily gone too early Georgia.

Oh, I can't believe she is dead.

But she was Ninety eight.

Yeah, but I just thought she'd go on forever.

And break all biological laws and be the only person ever to actually be immortal? She couldn't even walk.

We are sat, the morning after the night before passed. A day gone by with our own rumour and gossip, our fantasies and thoughts all kneeded together into a rising ball of utter bullshit. We have nothing else to speak about and like bored admin staff in a less than busy office, we have gossiped and invented our way into a frenzy.

We were given no explanation, and much to my own disgust, no party, which I had not wanted to go to, but now that it was taken away from me I was incandescent with rage at the snub. Bastards.

The day has gone as they always do: long and boring and no sign of the presenters. And here we are sat around a camp fire not really aware of what is going on.

Finally, Molly comes in, alone, and angry. She is hiding it poorly but she is looking everywhere, her concentration gone, and as fidgety as a kid who really needs a wee. She is carrying a large satchel that were it red and embossed with a large white Merry Christmas, would be the most amazing sight. However, it is neither red, nor printed and resembles a potato sack. There is some clapping in excitement, and a few whoops of delight, none of them from me. I sigh like a father who sees all the kids at the party playing and having fun and then spot my own small son who is bent over and eating mud. We had been promised a party and instead we get this?

"I know we promised a party last night," Molly says, "But unfortunately, due to unforeseen circumstances, we had to cancel."

"What happened?" Anthony asks with the voice of Bart Simpson upon inhaling helium.

"Nothing important. Nobody died," Molly says in such a way as to make me think someone has nearly died, is dying, or is about to die. "However, to make up for the non-party event, we have brought in the letters!" she says, trying for excitement, but managing to hit the tone of a man explaining to his mates down the pub that he has just been dumped by text by the woman who was so far out of his league as to be investigated for bribery, but it doesn't matter because he is fine. Really fine. Not upset at all. It happens. And can I order a double of everything on the top row as a celebration for this actually positive moment. And no, I am not crying.

I stare at the bag.

Oh, Jesus wept, here we go. But at least I might get conversation.

I have passed a day in which no one spoke to me in any way beyond asking for me to spout imaginative scenarios of the previous evening's events. No one listened as no one wanted to believe my idea that this is a modern day Logan's Run and we are all executed on the way across the bridge by rich middle-aged bankers who have paid a fortune to feel the rush of physically killing someone in a flash. The head of TSB is waiting with a Rambo knife because he needs to release the anger he feels for only getting a four million pound bonus this year.

The day had been normal for a while. Katherine and Jonny went off on a challenge together, all giggly and happy and flirty. Sadly they came back in an even more heightened state of early lust all giggles and

156

pats and, "you'll never guess what we did next?" and we don't because what happened next is nothing new or interesting and is essentially generally along the lines of, and then he said this, which was an obvious and direct answer to what I said, which was absent of all humour but we are giggling at it anyway. I want to be sick. We received our call, and were asked and then answered the easiest question correctly, something along the lines of What is Ben's first name? is it a) John or b) Ben? We should have come to a conclusion quite quickly after once again explaining to Gaz that is isn't a trick question. But we still had to fucking debate it though, didn't we? And go off on tangents whereby anyone and everyone could namedrop celebs they know, met, worked with, blew or all of the above.

The utter gleeful chaos they came back to was like a combination of fans at a Rolling Stone reunion gig, the euphoria of winning a gazillion quid on the EuroMillions, and being told that the nineties Meg Ryan wants to be naked with you and you alone. They came back, not with half a Jacob's cracker each but with Strawberries and cream, loads and loads of strawberries and cream. Not just one or two each, but bowls of the stuff. This should have been illegal but no, the production company want these two to be as popular as can be and the easiest way to do that is by bribing the whole group with tasty fruit and absolutely perfect cream. They are everyone's favourite. And I am not. My dislike did not extend to refusing the treat, and this left me feeling both dirty and warmly full.

It also makes us forget to the point of not caring about the possible death of our recently departed colleagues.

They all scoffed their faces, licked fingers and gloried at just how amazing strawberries are. Gaz, I think, had an erection. They spoke and asked each other questions on the crest of a double cream high. I was asked nothing at all. I was on a level with the pub's glass collector who has picked up a pint that has a couple of sips left in it and you don't want them taken away. As disliked as can be. Although I listened, and I now know enough about most of them to be able to find their houses, gyms, places of work and make a pretty good guess at who is having an affair. No need to trawl through their Facebook pages anymore. I know everything I am likely to need. But most of this will be cut from the broadcast because it is inappropriate and monumentally dull.

A quick recap: they all live in gorgeous houses, not too ostentatious obviously, they aren't those type of people, despite clearly being those type of people. It is just nice to have a swimming pool, gym, sauna and home cinema, why wouldn't you treat yourself if you could? They are all humble braggers, except Katherine, who is about the poorest person ever to appear on the show. However, she would happily sell her vagina for a mansion, and, I believe, intends to do this with Jonny. It isn't worth the cost, Jonny.

But what do I care, right?

And there we all sit, full and content, the doubts and disappointments pushed away through full bellies and a communal love-in as we laze about.

The evening has come, it is now very late and very dark. We have eaten rice and beans, but that is Okay, as everyone keeps saying because we are all stuffed on Wimbledon snacks, and stone me if they aren't all a happy bunch.

The big bag of letters from home arrived, brought in by a comatose Molly.

So we are sitting around the fire like it is a scout jamboree. A very sad scout jamboree and lacking uniform, a just-out-of-tune guitar, and the desire to sing some semi-religious songs about rays of light and the Lord.

But that is, in hindsight preferable to this.

I sit, listen and watch as one after another irritatingly emotional letters are read out to a sobbing contestant. They can really sob. There are strings of snot galore.

They are crying. One after the other. Crying over words written by someone they know very well, and last saw just over a week ago. And in the case of Katherine and Jonny, two days previously. We are all coming out alive, we are all free to return to our loved ones. We have chosen to be here and the letters are just a load of jizz. High-grade, nuclear level, tear-inducing, play-on-emotions paragraphs of love and missing. They are all variations on a theme. We miss you, we love you, we need you, we are proud of you, presumably for being paid a fortune in cash to sleep in a jungle for a week or so. We have not just spent the last ten years of our lives on death row for a killing we did not commit. We'll all be back down Wetherspoons by the end of the month. When they are on holiday in Dubai or somewhere else expensive they don't cry. They send postcards home. Not the other way round. On the beach and a courier gives them a letter from home telling them how they are missed and that they need to come back safe and not sunburned. But here, around a fire, darkness setting in, they are raining salty water down on the ground and sobbing so hard they cannot breathe because a letter arrived from someone they recently saw stating the obvious because no one, with possibly one exception, asked a total arsehole to send them a letter.

Production team: "Who would you like to write you a letter?"

158

Celebrity: *"My mum as she will send the letter I have already dictated to her stating all the reasons why I am so amazing."*
Production team: *"Excellent."*

We wait for what seems like an eternity of sobbing from Gaz as he is told by his daughter what a wonderful dad he is, what an inspiration, and general all round super hero – her own superhero – yadda, yadda, yadda.

They go for coffee every other day. She has never had to work a day in her life and is rich off her dad's wealth. Superheroes used to be of such a higher quality. With capes and lacking cholesterol.

"Here is a letter for Anthony," Bob says.

I swear, just upon hearing he has a letter from the person he told to write him, he wells up, a tear breaking on his cheek. How is this emotional?

"It is from your girlfriend," Bob says, and Anthony starts to sob, and I believe it is because he realises he has to go back and see her.

There is a pause, as we wait for this man-boy to stop choking on his own inability to cry properly. It is a wait that drags on too long.

"But aren't you gay?" I ask.

This does not elicit the laugh it would have had it been said by Bernard Manning in 1973.

"No, I am not gay," he says, in a way that if we are all being honest, would definitely be described as gayly.

"Ok. Sorry," I hold up my hands. "Nothing wrong with gays. I just thought that, you know, you were that way. Inclined. In that you liked-"

"Shut up, Ben," Jenny thankfully says as I am about to start on an idiotic middle-aged man's non-insightful explanation of what many of my peers would call, them there poofs.

He gets a teddy bear. Not a new one, his actual teddy bear. The one he sleeps with at home, when his girlfriend is with him. I think his girlfriend might be goldigging, or has mothering issues. I stare and open my mouth to say something but Jenny shoots me a look that hits so hard I feel my teeth grind.

Racheal received a chocolate bar, an eighty-five pence chocolate bar, which makes her cry in such a way as for me to check my maths and figure out she hadn't been a child in the second world war and this did not represent VE day and is therefore a symbol of all of the heroes who died to save us. She just likes chocolate. Chelsey gets a slice of her favourite cake from her sister, "Just a single fucking slice?" she sobs, stuffing it all into her gob and then chewing with her mouth open to gulp in air for five minutes. Pulped up lemon drizzle is not a pretty sight. Jenny gets a picture of her children in a frame and a lovely letter about how they miss her and that she is doing fab. I consider possibly doing less swearing for their benefit, but decide against it for the simple reason I do not care. Kieran receives a quarter of Cola Cubes, which seemingly had a deeper meaning than expected because upon seeing them, he broke into floods of tears about his childhood growing up that led him to a lifetime of TV and extensive dental work.

I wonder if we have all been drugged and we are hallucinating feelings that do not exist.

Bob places his hand into the large bag that contains the letters. He pulls out a parcel. "Ben," he says in just the same way my gran used to, after I had broken something in her well-kept garden. A gnome or a Buddha statue, the entire fence or when I set fire to the cherry tree.

Jenny leans across and takes the package.

"I'll read this," she says.

She takes her time unwrapping.

"Do you know who this is from?" she asks.

"A close confidant," I say, leaning back and getting ready for the words.

I had no one else to ask, which on one hand is quite sad really, not having a close relative to write kind words, but on the other hand it could be viewed, in the right light as also monumentally pathetic. Probably a combination of both to be honest.

I have never been married because a) I don't want to b) no one would be stupid enough to say yes but mainly c) I am terrified no one would turn up on my side of the aisle other than a dog I sometimes stroke outside Spar.

She finds the envelope inside, opens that and has a good, smiling look at the contents. The package is way too small for the object I requested, but then I should never expect anything different. Any friend I have is simply going to take any reasonable opportunity for revenge.

Jenny sits up, unfolding the letter in front of her.

"It looks like you should have those glasses old people have, the ones on chains around your neck. Maybe two pairs?" I tell her.

Jenny looks at me, stares like a headmistress, shakes the letter in her hands, coughs and starts to read.

"Dear Ben," she starts, smiling. It is as if she is auditioning for Jackanory in the early 1980s. She is a horrendously coloured tank-top away from being a member of rent-a-ghost. "I haven't watched any of this

160

insulting tripe you agreed to come on, and absolutely do not plan to either," she pauses. "However, I am in no doubt you will have been rude, told your 'Jokes', whereby you insult everyone in the hope that by reducing them to insignificance through sarcasm, you will seem bigger and better in comparison (please, please, please punch the male presenter in the coupon as he is an irritant. Here, we have started calling him Thrush.) Look forward to chatting about random shite with you when you are back, you knob.

Yours,

Ian.

"Lovely bloke," I explain as if I am making excuses for my drunk mate who has fondled a woman's bottom because no rules apply after seven pints of Stella. "Landlord at my pub. And as such, my best friend. Strictly heterosexual relationship, I should add." I say looking at Anthony.

"I am not gay," he says in a way not too dissimilar to a big homo.

"There is more," Jenny tells me.

"Oh, good," I say, knowing I wasn't getting off that lightly.

"P.s. Pat and Ron have broken up again, although this time without resorting to stabbing."

I feel all eyes are looking at me, but not in the contempt of before, more shock that they have seemingly let the king of the chavs onto the show.

"Can't have been that serious," I assure with conviction. "They'll be together again by the time I'm back, vodka, after all, no matter how many bottles are consumed, cannot destroy the bonds formed by true love."

They are still staring at me and I feel I should do a booming laugh to pretend it is all a joke.

"What has he sent me?" I ask instead. "Because it sure as hell doesn't look like the pillow I requested nor the three kilos of coke I require."

Jenny, grinning away like a first term uni student coming up on Ecstasy.

"And in the parcel is a packet of Scampi Fries." She looks at it closely. "It says, I know you said send a pillow but unfortunately I couldn't be arsed and we had a run on the pork scratchings, and the peperami are still popular."

I laugh because I like the guy.

"I hate scampi fries," I tell everyone, because I really don't want people associating me with this weird, in-the-pub-only, snack of lemony fish flavoured breadcrumbs.

It is a redundant phrase because you'd have to be on the verge of starvation and/or so drunk that laziness has set in and a walk to the food shop round the corner is simply out of the question. I need to soak up some of the booze and I choose, not cheese and onion squares but a small packet of scampi fries so my breath will stink of beer AND fish. Nice. Hello ladies.

"I absolutely hate that pub," Katherine says to no one but everyone.

"Because it didn't serve posh food and drinks?" I explain.

"No, because it is, wall-to-wall a den of despair and moaning."

I choose to ignore her.

"It is paradise on earth. Brass objects on the walls that I think are for horses or cows or something," I eulogise. "Patterned purple wallpaper, a carpet that has fag burns, gum and blood, despite a smoking ban being in place for two generations. The white walls are yellow. Real ale, house doubles, and an old man named Arthur who has been coming in for twenty years and always telling us he doesn't have long left, which we no longer believe as it has been twenty years. He drinks Woods Navy Rum with a splash of peppermint and can only speak in the voice of a very dull accountant. So many characters."

"P.P.S," Jenny reads from the back of the paper. "Arthur has finally died (LOL), which is a shame, although the locals have taken it well and there is a real positivity and happiness about, which really does show you that Arthur was, let's face it, a monumentally boring prick. See when you are back, you twat."

They are all staring at me.

"We can share the Scampi?" I say, and I notice there are no more tears anywhere.

THE PRESENTERS : DAY 09 : STRUGGLING

"They what?" The Welshman says, loudly between clenching teeth.

He is shouting at the production executive, a woman named Lynda, who dresses like she will be off to a Home Counties church fete just as soon as her Chocolate Gateaux is ready. It would seem, she is hating her first act as messenger. She had passed the information to Molly, a whispered explanation, a quiet voice. Molly had played along, smiling inside, hoping she had distanced herself enough. Maybe she hadn't, maybe a misstep had been taken but it was rolling now, she was caught up and she knew that the only way was forward to see how it all plays out. She was excited, and scared, and ready.

The Welshman, her husband for the foreseeable, was pacing, in the portacabin that was the operations office, thick wires, TV screens, and blue swivel chairs.

"They have threatened to shut us down, take us off air, and essentially crucify us, the team, and anyone remotely connected to the show if we do not immediately change our editorial direction," Molly says, reading from the email she has received from her agent.

"Have they seen the ratings? We are the biggest show in the country," he says, like he always says. "It is all about the ratings, the more people watching the better we are. Numbers say it all."

"Because we are hated," Molly says, grabbing his arm to stop his movement.

He stops and stares down at her, the face of a child on the verge of tears because he won't be bought what he wants in the toyshop.

"People are watching in morbid fascination," Molly explains as the producer edges backward toward the flimsy door. "They actually want to see someone die. Bookmakers are taking odds on will there be a death? People are placing money on it. We are popular through being detested."

He stands and shakes his head.

"That is just your opinion," The Welshman says.

He turns to the producer.

"What's going on, Lynda?"

"They are meeting. The top brass. All the big boys. We have never had this many complaints. No one ever has."

"But everyone is watching," he shouts. "Everyone."

"Mostly to see something they can complain about," Molly explains.

The Welshman stares at her and she looks to the floor.

"It isn't the image we choose to portray," she whispers to a carpet tile. "We do the happy, silly, non-serious, definitely non murdering TV. We don't do this type of TV. We have stepped over the mark. They are meeting now."

"Now? It is too early to meet now?"

"They are in a different timezone you tit," Molly points out.

"To decide what?" The Welshman says wafting the timezone fact away with an airy brush of his hand.

"Whether to pull the show right now," Lynda tells the crumbs on the floor.

"Without warning?" Molly asks.

The producer lifts her head, stares at Molly, her mouth dropping open, a vague attempt at conversation makes her look like she is chewing air.

"You had three," she finally says as her jaw and tongue return to functioning. "Yesterday a paper said our show, on our channel was akin to tattooing a swastika on the queen's face."

Molly turns to The Welshman. He looks for an exit.

"Don't you dare run," she shouts. "What warnings?"

Lynda looks to the Welshman, to Molly, back to the Welshman, into her very soul looking for any self-respect she might have left after having given it all away to be part of all this.

The Welshman nods.

"Oh, you don't need his permission, Lynda, you need to speak or I'll rip your face off. What warnings?"

"They've been coming through daily. The viewing figures are great, but it isn't like the old days when it was all fun and chummy. They aren't happy with the direction. The directors. The figures are great, but the pockets of discontent from academics, psychologists and the demographic that have any sense of empathy. They are not so happy with the creative decisions this year."

"And why am I hearing this now?"

Lynda looks to the Welshman again.

"Stop. Just stop looking to that mentally challenged tit for conformation. Why am I hearing this now?"

"He told me he would tell you."

It dawns on her, the fuckery this man is trying to pull. She won't shout, not yet, nor swear, but she knows she has to act immediately.

"And you actually believed him, or did you just say nothing in the hope he would make everything all right? I am caught up in this, this absolute stupidity. Me. I do not want to be tied to this incompetent jumper man."

She turns to the Welshman and pushes her right index finger into his chest.

"You are an absolute disgrace. You do not have the brains, imagination nor vision to lead anything. You are an absolute tool." She turns to Lynda. "And you, if you think by doing everything he says you'll end up in a relationship that will further your career, or in some way make you the nation's darling, you are insane. What do you see in this absolute void of empathy?"

Lynda stares at her, lips not trembling, but trying to say a word, something somewhere in her miniscule mind is stopping her from using the words.

"Come on," Molly says. "Tell me."

"You married him."

Molly nods.

"Which makes me the biggest fool of all."

She looks up at the Welshman and he is smiling away as if his grin can erase all awkwardness and set them all back on the path of adulation for his stupid fucking face.

"When are they deciding?" Molly asks.

"Now. I think Brian has spoken out, and Georgia almost died. It isn't looking good."

Molly turns to The Welshman.

"We are going to return in shame. We'll have to become hermits, separately. You have tarnished me with your bullshit."

"I can fix this," he says. "I have a plan."

"No you do not have a plan. You have a misplaced sense of your own genius – Spoiler, you discover at the end you don't have any - Why are you so deluded?"

She makes a sound like a dragged out reaction to being kneed in the thigh. Arghhhhh.

Molly crouches down, her thoughts spiralling, her plans absolutely choked because information she needed was not passed on. Her mind races and she tries to piece together a strategy, anything at all to be able to make an exit in which she doesn't become a hate figure for the left and the poster girl for fascists.

She swears loudly, dragging out the U for many a second.

DAY 10 : MORNING : BORED AGAIN

The cameramen and sound people and the people who lift wires and are dressed in camouflage but are very noticeable as they are not trained in the arts of deception and are generally noisy, sweaty messes, seem to be on edge. They are not chirpy in the way they normally are, that faked happiness and positivity of Nursery teachers who balance out the day of smiling at the torturous behaviour of other people's children when they get home by drinking wine and crying in a darkened room about how they simply can't do this anymore.

165

We have been left alone, no morning check in from the presenters, no challenge set, no news of any type. We have been on edge, by instinct, knowing the time they normally appear, like a pet dog who knows a bowl of processed, dry biscuits that have been flavoured with a chemical compound that resembles chicken, because all wild dogs love a good KFC, should have already arrived by now. But nothing happens and nothing materialises. We slowly slope back to our hammocks, put our crocodile Dundee hats over our faces and doze.

Something isn't right.

It never is. But today is strange.

The dozes finish and the groups start to emerge.

Each person venturing off to hang out with those they like and whose opinion they rate. I, rather weirdly, am left alone. Jenny looks across now and again, but her eyes are generally for Jonny Boy and his incessant chat to Katherine. He probably thinks he is the level of wit of Oscar Wilde, what with Katherine giggling and laughing and smiling and batting eyelids. He isn't, she did this with me, does this with everyone. She can laugh and smile with the best of them, which helps seeing as most of what I said was bitter moaning wrapped up to look like jokes.

But I'm staring too, even though I don't want to. Staring at a woman who until not so long ago shared my bed, my life and the thoughts I was willing to show – which is admittedly not a high percentage as I'm afraid most people given an inside track on my thought process would be in equal measure appalled and bored out of their brains. I once had a twenty minute internal discussion about which is the best way to eat salt and vinegar crisps. I was in a cinema, watching the premier of some science fiction tosh and drifted off near the end as the trailer had told me the whole story and contained all the good bits. Turns out those two minutes were all the scenes that made sense. The other two hours were actors using words to send me into the concussion protocol. Although there was a woman, with green skin, antennae, and a tail who, and I still have absolutely no idea why, really did it for me. Were I to wake up in Star Trek the Next Generation I'm pretty sure I'd be a sex pest.

Ooo, newly discovered planet where women look like zebras and have a hoof for a nose.

Cor, I'd have some of that.

There is probably a niche porno in there somewhere.

Katherine and Jonny are on fire with chat. Once, long ago, when I had even less self-confidence than now, I took a woman on a date to an Indian. The couple at the next table were hilarious, properly funny, and drunk, and in comparison my own words sounded feeble and boring and weak and without any humour at all. The guy looked across at me a few times, turned back to his girlfriend and made jokes I could not hear at my expense. Oh, how they roared with laughter, and oh how I panicked and drank about a litre of very, very dark red wine from a jug and vomited in the toilet.

I think I got away with it until outside her house.

I kissed her and what was left of her smile left. I think she tasted the bile. I wasn't invited in, and I am sure I was in such a weak position as a romantic future that I would have had more chance of getting through the front door and getting naked if I had asked if I could nip in as I needed a massive shit. I never spoke to her again, nor saw her and was worried that she had been murdered and I would be accused of killing.

But I stare at them, not directly, sideways glances that I think are surreptitious looks of interest. And maybe I linger a bit too much.

"Why are you staring at them?" Jenny asks having snuck up on me like a freak.

I jump, startled, and let out a bit of gas. It's like women who talk about not being able to go on trampolines after giving birth as they will definitely wet themselves. As a middle-aged man, walking along, generally in posh supermarkets, a bottom burb belches out without warning or build-up, which is added to by my poor level of hearing and I assume I've got away with it until the young children giggle near the dairy section.

Caught out I opt for honesty, of a sort.

"Fascinated by it all," I say trying to imitate the tone of a presenter on Question time. I'm not fooling her. "Strange, isn't it? You spend time with someone, get feelings, have vague ideas about a future, undefined, but there all the same, get cheated on, collapse in a broken heap on your kitchen floor in tears – in a manly way – sadness flowing into anger into self-pity into pretending it never happened and hoping never to see them again. But then, you somehow end up on a celebrity torture show as far from home as is possible to be while remaining on planet earth, and she turns up, and starts to pull all the moves she pulled on you in front of your eyes with a bloke with more fame and intelligence than you would ever have."

"It is my husband," she wines.

I look at her, tears welling in her eyes, my own sadness etched into my face. We lock eyes, sharing a pain, sharing something most people

167

have experienced, sharing that knowledge of pain and difficult lives. I lower my head and look at the ground.

I whisper, "It's not all about you."

She stares at me a bit more, her eyes becoming dry.

"Selfish," I add in a quiet voice.

She smiles, which is a relief as in other circumstances the attempt at humour may have been missed and she would now be hammer punching my teeth into my throat.

"How's it for you?" I ask.

"I'm still married to him, whatever that means. And here he is, being the big man with the money, the power and the influence. I am small in comparison. He couldn't let me just crack on, had to be involved, had to influence, probably has a team of recent marketing graduates working away for free to spin the shit out of this trip. They are probably all female, all impressionable, all ready to do absolutely anything for him and his amazing ways."

"He sounds a top bloke," I say, "probably a proper good story teller down the pub."

"A story teller, without a doubt."

This is something I want to investigate, to learn and to know. I have a list of questions running through my mind like they are all written on separate pages of an old Filofax. But I can't ask, can't speak because through the bushes come Molly and The Welshman looking furious. But I am no mind reader, understander of body language or even able to tune into auras like those hippy shits who tell me about my glow – generally starts as green and then after a few minutes conversation they correct themselves and tell me it is the blackest of blacks with molten lead flames bursting through. I have never given it too much thought but I assume, in their peaceful, pacifist, non-aggressive way they are saying I am the Devil made human. Well I think they should all fuck off, get rid of flowery clothes and stop pretending to be at one with nature and an empath and get a proper hobby.

Are you really tuned into other people's feelings? Can you truly feel what I am by being near me? I don't think so, because if you could, you'd be punching yourself in the face and trying to nail gun your tongue to the engine of a jet plane.

Oh, do you sense anger and frustration? Good, so fuck off and take the smell of cheap patchouli incense with you, you hippy. You smell like a drug dealer's satchel.

"Gather round," The Welshman says in tones he has never used, they seem almost defeated, apologetic, embarrassed. All emotions I thought he had surgically removed from his brain, along with insight, intelligence and a realistic opinion of himself. For the briefest of seconds I think it may be an impersonator. But it isn't, it is definitely this personality void and he is definitely still Welsh. Molly stands next to him, trying at sad, but seemingly having had a giant take the massive weight of her marriage from her shoulders. I think she might giggle. I think she might go off the rails, I think I want to be there when it happens.

We all trudge over, around the fire, The Welshman holding court.

"We have some good news," he says, "And some bad news," he adds in a way that makes me suspect he believes he is the first person to ever say these words.

"The good news," he says, totally missing out the customary question of which we would like first, "is that there is a party, a feast, a celebration, if you will, with food, drinks-"

"Alcohol?" Gaz asks.

"Alcohol, yes," Welshman confirms. "Unlimited really. Or as much as you can drink," he smiles.

"Which amounts to the same thing," I say and Gaz, caught up in the belief that the more you can drink the more of a man you are, nods smiling as if this ability to imbibe booze to levels that would intoxicate small towns were it released into the water is as special an achievement as being ranked number one in the world for a game of hitting balls about on baize.

"A huge unlimited feast, to which I will be attending," The Welshman adds.

I turn to the contestants and people I really can't call team mates. "And that is the bad news," I tell them. "Let's get ready."

Molly steps forward,

"No, the bad news-"

"Will be revealed at the party," Welshman finishes. "We'll tell you at the party. So if you want to put on your going out clothes, get your pulling pants on, and we will meet you in the clearing."

THE PRESENTERS : DAY 10 : STRUGGLING

Molly knows what The Welshman is doing, knows it all, that belief that he can turn this around, use some weird voodoo charm, or pray to every single God he knows including the ones he has seen in comics, to make a celestial intervention. Thor will be in there, he'll pray to Thor and some other utterly ridiculous nonsense, like a half-man half-plant from the other world in a cult, barely seen sci-fi 'classic' from the sixties. He'll pray to them all, demand his brilliance be repaid with a reprieve, a call to say, you know what? We were wrong, you were right. Carry on with the show and here is more cash.

The contestants are getting ready as the crew prepare the feast, the long table, the litres of wine, the chairs, the throne at the head in which The Welshman will inevitably sit. The music, the plates, the table cloth all chosen by him, all selected based on his tastes, and all you'd expect if invited to dinner with a posh serial killer called Tarquin, who once went to Eton, and got bullied, and by bullied I mean rogered by the hockey team for the bantz.

He paces, his phone pushed against his ear, then removed and messages typed, long desperate messages she assumes to people whose ear he might have and who might be able to reverse the decision. He is working, pulling out all stops not wanting this to be the end. He can't accept, won't believe that his moment is done.

She thinks of the chaos back home, the papers running with their break-up now running with their career ending cancellation mid-show. The shame, the dishonour, the absolutely appalling choices on content. There is no coming back, no way to see a future beyond appearing on desperately poor quality radio shows or slumming it on podcasts, not for the money, but for the chance, the remote chance, of saying the right thing, being the right person, and having one more shot. That constant, look at me, I'm still here, do you need me for anything? It isn't the money, they have so much, it is the fame, the presence, people having his name on their lips and his image in their minds and the desire to see his cock.

Her retirement has come, she knows this. Maybe when she is older she can pitch an idea about the return of a once famous has-been. Maybe in the future a similar show will become popular and they will ask her to come on and maybe him, and maybe they could be the new stars, the nostalgia overtaking the reality of their own incompetence. It is all a possibility, but this is the end, and this is her way out. No silly games required. The relief is there, the destruction of careers, the absolute self-inflicted career wounds of the terminally thick. Congratulations, your choice words and actions have stopped your fame right here, and with it you have brought down everyone associated. People will be erasing this job from their Curriculums.

170

He still can't make that call, can't make the announcement, to tell them all it is over. The last minute wait, the hope of a last minute reprieve.

Maybe, she thinks, he can pull this round by one last blow out of insanity. But it won't matter, the filming is cancelled, the cameras should not roll. The word has come, the decision made. The show will not be broadcast, certainly not live and certainly not played later today with the swearing edited out.

DAY 10 : THE PARTY : BOOZE

We walk into a clearing and the table is one made up to look like a castle feast in the Middle Ages. There is the sweet smell of actual food, the juices of animals who have been roasted in oil and vegetables that have been cooked to perfection. The aroma of a street food festival concentrating on the best open air barbeque in the history of mankind.

My mouth fills with saliva to the extent it is difficult to swallow.

"Dear God that smells amazing. It actually smells like real food, a Sunday roast," Kieran says, as strings of spit appear at the corner of his mouth making him look like Disney's attempt to render Labradors human.

Gaz, I believe has been struck dumb as his mind races through the possibility of gorging himself until he can eat no more and the only possibility for further food delight is to take the dessert and shove it up his arse.

Chelsey looks on, and while her gym clothes indicate she may be someone who has a selective eating habit, she takes it all in and says, "Oh, fuck yeah," at the sheer volume of food and, I believe, alcohol sending her into a state of hypnotic bliss.

They are all overwhelmed, the idea of bad news coming is lost in their eyes as they all stare at food and booze. It is like a bank holiday weekend dream for the masses. Drink all day, get sunburned and eat three months' worth of food for a four-person family in the space of six hours and then pass-out, and wake up ill the next day while messaging your mates about what a great day you had and can you believe we got asked to leave the The White Hart? We were only being hilariously funny by singing Bohemian Rhapsody with rude words.

Molly is very distant from the Welshman, a physical distance as well as no looks. I've been there myself, the obligation to be somewhere as a couple but the absolute conviction that your other half needs to exposed for the utter cretin they are. And to be honest, and self-aware, I am also often the cretin.

They pile in like a human wave of desperation and hunger. They take their chairs, some grabbing at food, all of them grabbing for alcohol. I look at Jenny, she looks at me.

"What is your tipple?" she asks like a barmaid in an Ealing comedy.

"I don't drink," I say, in the way all male Brits do, apologetic that I don't drink booze, get drunk, need to be a dick, or indeed have a minor problem with an easy to buy drug. I am the weird one.

"But your best friend is a barman."

"I gave up, not too long ago. I don't think he believes I will last as tee total."

Hopefully the normal conversation doesn't break out.

What, you don't drink? Not even a glass of wine? Are you ill? Why not? That is weird.

And it is, in the context of the United Kingdom, and a fair few other countries too. Saturday night in the British highstreets is a flow of adults in stages of inebriation, most of them paid professionals, fathers, mothers, educated students, plumbers, shop assistants, all out to have a laugh and let off steam by imbibing booze so inhibitions drop, co-ordination goes and every fucking sound is hilarious.

She stares at me as if I am weird.

"I used to," I explain, "a lot. But, you know, I got bored. And as you very well know, I am THE most annoying gobshite when sober, can you actually imagine the crap I spoke when drunk?"

"Do you miss it?"

I've thought about this a lot, and I have an answer, a real answer.

"I wish I'd quit sooner."

"How long?"

"About six months. I think now, if I started to have a beer here, I'd eventually wake up on a beach, naked, with an international arrest warrant in circulation and unable to remember my surname or why I now have Sharon tattooed across my foreskin."

Jenny holds up her thumb and index finger so close together it looks like a slow motion click.

"In tiny letters," she tells me.

"Braille," I correct.

She smiles.

"What made you quit?"

172

"The kitchen floor is very hard and cold and it was giving me backache sleeping on it so much."

"Any reason for that?"

"Five pints of strong Belgian lager followed by a couple of bottles of Lambrini and the inability to stand up."

She stares at me. "That is the chosen drink of all teenage girls," she informs me correctly, and I believe this is the description on the label. Cheap, fake wine made from pears and only to be bought for or by teenage females. Waitrose do not sell it as their clientele is aged ladies in floral dresses who only drink Pimms and ethically sourced Peruvian Pinot fermented in the stomach of peasant children.

It adds a sweet aftertaste, Doris.

"You know when times are hard, and you've broken up pretty badly with someone you essentially lived with and you are alone, no family nor friends, and obviously not depressed enough to need actual medical help that would cut short the suffering but mark you out as a wimp? And you remember all those fun days as a young adult getting drunk, setting fire to coffee beans in shots of Sambuca, or necking Drambuie."

"Nope," she tells me, shaking her head as if I am the weird one.

"Really? Odd. Anyway, I chose to self-medicate, in the way that I upped my self-medicated medicine content from mild alcoholism to raging drunk. You'd be surprised at just how bad an idea that is."

"I don't think I would," she says, although I suspect she hasn't given it enough thought.

"I couldn't write, understand what day it was and had only a fleeting relationship with personal hygiene. Fun times."

We stand, rocking back and forth on our heels, staring at the carnage as celebrities try to force unchewed meat down their throats with the help of what appears to be expensive dark red wine. Litres of the stuff are leaking down chins.

"It's like supermarket sweep," I say, "only in this game you don't need to get as much into your trolley as you can, you have to force food and drink into your gut without chewing or swallowing. I haven't seen any prawn Vol-au-vents, which is very distressing. What type of buffet is this?"

"A shit one," Jenny says, succinctly and correctly.

But our stand off and superior air has not gone unnoticed.

"Are you not joining us?" the Welshman asks from his chair at the head of the table that is actually a prop throne.

He is, as we should all have guessed, drinking from a gold goblet as if this is the last super and he is the hipster Jesus. One arm back and over the chair, legs akimbo in the belief, I assume, that giving everyone his man spread and line of sight straight to his cock and balls is going to act as a means of distracting everyone from his totally vacuous warbling.

I see a lobster, a whole lobster, a poor dead lobster to which I feel an affinity. The beef from a cow and chicken leave me feeling nothing which means I rank seafood well above farm animals in my newly discovered 'animals I won't eat' chart. Would I eat a dog? Probably, but maybe as a snack, like the fried leg of a Chihuahua, at first and then work my way up to a St. Bernard. I sit near it, in the middle of these celebrities acting like sharks competing to chomp on the carcass of a dead whale and just watch as they leave restraint at the camp and just go at it like Augustus Gloop in Willy Wonka's chocolate factory.

Jenny remains standing, watching us all and I follow her gaze to the love fireworks that are exploding from Political spin master Jonny and the totally uninteresting and absolutely nothing special at all Katherine. I am shocked to think that they are causing Jenny more pain than me. Is it their lack or care, the apparent contempt? Should that actually be a thing? We are all free of relationships, we don't owe anybody anything, and if I am honest with myself, which I am often as my internal voice scolds me for being just about the worst human being alive, I hate that she moves on easily while I still can't spend a day without telling myself I am worthless and deserve to be alone forever, living out my days on the thirty-seventh floor of a tower block that smells of piss, my own piss as I have become senile and incontinent and opened my doors to the local crack dealers just for the company.

Gaz is dancing round the table with a bottle of gin in each hand, so two litres of gin, all for him, he has laid claim, and while he has, like the others, drunk a couple of glasses, he is acting and talking like he has been on a session for the last two hours. His anticipation of being pissed has raised his happy game to a level commensurate to a rich single-child seven-year-old on Christmas day. All these gifts and all just for me. He is dancing in the way middle-aged pissed men dance, in that he is moving his arse side-to-side, his arms up and down and his feet are struggling to remain in contact with the floor in a way that stops him falling forward and smashing his face on the ground as he strives to protect the glass bottles of alcohol rather than his own teeth.

Kieran is sat, two beers in, his head back, clearly in need of filling his stomach as his head lolls and he is laughing the laugh of a man coming

174

up on mushrooms. He takes another swig of his bottled Mexican lager and I notice he has placed a quarter of lemon in the glass neck like the men in beer gardens used to do when such things were fashionable for those ten minutes that summer before everyone rightly decided it was the sign of a total tit.

Anthony is on the whiskey, or possibly southern comfort, but not straight, no, that wouldn't be right. He, I am absolutely certain, states to anyone who cares to listen in any pub – after they have asked him for ID, or invited him to the playroom – that he only drinks the original as the taste of cheap supermarket crap just doesn't do it for him. He has clearly no idea whatsoever as he proceeds to drown the expensive stuff in rola cola. It's like saying you only appreciate the delicate taste of the finest of risottos, possibly one with an experimental combination of strawberries and radish that has won awards throughout Italy, only to say, but I can only eat it by adding half a cup of mayonnaise, bought from Poundland.

Chelsey is on the prosecco, because she is, in her own words, mind and world, classy. It appears she doesn't actually like the taste though as she is pouring glasses of the stuff down her neck without any of it getting the opportunity to hit her taste buds. She laughs the laugh of a character from Macbeth, specifically the main witch.

Racheal, with her calm and expertise is eating with a knife and fork and sipping on Belgian beer. She really is a dab hand at this reality TV nonsense.

Molly stands near the table, not looking into cameras, not drinking, just stood, smiling, moving her eyes but not her head. But they always come back to her husband and his current desire for all attention.

I look across the table and Johnny boy has sat, after pulling a chair out for Katherine. He doesn't pull it away at the last moment so she can fall on her arse, which disappoints me bitterly.

He picks up two bottles of foreign lager, possibly Japanese, silver bottles with symbols that look like those tattooed onto a whole generation of men who played football during David Beckham's peak years.

Oh, what does that say?
My child's name.
How do you know?
The tattooist told me.
Japanese was he?
Scouse.
"I don't drink beer," Katherine says. "It gives me gas."

175

"And they stink," I shout, hoping it was my internal voice, but realising from their stares that it almost certainly wasn't. "Like a ton of rotten vegetables have been pulped into a paste and spread on the inside of your nose," I add, definitely out loud and in her face.

They stare at me, possibly trying to understand what mental illness I am displaying currently, or, as their expressions would seem to show, wanting me to fuck off out of it. I waft my hand in front of my face and look away discreetly because there is a noise I hear.

There is a chink of a glass and I turn to look. No one else does, they all carry on in sweet ignorance as I hold eyes with the Welshman. He taps a glass again with the same response as before, which he doesn't seem to like, so he taps harder. They ignore him again.

"Hey," he shouts, his voice creaking and breaking twice like a teenager who is having difficulty getting his balls to drop all the way.

They all stop, silently swearing because they have no need to stoke this guy's ego as they have already obtained the holy grail of booze and food. Someone, somewhere is preparing a spit of Keebab meat so we can all stand swaying next to it at two a.m. while shouting random obscenities at our friends thinking it is on-point observational comedy.

You see that?

Yeah.

Well, you're a twat.

"Can I have your attention?" The Welshman states like he is the best man at a wedding in which he is probably shagging the bride, and quite possibly groom, the pervert.

"Gather round," he tells us.

No one moves.

"Come on in," he says using different words for the same simple concept.

"I can hear you from here," Gaz shouts, bless him, glugging directly from a bottle, which will not now be touched by anyone who has seen this. The booze is in his veins, and without a doubt in his liver, along with late stage cirrhosis.

"I have something important to say. I'm not sure how I can word this. How-"

He breaks here and either he has learned the art of sobbing to get his own way as a child or he is genuinely upset.

"-I, I, I just can't actually say this. I don't know-"

Molly steps forward.

"Oh for fuck's sake," she says, glaring at her husband, who, I assume is about to be filed for divorce. "We have been cancelled."

Everyone stares at her. The eyes not truly understanding what is going on.

"There isn't going to be a show next year?" Anthony squeaks,

"No, there isn't. At least not with us," The Welshman says.

"But there is also not going to be a show this year either," Molly adds. "The company has pulled the plug."

"We have the best ratings ever. And I mean Ever," The Welshman says. "More than when we first started, more than the fifth and eight seasons when we had actual famous people on-"

"We understand the concept of ever," I say. "And are we still getting paid?"

"The money is guaranteed, no one will be out of pocket," Molly tells us.

"In which case, I don't care," I say, sitting back into my chair.

Bob, is pouring a pint of bitter down the front of his shirt. I'm guessing he wants it to go into his mouth, but shock has a tendency to make Bob really very weird.

"We aren't on TV? Then why are they filming," Jonny asks, showing observational skills beyond us mere mortals.

"Contractual obligation," Molly tells him. "This, I'm afraid, is the end, the last part. We are done and our spot on TV taken up by films that were shown over Christmas."

Everyone sits down, or remains sitting, except Gaz, who stands, swaying and swigging.

"We have this to film, this feast to have and then we are done? On our way back to the real world? It is over?" he asks, smiling.

The Welshman nods and lowers his head like he is about to say Amen at the end of Nelson Mandela's Funeral Eulogy. But he can't hold the humble. He stands, looks right at his wife.

"We have the biggest audience in the history of this show. But the largest number of complaints so advertisers jump ship, complain their brands can't be associated with this. Two of you have nearly died, they say, and the language has been too choice. And the tasks too vicious. The easily insulted have complained loud and hard, the soft leftie halfwits have chirped up with their wokeist drivel and we are now done. Mental health, they now say, is paramount. Well, it never used to be. Snowflakes."

We sit there, Jenny smiling, me thinking of the legend that will be for this end to the most popular show of all time. We have made history.

"I feel proud to be part of TV gold," I tell her like a father congratulating a child on graduating from University.

We all sit for a while soaking it in, the end, no winner, no losers – well, not in the classical sense – and I feel a relief, a stress gone, a worry resolved. I sit and watch them all unfold, making small talk with Jenny about nothing at all and loving it more than I should.

We watch, increasingly in silence because while I am sure I heard and understood the small speech by the presenters, or soon to be ex-presenters, others here seem to have interpreted it all differently.

I turn to the equally observant Jenny,

"He might as well have said, the show is cancelled, so let's just go frickin nuts."

That is what most are doing. An end of season party, an explosion of shackles that were holding in self-restraint. They have gone mad.

"This takes me back," Jenny says.

"Did you used to hang out with failed celebrities as they got drunk, will inevitably be sick and cry and possibly, and hopefully, start to get off with each other. I think Gaz fancies his chances."

And he does, the gin has changed his body language from edge of despair and physical ruin, to aged Italian man on the beach with leathery skin, hairy chest, a gold medallion resting on the top of a bulbous gut and concealing only two percent of his flesh with a pair of black speedos. The white laces, obviously, are hanging down, stating, I could whip these off in a jiffy if you just give me the nod. I wonder if I will ever reach those levels of ignorant arrogance and the self-hypnotism of thinking I look lithe and sexy when in fact I look like grandad who has spray tanned himself to the point of death after sitting on a pump.

"Teenage parties," she says. "In fields, or remote locations, where all teens having their early experiences with Special brew, luminous drinks named by initials only and screw top wine, and the hidden demons within everyone slowly slipping out through words and actions."

"Great times," I reminisce.

She laughs.

"They were, but why the actual hell you'd want to recreate that week after week as an actual adult is beyond me."

"It is fun to watch."

"Did you do all this until you gave it up?"

"No, for me to be able to have done this I would have needed friends and to have received invites to social gatherings. I generally supped beer in the local, talked shite, walked home where everyone assumed I would go to a deep alcohol sleep, but where I surfed the net while drinking wine as quickly as I could."

"Fun times?"

"I have absolutely no recollection of any emotion other than that sick, paranoia and the desperate self-loathing of the truly hungover. I watched films I do not recall, and for the sole reason to hear people's voices as I drank."

She stares at me, that lack of understanding, that total shame she has for me, the unbelieving notion that I would have wasted so much time in pursuit of oblivion.

"I know," I say. "I know."

"Good times?" she asks knowing the general gist of what my answer will be.

"I have absolutely no idea, just a long blur of bullshit. Could all have been the same night, could all have been multiple nights. Just a long up and down of sober mornings running in to alcohol afternoons."

Then I hear it. Those words that usher in the absolutely worst of all nights.

"Marry, shag, or kill?" Gaz says between poorly suppressed belches.

"Oh dear lord," I say despite not having been in a church since a primary school choir appointment. All those assemblies singing religious songs on a hard wooden floor. Words I can still remember and have even less meaning now than then. Something about magic pennies and rolling all over the floor.

But here we go, we have reached peak pissed, the verbal sparring, the game that reveals your loves, interests and hates. All those emotions happily blathered out in slurred tones so that everyone can stake a claim to feelings they have for someone else in the room. It'll start with famous, verge into the absurd and then finish with the people here. Everyone will know who likes who and no one will have to have an uncomfortable conversation. It is, after all just a game. A game for emotionally illiterate teens but now the mainstay of pissed adults who can just get out of everything by saying, *But it was just a game, I was joking, and what else could I say? It was the alcohol, not me.*

"Five quid says Gaz will shag anything, and that Jonny boy and Katherine are the power couple of the day."

Jenny sips on a glass of white wine, holding the stem. She takes a bigger swig than previously.

"If he can make this into some type of fame he will."

"It's over," I say. "No more of any of this."

She shakes her head.

Gaz has shown everyone in turn his testicles, apparently because they are as big as coconuts. I declined the offer but Jenny did confirm they were rather large. He has rapped a song from the 1980s, word for word, and expected an applause at the end, despite it being a one hit wonder with the line, look up my bottom, and fallen over three times, the last one on his face. The male pop star has started crying, apparently because this is what gin does to him and is in no way connected to his deep seated despair at the emptiness of his life, soul and personality. He hasn't sung because I suspect, he cannot, and that all his recordings are by a ghost singer. Small blessings and everything. Exercise woman has revealed details of a few minor celebrity men, and one who went on to be big in the pop industry, and by details I mean specifically how good they are in bed, and how they all just used her for her body and exactly how they used her body in graphic detail. There really could be no other reason for them to have been in a short relationship and then run off. She could see no other rational explanation, despite her own insistence she didn't want anything serious, or rate any of them at all in any way.

Bob has talked of future glories in detail and without stopping, part performing songs and jokes from a bygone era of black and white TV, choc ices, and families not owning refrigerators. It would seem the future for him is a return to the nineteen sixties. He has also cried, possibly to elicit empathy, or possibly because he too can see the future of fading away into insignificance and a worldwide shortage of man mascara.

Cool presenter Kieran on a desperate attempt to regain fame is half way through a mental breakdown. He is angry, ooo, is he angry. The conversation is not to his liking, we all need to grow up, speak about important things, and he absolutely does not need to see Gaz's hairy ballsack nor hear about celebrity shags. And no, he would not sleep with Chelsey as she isn't his type because she has in place of a personality a vacuum of nothing (I didn't interrupt to point out that is exactly what a vacuum is, as he was on a roll.) Nor would he participate in stupid games about who he would potentially marry, shag or snog. Chelsey consoled Anthony by cuddling him and engulfing him in plastic tits.

If the evening had been a film, I would have got it on DVD as a motivational movie entitled, "Don't do drugs."

Katherine is crying too, sobbing at the horrible misfortune of it all.

"I can't believe I come on here, meet someone like you, and then that's it. The end as soon as it starts. I've never felt anything like this for anyone before," she says, and certainly lies as I am sure she has felt nothing for loads of blokes.

I look to Jenny, who is also listening but trying not to show it, and mouth "What?" as I point at myself.

She points at her temple and swirls her finger around while making her eyes loll.

I take this as the sarcasm it is meant to be.

Jonny leans across like a Father Christmas who thought he should get into shape in the off season. He places his hand on her knee, and cups her face with his other hand. I actually want to be sick. I place my hand on Jenny's knee and she grabs my hand in hers, squeezes, pulls my hand up and off her thigh and throws it back at me. I pretend this never happened.

"I mean, we have this opportunity to do something different, something fun, in a place where few have been-" Katherine sobs on.

"Except every soap star who lost their job over the last two decades and other people searching for a way back into being of importance," I correct.

Jonny stares at me as if he is the hardest man in the pub and I need to shut up or have my face slapped. That pub would be shit. Katherine looks too, tears in her eyes but still managing the look of someone who would quite happily throw me in front of a speeding combine harvester.

They continue speaking but in hushed tones, which is so ignorant as I can't genuinely hear a thing they are saying.

THE PRESENTERS : DAY 10 : ON A BIT OF BOOZE

The Welshman has sat and watched and drunk more than he should. He likes control and being drunk leaves him open to failure. Two bottles of beer is a maximum and he has swallowed past to the edge of slightly pissed. He has been silent watching these fools get drunk and humiliate themselves. Jenny and Ben sat watching, making quips, laughing and staring. But neither can take their eyes off their pasts. They watch Jonny and Katherine all the time and are addicted to deciphering

181

words and language. It doesn't take a genius, it is an old scene playing out in the today. Two jealous exes watching a young woman work her way, using emotions, into an old man's heart, an old man that needs to know he still has something to offer. Maybe she does like him, but her tears are not for a sadness of a relationship that might not hold in the real world, it is for the end of a chance at fame. The show at an end and she hasn't had enough time to become the most talked about beauty in the UK.

She has edged with every sip to the point of tears and the eliciting of a caring embrace. And now Jonny stands.

He walks over to where Molly and The Welshman sit, at the head of the table, him in his throne and Molly two chairs down in silence as the cackle and chokes of contestants ring out and Gaz sings something no middle-aged white man should be allowed to sing about: L.A and AK-47s on a good day.

Jonny crouches down in front of The Welshman, he knows the reverential pose is all that is needed to gain favour. He'll think he is a descendant of the Godfather, and is receiving his respect.

"We are definitely cancelled?" Jonny asks.

The Welshman nods his head still holding his goblet.

"I need my phone," Jonny says. "There is a shot I'd like to take."

"A shot at what?"

"A shot at getting through. Are you recording all this?" he asks, spreading out his hand indicating the carnage.

The Welshman nods, leaning forward, drawn in by the voice.

"So this party, that can be edited, made into something before it gets into prime time TV in the UK?"

"That is how it always works," The Welshman explains. "But we've been cancelled. They are not having us back on TV."

Jonny nods.

"They may not," he says, "and possibly, if not probably all channels won't touch you. But there are always a few that broadcast controversy. Those that actively need to show stuff that polarises opinion."

Molly knows he doesn't understand what Jonny has said, knows he won't grasp the meaning of polarised. But he'll hear enough to realise there is a chance.

"What do you mean a chance?" The Welshman asks. "A chance at what?"

"Get me my phone, I can make a call, and we can see where that can go. But this conversation, and the one I have on my phone, that can't be recorded or put out anywhere. You understand that?"

The Welshman nods and stands.

"I don't understand," he says and Molly smiles. It is the first time she has heard him say that in years.

"Look, no promises," Jonny says. "But I can make a call. I have an idea. We could keep going. But I need to know a few things."

Molly stands and takes a step closer to them.

"What do you need to know?" Molly asks.

"Who owns this show?"

The Welshman looks lost, because he knows nothing.

"Our production company," Molly explains. "They pay us to make this and we deliver."

"And that is the rights to everything?"

"I think so," The Welshman says.

"I can't work with think," Jonny tells him. "I have to know. Who owns all this?"

Molly steps in.

"Our production company sells the show," she says. "We get paid, the show goes on national TV."

"But now they have backed out. Dropped you?" Jonny asks, looking for all the information he needs. "And the agreement is scrapped. Leaving you in need of a new distributor?"

"The legalities of it all, the documents. I don't know," Molly says.

"But there is a chance you are free to sell what we are doing now to an alternative bidder?"

"This is drunk talk," Molly says, "we are hypothesizing over something that can't happen."

"Who edits for the show?"

"Our team back home."

Jonny stands, and turns. He smiles at Katherine, and her face is waiting on his word.

"I need my phone," he tells them. "I can take that shot. How long to get an episode together and out there?"

"Seven hours," Molly tells him.

DAY 10 : NIGHT : DRUNK PEOPLE ARE ANNOYING

I watch them because I have followed Jonny walking, losing balance and clearly drunk. But his is a refined drunk, almost certainly

183

normally drinks beer from a tankard. That man at the bar who entertains the staff and locals with in-depth explanations on things he does not understand, spouting his own version of deep and meaningful that would be, on even the most rudimentary TV chat show, shown up to be shallow contradictory bollocks, a patch-work of non-compatible philosophy that isn't questioned because people are just there to get drunk. He is, in essence, a shit jukebox.

But he is saying something of great interest to the Welshman. That defeated but smiling face, that silent thought process of, oh well, their loss, I am already rich, I will go onto bigger and better things like the first person out of a boy band who has one hit record off the back of his fame and then drifts into obscurity finally settling down with his biggest fan on a farm in Kent, becoming a hermit and breaking all contact with the outside world with the exception of his dealer and an endless supply of cocaine.

What has fame brought you??

A passion for cattle and the disintegration of my nasal septum.

The Welshman is holding onto the most punishing of feelings, it is the hope that will kill you. Something Jonny said, something he explained, a drunken promise or a drunken plan that only the drunk can believe because your brain needs to be scrambled to see any logic.

Shall we break into that zoo?

Why?

To stroke a honey badger?

Yeah, man.

Shall we see if we can jump from the balcony on this tall building onto the next one?

What happens if we fail?

We'll die.

Let's give it a shot.

Jenny is watching too.

"What do you think that is about?"

Jenny looks all around the party, the competitors pissed and being an exaggerated version of themselves, which is quite something as they started out as exaggerated versions of a human in the morning. The carnage of those with serious self-delusions. The food that is now strewn everywhere, the open bottles, and cans, the dregs floating at the bottom. Everything tried but nothing finished.

She looks at the sobbing Katherine, at Jonny walking away with the Welshman, at Molly not moving, trying to hold an expression together that doesn't shout, "Fuck!"

"He has a plan," she tells me as if her heart is breaking. "He will always have a plan."

"Do they work?"

"They usually involve calling in a favour, usually to someone he has the dirt on."

"Less favour, more blackmail?"

"Pretty much, but that is how it all works. Favour for favour, misdeed creates a debt. The debt is paid, a favour is owed, or the debt remains. A silly game for posh kids who have all eaten each others spunk through losing a game of soggy biscuit."

"I think you still love him."

She turns to me and smiles.

"I think I would happily reveal all his secrets."

"I'm happy to ghost write. Add a bit of creativity and word play."

"I'd like nothing better. But, there are some problems. No one would publish it as it would mean the end of their business. I would be ostracised and hounded for the rest of my life, and probably the most important, I have signed a non-disclosure agreement which binds me to keep my mouth shut. The only way I could get that information out there would be if he were dead."

"So, if I've understood, and correct me if I am wrong. You have got me drunk and seduced me with your sexy talk for the sole reason you want me to somehow get away, on live TV, wearing a microphone, with murdering Jonny."

"Could be done," she laughs. "Drowned in the dunny."

"You've actually thought about this more than you should."

"No cameras in there. Could be made to look an accident."

"Sorry, officer, he walked in on me having a poo, and he tripped, fell through my legs, down the hole in the plank and headfirst into the urine and faeces receptacle below. I was in so much shock, as I stood up I fell over the underpants around my ankles, knocked myself out and was thus unable to call for help until after he had drowned in our combined bodily waste."

"Yes."

"Not even Sherlock would be able to crack that."

We stare at each other smiling. Having a moment. It is here, as a teenager, I'd blunder. The subtlety would go, the jumping the gun and moving too fast would happen. I move slowly, I'm pretty sure I am right, although the lingering doubt remains. She probably doesn't want my advances, and maybe only does now to piss off her husband. But she isn't moving as I lean my face to hers. She is smiling, and very positively, is not gagging. I think we are going to kiss off the back of flirty chat about murdering her husband in human slurry. But then we hear the lyrics of Gangster's Paradise sung loud inches from our faces, and feel the warm spittle of Gin Saliva. We look and Gaz is there, bashing out lyrics, having removed his shirt, revealing his body of white blubber and moobs. I imagine he has to wear a bra when playing snooker or he'll be touching the table every time he leans down to take a shot. Thankfully he still has his trousers on, less thankfully I think he has the intention of not going just through this song, but the entire album and possibly an entire series of Top of The Pops.

"Shall we go?" Jenny asks me, taking my hand and not inflicting any pain at all.

"What about Gaz?" I ask, genuinely worried he might attack us if we don't listen and applaud.

"I don't think he'll notice."

And he doesn't.

DAY 11 : MORNING : THE HANGOVER

Waking in a hammock is difficult at the best of times. The quick word with yourself not to move violently or make any sudden roll is paramount to safety. Waking up with another person in a hammock is a whole other level, especially when the other is Jenny. I open my eyes and she has her eyes open and is staring back at me. We have no cover, and we are in our clothes from the night before, a dry sticky sensation in my mouth, a nervousness would be one explanation, the after effects of dehydration through sweating kilos during the night another. The lack of fluids in my body make my lips smack and my mouth furry.

I go to speak and she places her index finger near my lips.

"Don't ruin it," she whispers. "Say something that isn't annoying."

I pause, trying not to say something stupid, unfunny, and a means to deflect attention away from what I am genuinely thinking.

"How did we manage to get into the hammock together?" I ask because it seems like we have achieved the human equivalent of moulding water into a sphere.

"Timing," she says. "Can you not remember anything?"

I try to throw my mind back to the evening before, but go too far and pull a face like I've looked on the bottom of my shoe and found I have stepped in every type of animal excrement available in the countryside including a badger.

"I see it is all coming back, thanks," Jenny tells me.

"I was remembering the party, not us. I have a vague memory of laughing and taking a jump."

"That was the first attempt. You will probably notice a bruised hip soon enough. And ego."

"I crashed right out," I tell her, and realise I am actually speaking normally to a woman I like who is pushed up against me, her face not inches from mine, half-wrapped up in a canvas sheet wearing smelly sweaty clothes a man who has fallen in to a barrel of piss would refuse.

"This isn't particularly romantic," I add, redundantly. "And as much as I'd like to stay in this position for a long time yet, having flash backs to weekends at festivals where I didn't wash, change clothes, or use deodorant for five days, I do actually need the loo, and even if you insisted, I am never getting into golden showers."

"On the count of three," Jenny says. "We'll sit up. Together or we will fall. Ready?"

"Yes," I say, sitting up, feeling the hammock move in ways Newton couldn't have predicted, my legs, as I swing them over the side of the hammock, lifting up like I've lent too far back on a swing, and toppling out of the back, landing on my neck, but the momentum of my idiocy taking my ankles and legs over my head so I do a backward roll into a rucksack, which seems to be filled with pointy rocks, and a bush made entirely of Australian nettles, which are like normal nettles but sharper, stingier and designed by nature to rip through my flesh and sit there pouring poison into my muscles.

"Fuck," I say with a level of restraint I have never shown while in a mildly grumpy morning mood.

"Count of three," Jenny says, sitting up quickly from the heap she has made on the floor. "You total tit," she adds correctly.

But I have no time to answer or defend myself as I have spotted a large white mass on the camp floor, like Moby Dick has fallen from the sky and squished itself into a ball. And while what I assume is its mouth is hairier than I had imagined from reading the book, I quickly realise that it is in fact the curled up form of Gaz, next to the fire, and completely naked. And that isn't a jaw line but the sight of his hairy arse crack.

"Gaz? You ok?" I ask, immediately regretting the decision as he rolls over to face me revealing his bulbous boobs and hairy nipples. His large drinker's gut flops to the floor in such a way as to reveal to me, and anyone in proximity, his monumentally hairy cock and balls. I watch, fascinated as he climbs to his feet.

"Yeah, I'm good," he says. "Cracking night that was," he adds while for a reason only known to him, checking the state of his scrotum with his right hand by shaking it all violently.

He looks around, turns, takes a step away from me.

"There they are," he says, as he bends down as if touching his toes to pick up his pants.

David Attenborough could not create a voiceover to make this an interesting insight into the animal kingdom nor sooth my eyes with his dulcet tones as Gaz does a passable impression of the backside of a cat.

I stand and walk as Gaz hops around, nakedly, trying to get his left leg into the appropriate hole of his underpants, every bit of him flapping up and down, the noises like a one-man band busking on the street with instruments all made out of meat.

He falls, landing like a cockroach on his back and chooses to remain lying down to pull his briefs over his feet and up and covering his modesty. To celebrate his success he belches. I would not want to share a house with him.

"I think I might still be pissed," he says in a way that doesn't seem to come as a shock.

I look down at him as I pass, avoiding the desire to look into his belly button.

"To be honest, Gaz, since the age of about thirteen, I don't think you have ever technically been sober."

I walk to the toilet and look at the rest of the camp, everyone out cold, sleeping in ways that are not natural, half in and half out of hammocks, young pop star is asleep under his, a face full of teddy bear. The smell of booze so strong I half expect a rain of birds to fall from the trees above as they pass out through fume inebriation. The camp smells like a pub's carpet. I glance at Katherine because I can't stop myself. She is asleep, face down, eyes puffy from crying, her mouth wide open, and I can see right up her large nostrils. This used to be cute. Jonny boy is nowhere to be seen, hopefully unconscious in a puddle of his own vomit and being live streamed to the world at large on a twenty-four hour feed.

I sit inside the hut they call the Dunny, trying to wake up, trying to figure out where I am and where I stand. The show is over, we are going home today. It is like being on a summer camp and the last day has arrived and I still haven't told the girl I like that I do in fact like her. I may have shown off, definitely said idiotic nonsense in the hope she understands, might even have made fun of her to show through some childish reverse psychology that I am so into her it hurts. But this is it, this is where I need to say something, to tell her, to tell Jenny that not only do I want to hang out away from here, I actually think I need to, that the idea of not meeting up scares me, that not having her about is going to cause me a fair bit of anguish. But I don't know if this is because we have just spent quite a few day together and you get that weird bond through isolation and lack of choice, or that it is something real, something worthwhile. Maybe I am rebounding again, and she fits the mould of what I'd like: female and not repulsed by me, maybe it is all just a sham. But I don't think it is. But then I don't even know where she lives, what she will be doing, how her life is away from here. I know I want to find out. Would she like to find out about me? Why the hell would she? All she would find out is that I am boring, that I do nothing but hang around in pubs, not drinking to the point of unconsciousness anymore, but continuing on with the moaning and complaining. She did sleep in my hammock again and I don't think it was because she was afraid that Gaz might sneak in naked to hers. At least I don't think it was that. She must like me. It can't all be in my head.

I look up and stare at the door, which isn't a door but a heavy curtain made up to look like a very old, worn red and black blanket.

"You've got to tell her," I say, to me, out loud, like a weirdo.

"But what if she laughs in my face?" I ask myself, again out loud, as if I am two people, and one of me has a voice of reason.

"Look at the facts," I continue out loud.

But before I can answer myself, or highlight how my own argument and ideas are wrong by having myself point out the flaws in my own logic and ridicule myself for thinking that way, I hear a voice, not in the weird, oh shit, I am mentally ill, hearing voices in my head way - God isn't telling me to educate the world in his ways, or that I am his son and nor is he pointing me to a burning bush. There is an actual recognisable voice.

"Are you alright in there?" Bob says from outside.

"What?" I say, having heard him perfectly well and trying to start an idea that I haven't been talking to myself like a man staggering through the high street off his tits on Spice.

189

"Are you alright? You seem to be talking to someone, or yourself. But if you could get to the end of that quickly, as I need the toilet. To be sick."

Fuck you, Bob. I think. But make a decision to tell Jenny, as I stand from the plank and pull my trousers up in a way Gaz can only dream of.

THE PRESENTERS : DAY 11 : MORNING BLUES

The Welshman is pacing, the news he needs and wants should be here already. Jonny is standing close, relaxed, leaning against a post. He is a cigarette away from being the Marlboro man. Molly assumes he is playing a jazz tune in his head. Jonny also has his phone.

"Anything?" The Welshman asks again, as he has every minute for the last hour.

Jonny shakes his head, smiling down at his phone, on which he is reading the news. The papers splashed the whole show, the feedback to the change in channel, the idea that a satellite station picked up last night's episode as a one-off to give the baying public what they wanted, a send-off for the stupid people they love, hate and absolutely do not admire.

Jonny had been smart enough to stay close to sober, to stay out of shot and to be kind to Katherine, calm, caring and considerate. He made sure all of his positives were in the cut that was broadcast on a channel that had been set up to broadcast right-leaning news, but had, upon appalling viewing figures, simply thrown any old nonsense onto the schedule to find an audience that wasn't Mr and Mrs. Retired, well-off and hateful.

The papers were raving, but then the guy Jonny had contacted, owned all the papers too.

"Have you seen the figures?" The Welshman says, reading the same article as Jonny.

Molly had read the papers already and she had a memory so didn't need to read them again. She knew they were fake, an exaggeration to build publicity. But even the real ones would have been huge. The biggest show they had ever had, which, she knew wasn't saying much, as they only had to beat the breakfast chat show hosted by a man who disliked most things and those he didn't he hated. He loved to describe in great detail why we should all hate like him.

Millions had come across to see the party, to see the famous get drunk and show themselves to be just like normal folk when drunk: loud, unfunny, tearful, aggressive and above all absolutely embarrassingly stupid. Car crash TV at its finest and she was hosting with a man, The Welshman, who she truly now believed to have evolved into one big ball of spittle spewing delusion.

"Millions," The Welshman says. "Millions watched it. No one complained. The millions who want this, who have bought into my vision, they paid cash to subscribe and watch the party. I knew it was a brilliant idea. I knew it. Celebrities, alcohol, inhibitions gone and you have absolute TV nirvana."

She is impressed with his vocabulary, which means he is repeating someone else's words.

"They have to pick us up, they have to let us go on, don't they?" he asks in welsh desperation.

"If those figures are right then they would have made some money. The phone in to have messages come up on the banner at the bottom. That was a good move. Insults, jokes sent in at a pound a pop and shown in a loop. That would have made them money," Jonny says glowing in the knowledge that it was his idea.

"What do you think?" The Welshman asks, the excitement building like horse after horse keeps winning on his eight bet accumulator.

"I think we have a shot."

"So when is the call?"

"Soon," Jonny soothes, and she is impressed with just how cool he can be.

But she has to think, because she has read the papers, and while her relationship with the Welshman is still news, it is on the inside pages, in a small column of gossip and tat. No one cares right now about the break up, they all want to know about if the show continues. The old school mainstream TV is being slated by those who think its morals are all Victorian age and need to be replaced. The show is a new wave of reality, torture TV or embarrassment TV is what they are calling it. Her life and career tied to this.

She knows it is a minority with a loud voice, a minority that will spend money, will watch the show, will want someone to get hurt or die. A minority in the sixty million people in the UK, but ten percent is six million and if they all spend money, then they are the audience that counts. Principles and morals be damned. She knows this. They know this, the Welshman and Jonny. They don't need to be liked by the masses, they need to be liked by enough who will part with their money. Those that write and complain, won't pay to watch and therefore will never see.

She is stopped from thinking by Jonny answering his phone. The Welshman stands, staring, trying to listen in as Jonny nods and says nothing. He listens for a long time, to the point where she thinks the call has ended and he is pretending to listen as he thinks of something to say.

"I understand," Jonny says like a British Gangster in the Italian Job, the sinister smile of a classically trained thespian who has cashed in on roles below them. "But it is an acceptable amount."

He presses the screen on his phone and turns to The Welshman who may as well be panting like a dog ready for a chewy treat.

"Here is the deal," Jonny says, still playing the king pin. "They will take the show, to its conclusion – they made a lot of money last night, and their lawyers say there is no comeback from the behaviour of our stars, they signed contracts to be filmed and their actions are their own responsibility. But, and there is always a but, they need controversy, no peaceful prime time show for the oldies and boring. They want conflict and they want torture. But not on me. I get to win."

Molly stares at this guy, this absolutely vain piece of human that will cheat himself to victory and call it a triumph, glowing in the adulation that does not really exist but is a fabrication created by the production team.

"In return," he says, pointing at The Welshman, "you get creative control. You run the show. They like your ideas this series, but they want you to crank them up. They want real pressure applied. They need to hear your ideas for that in the next couple of hours. They are sure they will be good, they just want to check. And when that is done, the end of the show is broadcast on pay TV to the hundreds of thousands who have paid their money to be part of TV history."

She looks at The Welshman and knows he is on the verge of tears of joy. She doesn't know what to do. She can quit, but that makes her a loser, that takes her away, means she is no longer on production, no longer getting the money. But she has to leave, she knows that.

"One more thing," Jonny says. "Katherine gets to stay unless I get bored or she becomes annoying or just a burden. The love interest is always a good angle, particularly with my wife there. But if I miscalculate, she goes out on a vote, a bit of sadness from me, promises to meet up in the real world and so on and so forth."

Molly cannot stand this man, his playing, his games and his manipulation. A man with a natural ability honed to perfection in his world of vices based on Machiavelli.

"Are there any more demands?" Molly asks, hoping to hit a sneer that might make just the smallest of dents in his shield of superiority.

Jonny turns to her, smiling his smile, like he has been asked a question he doesn't want on a live broadcast to the nation, but he has an answer all the same.

"You need to play along and just be you," Jonny says, the smooth gone, the bark in evidence. "The whole relationship breakdown angle you are playing, and admittedly playing well, needs to stop. There is a bonus in it for you, and the papers will back off and not try to assassinate your character nor dig up secrets that would embarrass you and your family. Your innocence is your selling point. They break that and you are worthless."

"I don't have any skeletons," Molly says, knowing she does.

Jonny smiles like Laurence Olivier playing a Nazi.

"Yes, you do, and they are ready to go to print."

The Welshman looks at Molly, then to Jonny.

"They don't involve you," Jonny says, and she knows that technically that is correct. "So play along, dear, and all is good."

DAY 11 : STILL MORNING : BUZZING

I am full of confidence, I am strutting, I should be accompanied by a Bee Gees soundtrack, although definitely not while wearing a white, silk and flared cat suit, that would be a difficult thing to pull off with cool outside of the late seventies and New York.

It is in my head, the words, the honesty, it isn't a deep unveiling of my heart and emotion, it is just a simple question, an aside, a polite, friendly enquiry into whether or not, regardless of where Jenny may live, if she would like to meet up and hang out and chat and remain in contact after we have left this hell hole, which should, all things going well, happen today.

Bob rushed into the dunny looking as ill as a man who has drunk like a twenty-year old and forgotten that he is in fact much closer to sixty with a body that will not recover quickly, forgive his excess, nor play along with his insistence he is only feeling a little rough. I'd say holding his face over the hole in the wood, getting a wiff of the bucket below, and inhaling what would be the equivalent of the fumes emanating from a music festival portaloo on the last day of a month long party, would be enough to trigger throwing up anything from his stomach, large and small intestines and possibly powerful enough to force bones from his feet out of his massive blathering gob.

But he is not my concern.

I walk through the camp seeing that Jenny is still lounging in my hammock, and I take this as the jungle equivalent of a girlfriend wearing one of my t-shirts to sleep in, possibly a branded one that cost too much and I have worn into a frayed mess, or a previous favourite that I ruined by spilling bleach on it. She is in my hammock and she is looking at me and smiling. I am not imagining this, although I do quickly check to see if I am trailing toilet paper on my foot, haven't pissed all over my trousers, or have my fly open and a bush of pubic hair is sticking out making it look like I have a vagina. None of these things seem to be the case so I can only conclude she is smiling at me coming back, although I have been told I walk funny, like an elastic chimpanzee who has just stood up after inhaling the entire contents of a three-foot bong.

But I talk myself out of the negatives and into the positives. She is in my hammock, she hasn't legged it and gone on a massive jog of shame out my front door, down the road in bare feet, holding her high-heels upon realising that there is actually no future in this relationship formed over shots of tequila and a conversation nobody can thankfully remember.

The camp is stirring, everyone awake, everyone a shade paler than normal, nobody moving quickly, everyone trying to search through the previous night's escapades in an attempt to create excuses for things they said, actions they took and embarrassing ideas they spouted as fact. The looks they all perform, glancing left and right, hoping for a smile from another human, a nod and that tacit agreement that all was well. Gaz has his clothes back on and is sat sipping coffee, although each mouthful provokes a blowing out of his cheeks and a belch and a deep breath. He is very practised and doesn't throw up over the fire. He gives me the thumbs up, I presume telling me he is Okay, and assuming that I actually give a fuck.

I have slowed my pace like a wimp, I know this, but I haven't taken a bizarre and unnatural detour at the last minute and looked like a fool with the courage of a member of the Wizard of Oz team, that man dressed up as a lion or possibly the man dressed up in metal. Maybe a combination of the whole lot, including the drug-taking, sexually deviant Umpa Lumpas.

Jenny has sat up, still smiling, leaving me space to sit down, and I try to remember what exactly I said to her last night. Have I bribed her? Have I promised something I clearly don't have? Have I agreed to marry her or something equally stupid in the pathetic attempt to get her naked?

194

This feels off because it quite frankly never happens. I'm a slow burner usually, women have to build a resilience to my nonsense rather than simply accepting me as I am, unless of course they are drunk, in which case I am hilarious as is anything, anybody and any joke. Alcohol, that great humour equaliser.

I sit next to her.

"What's going on?" I ask as soon as I sit, and feel confident enough that the slightest alteration in my bodyweight placement won't result in me doing another backflip over the back edge.

"What do you mean?" she asks, smiling in a way that makes me certain she has a whole conversation set up that will give her the greatest pleasure through watching me squirm. "Nothing," she says in that way women can but men can't. Nothing, a word that means, from her mouth, that everything is meant but you clearly can't understand and this fact is giving me great pleasure, and clearly highlighting my intellectual superiority.

"Nothing?" I repeat while making it into a question and somehow making me sound like an even bigger idiot than before.

Her response is a smile that has changed imperceptivity from friendly to condescending in the most lovely of ways.

I wait for a second because I seem to remember that socially this is a prerequisite in these situations, or it could be that I am seventy-five percent coward and don't have the guts. I take a deep breath.

"Look," I say, and she is staring at me now with a grin that her face cannot physically make any bigger. "Today, it all ends, although they haven't actually told us exactly when or how," I add, in a deliberate and conscious effort to avoid the words I am actually trying to say. She grins away enjoying it all.

"Look," I say.

"You've said that already," she informs me, although I don't think it was helpfully.

I do like her smile though, I think, and smile myself, which she counters with an eyebrow manipulating quizzical response, and I am, in terms of an ability to hint at feeling through the subtle movement of facial muscles, so far out of my depth, I should be curled up in a defensive ball.

"Look," I say again, before adding, "Yes, I know I have said that bit before, it is the next bit that I haven't. I was thinking, me and you, after this has finished, today, although we don't know when etc etc etc, if we, or you, as I would definitely be happy to, if you, with me, obviously, would like to, you know, kind of, meet up, sort of thing."

And she just keeps smiling at me, but somehow altering that smile to mean a million things in response to me being unable to ask a simple bloody question.

She nods, which is a good sign, although it could mean that she just understands my question I have hidden beneath too many words of irrelevance.

"Well," she says, leaving too long a pause, way too long as it happens as the whole camp turns to the opening where the path comes into camp.

"Good Morning!" The Welshman, either high on adrenaline or methamphetamine, bellows as he walks into camp throwing his arms out wide.

He is accompanied by the weirdly gurning Molly and worse of all, the smooth smile of Jonny boy. Bollocks, I think. I turn back to Jenny and she is staring at them and not me.

"Lost the moment?" I ask, imagining I look like a helpless puppy.

She nods, not taking her eyes from the three.

"We'll get back to it," she says, which I take as a promise as she squeezes my hand. In other circumstances this could be seen as patronising, but here, like this, I take as a definite sign she is in to me. Probably. Eighty percent sure. Or maybe a little less. A good sign, anyway, almost certainly. Although I will be talking myself out of this conclusion in the next ten minutes.

THE PRESENTERS : DAY 11 : NO IDEA WHAT IS HAPPENING

The Welshman is mad, Molly thinks, and knows, at the very least, he is definitely out of control. The Welshman has clapped and whooped and paced up and down interspersed with the occasional skip. He has not, she notes, yet jumped up and tapped his heels together, but this is more to do with it being beyond his physical capabilities rather than him thinking it inappropriate.

"We are back on," he shouts, "Back in the game."

"What are the viewing figures?" Molly asks, in an attempt to bring about some semblance of normality to this absolute shower.

"Probably Three-hundred thousand," Jonny tolls them. "Definitely not the millions claimed."

"Doesn't matter the number," The Welshman shouts. "It matters the money, and these people are paying to watch and then paying to text. This is the beginning of the next move. We are pre-empting the future,"

196

The Welshman adds, oblivious to the fact that TV shows have been doing this for years, that their TV show, the one they are currently doing, has been doing this for years.

"Let's go tell them," The Welshman sings.

DAY 11 : MORNING : HOPEFULLY OVER

"I have news," The Welshman says, "news you will all appreciate. So sit down, the mics are off, no recording for this moment in time, so open discussion is welcome."

Jonny slips off and walks to Katherine, he puts his arm around her shoulder and whispers something, something almost certainly made up, thought out and a tool to manipulate the here and now. Molly sees Jenny watching too, and that small shake of her head, more at herself and the days gone by than for Katherine. It is horrible when you are knowing.

"There has been a change of direction," The Welshman says, short of a shout and so full of happiness. "The contracts stand, but we have moved to a pay-TV channel."

We all stare at him, everyone knowing about contracts and the reasons we are here.

"What does that mean?" I ask, sounding like a spokesman.

"It means we are breaking with the normal format, in a way, while keeping with it in others. Now, you are free to leave but that would be breaking contract and a probable loss of earnings, legal stuff, you know, difficult things. If you stay, and decide to be paid, then we are going to speed things up a little, eliminate more people. We don't have as many days left as we normally would."

I can tell from his words he has only just been made aware of this and from here on in, he has not a single clue, which is only a slight downgrade on his normal way of being.

"We are about to go on a journey. Two groups competing, winner stays on, losers go out. And our viewers," he lies, "have chosen the captains. On the right, and what will be the yellow team, is captained by Ben and Jenny – our love birds for the season, and on the left, we have Jonny and Katherine, our mature lovely couple who are doing things right, unlike some, who are doing it wrong, on the left wearing red. Obviously not right now, but boiler suits will be provided."

"Who picks the teams?" Bob asks, way too urgently for my liking. I think I see a sweat break on his forehead.

"I choose Bob," I say. "Team bonding is important."

"Not a chance," Bob tells me. "Not a chance."

197

"You are all going to be selected by the team leaders," Molly says in a way that suggests she has recently been told of her pet dog's death. "A creative decision," she adds, looking at The Welshman and having decided to give up on any form of pretend respect. The Welshman, being The Welshman, misses the whole thing and claps.

"Let's get to this," he says, despite not having really explained what the hell is going on.

It is like some weird reverse of lining up at school and the best kids getting picked first and the unsporting, total ineptitudes standing waiting for it all to end and being selected on the team who picked second. Only here, as team co-captain, every single person is actively seeking not to be selected by me. Were we all able to select our squad, I would be alone – as I think even Jenny would prefer a couple of days with her soon to be ex-husband than me. They are all in-it-to-win-it and associating with an absolute arse clown like myself is a sure fire way of not only being eliminated but being eliminated through a long, slow painful deconstruction of your own reality and sanity. So I can't really blame them, although I know I will. As do they.

Jenny and I are dressed in yellow boiler suits and Jonny and Katherine in theirs of red. They are surrounded by campmates, all trying to weasel their way in to affection. I, on the other hand am stood with Jenny, who keeps looking over to where the cool people stand. We look absurd, and the boiler suits are just that little bit too small, so we are both standing to avoid appearing to have a serious case of the camel toes.

"Who should we select?" I ask, not because I want an answer, but because I want to give the air of someone who might actually give a shit.

"I don't think it really matters," she tells me without looking. "Every single one of us is void of skill and talent in these circumstances-"

"And many others too," I add, "mainly involving light entertainment."

"Bear Ghrylls we are not. And I am working under the assumption this is rigged for Jonny to be winner, and Katherine to be the new first lady in all his publicity. Look at me, a mildly attractive middle-aged man and my trophy girlfriend you all saw me woo on live TV. That will get him access to all manner of shows."

She is right, I have had much the same thought myself.

"I think our only option is to build a team that could, should, and really will try, to cock all this up for him."

Jenny shakes her head.

"That would take effort, Ben. Desire and some form of plan beyond saying stuff to irritate, and being mean. I am once again trapped in this man's game of life and I will, as always, be left the loser while he parades around victorious having cheated his way to the win. And it is all about the win."

I think about this, as I have already thought about this, and know she is right, know we are being set-up to fail, to be the abject joke in comparison to the intelligent, articulate organised one.

"Who do you think they would want? And then we can steal them."

"He won't want or need anyone. He has Katherine, and he will play the white knight to her damsel, and the supporting cast will be there just to pay homage to his brilliance. They are all already there, mainly, I think, not because of Jonny's brilliance but because not a single one of them can bear the thought of having to spend a full two days in your close company."

"I do need to work on my first impressions," I explain, trying, for whatever reason to sound posh.

"No, you need to take just a little edge off – not much, I'll be honest – but their reaction to you is about their insecurities and failings. That façade of fake chirpiness, and intellectual brilliance because they have achieved some type of fame. No, Ben, I initially thought you were a total tit, then discovered you were in fact, actually a complete tit. But somehow, and in some way, I like you. I would have hated it here without you. Whatever that means."

I look at her, and she is being serious. I feel the anger she has though, that anger at someone who has interfered too much in her life and who has influenced decisions and direction. I think the feeling is a recognizable bond through melancholy.

"And me you," I say, as close to being emotionally honest and open as I can comfortably be, and that is not comfortable at all.

"Two days," she tells me despite me knowing. "Two days as a group working against the other. And it is rigged in their favour."

I am not letting this go.

"Rigged because they think we will play by the rules. I have absolutely no intention of doing so. I am, despite myself, going to make a promise here, and tell you, for what it is worth, that I am going to put in everything I have to try and destroy whatever they try."

She looks at me, sad eyes, but a hint of a thanks in a small wry smile.

"I know it won't work," I tell her, honestly, "but I just need to have tried, need to have had a go at smashing that public school face into the ground."

"He went to a comp," she informs me, showing up my prejudices.

"What?"

"Normal comp, where he was king. He wasn't educated into being an insufferable cock, he was born that way and just perfected the skills as he went along. In another life he is the world's number one Window salesman."

I look at her, disbelieving.

"It gives him the right to be a man of the people. Made his way on the hard road. Fails to mention he went to a comp because his ridiculously rich parents thought pumping money into his education would be a waste of money. They just bought him expensive stuff."

I can say nothing to that.

They are actually lined up, in a row. They don't have their backs to the outside wall of a red brick primary school built in the seventies because there isn't one about. But the set-up is the same. Every one of them has tried to edge toward the red team to the point where we, the yellow team, have had to shuffle across so we can actually see them. They learned this routine when they were seven, and have had no reason to modify in their adult life so we all fall back on what was successful before. It's like watching parents file into a classroom, they all, to a one, go and sit where they sat as kids. The front filled with the eager beavers and the back row rammed with dickheads.

Red to select first.

"Kieran," Jonny boy says, logically. A tall strong bloke who keeps his mouth shut and doesn't aim to be king. Good call.

"Racheal," Jenny says.

"What?" I ask, incredulously.

"I need someone to talk to that isn't you," she tells me, which is a fair point, and quite frankly she is no bother to the point I'd forgotten she was here.

"Bob," Katherine says, and Bob, bless him, is so happy I think he may write her into his will.

"I can see their plan," I say loudly, pretending this is for Jenny. "They are going for male muscle, but forgetting that these tasks will almost certainly need some level of intelligence."

200

They look at me and smile as if they know something I don't, which they do, quite a lot I'd think, I am, to my own admission, for example, totally shit at identifying flags.

"Gaz," I say.

Jenny looks at me.

"I need someone to speak to as well, that isn't you and your banter about girly stuff, like feelings and emotions and make-up."

"Anthony," Jonny says, and their team is complete, leaving us to tut and roll our eyes and say, "Chelsey."

"Dream team," I say.

No one high fives and I am left with my hand in the air.

I hand out the boiler suits and we collect our supplies. We have a Land Rover to fill, and a map to follow. We have two hours to get to our first check point. Who arrives second loses rations.

"There will be," The Welshman says like a gameshow villain, "Challenges and surprises along the way."

We are five people looking like large bananas packing tents, sleeping bags, and clothes onto the outside of a yellow Land Rover. I can't help but look at the red team, in their well-fitting boiler suits as if they were made by a tailor, and the extreme efficiency with which they work. Jonny ordering in the most pleasant of ways and his team, like a well-drilled group of worker ants, acting in unison to pack up their vehicle and belongings in the shortest time. Their Land Rover looks like it is about to go on a month's safari in the Serengeti, while ours looks like we are about to partake in the first of many trips down to the local tip because we are clearing out a recently deceased hoarder's house.

"Shotgun," Gaz shouts, getting into the passenger seat, not realising it is a three door vehicle and he'll need to get out to let someone in. I am not working with genius.

"Ok," I say, in the role of team captain, clapping my hands for attention for the simple fact I don't have a bell. They all stop what they are doing, which is mainly milling about and avoiding work, and listen to me.

"Here is the plan," I tell them. "Jenny you drive. Chelsey, if you sit in the back, where the suspension is best, which will make it so much easier on your breasts and reduce the level of distraction for male eyes. Racheal, if you sit in the back too, with the map, giving us directions and having full responsibility for getting us to where we need to be, and are thus our de facto scapegoat. And Gaz, if you could sit in the front, silently, and try not to be car sick, get naked, stare at boobs, or touch anything on the dash, that would be ace, while I will also be in the back next to the window, trying my best not to engage in eye contact or conversation. Are we agreed?"

They nod, all of them, as if I have said something intelligent, which freaks me out a bit.

"Okay then, let's get in?"

Jenny drives us up to the starting line, we are two metres from the red team in their red Land Rover, which has all its surface covered with things we chose not to bring, didn't realise we could bring, or simply had no way of figuring out how to attach to a car. Everything we have, we essentially threw on the roof and tied down as best we could with elasticated rope. We now look like a double decker, the second floor being made up of an out of control washing basket consisting mainly of socks.

Jonny is driving, and he is, like some absolute tool at the lights in a souped up hatchback, probably made by Peugeot, with body kit, rear fin, and weirdly angled wheels, revving his engine like we are about to start a drag race.

"He is just wasting petrol," I say, like a middle-aged dad with no sense of fun.

Gaz takes a sip on his steel water flask and gasps, breathing out with a rasp.

Jenny throws him a look of contempt.

"Just how much gin did you steal at the party?"

"Not enough," Gaz replies in a way that indicates his larynx has just undergone a chemical burn.

He offers his flask around and the pungent smell of ethanol fills the cab.

"It is the morning," Racheal says.

"Which is why I am sipping. I'll save you some for the afternoon."

We sit in silence for a few more seconds, possibly contemplating life and how absurd it is to be trapped in a car with these people, how Gaz is able to operate daily while being drunk, how I have been put in charge and just how we are going to manage the next forty-eight hours being trapped so close to each other. I hope everyone has packed deodorant.

"I don't think we are going to win," Chelsey says breaking the silence and rubbing her chin like she is a Greek philosopher.

We all look at each other, one to the next, like we have to chink every other glass at a celebration, but instead of expensive crystal flutes we have only our sad eyes and knowing nods. Eventually we look at our rivals through the windows, all of us hoping Gaz doesn't start licking them, we see their serious faces, their concentration, their absolute eagerness to accelerate away and become champions of driving a car to another place in a quicker time than us. Their zoned in, competitive edge of a single determined effort to be the best by getting there first is filling the very air in their car.

"No," I say, "we almost certainly won't win, not in real terms, not in the classical sense of being first, but, and I don't want to sound bitter or twisted – or, actually seeing how you are looking at me now, I should say, more bitter and twisted – I think we, as a group, need to leave our mark. We are doomed to failure, in the games that lie ahead, but I think, and it pains me to say it, and this may be used in the future as a motivational speech by coaches and trainers at the highest level of sport, and I'm thinking World Cups and World Championships, we have to make an effort to simply make it as difficult and humiliating for the red team as we possibly can. I am not about to be humiliated and bullied out of this by a group of tools in red boiler suits."

Another silence ensues and I am worried I have picked a team with serious mental processing issues.

"You are actually saying you are going to try?" Racheal finally asks, seeing the possible flaw in my argument.

"In my own special way, yes. I am."

"I'll stay involved just to see that happen," she tells me smiling.

"There will be, without a doubt, a song in it for you. The ballad of Ben," I say.

"The boisterous yet boring bellend," she finishes.

And they laugh, at me, and it is cool. I feel a small moment of team bonding, a sense of being a father figure to abject failures, like a man taking on the boys from borstal. I probably should have a word with myself.

"Here we go," The Welshman shouts and jumps up in the air in front of us, and as he comes down, he moves a mini flag about, in the way a scantily dressed woman does in every single one of the ten million editions of The Fast and The Furious. I am sure I am not the only person who finds this weird, although Anthony is possibly reimagining the scene in his head with The Welshman wearing a two-piece bikini.

The red team accelerate away as Jenny turns the ignition key and starts the engine.

She slips the car into first, very smoothly I should say, and we don't exactly accelerate away but more move forward as if we are in neutral and the world is simply revolving under us.

"Slowly, slowly catchy monkey," Gaz says and giggles to himself like a pissed tramp.

"Where should we be going?" I ask Racheal.

"Well, to start with," Racheal explains, looking at the map, "it would be quite a good start to simply go forward significantly quicker."

Jenny turns around and stares at Racheal.

"She is making a good point," I say in my mediator role, "The red team have, it seems, already disappeared over the horizon, while we, or specifically you, have developed a phobia of the accelerator pedal."

"Do you want to drive?" Jenny asks me in a way a wife barks at a complaining husband who is in the passenger seat, much like Gaz is, because he is half-pissed and it would be illegal for him to do so.

"You keep going," I say, and within five minutes of angsty silence the awkwardness has dissipated and Jenny finally puts the car into top gear.

Gaz cheers so she slows down.

The drive is endless on roads that are dry red dust. Luckily the red team are so far in front that the dust they have thrown up has long since settled by the time we pass through. There is a mark on the map we have been given and it would seem there is only one road leading that way and as we are on it, no navigation is necessary. Racheal really landed on her feet there.

Normally a radio and its music would fill the voids of empty space where no conversation takes place, only the radio has been removed from this car and replaced with a large speaker, a speaker that has mercifully remained silent of all noise and specifically a loud booming Welsh voice spouting self-reverential tripe.

We are motoring along at a safe speed - safe for animals because we are in no way possessing enough momentum to knock even a pug down in a head-on collision - in silence, staring out at the scenery, which is quite frankly repetitive and boring. A large flat area reaching to the horizon of red-brown dirt, dehydrated to the extreme, an occasional tree, and sometimes, in the distance what appear to be large areas of yellow as the greenery has been starved of all water. We keep on trundling forward, not even a film crew in sight. We are alone, the cameras inside the car watching us at all times and seeing five people bored out of their minds on a long road trip to parts unknown.

No one has dared suggest a game, nor made any jokes. I fancy a nap.

"Hello," a voice booms from the dashboard, Welshly, loudly, annoyingly and, for Jenny, distractingly. We veer off road to the left as Jenny shouts a rude word at The Welshman, she compensates too much, and we swerve back the way we came, across the road and out in to the rough on the other side. Tyres on one side of the car lifting from the ground. We all scream. We bump and swerve several times more as Jenny swings the wheel clockwise then anticlockwise with increasingly less panic as we finally right ourselves and head in a straight line on the road once more. It appears that Australia doesn't need tarmac, just tightly compacted dust that provides absolutely no grip when the driver freaks out and thinks they are playing an arcade game with unlimited credits, but flies up and covers any human in a thick layer of orange if you take just the merest of missteps. Knowing Australia this dust is probably poisonous, or alive and poisonous, or most likely angry, alive and poisonous and hungry for mildly flabby British flesh.

We are all holding on for dear life to handles, seats and doors, while Chelsey is holding her breasts, for fear, I imagine, that the violent bouncing might drag them down too far and result in unwanted sagging.

"What the hell do you want?" Jenny snarls at the microphone.

I do not believe this is the opportune moment to mention that The Welshman isn't behind the gauze but that it is radiowaves that make it appear he is hiding behind it. Although I too would punch the speaker to make myself feel better.

He laughs, booming and at that pitch that grates on my very soul.

"To break the monotony of your travels, we have our first little challenge. You will obviously realise you are late, much behind the red team, who have spent the last twenty minutes attempting the task at hand. They are nearing the end. So if you take the next left, travel a few hundred metres into the small wood, you will see the challenge and also your competition."

The speaker clicks and the voice is gone.

Jenny turns into the road, having slowed to the point just short of reversing, looked around to see if any traffic has miraculously appeared out of nowhere in the ten mile radius we can see, and even fucking indicating.

"Have you ever been fined for speeding?" I ask.

205

"You were the one who asked me to drive."

"You could have said, no, that is a bad idea as I am unable to make rational decisions above the speed of a beach ball rolling up hill on the back of a light breeze."

"We got here, didn't we?"

"Yes, just about a day behind them," I tell her pointing at the high-fiving, dancing, gleeful group of red boiler suits all skipping and leaping back into their Land Rover as we roll slowly down the track to an area with three trees and a pond.

The Red Land Rover passes us as we head to where they were, and I can't help but look and they are all chirping away, gabbing to one another and patting backs, and slapping hands and Bob, bless him, smiles in my face while raising his middle finger at me as they zoom on past.

We stop and Jenny puts on the handbrake.

"I thought you hadn't taken that off," Gaz says, and I laugh, as do Racheal and Chelsey until Jenny looks at us all and we stop and look at our shoes. Scary woman it seems is our Jen.

We step out of the Land Rover at which point The Welshman's voice booms out into the area we are in. There is a large number pad in front of us resting on a tree, it is the height of a ten-year old with large buttons and a screen. There is a TV next to it with The Welshman's face, and behind him is Molly, looking like a person who is trying, quite successfully, to hide at the back of a family photograph to avoid being in evidence they are associated with this group of wankers.

"The Red team have just left having completed the challenge," The Welshman says redundantly because we just watched them do it. "Next it is your team's chance to gain extra time. Whoever answers these questions correctly, and quickest gains ten minutes travel time. And I should add, Jonny got all the answers right and quickly. So here we go. It is a maths challenge, a calculator is not provided. Maths questions of increasing difficulty will appear on screen, all you have to do is input the answer you think correct into the keypad. All good? Here we go."

I look around the group and wonder if any of us has any qualification considered a pass in mathematics, or any aptitude or skill with numbers. My initial thought is abso-fucking-lutely not, but I think again and realise we are royally shafted, we need questions on irrelevant stuff, and obscure facts no one knows because no one cares. We'd be good at that.

The first number pops up which is a five with a small two sat on its right shoulder.

"What does that even mean?" Chelsey asks.

"Twenty five," Gaz answers and smashes the buttons on the pad.

The next comes, a six with the same little two. Gaz smashes the buttons and we move on as he is correct. This keeps going to fifteen and Gaz smashes the answer, going as far as imitating Sugar Ray Leonard by throwing quick jabs at the large numbers.

"Please don't do that," The Welshman begs, "You'll break it."

"Shut up," Gaz tells him, "and get to the difficult ones."

There follow a series of multiplication and division questions, all of which I would need a calculator and possibly the help of a teenager currently sitting A-level Statistics to answer, but Gaz, just nails them, one after the other to the point he is waiting impatiently for the next one to pop up on screen.

"Hurry up," he says, repeatedly and to my mind hilariously.

"What the hell is in his flask?" I ask Jenny quietly.

"The liquid spirit of Albert Einstein," She answers, staring as we all are at Gaz, wondering if he is that bloke from a Beautiful Mind, or possibly the basis for the film Rain man.

The questions keep coming, longer numbers multiplied and divided, added and subtracted. Not high level weird maths of quadratic equations, and calculating the external angle to a dodecahedron, that they teach you in school for no discernible reason other than to make you all look thick. Nor is it algebra where letters replace numbers so calculations allegedly become easier, when in fact, Mr. Maths teacher, they have just pushed mathematics into the realm of science fiction and induced a level of dyslexia I never thought I had. Gaz, nails them all, with minimum thought. He multiplied a three digit number by a two digit number without paper, pen, or even thought. Question asked, answer punched into an increasingly rough looking calculator. Then the questions stop.

"Hurry up," Gaz shouts. "Come on, I'm enjoying this."

"Erm, that, I'm afraid, is the end of that," Molly says, and I am sure I hear a splash of laughter and lightness in her tone that I have not detected in a while. "You have answered all the questions correctly, and in a time significantly shorter than the red team. Congratulations, you have gained the time and quite frankly Gaz, the accolades. You are free to leave and head to the next check point."

"Right, let's go then," Gaz tells us, walking as if he is a Sergeant Major in the Boer War with his chest puffed out anticipating a medal.

"Have you by any chance, in your life, at any point, being diagnosed as an idiot savant?" I ask.

"Mate," he tells me in a way that is justifiably patronising, "I have worked with numbers all my life. Snooker, darts, and over the last several years, to the detriment of my mental health, liver and more importantly bank balance, high stakes poker. Maths, and quick calculations are my life."

"They are indeed," I say.

"But if it makes you all feel a little better, and less inferior, I am, in the words of my lovely partner, incapable of functioning as a mature adult."

He takes his flask out, unscrews the lid, raises a toast to whatever is going on in his brain, and takes a gulp. He smacks his lips and rasps.

"Are you sure that isn't petrol?" I ask.

"A cocktail of dregs," he tells me. "Quite a kick to it and almost a perfect taste, although I admit the Tia Maria was a mistake."

He offers me some and I shake my head so he drinks the bit he believes I should have.

"I imagine not smoking until at least five minutes after sipping that is a rational choice for fear of exploding into a ball of flames."

Gaz nods, apparently because his drink has rendered his vocal chords into a vibrating mess of pain.

THE PRESENTERS : DAY 11 : MILD PANIC

"Well that was unexpected," Molly says, as she watches The Welshman stare at his monitor with his mouth open as if he has dropped into a catatonic state after a particularly poorly calculated dose of traquiliser.

He turns to her, closing his mouth but fixing the white teeth smile.

"Why did we not know about Gaz and maths?" he asks.

The production team stare at the floor.

They have gone mobile, a large camper van of media equipment is their base, and the two buses that follow provide accommodation. A six man crew and Molly and The Welshman sleeping in bunks on a bus like students on an overnight budget road trip.

They have cameras in the Land Rovers and cameras at the stop off points. They are staying well back, giving the contestants all the space they need to mess up and fight, and hopefully, for the ratings, have a full on mental breakdown requiring medical intervention. This would be great, and even better than any of them being attacked by a particularly irritated gang of rats, and finished off by a dingo, whatever the hell a dingo is.

"We can't account for anomalies," Molly says. "I would have said his skill lay in eating rancid animal parts without being sick and drinking more alcohol than the Balkan states combined without appearing to suffer any ill effects. Certainly didn't expect him to have the maths skills of a university lecturer in astrophysics."

She knew, but she hadn't known how good. She had seen Gaz live at an exhibition many years before where he had pulled off trick shots that looked impressive but were simple set ups with balls in specific places doing specific things on repeat. But he had hung out with the crowd after, and while she was wrapping up her local report, he had been talking to old ladies and they had challenged his intelligence. He had asked them to throw numbers at him and he answered them all, double quick, and the old ladies loved him more.

"Who did the research on Gaz?" The Welshman asks in a shout at the six crew members. They all look at each other, shaking their heads and shrugging.

"So, nobody? Brilliant. I have no doubt he'll be invited onto celebrity Countdown now and out-perform the woman who has a PhD in advanced number sorcery and has been chosen as she is the only woman with such a qualification who would still resemble a human when wearing a bikini."

Molly smiles at his lyrical play, something she hasn't heard in years.

Molly knows the games are rigged, or at least should be, in Jonny's favour. He is good at maths, and certainly proved it in the challenge, but the shame he will feel when he finds out that "drunken Snooker chav" as he called him, is a significant step up in the number scale.

"It doesn't matter," The Welshman says, fooling no one, but mainly himself in a way of convincing the plan will work out in the end. "We'll trip them up at the next one. How far are the red team in front?"

The geeky guy, who has embraced geek life fully in his blue shirt with short sleeves, pens in his top pocket ordered in the correct colour sequence of the visible part of the Electromagnetic Spectrum, and thick black rimmed glasses, presses some buttons, which Molly suspects are not connected to anything but give a hint of gravitas, and speaks.

"Technically they are five minutes behind," he says, "After Gaz's impressive display."

"Fuck!" The Welshman says as he has promised Jonny a win and an easy ride to that victory. "How's the big challenge going?"

"Still being set up. We don't have permission to use that much water out here. Short supply and we are in the wildfire season," Geek boy says in a way that seems to be impersonating the love child of Bill Gates' Personality and Stephen Hawking's voice

"I don't care. Get it set up, we'll just lie about the amount of water," The Welshman says as if he has become Prime Minister on the back of an overwhelming popular support of The United Kingdom of pricks.

"We need a couple more hours to get it ready," blue short geek man says, possibly concluding that his lunch times at school could have been better spent doing something other than playing with a twelve-sided die and embodying a character called, Argor the magnificent, the last of the fire stone killers from the Forest of Trees, or something that when heard by someone without a liking for putting on strange voices, translates as cock.

"A long drive, in this heat, all crammed in a car should set something off. And the second challenge they cannot win. Needs muscle. That'll put them back level pegging and the final challenge, well, there is no way we let Ben and Jenny's lot win."

Molly nods her head like all the others, compliant and submissive. Her chance, she thinks has gone. She needs to ride this out and come out scathed, scarred and maybe in good enough shape to hide out and recover, wait for people to forget and then step back into it all. She knows this is the last time she will be the other half, the female in a double act. She needs to ride this out, and she can, she knows that. If the papers and media go after her, and Jonny can see that is the way it goes, then there really is no way back. Support, or manipulation of facts in popular press makes or breaks. The Welshman had come back from devastation, having done what others were sent to local radio for doing, he did interviews, and papers manipulated stories and he came back rehabilitated. She knows she doesn't want the pain and humiliation. Maybe a simple, quiet leaving of the scene is all she can hope for now so she nods her head and The Welshman, she knows, thinks he has her until he doesn't need her anymore.

But she knows the next test, the one she helped construct, is not the easy win The Welshman wants.

DAY 11 : AFTERNOON : THE CAR IS HOT AND SWEATY

We drive, nice and steady, and Jenny is growing in confidence – the odometer hitting and staying at fifty. A nice cruising speed. Thankfully The Welshman's voice is absent from our travels. The windows are open, the air conditioning unit suspiciously unable to do its job, and the noise of the wind smashing around inside makes conversation impossible as every word spoken is blasted in to incomprehensibility by the speed we travel. Our hair is flying, we are relaxing, sat back, smiling as if we are all hippies high on acid and taking in the beautiful scenery that is just the weird side of real. The red Land Rover is ahead, probably by a mile, but we can see it and the dust they throw up, and we know all we need to do is follow. Jenny takes her eyes from the road, briefly, as her confidence isn't yet there and she smiles and it makes me feel happy. It also makes me feel as if we are two middle-aged parents taking our teenage children on a long drive to visit relatives at Christmas. These teenage children, who I should be disappointed in, who are not what I expected, but who are mine and I just have to go with it. They seem like teens who have started to experiment with personality and attempts at taking that step into adulthood. Teenagers who are doing this badly, the layabout drunk, the smiley happy performer and the sullen make-up girl, and they are led by me, the father, an abject failure of a grump who is just winging it as best he can. I look at them all and smile, and just like actual teenagers, they pull faces at my serene smile and attempts at bonding, and roll their eyes and are certainly thinking, Wanker. But stuff them, I am actually having fun.

The voice of The Welshman takes an edge off but not enough for a frown.

"Sorry to break your happy calm," he booms, clearly lying, which he does a lot to be fair. "The turning you require for today's second test is a couple of miles ahead. I hope you are ready."

We all look ahead in no real rush, like a chilled out cat who rules the roost and has opened an eye to see which human has entered his house. The red Land Rover is heading left, the dust riding up behind it in a plume. We will follow, get there later. For whatever reason I feel no need to rush.

"I doubt it will be maths based this time," I say out loud.

"Probably be a physical challenge," Jenny says, looking ahead, eyes flicking between the road and the speedo. It seems she is currently operating under the belief that if she keeps the needle exactly on fifty

211

then nothing bad can happen, like walking to school before an exam convinced if you don't step on a single crack then you will not fail. Logical illogic of the most absurd minds. I'm buying in.

We pull up into the clearing at the beginning of what appears to be a military assault course of walls, ropes, tunnels and the obligatory swampy water, mud mixture of hilarity. There are four people in camouflage milling around which brings no comfort as I believe they are there in the capacity of higher level life guards to protect us from suffocating to death on live TV, or to sew limbs back on after they have been ripped out at the socket on the zip slide covered in razor wire. We clamber out of our Land Rover and see the Red Team way down their track off to the left. I can hear them, all chatter and back and forth, but it doesn't sound harmonious, it sounds like they are having a proper debate about how the hell they are supposed to get over a sheer wall that has a single knotted rope.

"Hello," The Welshman booms from a speaker in the trees. "Welcome to the second challenge. This is more physical than cerebral, so Gaz the Wonder Man won't be of so much help." The Welshman laughs at this, while Gaz rolls his eyes and moulds his hand like he is carrying an invisible lead pipe and shakes it up and down.

"There is an assault course, on which you will need to work as a team. At the far end there are objects that you must bring back to this end. When here they must be constructed and upon completion you can leave. Any questions?"

"Yes," I say, looking into the water to my right. "There are alligators just over there."

"There are no alligators in Australia," The Welshman patronises, "Only Crocodiles."

"Vegetarian are they?"

"Let's hope we don't find out."

I look at the eyes above the water, the snout protruding too. He is, without a doubt looking at me, already weighing up who it would be best to eat, and realising that it is me as I offer the best flesh to bone ratio of the lot. Gaz would probably destroy its liver, Chelsey would essentially be chewing gum, and the other two are significantly smaller than me.

"Away you go," The Welshman says, laughing like a maniacal Blofeld about to blackmail the Earth because he has built a secret laser in space and no one noticed.

"Any ideas?" I ask.

Racheal steps back and to the side, looking all the way down our assault course. She looks and thinks and ponders and finally, to the point my stomach turns and hits full on butterfly, she smiles.

"Looks doable, nothing new, nothing out of the ordinary," she says. "Gaz, you stay here and whatever we bring back, you try and stick together or build or whatever will need to be done. Chelsey, you come with me, and you two," she says pointing at me and Jenny like we are the left overs and she needs to pretend to give us a job of some significance, like making sure the sun sets and then rises again as it normally does, "follow along at your own pace?"

"I feel mildly insulted at that," I tell her in no uncertain terms, "but at the same time enormously grateful. I still have no idea what the plan is, but it does, in its strange incomprehensibility, sound like a great one. Let's go."

I put my hand out, arm straight, palm down.

"Can I get a go Yellow team?" I ask, with the answer not given verbally but through action as they all fuck off, except jenny, who smacks the back of my hand with her clenched fist.

"No, you cannot," she tells me, and we walk slowly toward the first obstacle of horizontal poles at various heights that we are not going to get over any time soon, and especially not in the way Racheal and Chelsey are doing. They leap, like gazelles in boiler suits, legs coming up and over and for fleeting moments they appear to float, or have legs like Tigger's bottom, all made of springs, and clearly suffering from ADHD as they bounce, leap and pull themselves through the first obstacle in seconds. I hit the first pole, put my palms on top, as it is at chest height, lift my right leg up so my ankle is on top with my leg straight out to the side. I then jump up a little with my left leg. I come back down exactly to where I started, so, in my great expertise and analytical skills, I repeat the little jump with my leg up on a pole like an arthritic ballerina, and, weirdly to my own complete surprise the same results happen. I am essentially hopping with my right leg forced up at an angle on a bit of scaffold.

"Oh, for Christ sake," Jenny says, grabbing my arse and then pushing me up and forward so my balance is shot and I fly straight over like a heavy rope slipping off the edge of a dock. I hit the ground in such a way that I believe I have tied my limbs into a reef knot. Jenny jumps down after me.

"I think I might try and get in shape," I say.

"You can start by trying to get up."

I hold out my hand and she grabs it and pulls me to my feet as I say, "Go Yellow team!" so she lets go and I slump to the floor again, like a sofa being pushed out the back of a truck.

We continue to try and cover the other three poles, and manage this in a matter of minutes, about ten I reckon, which means neither of us is eligible to enter into the training for elite SAS. This does not make me sad.

I look up at the cargo net that reaches so far into the sky that were it to rain the top would remain dry.

Incomprehensibly, as I stare up at the top I have no intention of going near, Racheal and Chelsey come into view scrambling up and then down the cargo net carrying what appears to be three large wooden spheres all stuck together in a row. The balls are about half a metre wide and have no discernible purpose other than to be large, unwieldly and heavy.

"There are a few of these things," Racheal says, breathing heavily, "at the end of the course."

Chelsey, having yet to break sweat, adds, "They are a bit heavy."

The reason she hasn't broken sweat is that she is covered, almost entirely, by fast drying mud in the way most Labradors are when let off a lead in a wood after a heavy rain.

"That looks like it'll be good for your skin," I say because I have seen videos of Spa retreats where people pay good money for pervy, unqualified people to smear what they call volcanic mud specially imported from Tibet, but which is, more likely, the scraping taken from the local farmyard slurry tank. Call it by a foreign word, however, and that shit sells for great money.

"Are you having trouble with the obstacles?" Racheal asks, smiling at me sweating, hurting and on the verge of quitting after essentially doing the equivalent of clambering over a countryside style.

"You two don't seem to be," I say, as humbly as is possible, which is admittedly not particularly much.

"I do this for fun," Racheal tells me in what appears to be a brag rather than the ravings of a loon.

"Fun?"

"Obstacle courses, fun runs, all that diving through inflatables and getting stung, jumping from up high and landing in freezing, dirty lakes. I love it."

"Love it?" I ask her, pulling the face of a man desperately trying to get out of a conversation with the mental drunk Scot at the bar.

214

"Over the cargo net, there is a mud slide," she say as if this would excite me, "a tunnel through dark water, a crawl through thick mud, then a climb up to a zip line that you have to jump from at the end into freezing cold water. You'd have to pay thirty quid to enter a race like this."

"And you do that?" I ask, slowly so she can understand what I am asking. "For fun?"

"Obviously. It is a bit trickier coming back, there are these balls to carry, but you have these, and we'll head back for the next. See if you can meet us a bit further toward the end next time, eh?"

"And you?" I ask Chelsey, to her face as her boobs are now brown with white cracks appearing everywhere like someone painted them ten years ago and they've been left untreated out in the back garden ever since.

"I'm just following her lead, a nice bit of cardio really. Like a circuit class but dirty."

"I don't understand what is going on," I say. "I am officially not getting any of this, but we'll take this back," I tell them and try to lift the three balls stuck together. Realise I can, but I have absolutely no chance of walking if I hold them on my own, and ask Jenny, "would you mind?"

The women look at each other and smile that knowing smile, and I nod my head because they are, as always, right.

Jenny takes the other end, and I manoeuvre so she gets the heavier bit as the two sporty women, run off laughing and skipping and whooping to go through the torture course once more. For fun, the weirdos.

"I think we are going to have to chuck this over," I tell Jenny, as my arms and shoulders start to feel like they have been doused in lighter fuel and lit with a Zippo.

"Three, two, one," I count down as we swing them, and then chuck them over the pole. Jenny gives me a bunk up, and I manage not to fall off into a heap, but I do forward roll, feet over my head and land on my arse. Jenny jumps down as if she used to compete in the all-round gymnastic programme at the Commonwealth games. We ignore the fact I am a lumbering heap of embarrassing flesh and we lug the balls to Gaz, who watches but doesn't make any move to help us. To him, his work is done.

"What the bloody hell are these for?" Gaz asks.

We shrug and tell him to watch them for no reason whatsoever other than to give him a job to do so he doesn't wander off, get lost, and only be found again in twenty year's time when he has, miraculously, become a god like figure to a group of people hiding out in the bush, ninety percent of whom are wanted for murder.

"Don't let anyone so much as touch them," Jenny adds, presumably imaging that Gaz would fight anyone. He would be the worst guard dog, one that would growl but suddenly become your friend and loyal companion if you offered him a slice of ham, and a metallic bowl of lager.

THE PRESENTERS : DAY 11 : PANICKING MORE

"What the hell is going on?" The Welshman shouts.

Molly is watching along with the crew on a monitor in the van. Chelsey and Racheal, are nailing the course, exerting the same amount of energy as an average male would use walking to the local corner shop to buy some baccy. They are in very good cardio shape.

"What the hell is Jonny doing?" he asks them all, but the only answer is, cocking it up.

They all watch in fascination as Jonny makes one bad decision after another.

"Did he not listen to the rules? They don't all have to go to the end of the course."

And it is true, no one said they all need to go, they just need to get the objects back one at a time and put them together.

Ben and Jenny are cutting the course shorter for Chelsey and Racheal, and Gaz is sat looking at the sky and sipping on his flask probably wondering if the birds that circle above are vultures or a rather scary hallucination.

Jonny's team are all struggling to get down the zip wires and they are no closer to completing the task than when they started. By accident or design, Ben's team is miles ahead. Racheal and Chelsey drop from a height into the muddy water and squeal with delight, like two kids in their new wellies jumping into puddles. They trek up the steep hill, hands on knees, grab the next set of balls, take a deep breath, make a joke about Ben and Jenny and sex and then chuckle off on their way back. They are doing all the work, but nothing as difficult as trying to get Gaz to this point and then getting him back. It would be akin to moving a massive, water-filled balloon, without spillage, to the end of a road that was covered in carpet tacks.

216

Ben and Jenny leap over the initial barriers, or in Ben's case, slide over ungracefully, and he lands every time on a different part of his anatomy. The only one he has yet to use are his feet.

"They are going to lose," The Welshman says.

"I don't think they are actually going to be able to finish," Blue-shirt geek boy says, in what is a voice growing in confidence and authority. Tomorrow, no doubt, The Welshman will have him holding the three metre mic boom, or, if he chirps up too much more, have him serving slop in the canteen.

They watch in awe, and in the Welshman's case, horror, as Chelsey and Racheal breeze through the obstacles holding three giant wooden balls that are glued together.

"Why are the men not winning this?" The Welshman shouts.

They all watch as the entire team reach the top of the hill and they see the objects they need to bring back. They are all head-to-toe covered in mud, their boiler suits ten kilos heavier with the absorption of water. Bob collapses on the ground, Kieran bends over, his hands on his knees, young pop-star falls and lies on his back.

Jonny tries to rally his troops by telling them in his best general voice, "Only have to do that five more times," as if that is an incentive.

No one answers, or moves, and Kathrine stares at him, her eyelashes still protruding with thick, glue-like mascara, opens her mouth and nothing comes, not even a whistle.

Kieran picks up the three wooden balls.

"These aren't that heavy," he says.

"They will be when we try to get it over the cargo net," Bob tells him factually.

Kieran lifts the balls up onto his right shoulder and starts walking down the hill. They all watch him for a few seconds, then one by one they stand, take deep breaths, hoping the air they inhale has traces of amphetamine, and they trudge after him in silence.

"Worse things happen at sea," Bob says, smiling through his mud-caked face.

Katherine looks at him while still pacing forward.

"Shut the fuck up, Bob," she says, and the others nod.

DAY 11 : AFTERNOON/EVENING : THINGS ARE EASY

"I think we should wait here," I say at the bottom of the cargo net that appears to be getting higher every time I look. "We'd only get to the top, pretend we could hold the balls, realise we can't, and then let them tumble down, watch them smash into a million pieces, and then have to glue them together in the correct order with our own blood and tears."

"You are such a lazy sod," Jenny, once again incredibly accurately, tells me.

"I just want to win," I lie, more or less, but know there is truth in there, which is annoying.

We watch Chelsey and Racheal climb the cargo net with heavy balls, reach the top, and shout something I imagine to be, "Catch!" as they let the thing go and it comes sliding down, directly at us as they chuckle and bond and move away to try and pick up others and me and Jenny move quickly out of the way.

We pick up the balls, carry them over the poles, I inevitably end up on my arse and Jenny looks down at me.

"You'd think you'd have started getting better at that already," she tells me, pulling me up to my feet as we roll the balls the rest of the way to Gaz.

"How's it going?" he asks.

"Just leaving the girls to it really," I say. "They seem to be enjoying themselves. Heard anything from the Red team?"

"They seem to be stuck down the other end there. All of them. Strange plan. They haven't the brains to work out what to do with these things like we have," Gaz says, possibly in an accent he believes all high-level university lecturers use when overcome with a desire to patronise the freshers on their first meeting.

"No need to think, Gaz," Jenny says very, very slowly like talking to a small child who doesn't speak the language. "It is a pyramid."

"A what now?" I ask looking at the two sets of wooden balls on the floor.

"A pyramid. You put them together in such a way as they form a pyramid."

I stare at her, hoping my facial contortions indicate that despite me being able to pass my A-Levels, I still have absolutely no clue what she is badgering on about.

It is her turn to look at me the way she looks at Gaz, slightly mothering, but mostly feeling sorry for my intellectual disabilities.

"The brain toys, bits of metal linked together and you have to separate?" she asks expecting me to nod.

I shake my head.

"The wooden toys that are shapes that only fit together a specific way?"

I shake my head again, only less vigorously as this does ring a bell. "Rubik's cubes?"

"I know what they are but they are not this."

"We used to play with them at Christmas, new ones each year, try and figure them out. After the Queen's speech?"

"Christmas can be boring, but it has never been that boring," I say.

"Most people just get drunk," Gaz explains. "Eat too much, realise they don't like most of their family when sober and absolutely hate them on the back of all-day drinking from cans and a bit of after-lunch sherry. Nobody builds a pyramid."

"Monopoly?" I ask, hoping it wasn't just my family that ruined Christmas by engaging in the longest board-game in history to avoid conversation and have a Christmas day winner.

"You've never done the mind-exercise games?" Jenny asks as if we are the freak.

We shake our heads.

"Doesn't matter. These are to build a pyramid."

"You had these in your house?" Gaz asks.

"Like these but smaller," she explains.

I'd like to find out more about what sounds like even worse Christmas than mine. I bet they didn't even have a cracker, or a fortune telling fish, let alone a plastic magnifying glass. Posh bastards. But we are interrupted by Racheal shouting for us to get to the bottom of the cargo net and pick up what appears to be four balls together.

"It's bigger this time," I tell Jenny, fully confident I am blowing her pyramid theory out of the water.

"Four?" She asks, without looking but already knowing I will answer yes.

I nod.

"Pyramid," she tells us, turning around and marching to the poles, and then the balls in a manner that makes me think she may be imitating the footage of the Hitler youth.

"It is not a pyramid," Gaz says, the professor in full swing.

But it is.

Chelsey and Racheal bring all the pieces back, they climb over the poles and don't fall, which, from my own experience can only have happened by chance. We stand and do what Jenny tells us, placing the rows of balls together in such a way as a pyramid, like a pile of ordered cannonballs, appears. We stand back and nod, looking around to hear a

219

voice confirming our brilliance and hopefully mentioning Jonny in passing and Katherine specifically as totally ineptly shite.

"Congratulations," The Welshman says like he is the King of England having to award the world cup to Germany after they have just beaten the Three Lions in the final on penalties, at Wembley, coming back from three-nil down and discovering on the final whistle that the entire team have been receiving sexy texts from his wife. The enthusiasm is lacking but he is duty bound.

"The red team are still finishing the task. But you are the winners. If you enter your Land Rover, your final destination will be revealed and we enter the last part of the elimination tournament, a part we have named, The Elimination."

"Some people just have that spark don't they," I say. "That brilliant imagination that others, like me, just cannot match. The Elimination. Wow."

"Just get in your Land Rover," The Welshman tells me. "The Red team will not be too far behind."

"If they aren't it is through the art of editing because you know as well as I that they haven't even got three pieces back yet."

"Get. In. Your. Land. Rover," he tells us all, but me in particular, in a way that reminds me of a man I once saw in a pub get so angry that his face went red, his eyes rolled up and he collapsed on the floor shaking. He didn't die, in fact, he was back in the pub two nights later, only now he was referred to as Pass-out Pete or, if you really disliked him, Mr. Stroke. I tried a few times with 'brain-fuck,' but it didn't catch on, arguably too deep for the average Wetherspoons, and maybe a step too far as his speech was permanently slurred.

We all do as we are told, but smiling and happy, and dare I say it, a team.

THE PRESENTERS : DAY 11 : ANGRY

"What the hell is going on?" The Welshman shouts at a level that surpasses the previous ten minutes. He has cranked up from terse to voice-breaking booms.

"The red team aren't very good," Molly tells him.

"Or particularly smart," Blue-shirt geek-guy adds. "I mean, they appear to be trying to make Jonny and Katherine seem like winners, but are just presenting themselves as fools."

The Welshman stares at little four-eyed speccy tit, and the response he gets is a shrug that says, doesn't matter how much you stare angrily, that is the truth.

Molly nods, and is loving the outcomes. They are better than anything she could have hoped for. She knew the girls were fitter, if not stronger, but it was a test of endurance not power, she helped push the task in that direction. Those little percentage advantages add up. Jonny trying to have total control over every aspect like he has a disorder forcing him to have the final decision on every point. She knew the only way to go fast was teamwork. Ben is too lazy to take control, and that would leave him without the option of taking the piss. She knew they would gel, she knew Jenny would make them better. Jonny blew it, his lack of faith in others, while probably well founded if they were all to get into politics, was out of place here. An old man ordering about celebrities without a clue was a thing of beauty.

"They are still trying to finish," Molly tells him, smiling away, watching their increasingly frustrated faces fall and fail and be nowhere near finishing.

"This is absolute bulllshit!" The Welshman shouts.

He grabs a microphone and presses a button on the large electronic console in the van.

"Just stop!" he shouts and Jonny's team all stop what they are doing. "Call it a day. Get in your Land Rover and head off to the next stop. We'll edit this out to make it look like something positive happened. If this had been live we'd have been absolutely jiggered."

"Isn't that cheating?" Bob asks.

"Yes, Bob, it is cheating as you and your team are totally inept. The yellows finished and have left. Get in your car. The Elimination is next."

"The what?" Jonny asks.

"The Elimination," The Welshman says slower as if this will help them understand the game he hasn't described, nor spoken about and only just recently named.

"The Elimination," he says again.

"Which is?" Jonny asks, his face showing patience but his voice growling insults.

"The final encounter. Winner takes all. The normal final task, changed a bit. Water jets. Tidal waves. Heavy rubber balls. A race to the top. You know."

"The water challenge?" Bob asks.

221

"Renamed the Eliminator," The Welshman tells him. "Similar to the Water challenge, but different, which is why it is now called The Elimination."

"How has it changed?" Kieran asks.

There is a long pause while The Welshman thinks.

"It hasn't, really. The same but instead of production staff trying to stop your progress, it will be the other team."

"And that required a name change, did it?" Anthony asks, presumably showing how angry it is possible for him to be.

"I am trying to help you win," The Welshman shouts, his voice falling away from authority into a pitiful apology in the space of four syllables.

"Well it isn't bloody working, is it?" Jonny says, in a way only the truly posh can say.

Molly smiles. It isn't working despite the best efforts of the The Welshman and production team. The water challenge, or should she say, The Elimination, as if this is some type of knock-out tournament in American Wrestling that she knows he still watches on his phone, in secret, because he is embarrassed by his tastes. The Elimination is live, broadcast as it happens, medics present, ambulances ready, and chaos on TV. The idea stolen from "It's a Knockout" the programme he loved as a kid. No original ideas, just twists on what has already happened. Maybe that is his genius, taking what is known, what is familiar and altering so it looks new, looks fresh, looks like something. Always similar but different. Her replacement will be that, similar but different. Recognisable but altered enough to be separate. He will find a replacement, someone to act as his foil and someone to front shows. He won't be single, won't want to be a playboy. He needs the relationship. It won't be with her. The papers will dredge up all her past and she will vanish. It is what is written. Jonny and his pals can all go to hell.

DAY 11 : NIGHT : GOOD FOOD

They fed us with some quality food, and by quality I mean what would normally be considered bog standard dinners in the form of burgers and chips, but it was welcome. None of us wanted to refuel on beans and rice and drink warm water from Jerry cans. We sat mostly in silence, smiling and eating, talking about the water challenge that had inexplicably been renamed The Elimination as if the original name was copyrighted and the TV channel in a fit of stupidity decided not to let them carry on with it. It didn't matter, the game was a mixture of old physical game shows where people dressed in oversized costumes while being pummelled by water, carrying large foam stars to places they couldn't stay because high powered water jets would be aimed into your face if you so much as came close to the right place before the adverts were due to start. Only this year, for them, they would get to run the course and also get to aim the water and fire the rubber balls at their opponents.

"We'll have a head start, surely?" Chelsey says having seemingly inhaled the burger and chips into her stomach without them touching her tongue or throat.

"Who knows?" I say. "We won the challenges, but I think we won by hours rather than seconds. We could finish the course twice with the time we gained."

"They must have been truly awful to have lost to us," Gaz says.

For whatever reason, this tugs at my soul.

"I think we did really well. A collective of responsibility taking, no one in charge as such, no one really able to do everything. It all worked out. We had the two girls there in actual shape, you with the numbers, Jenny with the very sensible driving skills, and me with no sense of balance, ability to provide a positive input or in fact contribute in any meaningful way, and arguably seen as a drag, which, as is the way of the world, qualified me without question as the obvious choice as manager."

"Any more incompetence and you'd be promoted to the board of directors," Jenny says, from experience.

"Where, I believe I could well and truly balls things up."

"You are so talented."

"I prefer to refer to it as a gift."

"Do you think we will win?" Racheal asks, her poshness coming through.

"Not a hope in hell," I say, half way through a gherkin. "We have got away with one so far. It'll be rigged in their favour. Heavily rigged. But we might have a shot. I think we should all have a good go at it."

"What?" Jenny asks, spitting, and choking which is a great combination when eating chips. "Did you just actually try and promote a bit of effort?"

"I believe I did. Look, I don't like them, I don't like The Welshman, I don't like this TV show. But I do like you, for whatever reason that might be. And it definitely isn't a sexual thing."

"Not even Jenny?" Gaz asks.

223

"Jenny, absolutely sexual. Pure unadulterated animal passion in a caveman type of way."

She stares at me and I'm not too sure if it is with violent intent.

"With flowers and a nice meal first, obviously," I add, she nods, I inhale.

"However," I continue on a verbal roll, "you lot I do not want to see naked, although, to be fair Chelsey, there is very little of you I haven't seen. Possibly with the exception of your left hamstring. However, you guys want to stay on, and win, I think. So while I believe we are serious underdogs, and the game is rigged. Let's go for it."

They are staring at me, smiling, not really wanting eye contact.

"Don't do that," I tell them, like I am their dad. "I'm not saying lets go snarling angrily into combat mode, but let's have a crack. The other games were rigged for them too and look how far that got them. Let's have a crack but be mindful to be aloof and sarcastic at all times, even to each other, I believe in method acting and we shouldn't really be breaking character."

They are staring at me, eye contact now engaged.

"Just eat your food, you bunch of wankers," I tell them, and the immediate universe seems to have returned to normal.

THE PRESENTERS : DAY 12 : THE ELIMINATION

"Just to reiterate," The Welshman reiterates, "Ben's team cannot win. Come close-ish, not a problem. But they lose. I don't care how this is achieved, although make it look like a genuine result, obviously. But at no point must they win. Totally not allowed. Are we all clear?"

The Welshman is holding court to all the medics, technicians and staff, about twenty in total. The contestants have returned close to the original camp, the water course is ready to go, and the live event is what gets them the biggest viewing figures. The public, it seems, love to see celebrities humiliated in events involving being smacked in the face, nearly drowned, and repeatedly falling over in oversized clown shoes. Molly is pretty sure these same people find fart jokes hilarious, and believe falling down a hole in the street to be comedy perfection. Laurel and Hardy were gods.

The production team have been told numerous times that the winner is Jonny. The technical team have been told the same. We must all cheat, or bend the rules so that Ben and Jenny are humiliated into a defeat that will not only ruin their image but hopefully their future mental

224

wellbeing. Crushed, is the term The Welshman uses, both physically and mentally.

He is in charge so they all nod.

Molly listens, knows she has to play along and knows her interventions are not likely to work. She cannot control the people here, and knows they will all play along with her husband for the easy life and potential future employment.

She has walked the course, like she has every year, a five hundred metre long water slide like those you buy for the back garden, a long strip of plastic that is sprayed in water and soap so kids can aqua plane along until the plastic runs out and they slide onto grass, or into a strategically placed inflatable paddling pool. Only they are not looking for that level of fun, they are looking for that moment later on in the day when a drunk adult, whose decision making logic has been temporarily obliterated by booze, thinks it'll be fun to have a go and so runs up, dives head first, while still holding a can of supermarket lager onto the soapy surface, slides, grinning and smiling, starting to spin slightly, panic seeps into the face, the grass comes speeding forward, they hit it, their face acting as a friction brake, their legs flipping up and over their head, bending their neck in all sorts of wrong angles, as they flip and forward roll straight into the trunk of a cherry tree as their equally drunk mates look on laughing and cheering as they fall unconscious to the floor, somehow not having spilt a drop of beer, only blood from their nose.

This is the type of comedy action the public want to see, like a 'you've been framed' of anticipated carnage.

The catapults for the heavy rubber balls line the side of the shoot, along with high powered water jets, and the sluiceways that will release massive deluges of water on celebrities who waddle along in their costumes trying to place foam stars in a net and make it back to the start so a team mate can take their place and have the same torture applied to them.

The slide has been adapted over the years, but in essence it is all a load of nonsense stolen from other shows wrapped up as their own. This is the highpoint of the show, the one event, beyond eating live animals with claws, stings and massive eyeballs that the public love. For her, the only pleasure is that this is always two days from the end of the show and the ability to get on a plane and go home. The last two days are generally a love-in of the remaining contestants who all think they have a chance to be crowned king or queen of the show for a year. The last two days are dull for the public but happy for her. She smiles as it is all very nearly over and whatever happens back in the United Kingdom she will face and work through, alone, and almost certainly out of the limelight. The Welshman is no longer her concern. They have no children so no staying in contact is needed, and their finances have always been separate. A solicitor's letter, a goodbye and a new life.

She smiles because there is part of her that thinks it will be that easy.

DAY 12 : LATE MORNING : ELIMINATION TIME

"What the hell is that?" I say at a large head I am supposed to put over my own. "Who the hell is that supposed to be? It looks like a deformed lump of cheese with eyeballs."

Jenny frowns, looks at me trying to see if I am setting up a punchline.

"It's you, you nob," she informs me.

I look again, squint and then nod. Yeah, once it has been pointed out, it is in all honesty, a pretty fair likeness.

We have all been allocated large foam hands that are designed so as to make it almost impossible to pick anything up. We have massive clown feet also, which make it impossible to move at any speed, or stay upright for anything more than three steps, and a large head that rests on my shoulders in which I can see nothing in my peripheral vision other than inside and a limited view forward. We are to use these to run up the impossibly slippery slope while our opponents fire water, balls and other such nonsense at us. We in turn have to carry stars to the end of the course and place them in an oversized basketball net. Simple really. Practically impossible, but a simple premise all the same. The first team to get five into the net are the winners, or at the end of the time limit the team with the most is champion.

"We need a strategy," Jenny says.

"I think I should shoot the cannons," Gaz says all too eagerly.

"We all have to attempt a star run. We have to get up close before we are allowed to call it quits," Jenny informs us as if she has written the rules.

"Shit," Gaz says. "I don't think I can get that far."

"Just leg it, and then crawl, and roll. It'll take a bit longer but at least we can move on. You'll be great on the water jet," Racheal says, hopefully in a way that will make Gaz feel better and maybe just get him off the course as quick as we can possibly remove him.

226

"See if you can make it close," Chelsey says, in a way that indicates she has studied and thought about strategy for the event. "Throw the thing and then get back to us. It isn't like their team is full of superstars."

"What order are we going in?" Jenny asks, and they all look to me. I do not like this responsibility.

"Gaz, Racheal, Chelsey, Jenny, and then me, in the hope you guys get the stars and me and Gaz don't drown. All ok with that?"

They nod and shrug which I take as an Okay. I don't think the order will change anything, certainly won't decrease or increase the chance of winning.

We walk to the start like a group of really shitty children's entertainers, and we'd move quicker if we were all crowded into a clown's car with square wheels, each carrying a bucket of tinsel and honking air horns. It's like I have involved myself, against my will, in the absolutely worst themed fiftieth birthday party ever.

Go on, Ben, it'll be hilarious, us all dressed up. There will be a smoke machine and a DJ. We can all get blootered on Drambuie. What can go wrong? We'll dance, it'll be ace.

No, it will not. It will be a horrific mess of old people trying to regain their youth by being bellends. We might all as well go to Magaluf in T-shirts with nicknames on the back like Big Poof, Dr. Studd and the Twot and ignore the fact all the young people are staring at us like we are some type of freak show as we imagine we can shag the hotties. It is over, move on, accept your age.

Gaz stands at the start line and he is up against Bob, whose massive head looks very similar to his real head in that it has weird eyes and eye lashes thick with black mascara. On one side stand Jonny and his team behind their catapults and water jets and on our side we stand behind ours. There is a silence, a proper pre-battle nerves.

I feel I should give a speech, maybe walk up and down in front of them mentioning King and Country, or channelling the energy of William Wallace, say something inspirational that will give us that extra one percent that would be the difference between winning and losing. I formulate words in my head as the de facto leader.

"I will pay twenty English pounds to anyone who can get Bob square in the bollocks," I say, profoundly and a touch philosophically. "Forty if you smash his face," I add with an eloquence few could match.

The buzzer sounds and we are off. Gaz takes a step, slips, feet up into the air, landing on his back and sliding further from the start. Bob laughs for a split second before cursing loudly as Gaz's legs swipe Bob's from under him. Bob falls too and it is a sliding race in the wrong direction. Gaz gets on all fours and starts to crawl like a ten month old baby heading for the ornaments near the Television. He moves his knees and hands rapidly, but friction is not his friend and he moves forward with rapid movements equating to small fairy steps. Bob stands, and tries to run, but I hear a ping from my right as Jenny releases a large rubber ball, and then a thud as it smacks Bob on the side of his fake head, which knocks him over, spins him round, and removes the fake head from Bob's shoulders. I see my chance, press the button in front of me and fire a shot of water, a very high speed jet of water straight into his face. His mascara doesn't run, but his head tips back, and he too drops to all fours. Gaz, is somehow making headway as the team on the far side try to hit him with everything they have got. They miss, with rubber balls bouncing close but not on him, and water jets making contact but not forcing him back. Gaz's shoes fall off. But he makes it to the stars which are contained within a box. He reaches in and pulls one out, he is standing, but not for long as without being hit, he slips again, and falls on his side in such a way as I believe he may have pushed a rib through his lungs. He crawls forward and the balls are pinging off his body, seemingly with little effect. The mass of the man is holding him steady.

My eyes, and the eyes of everyone on my team are on Bob, who is up and without big clown shoes, is making quick progress forward, albeit like a novice on ice. He reaches his box of stars and pulls one out with his big foam hands. Chelsey, I think, forces a rubber ball into the side of his head, but it pings off, only making his hair flail in all directions and he stares at Chelsey, which is my opportunity to fire a jet of water directly into his mouth.

Gaz is crawling forward, getting closer to the line from which he can return. He makes it past, crawling his way along on his stomach like he is in the army and trying to sneak up on a pillbox at night. He stands, the star between his big foam hands and he chucks the thing high up into the air, we watch him, and the arc of the star as it flies up, spinning, moving forward, not dropping, and we are transfixed, literally unable to take our eyes off a large, yellow foam star that spins, having been thrown by a man half dressed as a loon, and clearly an alcoholic. The excitement, I hate to admit, is killing me. We watch it come down, bounce on the edge of the net into which we all desperately want it to go, we watch it bounce up, still spinning and then come down into the net. One star. We cheer, look at each other in disbelief. We have made an error though.

We have taken our eyes from Bob, who has crawled up to the net, stood and is placing his star inside without throwing. I fire water, as does Racheal, Chelsey and Jenny firing large rubber balls all of us screaming as if we are in a slow motion action scene in a film depicting the horrors of Vietnam. We are all too late as the star drops and Bob raises his hands as he is simultaneously hit in the throat and thigh by high velocity balls, and smashed in the chin and ear by water jets. He drops to the floor and slides back to the start. Gaz is already there.

"Next," The Welshman shouts.

Racheal sprints off leaving a gun unmanned. Gaz is collapsed in a heap on dry land away from the start.

"Gaz," I shout, "Get to the gun."

He looks my way, tries to stand, does for a second, collapses and says,

"Give. Me. A. Minute." He takes a massive gulp of air between words.

Racheal is graceful, like a dancer, or someone who knows how their body should move. She races to the start, despite her massive clown shoes, huge head and ridiculous hands. On the other side Kieran jogs down, although his head doesn't seem to be firmly attached as it wobbles all over on each step. They cross the start line together, neither of them appearing to have any difficulty with the slippery surface. Racheal gets smashed in the head with a ball and drops down. Her head flying off. But she jumps up quicker than would seem possible in such a costume. Kieran is weaving, I think by design, feet flapping, legs going out to the sides, hands clapping. Racheal is on his tail, her massive fake head slipping back to the start. They are getting hit but riding it out and they dive to the boxes. Racheal is up first, the star pressed firmly between her huge foam hands. Kieran shakes his massive head and it flips off, his real face a grimace of determination and what appears to be pain. They skip forward, rubber balls bouncing around and hitting them on ricochet as they charge forward to the net. A siren sounds, I look to my right and a sluice gate opens and thousands of litres of water surge out on either side of the slope, flying toward each other and smashing up into a metre high wave then snaking left and downhill toward Racheal and Kieran. They see it coming, this mini tsunami but keep pacing forward getting closer to the oversize basketball net. The wave comes quicker, picking up speed and power, gravity helping it along, the mass of water pushing the wave up and out. Racheal jumps, as does Kieran and the wave hits them, Kieran just below the knees and Racheal in her thighs. They flip, up and over, like a small car has driven through their legs, Racheal releases the star, her head looking at the target whereas Kieran chucks his star up into the air and forward. They come crashing down into the backed up water behind the wave front instantly being dragged down the slope, past the start line and into a pit of water that collects at the bottom with all the rubber balls. I look back at the nets and each team has two stars inside.

"Next!" The Welshman shouts.

Chelsey is off at a canter, less graceful but more power than Racheal. On the other side the pop star, struggling under the weight of the costume moves slowly. Chelsey is pumping ahead and I am sure she will tell me later that there is a gym class that does something very similar like sesame street step aerobics where they all have to dress as big bird and work out for an hour without dying. She moves quickly and is at the box before anyone has fired. I am taking my time lining up the slow moving pop star who seems more concerned with staying on his feet rather than moving forward. We are pummelling him and Jenny finally manages to smack him in the head with a fastball. His head is knocked off and he falls to the side, slipping back to the start. Chelsey has a star in hand and is running forward, she gets within touching distance but is hit in the head with a ball and blasted in her stomach by a water jet and she spins and slips and falls, sliding away but she holds on to her star. The pop star is up, and maybe due to the encouragement from his team, which mostly consists of 'fucks' and 'get up' and 'wanker', he jumps toward the box and hangs on with his big hands. Chelsey is up and moving forward again, her head is off, I suspect she pulled it off, and is charging forward like racing into a strong wind, albeit in size 99 shoes. She passes the pop star, who shrieks, possibly in a bout of self-motivation, or possibly because he thought he saw a mouse, picks up a star and moves forward. Chelsey, getting used to being hit in the body with rubber balls and having her face smashed with water jets, reaches the net and drops her star inside. She jumps up in the air, landing on her bum, and slides back to the start in double quick time.

The Welshman shouts, "next!" pointing at our team, and Jenny is off, but falls over after two steps and not even close to the slippery bit.

"Shit," she says.

I lean down to help her, forgetting I am dressed as a massive tit and simply fall on top of her.

A cheer goes up and I take it to mean the pop star has made it to the net and dropped his star inside. I get up, look and confirm my suspicions as The Welshman shouts, "next!" and points at Jonny's team.

230

Katherine makes a dash for it, and unlike Jenny, doesn't fall over like she has replaced her legs with cheese strings.

Jenny is on her feet and waddling to the start as Katherine hits the slope, and much to my own delight, slips, feet going so far up in the air that she lands on her massive fake head. There is a moment when everyone pauses, thinking she has done herself some serious damage, a pause and intake of breath, but, unfortunately she moves and gets back to her feet, the absolute trooper. Jenny is now, inexplicably ahead and it is starting to dawn on me that I made a mistake in my decision on the order of contestants. I'm last. Shit.

The alarm sounds, I look at the sluice gates, they open, more water than before gushes out like a damn releasing an overflow, the water coming in, crashing together, smashing up into a froth of white, like a rapids where people on rafts in life-threatening situations with their entire safety and wellbeing in the hands of Charlie, the minimum wage kid doing a summer job with no actual lifesaving experience. But it is Okay, he is wearing a helmet and his parents are rich. The water comes rushing down the slope and Jenny and Katherine make the creative decision to crouch down into a small foetal position. The wave hits them smack on in their bodies, lifting them, carrying them with it at speed and then spitting them out into the pool at the bottom. Their faces, without the huge fake heads, pop up through the rubber balls floating on top and they scramble out making their way back up the course without the foam hands and shoes. Katherine slightly ahead, but Jenny tracking her every step.

They make it to the box at the same time, rubber balls pinging around and jets of water sprayed randomly everywhere. Both teams hitting their own mates with friendly fire. They grab their stars and crawl forward, unable to get any traction while stood. They pass the white line, getting closer, thinking about throwing and running, but holding onto their stars, too scared to fail. They crawl close, reaching up, grabbing the metal bar that holds the net, reaching up and dumping the stars inside. They dive forward like superman, onto their fronts, sliding down the slope, getting faster as they go, passing the start line in unison and slipping over the edge, head first into the collection pool. They pop their heads up at the same time.

"Next!" The Welshman shouts.

"Shit," I say. "Shitty, shit, shit," I add as I waddle to the start, watching Jonny on the other side moving quicker in what appear to be significantly smaller shoes than mine, and a fake head that falls off immediately, the cheating bastard. I try to wobble mine off but it appears

231

to be welding to my neck. Bollocks. I reach the slope and make the schoolboy error of walking on as if there will be no discernible difference in technique from walking on solid ground and walking on soapy slippery rubber. I fall heavily on my arse. Jonny has obviously given it a bit more thought and edges on, remains on his feet and starts to race forward. Shit. I get up, slip a couple of times more, try to shake my gloves off but they appear to be tied to each other like those mittens parents give to kids that hang by string and can never be lost. I look to see where the balls and jets will come from but there is no one on their side. Anthony, Kieran, Bob and Katherine are all at the bottom of the slope recovering from their exertions. I smile, thinking my team will help me here by smashing Jonny with everything they have got. I look to my team and they are all sat, lying down, like star fish. Nothing left to give.

Oh shit.

Gaz waves.

I am up, I have the face on, and I move forward, on all fours like a marathon man who has misjudged the pace and is now crawling to the finish line in humiliation with no energy left but the desire to make it to the end. Other athletes are running past looking at their watches. Jonny is nearing his box of stars but there is another siren, I look to the sluice gates, there is nothing, they are open. I look around and see Molly smiling up on her platform having pressed a button. The Welshman is staring at her, trying to move her hand away, but it is too late. I look up at the end of the course, the canvas sheet is lifting, revealing a wall of large, water–filled bouncing balls. Hundreds of the things. There is a moment where inertia keeps them still, but gravity wins out and they start to roll, pick up speed, bounce in unpredictable directions but somehow remain tight enough to be a massive solid wall of pain heading straight for us. I stare at their multi-coloured beauty as they hurtle toward me, like I am looking at the most amazing rainbow oblivious to the fact they are fooling me into a false sense of security before carrying out their evil plan and putting me into the trauma ward at the local specialist hospital.

The first one whips by my head accompanied by a whizzing noise I have only heard in films when a bullet flies past the protagonist's ear. Others, many others, soon follow. I see Jonny standing, moving side-to-side as if he is a trained ninja. He isn't. A big red ball smacks him clean in the gut, lifting him off his feet, sending him back, bouncing off his chest when he lands, and rolling away as he slides away from the box. I grin, big and wide, turn to get a star and get a big blue ball clean smack in the face. The big fake head smashing against my real one. I'm not knocked out, but

I'd be hard pressed to remember my address, I certainly forget what balance is, and hit the deck. I am sick, but being a man, I keep it in my mouth and swallow.

I sit up, although I am not too sure how long I have been lying down. I instinctively look left and see Jonny sitting up too. My massive fake head is off, my shoes are gone and my hands are free of foam. That ball really did a number on me.

We stare at each other, for three seconds, trying to communicate our confusion through a competition on who can look the most gormless. Where we are and what we need to do seeps in and we stand, gingerly, and head to the box. We reach our stars at the same time. We hold them, waiting for another punishment to fall upon us, like being shot in the face by an elephant hunter, but nothing happens. We race forward, slipping and sliding but keeping our forward movement. I touch the floor with my left hand but remain on my feet and I see Jonny slipping and sliding too. There are four stars in each net, five makes you the winner. Do I throw, or do I dunk? I watch Jonny, and he is having the same ideas as me. We are close, close enough to throw. An alarm sounds, I look to my right, a barrier is lifted like the lock on a canal at speed, a wall of water drops, smashing, flies up and is a second from me. The same is happening on Jonny's side. We look at each other, we look at the water, we know if we are hit we go back to the start, the time will be gone, it is all or nothing. We throw at the same time, the stars go up, and spin as we are smashed by water. I don't fight it, I try and float on top, watching the two stars spin and move toward the net. They look on target. They each hit the rim, bounce up in unison, look to come down at the same time into the net. A draw, it has to be a draw. I hear the ping, I look left, see Katherine at her catapult, a rubber ball flying toward us, but nowhere near hitting me. I look at the stars as they fall and smile. I see the rubber ball fly past smacking into my star, pushing it away from the net as Jonny's falls in. The siren sounds as I hit the deck and slide on my back, head first to the collection pool. I hear Jonny scream in delight, I hear their team shout. I slide, not fighting against the pull of the water and I am submerged. I wait, taking my time to float to the top. My head pops out and I see my team, heads down. I look away, look to the other team, who are jumping and hugging and celebrating. Jonny slides into the pool, popping his head out immediately. He smiles at me, a big shit-eater grin created off the back of years of experience.

"Loser," he tells me before climbing from the pool.

233

THE PRESENTERS : DAY 12 : THE GLEE

"What the hell were you doing?" The Welshman shouts. "The balls were only if Jonny was losing."

They are up on their platform, the cameras rolling on the contestants, the dejected faces of Ben and his team, the losers, and now to be eliminated.

"It made for better TV," Molly tells him, looking ahead at the camera, waiting for her cue to start spouting insincere blather about how there must always be winners and losers.

Her phone vibrates. She picks it up and turns on the screen.

"Don't look at your phone now, we are on air. Be professional."

She looks at him briefly, a disdain, a curled lip, a scrunched nose, ignores him and looks back at her phone. A swear would be a waste.

It is her agent. The internet is on fire with this, the message says. Molly presses a button and looks at the Program's feed. The words that are trending are Fix, con, and cheat. Molly smiles as she sees her pushing the button for the balls to fall were seen as an attempt at parity. There is talk of balls being fired with less power by Ben's team, water jets not reaching as far as Jonny's. They have all been seen, are all correct and now the conspiracy theories are starting. No one likes a cheat.

She smiles and places the phone down. She looks up and sees they are two seconds from being on air. The Welshman makes himself calm, the smile returns, the producer points at her and they are ready to go.

The Welshman opens his big grinning mouth but Molly speaks.

"Controversial," Molly says directly into the camera. She can see on the screen they are both in shot so she turns to The Welshman.

"That didn't seem fair. A lot of losing costumes quickly from Jonny's team. A lot of low power shots from Ben's. There seemed to be a bit of a disadvantage there. What do you think?"

She watches on the screen behind the camera as they zoom in on The Welshman's face.

"I don't think so," he says smiling. "We are always fair on here. Camera angles and luck always play a part. The cascade of balls at the end, our new surprise, evened out the field. So close, so fair, but as we knew from the outset, so very sad for the losers."

"You can all have your say on social media, for free," Molly says. "Get on our account and post away, ask anything and explain what you think you saw. No need to text, no need to spend any money. Just

234

straight to the program feed, or if that mysteriously goes down go straight to mine. We'll publish the best ones just as soon as we can."

"But right now, here is a highlight reel of all the shenanigans from The Elimination," The Welshman shouts.

The cameraman cuts away and they are no longer on air.

The Welshman turns on her.

"What are you doing? For free? What? Conspiracy theory. Our feed has crashed. We don't need that level of nonsense."

"Conveniently mine hasn't. I want to hear what they say."

"You just want to destroy all of this, don't you? All of this and all of us."

"There is no us, you absolute tool. We are done. I know you haven't noticed or particularly cared and have it in your head that you will somehow win me over when we are back home. But you won't. Thanks for everything, it has, in many parts been a blast. The last couple of years, not so much. I'd like to be in a relationship with an adult, a functioning adult, not Peter Pan on crack."

"I don't take crack."

"Not the point you stupid, fake arseface."

"Get off set," he tells her, flicking his hand out like wafting away a fart.

"What?"

"You heard, clear off."

"Get stuffed, you Welsh turd. This, as you have forgotten is fifty percent mine. I own half, the production company, the re-runs, the whole lot. I am, unfortunately liable for the utter bullshit you have played this season. I am, as your wife and partner absolutely up to my eyeballs in your endless pathetic drivel. So don't be ordering me about, or I'll pull the plug on all this, and bankrupt you."

"You can't do that, that is not an actual thing." He turns to the people watching. "She can't, can she?"

The production manager nods in such a way as to indicate it is a major possibility.

"If you want this to continue in some way, or for you to have a career with this company, or anything else in any way related to what we have built up, then you need to shut your face and just get on. I'm not intending to destroy you, just walk away with what is mine. That doesn't include you nor your entire wealth. But if you keep trying to be billy big brains when in fact you are a little bit intellectually challenged, I will push.

235

So, if you don't want me to be in your presence, it is you who needs to bugger off."

He stares at her, and she at him. Molly is looking up, and he down. The anger and tension in him builds and she can see it. He needs to release some of it, needs a release because otherwise he'll blow.

He points at her, words forming then evaporating away. He steps back and then forward, pointing all the while. His head starts to shake.

"Best viewing figures ever," he says, turning his back and walking off.

She can't resist and does a wanker sign behind his back. She looks to the crew and they are all nodding and smiling. She thinks some may applaud.

DAY 12 : NIGHT : DISAPPOINTMENT

They drove us back, no need for Jenny to meander along in a Land Rover full of tired wet, would-be celebrities, all quiet, all thinking and coming to terms with a loss. We were separate, two trucks, two teams, two different emotions. Silence almost all the way.

We walked the last mile to the camp, over the rope bridge, which shook as it always did, while not feeling strong enough for us all. We came across first but we heard the other group behind us still cheering, hollering and congratulating each other. We heard Katherine swear at Bob to stop shaking the bridge like a child. It isn't funny, she told him.

And there we were, two groups in camp, divided by an invisible line, the winners and the losers.

A few smiles were shared across camp, but we knew we were going. One more night in this place, the heat and the dry earth and the strange animals and people we, or rather I, do not like.

We moved quickly, the two groups sitting separate, one all chat and the other all pensive, most with fake smiles.

"I'm sorry," I say, as we are sat around in a circle listening to the other group laugh and blow off steam.

"Nothing to be sorry about," Racheal tells me. "We tried, and we came up short."

"It was fun," Gaz says. "Certainly prefer our team to theirs."

"Yeah, we nearly made it," I tell them. "But I am sorry."

"We don't care," Chelsey says. "Nothing to apologise for."

"I apologise for being rude. Being a bit of a dick."

"A bit?" Jenny asks.

I turn to her and smile.

236

"Ok, a lot. A total massive dick. At times."

"Most times," Racheal tells me, smiling sweetly as if she can do nothing else. "But it's cool. You're Okay, mostly. I know you don't mean most of it."

It is my turn to laugh because I am pretty sure I do.

"What are you planning on doing?" Chelsey asks the group.

"Right now?" I ask. "Right now, I'm going to hit the hammock for the last time. Sleep as well as I can, and wake up and walk out. Probably have to do that interview after, right? But at least there will be five of us, so less time on screen to moan and complain and make jokes at That Welshman's expense."

"Less danger of punching him," Racheal adds.

"I wouldn't punch him. I'm not like that. I would never start a fight with someone who is that much bigger than me. I only punch little people."

"What do you mean little people?" Jenny asks.

"I think the politically correct term is children," I explain.

"And when you all get back?" Chelsey asks.

"Eat," Jenny says.

"Get drunk," Gaz informs us, sipping on his flask.

"Sleep," Racheal says.

"Try and write something," I say. "And you?"

"Just chill for a while maybe."

We all sit, nothing else to say.

"I know the idea might fill you all with dread," I tell them. "But you are all welcome at my humble house. You can sit at my table and stay over. You don't even need to speak to me."

They stare at me.

"Yeah, I know. But I am an Okay host, if you like hosts that leave you alone and let you do stuff in their absence. Obviously a one night maximum limit on the stay, I'm not an idiot. But you are all welcome. Norfolk way if any of you are close, or have heard of it, and can locate it on a map."

They say nothing and nod. I smile.

"It is an open invite. Soon or a long time into the future. I've no plans to move. But I have reached the point whereby I need to sleep. So I will bid you all a good night, and see you in the morning for the walk of shame."

I get to my hammock, relatively expertly sit in it, flip my feet off the ground and lie back. I put my hands behind my head and smile. None of them are going to come, it'd be like Bob offering the same to his group. But I meant it, right now, probably regret it if they do, but right now, after all this, I mean it. I close my eyes.

"Ben?" I hear.

"Yeah," I answer.

"Do you want to budge up and make some space?"

I open my eyes and Jenny is looking down on me. I smile.

"Sure, " I say moving my body but not actually creating any extra space at all as it is a hammock and it would be physically impossible. "But no funny business, no touching. I'm not an easy tart, you know."

She slides in, and we exchange three words about our team, something like, they are actually lovely people, and we fall asleep, into what I think will be a lovely deep, relaxing sleep akin to being anaesthetised, a blissful black nothing, with the obvious removal of any actual operation. I don't fancy waking up having had my spleen removed or to discover an intern has jokingly augmented my breasts.

STILL DAY 12 : NIGHT : NOT SLEEPING

There is no way of checking the time. There are no clocks and no watches allowed. But it is dark, and that means, genius that I am, morning hasn't happened yet. Years of schooling got me here.

The voice and the push woke me.

"Ben," said quietly, and the shake barely touching me.

I don't open my eyes.

"I'm too tired," I explain regretfully. "You'll have to wait till the morning. I'm not sleeping with you now."

"I don't want to sleep with you," Gaz tells me, offended as if he is out of my league.

"What do you want?" I whisper.

"I think I've messed up," he tells me, and there is something there that makes me sit up.

"Messed up how?"

"I can show you."

I get out of the hammock slowly, untangling myself from Jenny's arms. Gaz walks off before I am on my feet. I smell the fire, see its burning embers, inhale the smoke, which is stronger when you first awake.

"Where are we going, Gaz?"

He walks quickly to the edge of camp and I see the flickering glow within the bush. I step in after him.

"Oh shit, Gaz. What have you done?"

238

"Just a fag," he tells me moving his hands around at the huge fire expanding in all directions through the tinder dry bush.

"It was smaller a minute ago," he tells me as if it is a possibility it will return to that size.

"Oh shit, Gaz," I say.

The fire is climbing up the trees, sprinting left and right through dry shrubs and the grass burns away like it is paraffin poured on a bar top.

"What do we do?" Gaz asks.

"We run."

The heat is incredible, the flames starting to wave and spit. There are pops and cracks. Gaz is staring as flames jump from branch to branch, tree to tree, and across the ground like napalm depicted in movies.

I grab Gaz by the arm and pull him back to the opening. The noise of the impending inferno starting to really hit the volume like a superhero film in a cinema.

"Fire," I shout, and my sleepiness is gone.

Everyone wakes up pretty quick, thankfully there have been no celebratory drinks, or party or drugs or anything other than being smashed around on a waterslide.

"Fire?" Jonny asks before looking from where we came, seeing the wall of flames and adding, "ah, yes, a fire."

Everyone is awake and shouting. The night is a time when the production team sleep too, when we are filmed by night-vision cameras, which use heat to outline shapes and will now all have blown because we are essentially standing near a flake that has fallen from the Sun. The fire is a wall and it is enclosing the camp.

"Rope bridge," I shout. "Move it."

There is a river way off behind us, a steep face to a hill behind the fire, god knows what to the left, although I would assume a sheer cliff face with a bottom made of sharpened wooden spikes. To our right is the rope bridge, leading us to the crew, the presenters and into open space.

"Have we got everyone?" I shout.

I look around and see most of them, The smoke is bellowing over the camp, the air getting thick. I see Racheal, Jenny, Chelsey and Gaz huddled together, justifiably bricking it, and figuring out the direction of the bridge.

"Just go," I shout, and take steps into the smoke. Jonny is there as is Katherine and Kieran.

"The other two?" I ask, hoping the answer is, there, right behind you.

"We're here," Bob says, dragging the pop star along.

"Rope bridge," I say.

"Is that wise?" Jonny asks.

"Wise? What the bloody hell do you mean, is that wise? Do we need to have a meeting. Look, fire there, no fire there. Let's go there, where conveniently there is a bridge. Let's go."

I start to walk and no one follows.

"Are you kidding me?" I ask.

"It might just be a task?" Bob asks.

"That is a real fire. It is very warm. The smoke is also very real. Now, maybe it is just a hilarious task, and we are all failing miserably. But you lot have already won. Let's get the fuck out of here."

I start walking again, and they all look at each other like I'm the serial killer Pied Piper, and if they follow me they will all vanish and I'll use their skin to make lamp shades.

"Look, as much as I dislike you all, and you all dislike me, I'm not really at the point where I think, you know what, I'll sacrifice my life to kill all of you fricking idiots. Stay here and roast, not in the porno way, or get to the bloody bridge. No one is coming to save us. And incidentally, the fire is frickin huge."

They turn, look at the fire, look at me, look back at the fire to double check which of that or me they detest most, decide as if they are connected telepathically, and then move toward the bridge.

I swear Jonny tries to jog the first bit so he is in front.

"Follow me," he shouts, "to the bridge."

And they all do, the awful little cretins.

I don't look back because I have watched films where people look back, and while it is usually at some possessed killer wielding a knife who doesn't really need to chase as they have an ability to transport themselves at will and also appear in dreams, but they catch up in the traditional foot chase because the person looks back and trips, or looks back and forgets how to run quickly, or looks back and the insane weirdo with a mask machete's their head off, which they couldn't have done if they had just kept looking ahead.

The fire, however, is loud, crackling and making the jog over jungle paths relatively sweat filled.

We hear the other group, my group, the better group, the lovely group up ahead. And while I love them all now, as valiant losing often does evoke that emotion in the Brits, I detect a hint of panic, which, engulfs me also when I get there.

The bridge is on fire.

Not totally, but on fire all the same. To the extent you'd have to be an absolute arse pop to contemplate going across.

"Shall we just make a run for it to the other side?" Bob, auditioning for the post of arse pop asks.

We all look at him.

"Nobody say, go ahead," I shout. "He will, he'll die, on live TV, and we will all be hated to the point where I won't ever be able to become a member of the masons."

"That is your dream?" Jonny smugs.

"No, it isn't."

I look around, as everyone does.

"Bridge was a shit idea, wasn't it Ben," Jonny tells me, having completely forgotten his rallying call from minutes before.

We see the wall of fire in the direction we came, the bridge starting to creak and crack and pop as the handrails, made from renewable natural fibres, start to burn with a smell like chemical vanilla incense crossed with combusting oil.

"The river is that way," I say pointing in the direction where there is no fire, and hoping the river is in fact that way and I am not leading a group of panicking celebrities into a pit of liquid petroleum gas.

"Are you sure?" Jonny asks.

"As sure as that way is fire, that way is plunging to our death on a broken bridge and that way is the only way we can go without becoming candles. Chelsey, you'd burn longest. Gaz, you would burn brightest. In fact, please do not try to urinate anywhere near the flames. The amount of alcohol in you would cause an explosion."

They are all staring at me.

"I'm sure you might have picked up on the fact I talk shite when I am nervous. Can we get going?"

"There isn't a path," Katherine says.

"Oh well, let's just stay here then, shall we? Oh, why did she stand there and just let herself become a crinkle cut crisp? Oh, because there wasn't a path."

She snarls at me, and the side of my face is red hot, but not from humiliation but the largest ever bonfire I have seen is chasing me around like the plot to an absolutely awful, straight to DVD, low-budget horror.

"Let's go," I say, and no one moves. They all look to one another seeking out a leader.

"Let's go," Jenny says, calmly and quietly and starts to walk through the bush.

Everyone follows.

We walk quickly, pushing our way through pretty scarce undergrowth. It is not the amazon, it's like an overgrown backyard on a house that has been empty and up for sale for fourteen months. I do not look behind through fear, and there is little point as we are getting running commentary from Kieran as to the direction, speed and distance from us of the fire.

"It's turned away, oh, no it hasn't. It's stopped, oh, no it hasn't. It seems to be dying out. Oh, no, hang on, it doesn't," are some of the phrases he throws out.

Essentially it is chasing us down, and we need to find some way of outrunning the thing.

"The water," Racheal shouts. "I can hear the water."

I can't, I can only hear the fire and smell my own fear. But she is right, and so was I miraculously.

"Told you," I say out loud so everyone can ignore me, which they do.

The river comes into view and it is as wide as I remember, which is very wide, and twenty metres along its shore are our rafts, tied to stakes in the land.

"I'm no scientist but If I remember correctly from high school, water doesn't burn. So, I say, let's get in the water, then to the other side of the water, and then sit there while the production company come to find us hoping we are all safe as the insurance company will, as is their want, describe all our deaths as an act of God and therefore outside their remit, and thus the quadrillion Australian pounds paid in premiums was a worthless waste of time."

"Ben," Jenny asks.

"Yeah?"

"Shut up."

I nod.

"Good point. Well made," I explain. "However, let's get on the rafts and talk insurance fraud later."

I look at Kieran. "How's the fire?"

"Big," he tells me. "And very close. Getting closer."

Despite there having been no breeze at all in the last twenty seven years in this place, there is one now, blowing toward use making

242

the movement of the wall of death fire all that much quicker. We all start to jog, even Gaz, although he gives up after two steps.

"You Okay, Gaz?" I ask.

"What will they do when they find out I started it?"

"No harm done. We'll all get out. We'll all get paid. Dumb luck. It is all good."

"What if someone dies?"

"Maybe we should leave the decision on who to kill up to the viewers?"

He laughs.

"Who do you think they'd choose?"

"Obviously me. To be quite frank, I'd be totally gutted if they selected anybody else. Has to be me. I'd insist. Don't sweat it Gaz. Besides, if we all die, no one will ever know. Hopefully they'll blame it on the Welshman."

I pull him along to the rafts. Jonny and his team are getting on the first, paddles all ready.

"It's not a race," I say. "We are all in this together."

They all look at me and paddle away from the shore. They make five metres out very quickly, panic often improves performance.

Bob sings his sea shanty, laughs and Katherine pushes him off into the water. She has the fury on.

My team are waiting for us, stood with paddles in hand, panicking as they should, scared, and impatient. But they wait for me and Gaz. Probably Gaz more than me.

We clamber on and the heat of the fire and the smoke is imposing. It is becoming difficult to see, white and black swirls of thick smoke blowing across the surface, making us all choke. I hear Bob's voice shout a swear word.

I look around our raft and see the rope used to tie it to the land. I pick it up and tie it around my waist. I know nothing about knots so I invent one that is essentially the simple knot we all know just done over and over again. We'll need a chainsaw to break it.

"Really?" Jenny asks. "A hero?"

I look at her and at me, and at her again.

"Go on, fuck off, superman," she tells me.

I turn and I cannot see a metre beyond me.

"Shit," I say. "Bob, I'm coming to you with a rope. Keep shouting. Sing a song or something so I know where you are. Not the sea shanty though."

243

"Okay," Bob shouts back, and then breaks into a pretty decent version of George Michael's Careless Whisper, pretty decent for someone drowning.

"Good stuff, Bob. I'll get there before the chorus. And don't worry, Allig- Crocodiles are deaf."

"Are they?" Chelsey asks.

"If they aren't, my only hope is that they have taste and swim away from this bollocks."

I jump into the water, which I had intended to be a dive, like Tarzan going to save Jane, but it turns into a Dad losing all confidence off the highboard at the local pool and just landing feet first as if maybe, just maybe, he can walk on water.

I'm in and my head is above the surface. I hear Bob warbling about his guilty feet and how he knows I am not a fool. I start to swim toward the noise. Then it hits me.

"Make sure the rope is secure on the raft," I shout, realising that in panic situations my decision making processes are a bit shit.

"Done it," Jenny shouts back and I can't see the raft.

Bob is now lamenting how he is never going to dance again the way he danced with me, which is helping, as I am getting closer, or, possibly, Bob is singing louder.

And just like that I am face to face with Bob, who has clearly done a survival course and is laying on his back, like a starfish, with his face above water.

"Do you want to get to the end of the chorus, or shall we just get back to the raft now?" I ask.

Bob starts to splash around because on the verge of help and saviour the best thing to do is thrash about and try and drown both of us.

"Bob, just grab the rope. They will pull us in."

He thinks, stops and grabs the rope.

"Pull us back in!" I shout, and feel the tug of the rope around my waist. "You holding on, Bob."

"For dear life," he says.

I laugh.

"Tonight the music seems so loud," I sing, badly, and with a bit of river water in my eyes.

"I wish that we could lose this crowd," Bob then sings, as if this is a broadway production.

"Maybe it is better this way," we sing as a duet, a tone-deaf duet like two nearly unconscious drunks in a pub who have just been dumped. "We'd hurt each other with the things we want to say."

Unfortunately for George Micheal fans, music lovers in general, and possibly even world peace, we bump into the raft and stop singing. The crew help us on, and we lie there wet, while I try unsuccessfully to untangle the rope. I give up. It'll make a nice belt.

"Why did you do that?" Bob asks me as we lie there. "You don't even like me."

"I don't know you, Bob. You put up a barrier of bullshit jokes. Everything you say has to be a humorous aside or something. It is annoying. I have no idea who the real you is."

"And you? How are you different?"

I nod, tapping the back of my head against the raft.

"See, now that is worth saying."

THE PRESENTERS : DAY 12 : THE END IS NIGH

"We are on fire," the Welshman shouts.

He has burst into Molly's hotel room, but she is dressed. She knows, everyone knows. TV channels, radio and the internet, all of them know.

"There are no cameras," he shouts. "We have the audio, but they have run away from the fire. We have no eyes on them."

"How unfortunate," Molly says. "They need to be rescued, not filmed dying."

"There is a car picking us up. We have a cameraman. We need to get down there."

"Really, I would have thought you would prefer to sit up on a platform and play your violin while watching it all burn to the ground."

The Welshman stares at Molly, trying to figure something to say, trying to figure out what she just said.

"But I can't play violin," he says.

"It doesn't matter. It really doesn't matter. I'm not coming."

"You have to come, you are co-presenter."

"This isn't a special edition," she shouts. "That is a genuine fire."

She stops, looks at him, looking to read him and his features.

"This is a genuine fire, right?" She asks. "This isn't another one in a long line of your shit ideas is it?"

"Gaz started it, threw a roll-up into the bush. Place just went up."

She stares at him more, reading him as well as she can.

245

"Go off, gain your fame in the flames reporting. I'll come in with the rescue team. I'm not making an episode out of this."

He shakes his head like she has made the gravest error.

"This will be TV gold. Awards, proper awards. Not teen favourite, actual awards. Danger, camera, all of that."

"You have gone genuinely mad."

"No," he says, trying to think of something intelligent and pithy and cutting. "You have."

He turns and runs away. She sits back on her bed waiting and watching the flatscreen TV and the news program and its rolling service covering the unfolding tragedy.

DAY 12 : PROPERLY IN THE NIGHT : ON A RAFT

We paddle, the smoke clearing like we have gone through a thick, mystical mist and there is an uncharted land ahead. It'll contain creatures that will kill us just by looking. This mythical land is called Australia. The other team is on the bank on the far side. They are sat looking across at us, but seemingly over and behind. I turn, and the fire is raging, all the way down to the river's edge it would seem. Smoke hides most but atop, flicking out are obviously huge flames. We paddle to the bank, I jump out and haul the raft in and we all fall down and sit on dryish land. The grass here is straw dry as well, but not even Gaz is dumb enough to light a celebratory cigarette.

"Do you think we are safe?" Jenny asks me.

I lean into her shoulder with my own.

"I think someone is coming to get us as we speak. Death of celebrities, especially burning them alive like we are witches, isn't a good look for TV."

We sit there, hoping we are safe, looking across the river at the flames and smoke, the air quality our side not great but definitely not as hot as where we camped.

Racheal hears it first, the beating of the propeller, spinning around to look. One-by-one in steps of age we all turn and see the helicopter coming in. We feel the wind, the smoke being pushed away and the noise of the engine and the thrashing of blades against thick warm air.

"I'm guessing that is for us," I say, "but keep your heads down. No one wants to be that guy or girl who has made it all the way through the film only to have their head lopped off just before the escape."

No one is listening to me, which is comforting.

246

We watch the helicopter land thirty metres from where we are. A man in a red boiler suit and yellow helmet steps out and waves us toward him. We all stand and traipse over. Inside there are seats for us all despite The Welshman and a cameraman being in the two best seats in the middle, far from the open sides. We get in, the red boiler suit man passes around and straps us in. All of us sitting like new born babies in a car seat. We take off. No one has said a word.

"So," The Welshman shouts over the noise. "How is everyone?"

I lean across, grab the camera from the man. He puts up a bit of a struggle but I think he gives up when he sees my eyes. I take the camera and hurl it out of the open side of the helicopter, and have a brief panic about it landing on a human and killing them, or a kangaroo, or camel.

The Welshman stares out the open space. He looks at me and I lean forward again.

"You're a cock," I say.

EPILOGUE

I walk in a cafe in the middle of a tiny coastal town in Norfolk. I see Jenny and sit down at her table. She doesn't stand, and we don't hug. The place is about as English as can be with old wooden chairs and handwritten boards telling you the food they offer, which is essentially scones or toast. They have a lot of tea.

"The place is so obscure my sat nav didn't have a clue how to get here. You know this place?"

"Came here on holiday when I was a kid," she tells me.

"Okay. Not exactly Magaluf, but I'm sure it was fun. What's the plan?"

"Coastal walk, see the view, hopefully see some wildlife," Jenny says.

"Oh good," I lie, and she smiles. "No sex then?"

She reaches across and grabs my hand. "We are booked into the rooms above. Hopefully be better than last time."

I laugh.

"Thanks," I say.

"It is always good," she says, trying to reassure my ego, "just here is a more pleasant vibe."

"True, less chance of passing out with the sea air. Good thinking."

We aren't living together, and maybe that will come, or maybe it won't. But it is cool, relaxed and cool. We stayed together after the TV show and flew back together. Twenty-four hours on a plane, admittedly in business class, is a real test of a relationship. We meet up a few times a week, and text each other almost constantly. Sometimes we actually converse, while other times we send each other memes, jokes, or really stupid pictures.

So far we have avoided any mention in the tabloid press.

Printed in Great Britain
by Amazon